Autumn Winds
Miners' Cut Mystery Series
Book Three

By
H.W. Peterson

Author's Notes

Although *Autumn Winds* is a work of fiction, the town in which our characters live, Ouray, Colorado, is a real town in Southwestern Colorado. Red Mountain, several miles up the Million Dollar Highway, is a mountain and the location of several mines. Yankee Girl Mine, where our fictional character Marcus Wright works, was a mine started in 1882 by a man known as "Mr. Robinson", who found a rock full of galena one day. He found where the rock came from and discovered a huge chimney of silver ore. In its day, Yankee Girl Mine produced silver, gold and copper, and was considered one of the most profitable silver mines in the entire United States.

In this book, Fred and Marcus travel to the Pikes Peak Region to meet with **Bob Womack**. Bob was a real live, flesh and blood rancher around Cripple Creek who discovered traces of placer gold in 1878. For years he believed there was much gold to be found in the area, but it wasn't until 1890 that he actually staked a claim in an area north of Cripple Creek called Poverty Gulch. His claim started the Gold Rush in the Pikes Peak Region. The story goes that he sold his claim one night for $500.00 and a bottle of whiskey, probably not realizing what a rich vein it was. He died a pauper on August 10, 1909.

On their trip to the Pikes Peak Region, Marcus and Fred stayed at the home of **General William Jackson Palmer**. General Palmer was the founder of Colorado Springs and co-founder of the Denver and Rio Grande Railroad. During the Civil War, he served in the Union Army, advancing to the rank of Brigadier General. After the war, he moved west to Colorado and founded the city of Colorado Springs in 1871, as well as several other communities in the area. He built his grand castle, **Glen Eyrie,** in 1871, just outside Colorado Springs, and a stone's throw from Garden of the Gods. He and his wife, Mary "Queen" Palmer, lived there part-time, as his business travels took him all over the world. Due to a fragile health condition aggravated by the altitude, Queen left Colorado Springs for good in 1885, moving to the East Coast, where General Palmer visited her frequently. General Palmer died at his beloved Glen Eyrie on March 13, 1909, following complications of paralysis sustained from a horseriding accident, at the age of 72. Glen Eyrie is currently home to the Evangelical Christian organization, The Navigators.

To Don:
Your voice makes the angel choirs stop and listen.
The world is a better place because of your music, honey.
Never stop singing!

Your love, God, is my song, and I'll sing it!
I'm forever telling everyone how faithful you are.
Psalm 89:1 (MSG)

Forward

I once heard a saying that went something like this: if you ever want to make God laugh, tell him your plans. Well, if there is any truth to that, The Great I Am must be ROTFL. For those of you who are not familiar with this acronym, it simply means rolling on the floor laughing. My husband said that I have now brought at least half of America up-to-speed on the use of this social media acronym, so kudos to me. LOL (laugh out loud, not lots of love).

Now that *that* is out of the way you may be asking why *my* plans would seem so fantastically amusing to the Almighty. Well, sit back and enjoy the tale.

Back in the day when I was a productive member of the workforce, one of the things I prided myself in was the ability to keep to a schedule and make my deadlines. I actually thrived in a make-or-break, down-to-the-wire arena.

Then I met Don. Don, who is an easy-going, it'll-get-done kind of guy, who can wait until the last minute to begin any project and not get bent out of shape about it. So here we are: Hazel = Type A; Don…not so much.

In July 2013 I had reconstructive surgery on my right foot from a fracture that had occurred almost two years earlier and simply refused to heal. I was released from my orthopedic surgeon's care around Christmas of that year, about the same time *Iron Fists in Satin Gloves* was published. I began writing this book in January 2014 and had completed less than one chapter when I fell in our driveway and fractured my right hip. And it was a doozy of a fracture. Being a Type A, I decided to make lemonade out of lemons and asked Don to bring my faithful laptop to the hospital so I could keep on schedule during my stay.

Well, let me tell you one thing: if you've never had a hip fracture you can't begin to imagine the inconvenience. What an ordeal! Until surgery I had to lie in one position, flat on my back, staring at the ceiling. I can't tell you how thankful I was for excellent drugs…and I'm not kidding even a little bit. Every four hours like clockwork here came the nurse, my new bestie, with a syringe full of a magic potion to be injected straight into my IV. After surgery…well, I'll just say that nothing about hip surgery or its recovery time is conducive to good writing. I stayed in the hospital eight days, my days filled with physical therapy and rest…and drugs. My computer never left its case.

It wasn't until eight weeks later that I actually opened my laptop and got back to work. Things were moving along quite nicely; three chapters poured forth and then the unthinkable happened. My motherboard crashed. Yep…that's right. I cried…and cried…and just when I thought I there were no more tears, I cried some more. Finally, I said, "Enough already!" By this time it was Springtime in the Rockies, which may or may not mean sunshine and flowers, so I bundled up, sat on the porch swing, which isn't on the porch at all but in the backyard, with a spiral notebook and purple ink pen and wrote until I got a new laptop. Oddly enough, I found handwriting stimulating; new ideas just poured out of me. I was actually sad to put the notebook aside when the new laptop came along.

I was pretty pleased with myself. By now it was the beginning of summer and I'd finished all my physical therapy, transferred all my hand-written notes to the new computer, and was on my way to finishing. I was beginning to think I might even make my deadline, which had changed from a thing that never failed to get my blood flowing to something that made me nauseous at the very thought of it.

Thanksgiving came and that's when the next trial set in. I had the dreaded writers' block. I couldn't decide which way to go with certain characters…mainly Reginald O'Keefe. People were begging me to kill him off. I panicked. What to do?!?!? These characters are a part of my life and even though he is a pill, I couldn't pull the plug on Reggie-boy.

So what did I do? I put aside the deadline. And guess what? The world did not come crashing in on me. I actually lived to tell about it and learned a lesson. The only person upset about the book being late was me…so I chose to get over it. And good thing, too, because wait until you hear what happened next.

Christmas came, Christmas went. Don wasn't his usual chipper self at all. He was tired, out of breath, and generally uninspired about his work, which is a bad thing as he's self-employed. He'd just gotten new insurance and needed to meet his primary care physician, so I made him an appointment, which he reluctantly agreed to keep.

A few short weeks later Don had a triple bypass. That's right, open heart surgery. I was in shock. One day my husband was home with me, the next he was in the ICU attached to all kinds of machines and yards of tubing fighting for his life. I don't think I slept for about a week. I know I went through the motions because I'm still here to talk about it, but everything is such a blur. It's now April and I'm still exhausted.

We've been traveling back and forth to Colorado Springs three times a week for Cardiac Rehab. He's stronger now and doing so much better. I'm seeing glimpses of the man I knew before he began to feel bad. I'm so thankful I made that initial appointment.

So did God laugh? Probably not...at least concerning Don's health crisis and my hip fiasco. Life got in the way of my plans but I had lessons to learn. I've learned to be more flexible; I've learned to trust God more. I've learned that if things don't pan out the way I want, life will go on and I will survive.

My self-appointed deadline for the completion of *Autumn Winds* passed me by like a whirlwind. All my life I've heard people say that God's timing is not as our own. I've tested the notion more times than I care to admit and always found it to be true. The writing of this third installment is proof that if we are faithfully persistent in our endeavors, we can accomplish anything. God's still small voice urged me on despite the difficulties of this past year. Like most Type A personalities, my plan was straightforward and to the point. I can now laugh at myself because there is nothing straightforward and to the point in the way the pages of this story came together. I can explain it no other way than to say it was a GOD THING.

Psalm 51:10

Reginald frantically paced back and forth in the rundown one room cabin, barely noticing the two young people crouched against the wall beneath the only window. Almost a month had passed since the fateful night he'd taken Sandy and John from the basement of the Wright's house. He knew he'd stepped into something from which he'd never be able to escape. Jesse and Luke had argued and hem-hawed their way into this mess, but only he would be held responsible, and that suited them just fine.

Sandy coughed bringing his pacing to a screeching halt. He turned and slowly looked down at the two, boring a hole through Sandy with his piercing eyes. She begged him for a drink of water. Luke abruptly howled with laughter and told her to get it herself, which started a whole other argument between he and Jesse.

Jesse was a country bumpkin and he grated on Luke's very last nerve. Just the sound of his whiny drawl put Luke over the edge, which sent Reginald into a tailspin as to how to quiet things before they got out of hand.

Reginald ran outside and dipped a bucket in the cold mountain stream just a few yards from the cabin and hurried back indoors. He poured a glass of water for Sandy and urged her to forget about Luke and Jesse. He whispered that they were malcontents whose opinions didn't really matter.

Sandy nodded, offered a barely audible thank you, placed the cool cup against her forehead and closed her eyes. She then downed the cup and asked for another. Confused and frightened, she huddled close to John.

For the time being, Luke was quiet. She despised the sound of his voice. For that matter, she detested them all. She found it difficult to keep most of the Voices straight, but always recognized Luke's and Jesse's. Luke antagonized Jesse and sometimes Frank. She was careful to listen to their banter and found that Luke picked on them because they were the most reasonable ones of the group.

Reginald leaned against the wall, crossed his arms at his chest and dropped his head. How in the world was he going to get out of this mess? Would anybody believe him when he said he remembered very little of the past year? Would anybody listen to his stories about a bunch of Voices who'd set up camp inside his head?

******

Washie sat cross-legged in the middle of Sandy's bed. She closed her eyes and thought of the last conversation they'd had. It was at the breakfast table on the day Sandy disappeared. They'd talked about what it must be like for the Archer family to finally be back together after such a long time. Now the Archers and Somers were living the same nightmare. As bad as the situation was for Washie and Alfred, it had to be a hundred times worse for the Archers. First Simon went missing and now John, all the doings of the same vicious man. Would they ever see their children again? She clutched Sandy's pillow and held it to her nose. She breathed in the scent of her daughter. *Rose water*, she thought. *My Sandy smells of rose water.*

She prayed and wondered if anyone was actually listening. She dared not share *that* with Alfred. He'd tell her that God was working, that she must have faith, and if God seemed distant perhaps it was because of a wedge of her own making. She knew those things to be true, but right now, in this very moment, she needed to be angry with someone. God could have prevented this. Why didn't he?

******

Susan and Clara puttered around the kitchen preparing the midday meal. Susan hadn't spoken two words since donning her apron, but went about the business of thinly slicing a roast chicken for sandwiches. Her heart wasn't in it; her stomach was queasy. Her mind raced with thoughts of the possibility of never seeing John again.

Just when life was getting back to normal on the ranch he was taken away. Simon blamed himself. The reality of the situation was that John would be home where he belonged if Reginald didn't hate Simon and wish to make his life miserable in any way possible. Most normal people would have let go of such a vendetta and moved on. No, that wasn't right. Normal rational-thinking people would never have carried out and continued a vendetta like this in the first place. She wagged her head as she continued slicing the chicken breast.

Normal. Just when life was getting back to normal…

Chapter One

We can't help everyone, but everyone can help someone.
~ Ronald Reagan

Fred grabbed the sack from the bottom drawer of his desk and his suit jacket from the back of his chair. *Free at last!* He hurried from the office and across the grounds, over to his favorite lunchtime getaway. He plopped down on a boulder on the cliff of the mountain and gazed at the beauty before him and breathed in the fresh mountain air. If he lived to be a hundred and one he'd never tire of the majesty and splendor of these mountains. He peeked inside the paper bag to see what Lydia had prepared, secretly hoping for a meatloaf sandwich and a few of those tangy bread and butter pickle slices from last night's supper. Inside was something wrapped in a napkin and he uttered, "Can it be?" He removed it from the bag and unfolded the napkin to discover his wish had been granted: a generous portion of meatloaf between two slices of Lydia's homemade soda bread with mayonnaise and pickle slices. He smacked his lips and took a generous bite from a sandwich half. "Heaven on earth," he said despite a mouthful. He crossed his feet at the ankles and dove in with gusto.

"Hard to beat Lydia's meatloaf sandwiches."

Startled, Fred turned, squinting in the bright sunlight and watched as Marcus approached. "Hey, my friend, come and have a seat. There's not a better view anywhere."

"Thanks. I believe I will." Marcus had enjoyed his sandwich at his desk while he finished a report that was due at the next partners' meeting. He bit into a juicy red apple as he sat down next to Fred and leaned up against a knobby bristlecone pine. "Say, if you're not going to eat the other half of that sandwich, I'll be glad to take it off your hands."

"Touch it and die!" Fred warned and then grinned.

"Say, Fred, you'll never believe what I just heard. I heard a new posse is being formed to look for our old pal, Reginald."

"You don't say. That means he's been spotted." Fred popped a tangy pickle slice into his mouth.

"That's what I hear. You know that old hermit that lives the next hill over? He came up here last night after we left and spoke with the night guard. Said he'd seen a guy hanging out at a deserted old cabin around the bend from his place. Said he didn't like the looks of him and thought somebody ought to check it out."

"Well, I'll be." Then: "Did he give a description?"

"I'm not sure, but something's up 'cause Sheriff Johnson wouldn't

13

deputize a bunch of men on a whim." He munched on his apple while Fred finished his sandwich. "You know, I wish I could get some kind of a clue about Reginald. He's not the guy I grew up with, that's for sure."

"I wish I'd known *that* guy. I've only known the Reginald we have now." Fred lifted his brows and pursed his lips. "He's not somebody to mess with. You know it. I know it. Heck, ever'body knows it."

Marcus thought on that. "I want to believe that somewhere inside him is the person I used to know. There has to be a way to get him back. There just has to be."

******

Sheriff Johnson dreaded deputizing another group of men. He propped his feet, boots and all, atop his desk, leaned back in his chair and pulled his hat down over his face. He closed his eyes and recalled the last time he deputized a posse. It was a nightmare from the get-go. Each man thought he had the best ideas for capturing the suspect, who was a man accused of attacking a woman walking home from a Wednesday night prayer meeting. One deputy wanted to go door-to-door until they found someone who matched the varmint's description. Another believed a deputy dressed in women's attire, wandering the streets at night in hopes of enticing the culprit to be the best idea. And yet another wanted to simply offer a reward under the notion that even crooks would admit their guilt for the right amount of money. Sheriff Johnson wagged his head. "Lord above, please sir, don't let me git a bunch a' idiots like b'fore. This here's a big deal an' I can't take no chances."

Hopefully, most of the thrill seekers weren't interested in hunting down a real life murderer and would stand down for this adventure. He only needed a handful of men and hoped for the cream of the crop. There was one man he would give his eye teeth for…Edward Savage. Edward was an expert shot, had a keen eye, was mild-mannered, and, most importantly, followed orders, never thinking he knew more than the person in charge. He was an ex-lawman who gave up the badge for family, but still liked to get his feet wet now and then. This would be just the kind of case he'd appreciate…rescuing a couple of young people from harm's way.

******

Fairie stood on the landing and stared out the big window that overlooked the backyard. George was raking leaves into a big pile for burning. She loved the smell of burning leaves. Something about autumn grounded her, cloaked her in contentment as no other season did. She wished her friends might feel the same comfort, but how could they. Augusta was hidden away in Pagosa Springs with her baby and nanny. Alfred and Washie were beside themselves with frantic worry over the kidnapping of their daughter. The Archers had just begun to transition back into family life after Simon's long absence when John was taken from them. How could she or anyone else be a solace to them? How could anyone comprehend the agony they must be experiencing? All she knew to do was be a constant in their lives.

She shuddered to think that Reginald had camped out in their basement. How long he'd been there was anybody's guess. *Did he have no qualms about invading others' right to privacy?* She sighed and rolled her eyes. *Of course he had no qualms about it; he was a criminal, for heaven's sake.*

******

Deputy Dan Stone was right proud of himself. He'd pulled together a fine group of candidates for Sheriff Johnson. There wasn't a noodlehead in the bunch. They could all read and write and claimed to be adept at using a firearm. Most of them were unattached and those who weren't were positive their families would get along just fine for a couple of days without them. Truth of the matter was that most of the men were bored out of their minds and anxious for a little excitement. If hunting down a danged old bad guy didn't qualify, well, by gosh and by golly, he didn't know what did.

Since Augusta and Nora were vacationing in Pagosa Springs, he was free to do whatever Sheriff Johnson asked of him, day or night, rain or shine. He had to admit he liked the idea of sneaking around in the woods, trying to get the slip on O'Keefe, but would stay behind and keep watch over Ouray. After all, it was his sworn duty to serve and protect. Besides, O'Keefe might just be the one bad guy able to give the posse the slip and show up in town. He imagined O'Keefe sitting in the back of the saloon downing a shot of whiskey unaware Dan was watching from across the room. When O'Keefe got up to leave Dan would nab him. "Reginald O'Keefe, you're under arrest." He smiled. *It could happen.*

*****

Early the next morning a rough and tumble group of men gathered in front of the sheriff's office to be sworn in. Sheriff Johnson looked them over, impressed with Dan's efforts, believing the young man had outdone himself. These guys might just do the trick. There wasn't a man in the group who didn't know Reginald O'Keefe; some even found him to be

15

a right likeable sort, but no matter. After speaking with each man one on one, the consensus was unanimous: a job was a job and they'd bring those young'uns in no matter what the cost.

Marcus and Fred happened by on their way to the train just as the posse members were mounting their horses. Sheriff Johnson waved and nodded and called out to them from the other side of the street. "Today's the day, fellas. We're headin' up t' find those kids. Hope that old hermit weren't jest waggin' 'is tongue."

Marcus gave the thumbs up and said, "Good luck up there. Feel free to stop by the mine for coffee and donuts and such. Cook's mighty proud of those clove donuts he keeps handy. Makes them fresh every morning."

"Mighty kind, Marcus. See ya up on th' mountain." He tipped his hat, looked ahead, dug his boots into the sides of his painted pony and took the lead, the others falling in behind. Marcus and Fred watched as the crew made their way up the first switchback, then the next, and then disappeared in a sea of blue spruce and aspen.

******

Annie, Faerie, Myra and Lydia gathered around the kitchen table with a pot of coffee and a plate of oatmeal raisin bars. Autumn had ushered itself in while everyone's attention was on the dire situation their friends found themselves in. Faerie called it the Season of Color, and for good reason. The vivid yellows and golds of the aspens against the dark evergreens and clear azure Colorado skies never failed to be a resounding last hurrah before the stark white of winter set in. However, even the breathtaking alpine autumn could not hide the fact that all planning for the holidays had gone by the wayside.

Baby Patricia squealed with delight as Myra bounced her on her knee. Lydia made silly faces at the wee one from across the table. Annie broke an oatmeal bar in half and took a healthy bite. Faerie sat back in her chair and enjoyed the amiable moment. Though the ladies around the table were her employees, she also held each one close to her heart as friends.

Hattie and Mattie sat in their high chairs and gnawed on halves of oatmeal bars. Faerie watched as Mattie chewed with her lips puckered together, her chubby cheeks a rosy red. "She loves these bars. She's usually such a fussy eater, but she's really going after it." She winked at Lydia. "They're a bit hit, Lydia. You've done it again."

"Thank ye, ma'am." Lydia blushed.

Faerie took a long draw from her coffee and gingerly set the cup back in its saucer. "I wanted to get together this morning and plan the holidays.

16

It appears time has gotten away from me this year." She furrowed her brow. "I can't imagine why I've let things go the way I have," she said with a snippet of sarcasm.

Annie snickered. "Goodness, Faerie. I can only suspect it might have a little something to do with the strange goings on around here."

Faerie nodded and gazed out the window. A whirlwind of aspen leaves lifted into the air and scattered, slowly dissipating into nothingness. *Not unlike my emotions these days*, she thought.

The ladies shared curious glances. Then: "Faerie, are you all right?" Myra asked softly.

"Wh-what? Oh, yes, I'm fine." Faerie clutched her hand to her throat. "I was just thinking how up and down my emotions are running these days. There's been so much…" She stopped midsentence. Then: "That would be the reason I haven't taken the time to meet with you, ladies. Please forgive me for being so remiss in my duties as mistress of this house."

"What're ye talkin' about, Miss? There's nothin' t' forgive. Ain't that right, ladies?" Lydia offered, beseeching assistance from the others with her eyes.

Annie took the bait. "Lydia's right, Faerie. No one can fault you even one tiny smidge. Besides, this house runs like clockwork. It's a pleasure to work for you and Marcus. I think I can speak for us all when I say we want to give you our best." Annie reached over and put her hand atop Faerie's and gave it a little squeeze.

Myra smiled. "Faerie, don't be too hard on yourself. Why, George and I were just talking about this very thing last night. We both said how grateful we are to have such benevolent employers."

Faerie grinned and said, "The truth of the matter is that each of you perform your duties well enough that my supervision isn't required at all. For that I am truly grateful." "Having said that, let's get down to it and make some notes of preparation for the upcoming holidays."

By the noon hour the ladies had waded through three months of planning. Annie, Faerie and Myra quickly fed the babies before carrying them off to the nursery for their afternoon naps. They were pleasantly surprised at how well the little ones did being confined to mothers' laps and high chairs for so long a time. Annie stayed in the nursery, choosing to lie down on the sofa and rest while the girls napped.

Faerie stood at the top of the stairs and gazed down upon the spacious floor below. She recalled thinking how ostentatious it all seemed when Augusta was decorating and readying it for the wedding. She recalled thinking it spacious and far too much house for anyone, not to mention pretentious and somewhat…no…*very* flamboyant. Yes, Annie hit the nail on the head the day she so mockingly referred to it as Monstrosity Manor. Even so, she'd grown to love it here. By dressing down the previous décor and adding her own special touches, Faerie had created a warm and friendly atmosphere, making this much talked about house a home.

She wandered down the hall to the master bedroom where a letter she'd begun to her mother days earlier sat on her writing desk waiting to be finished. She'd endeavored to complete it several times but the words would not come. At this point, she'd settle for just a few measly generalities but knew her mother wouldn't be happy with 'I'm fine, the girls are growing like weeds, and Marcus is doing well and is as busy as ever'. Her mother wanted meaty, lengthy correspondence full of life and descriptive experiences of the Wild West.

"Wild West, indeed!" she muttered under her breath. "The only wild thing around here is Reginald O'Keefe." The second the words escaped her lips she regretted them. She was so very tired of it all. She wanted Reginald to turn himself in and end this nightmare. She stood in the doorway and leaned against the jamb, her arms folded in front of her. If her mother wanted mystery and intrigue, Faerie would deliver. She would write a letter that would surely curl her mother's gnarly old toenails.

******

Faerie leaned back in the chair at her writing desk and stretched her neck and back. She stood and walked to the window and peeked outside. The clock in the hallway struck two. Had she really been writing for an hour and a half? She sat back down and picked up the pages. The letter was full of pleasantries and descriptions of the magnificent Rocky Mountain autumn. She bragged, like any proud mother ought, about her beautiful baby girls and how extraordinarily intelligent they were. She went on and on about her handsome husband. Then she delved into the seedier, darker side of things. She wrote about Reginald, the same Reginald her mother knew only as Marcus's closest childhood friend. She told of a man who'd slipped into a dark world of mental illness, listening and responding to Voices only he could hear, and seemingly bowing to their every whim and delight. Her mother would sit in the corner by the fire in her favorite chair and enjoy a cup of tea as she read the hypnotic tale of a man lost in a world that only existed inside his head, and she would thank her lucky stars that her own husband got help before the same thing happened to him.

18

By the time all was said and done Faerie had written a short story instead of a letter. She set the pen down and massaged her finger joints and the palms of her hands. She folded the pages and managed to fit them in the addressed envelope. She chuckled as she held the bulging envelope in her hand. *The size of it alone should be enough to ward off any ill will she feels at my neglect in writing,* she mused.

She thought back to the days when her father was living in the throes of his own psychosis. Hoarding food and tormenting the family with empty plates at supper was his idea of a good time. If not for a moment of clarity he might have continued down that path. She wished and prayed for the same kind of clarity for Reginald. She waved it off; she would not allow herself to wallow in this any longer…at least for today. She decided to take a walk to the mercantile to post the letter. She felt a twinge of chagrin. It had certainly been too long since she last wrote her mother. Back in her hometown of Boston, there was a woman checking her mailbox every day for a letter from her unruly-haired, feisty daughter in Colorado.

Down in the foyer, she donned a sweater and hat. Lydia came from the kitchen muttering under her breath about this and that. "Whatever is the matter, Lydia?" Faerie asked, most curiously.

"Oh, nothin', Missus. I jest talk to m'self ever' now an' agin." She chuckled. "Well…more often than that, I s'pose." Then: "Are ye goin' somewhere special?"

"No'm, I just need some air and thought I'd drop a letter in the post. I fear I've seriously neglected my daughterly duties when it comes to correspondence." She smiled sweetly and held up the envelope.

"I don't mean t' be a bother, but would it be ah'right if I tag along?"

Faerie lit up. "I'd be glad to have the company." She knit her brow. "I can't recall ever going out on the town with you, Lydia."

"No, ma'am, we ain't never. I can't recall ever bein' friendly with m'boss th' way I was with Miss Augusta." She blushed. "Oh, an' ye, too, Missus."

Faerie placed her hand on the door handle and said, "I appreciate that. And by the way, Lydia, I'd like to think we have something more than a professional relationship."

Lydia's face brightened. "Oh, yes'm. Yes, indeed."

They wandered out of the house, down the walk, past the wrought iron fence and onto the street. It was a warm afternoon with just the slightest breeze. Faerie soon removed her sweater, folding it and carrying over her arm. As they enjoyed their walk, Lydia chatted about her growing up years in Georgetown. Then Faerie animatedly regaled Lydia with talk of the years she and her mother spent designing and sewing ball gowns for Boston's elite.

"Maybe ye should consider doin' that here, Missus."

"There isn't much call for ball gowns in Ouray. I'd probably need to be in Denver to make a go of it." She giggled like a schoolgirl. "I *have* toyed with the idea of designing practical wear for women."

Lydia leaned her head to one side giving that a thought. "Now there's a right fine idea. Somethin' a woman could wear t' tea or a fine dinner."

"Exactly."

"Do yerself a favor, Missus, and think about it long an' hard. That's a winnin' plan if'n there ever was one."

They rounded the corner onto Main Street. People milled about everywhere taking advantage of one of the last warm days of autumn. They stopped in the Mercantile, which also served as the Post Office, and dropped off the letter and picked up some hard candies to enjoy as they strolled down Main Street. As they moseyed along, they met several ladies from Faerie's Sunday school class coming out from The Bon Ton, a local pastry shop.

"Have you heard the latest about Mr. O'Keefe?" Eleanor Rush was a mouthpiece from way back who chose to believe that idle talk wasn't gossip if it was true, even if said in a whisper and beginning with 'have you heard', unless, of course, the talk was about her and came from another source.

Lydia and Faerie passed each other cautious glances. "Can't say we have," Faerie replied kindly.

"A new posse was deputized this morning. They're up on the mountain this very minute!" Eleanor said enthusiastically. "Can you imagine?" She was practically giddy at the prospect of spreading the news. Her two friends stood behind her listening with stern expressions.

"No. Well, yes, I can." Faerie was dumbfounded. She'd hoped for this day, but was completely taken off guard. "We can only pray he lets those poor children go without harm."

Eleanor raised a brow and grinned deviously. "I forgot how you like him and all. Silly me!" she said peevishly with a raised brow. "Be careful how you choose your friends, Faerie," she said snidely. "I sincerely hope your half-breed husband has learned his lesson."

Eleanor nodded to her friends and off they went, leaving Lydia and Faerie standing in front of the shop, blindsided and in need of a midafternoon boost. They stepped inside the cafe and sat at a table on the far side of the room against a window overlooking The Beaumont Hotel.

"I don't know what to think about those ladies, Lydia. It seemed like they received some strange satisfaction at being the ones who shared the news with us. They know good and well about Marcus's relationship with Reginald. We've talked about it in Sunday School many times." Faerie's face flushed.

"That one lady? Eleanor? She sounded...*proud* t' be th' bearer o' sech news, all puffed up like a peacock. I don' mean t' sound tacky, but t' was like she *wanted* t' see yer reaction, t' see ye hurt. And that remark about Mr. Marcus? Trash, pure trash."

Faerie pursed her lips and stared out the window replaying the brief conversation in her mind. Then: "You're absolutely right," she said sadly. "She was proud, Lydia. She's never liked me since we moved to town. Now I know why."

Lydia wagged her head with a tsk. "She ain't nothin' but jealous o' ye, Missus. Yep, that's it, a right bad case o' th' auld green-eyed monster." Lydia tried to lighten the mood by wiggling her brows playfully.

A smile began to creep across Faerie's face and in seconds she was laughing. "I can't let that old cow ruin our afternoon."

"Why, Faerie Wright, I canna b'lieve I heard ye right. Did ye say *cow*? Why, yes, I b'lieve ye did. Glory be t' th' Saints and Mary and Joseph, too," she cackled. "Ye said cow, and a cow she is, Missus. Don't ye ever ferget it."

The waitress approached the table and said, "Faerie Wright, as I live and breathe. I'll bet you need a peach tart?" Jane had waited these tables day in and day out for years and Faerie was by far one of her favorite customers.

"How'd you guess?" Faerie teased with a broad smile. Then: "How are you, Jane? It's been too long."

"Things are as they should be. There's no rest for the weary. Seems there's more to that saying but I can't for the life of me recall it." She laughed. "Lydia, how's my favorite wishful Irish?"

Lydia blushed. "If'n I'se any better I couldna stand m'self."

Jane leaned in and said under her breath, "I saw that old bag, Eleanor Rush, corner you outside. My stomach turned over in its grave." Faerie and Lydia covered their mouths to hold down the guffaws. "She sat in here and went on and on about what a no good sidewinder she thinks Reginald O'Keefe is and how the noose is too good for 'im. Her lady friends barely lifted their heads from the table, they were so taken with embarrassment. What's *wrong* with that woman? I do declare!" She frowned and let out a big breath.

"All's I can say is 'er husban' has 'is hands full!" Lydia said flatly.

More laughter and then, "So we've established that Faerie has a craving for a peach tart. What about you, Miss Lydia?"

"I'll have th' same and a cuppa hot coffee."

"Same here," echoed Faerie, "with cream."

"You've got it! I'll be back in two shakes of a lamb's tail."

Faerie watched the spry woman flit across the cozy dining area and into the kitchen. "She's something else. Marcus and I happened on this place one Saturday afternoon right after we first moved here. We were unpacking boxes and there was paper everywhere with boxes piled up in the corners. We were hot and thirsty and irritable and desperately needed to take a break. We decided to go exploring just to see what we could see before we started picking at each other." She grinned impishly and added, "Amazing how the moving elves didn't come in and finish the work while we were gone."

"I love those kinds o'explorin'."

"Me, too. Anyway, we left the house...the one over on Second Street... and ran hand in hand through town like two young lovers. We didn't even take the time to clean up or even run a comb through our hair."

"How scandalous!" Lydia joshed.

"Isn't it though?" Faerie's eyes flashed as she relived the day so many years ago. "It's hard to believe it's been so long. How the time flies." She wagged her head and waved her hands in front of her face. "We looked a mess. Certain women, who shall remain nameless," she began with a crooked grin, "looked down their noses at us like we were ragamuffins. I shan't say who it was, but one of the glares came from a gossip we happened upon today."

Lydia's eyes got ever so big and she said, "Well, well, well. Th' plot thickens. She's looked down on ye from day one, just as ye said."

"Yes, well, I digress. Marcus and I laughed right in their grumpy old snotty faces and laughed and snorted and behaved outrageously...at least in the minds of the highly sophisticated women of Ouray. We went to the Mercantile and met Old Henry for the very first time. We stopped by the livery and got acquainted there and Marcus stepped in it, if you catch my meaning." She snorted causing Lydia to do the same. "That scent followed us everywhere we went until we stopped back by and asked if we might use some of his water to clean off the bottoms of Marcus's shoes." Again she snorted. "Oops! There it is again! I'm hopeless, I tell you, truly hopeless." Faerie covered her mouth with one hand and snickered.

Jane returned with their afternoon treat, implored them to enjoy and promised to check back in a few minutes.

Faerie doctored her coffee and took a sip. "Ah, just what the doctor ordered." She continued her story as Lydia munched on the delectable peach tart. "We'd skipped lunch that day and were famished. I recall desperately craving a glass of lemonade and incessantly whining about it until Marcus finally promised we'd stop at the first café, which we did…this one. Jane was our waitress. We became fast friends."

"Ye should 'ave 'er over, Missus."

"You're absolutely right. She'd get on famously with our little houseful of women." She caught Jane's eye and motioned her over. "Jane, I was wondering if you'd be free for an afternoon of cards and refreshments. It'd just be a small group. You, Lydia, me, and a few others. I'd like you to meet my friends." She reached over and squeezed Lydia's hand. "I have the most amazing friends."

Jane's eyes showed her surprise. "I can't think of anything I'd enjoy more. I'm off on Thursdays and we're closed on Sundays.

"How about this coming Thursday, say around 1:30? We'll have a grand time. Don't bring anything but yourself and an appetite for fun."

"I'll be there!" she exclaimed with a smile and then turned on a dime and headed to the kitchen.

Faerie stared at her peach tart with mouthwatering desire. She picked up the fork and dove in. She chewed slowly, savoring the flakiness of the pastry as it blended with the sweet, yet tart, peaches that she knew to be from the orchards just north of Montrose. She closed her eyes and swallowed. She sighed and said, "Lydia, there must be a way to convince Tilly to share this recipe. Jane told me Tilly's been making this recipe since before she and her husband opened the café."

Lydia heehawed and said, "Ye mus' be a'kiddin' me, Missus. There ain't no way on God's green earth she's ever gonna give up sech a secret. She'll take it t' the grave. But I think I can come perty close on me own. Tell ye what I'll do. Fer tea on Thursday, I'll come up with me own version an' see what Miss Jane thinks. Deal?"

"Deal." Faerie slowly sipped her coffee, savoring the aroma and its full-bodied taste. "The coffee here is sublime…and pricey, I might add. They have it shipped from Lion Coffee back in Massachusetts. I saw the label on one of the packages when I was here a while back. Mother and I bought Lion Coffee on occasion to treat ourselves when we'd completed an especially difficult deadline of ball gowns. Believe you me, we earned it. Even though we were the most popular dressmakers, we were still looked upon and treated as servants much of the time."

Lydia held her cup in both hands. "Now I understand. Ye treat all o' us like ye want t' be treated. It all makes perfect sense, Missus."

"Refill ladies?" Jane poured, winked and slipped away.

"Marcus and I never want any of you to feel like servants. He grew up on a reservation and knows the pain of being treated as an insignificant. I've been snubbed by the wealthiest of the wealthy. Neither of us wants anyone in our house to feel slighted or stepped on."

They drained the last of their cups, Faerie paid the check and they began their trek back to the house. It was two hours until supper but Lydia wasn't worried about a thing. She knew exactly what would be on the table when the family gathered together promptly at six.

******

Alfred took one last look around the kitchen before leaving. About now would be when Sandy would snatch a slice of ham and wrap it in a lettuce leaf, devouring it as if it were her last supper. The corners of his mouth lifted slightly as he thought of her teen-aged appetite and then, just as quickly, he was overcome with sorrow. His chest tightened so that he felt he might collapse under the weight of it. He managed a few deep breaths before he pulled the door open and stepped into the alleyway. Oh, how he missed that girl. She was his morning and afternoon sidekick. He especially missed her on the long rides home at the end of the day. She filled the ride with joy and laughter. Her teen-aged banter, the simple way she viewed life, hearing about school and the antics of the kids in her class: he missed it all, especially the way she could turn a conversation about absolutely nothing into the most interesting thing he'd ever heard.

After hitching up the team, he began the slow, arduous, silent ride home. He was anxious to arrive and tell Washie about the posse. She needed a little something to hold onto, a little ray of hope. In all their years together, he couldn't remember a time when she was so sad and beaten down. Even a small glimmer of hope was better than none at all. He tried to keep a stiff upper lip when they were together; he only let down his guard in the wee hours of the morning when sleep was an elusive dream. It was in those quiet, desperate hours that he crept into the family room and sat on the floor wrapped in a blanket and stared into the fire, his emotions laid bare before God as he begged for Sandy's life.

The sky was fading into darkness as he rounded the bend that led to the house. He strained his eyes searching for any sign of light. When finally he saw the soft, golden glow of a lamp in a window, his heart leapt within him. He was glad to be home.

He tried to imagine what Washie was up to behind those walls. He drove the team to the barn and unhitched them. After the horses were watered and fed he headed straightaway to the house. He sighed and wished for a nice big plate of hot cornbread fresh from the oven to be sitting on the table.

Chapter Two

Hope is patience with the lamp lit.
~Tertullian

Susan wrapped herself in the warmth of her favorite shawl and sank into the back porch swing. She longed for even a five minute reprieve from the frightening thoughts that plagued her day and night. She could only imagine the kinds of torture a madman might inflict upon his victims. She didn't want to think about it anymore. The smells of breakfast had turned her stomach so she'd stepped outside to catch a breath of fresh air. John was gone; he'd been snatched right out from under their noses. Simon was gone for a year yet she'd always held out hope for his return. All along she'd had a calm assurance despite the emptiness that often tormented her. Why were her feelings so different this time around?

The answer was simple, yet so complex in its very nature. John was her first born. She'd carried him for nine months, felt his movements inside her body, gave birth to him, fed and clothed him, kept him warm and dry. She'd nurtured him and watched him grow into a fine young man. She was his mother; she was supposed to protect him but believed she had failed him miserably. That's why this was different. He was her baby boy and she wanted him home. If given the choice, she'd willingly take his place.

She gazed up at the skies. Why had she not noticed how overcast and gloomy it was? Had she become so caught up in their circumstances that nothing else mattered? Yesterday was…she couldn't recall yesterday's weather at all. Was it sunny? Was it cloudy and cool? She didn't have a clue. She turned her thoughts to Washie and wondered how she was. She knew Washie spent her days alone on their farm. She feared her friend might be using her chores as a way to isolate herself. She and Clara should plan to visit her, but first Susan had to pull herself up out of the mire.

Her thoughts shifted to a quieter, more relaxed time when she and Simon spent countless hours in front of the fire reading to one another or playing checkers, laughing, and talking about their day. It seemed like a lifetime ago. Simon was quiet these days; he was hurting. She suspected he'd placed the blame for Reginald's latest escapade entirely on himself. She heaved a sigh and closed her eyes, the beginnings of a headache working at her temples. Did she have the strength to try and have yet another conversation about this with Simon?

Sometimes she halfway wished she could be like other people she knew who put their problems on a back burner until they chose to deal with them. Her convictions never allowed her such a luxury. Or was it a luxury, particularly when it involved relationships? Perhaps letting things lie opened a door for resentment to creep in. That's why she only halfway wished for it; ignoring a problem doesn't make it go away.

So there it was: the decision that might as well have slapped her in the face. A little voice seemed to whisper in her ear that now was not the time for waffling. She must stand firm, fight the good fight. More importantly, she must encourage Simon and emphasize he was not to blame. She must assure him that she was going nowhere; she was in this marriage come what may.

"All right, Father," she said, slowly standing, "I get the message. Thanks for the not-so-gentle reminder." With closed eyes, she lifted her face to the cloudy skies. The crisp autumn breeze soft upon her skin served as a gentle reminder of the constancy of God. He would never leave nor forsake her…or John.

She waltzed into the house with renewed enthusiasm. Clara caught a quick glimpse and said, "You look much better. Everything okay?"

"All is…*well*," she answered, sounding hopeful.

"And will be!" Clara responded. "Just wait and see."

Breakfast was on the table. Scrambled eggs, lightly buttered toast and chokeberry jam, applesauce, and thick slices of bacon set Susan's mouth to watering. "And to think just a few minutes ago, I felt sick to my stomach. All I needed was a few minutes alone with…well, you know."

"Yes…I do know." Clara nudged Susan's arm and gave her a under-standing nod.

Massaging her temples, Susan glanced at the table curiously. "Correct me if I'm wrong, but isn't there an extra place setting?"

Simon wandered into the kitchen and said, "Yes, there is. Troy will be joining us. He was in the barn when I went in to feed the horses and said he had news from town that couldn't wait. I invited him to breakfast. I hope that's not a problem."

"Not at all." She suddenly looked a trifle sad. "I just thought…I just thought maybe Clara forgot about…"

"Oh, honey, don't fret. John will be home soon and then we'll share many breakfasts with him." Simon took her in a warm embrace.

Clara cleared her throat and said, "Well, we should eat before it all goes to waste."

Susan wiped her eyes and gave Simon a little smooch on his cheek. "I'll run up and hurry Timmy along." Before Simon knew it, she'd es-caped his embrace and flitted from the room.

"Simon, that just about tore my heart in two!" Clara said solemnly.

"I think the reality of the whole situation is really beginning to take its toll. A word to the wise: we mustn't coddle her, Clara. That's not what she wants or needs." He coughed and then cleared his throat.. "I, on the other hand, could use some coddling."

"In your dreams!" she exclaimed flippantly.

******

Troy spooned a generous helping of scrambled eggs onto his plate before passing them to Simon. "Mighty nice of you to allow me t' break bread with you this mornin'," he said as he spread jam on a slice of toast. "I s'pose you'd like to hear what I have t' say. I've been waiting all night t' share it with you." He glanced amiably around the table; all eyes were on him.

Clara tapped her hand lightly on the table. "Why don't you tell us? Don't keep us in suspense."

Timmy looked up at Susan and asked, "What ith thuthpenth, Mommy?" The recent loss of a baby front tooth had given him quite a lisp.

Susan stifled a snicker and said, "You know how you wait and wait for Christmas and think it will never come? Suspense is like that. It can make us impatient."

His eyes grew big as he dragged out, "Oh. Tho grownupth are impathient, too."

Susan looked at Simon and shrugged her shoulders. "Why do you say that, Timmy?"

"'Cauth, Mommy, you tell me I'm impathient 'bout Chrithmith and my birthday. Ain't you impathient 'bout hearin' Mr. Troy'th newth?"

"Out of the mouths of babes," Simon chuckled.

Susan ruffled Timmy's hair and said. "You're absolutely right. So let's stop the suspense and let Mr. Troy tell us his big news."

"Thpill it, Mithter Troy," came the little boy's response and everybody cackled.

After Troy regained his composure and dabbed away the coffee he'd spewed all over his shirt, he said, "Yes sir, Timmy. My wish is your command." He winked at the boy who responded in kind, sporting a toothless grin. "Well, then," he began, "as you know I went to Ouray yesterday. While I was there I ran into Deputy Dan. He was fit to be tied. I couldn't resist asking why he was so excited. Seems Sheriff Johnson deputized a bunch of men and they've high-tailed up the pass to look for the kids. There's an old hermit up there who told the cook at the mine where Marcus works that he saw a fella checkin' traps. From the description he gave,

29

it sounded a lot like O'Keefe. The cook reported it to the guard, the guard contacted the sheriff…"

"And now we have a waiting game?" questioned Simon.

Troy nodded. He added, "That's all I really know."

Susan dabbed the corners of her mouth with her napkin. "When did the posse go up the mountain?"

"Bright and early yesterday morning." Troy could only imagine how agonizing this was for her. She was the best mother he'd had the pleasure of knowing…excluding his own, of course. He'd do almost anything to take away her pain. "Susan, if there was ever anything I could do for you, you'd let me know." He hesitated trying to read her face. "Wouldn't you?"

"Troy, you're very kind. John thinks an awful lot of you. When he comes home, he might not want to talk about…*things*…at least not at first. He thinks of you like a big brother. Would you be that for him? Could you?"

The pleading look in her eyes plucked at his heartstrings. How could he refuse? He offered her the most reassuring expression he could muster and said, "I'd be honored."

Simon coughed and lifted his glass of apple juice and said, "I propose a toast. Everybody raise your glasses." There were curious glances all around the table. "Oh, come on. This is good news. Heck, it's the only glimmer of hope we've received since the kids were taken. We can't give up now. So, come on, up with your glasses."

Timmy was the first to raise a glass. "I thay thith ith good newth. Mommy, you alwayth thay we gotta have faith."

"Can't argue with that!" Her sweet cherub's words cut to the heart of the matter. She lifted her glass high with Clara and Troy following.

"To the sheriff and his posse," said Simon. "May the Lord guide and protect them and bring our sweet John and Sandy back home where they belong."

Glasses clinked as Troy boldly proclaimed, "Here! Here!"

Later that morning as Simon and Troy mucked the stalls, they still carried on about Timmy's sudden burst of wit at the breakfast table. "He's always been such a quiet boy. He completely caught me off guard," said Simon with a chuckle.

Troy stepped out of a stall and leaned against the railing and crossed his arms. "He's really quite animated. With that lisp, a body can't keep from havin' a chuckle just listenin' to him. You better watch that one. Why, he's got such a way with words he might grow up to be a lawyer or a politician or some such nonsense."

Simon looked far off and thought. "Imagine it: Timothy Wesley Archer, Governor of the Great State of Colorado." He grinned slyly at Troy. "A dad can dream, can't he?"

"Absolutely. Just do us all a favor if that day ever comes."

"What's that?" Simon queried.

"Remind him every now and again that he puts his pants on one leg at a time like all the rest of us. Some of them politicians get too big for their britches and need to get knocked back down to size."

" I'll try to remember that." Amused, Simon shuffled his feet on the hay-covered dirt floor of the barn. "I wouldn't want the future governor to think more highly of himself that he ought. It wouldn't set well with all us country folk," he joked dryly. He stuck a long piece of hay in his mouth.

"Tim's a little tike yet, Simon, and still has a lot of growin' up to do. John, on the other hand, has one foot in his teen-aged years and the other in the beginnings of manhood. He's grounded; he's kind and compassionate. Come to think of it, I've never heard him say an unkind word to anybody."

"Me either, Troy. He's a good boy." He grimaced and then looked Troy dead on in the face. "It's no secret what I've put my family through. It's also no secret that John was forced to be the man of the house. I've been selfish where he's concerned. I told myself it would be good for him to see what it was like running the ranch while I went gallivanting all over Creation, living out some pipe dream. I made a lot of serious mistakes and set a horrible example for my boys, particularly John. I hope he can truly forgive me." He paused. "What you said about him being grounded is true. He doesn't say much, but I can tell he's still having a problem with the whole idea of trusting me. I can't say as I blame him. Until recently I haven't exactly been what most people would call trustworthy, but I came home a new man with a new purpose, and a new lease on life. John was beginning to see me in a different light. We were making real strides in our relationship until…"

"Until good ole Reginald O'Keefe took matters into his own hands again." Troy slowly wagged his head back and forth. "Somethin' in my gut tells me that new posse will find the kids, Simon." He and Simon walked toward the open barn doors. "I can't really explain this, but I've got a funny feeling that those two will be home sooner than we can imagine."

Simon chewed on his lower lip. "I hope so. I'm counting on it."

******

Washie cleared the breakfast dishes from the table and set them on the

31

counter. She heated a kettle of water on the stove and poured it into a dish-pan and set about the business of washing and drying. She mindlessly ran the rag over the same plate again and again as she stared out across the expanse of mountains before her. She wondered where O'Keefe was hiding Sandy and John. Wherever it was, Sandy didn't have a heavy wrap with her. The nights were getting cold here in the valley. It pained her to think about how much colder it must be up in the high country. Surely Reginald wasn't so coldhearted that he'd let them freeze.

She wished she could be an invisible rider on one of the deputies' horses. She wanted to be there when her little girl was found. She clutched the wet rag and twisted it, squeezing droplets into the hot dishwater. "What if...what if he killed them?" There! She'd said it...out loud. Now there was no need to ever say or hear those words again. In her mother's heart, she didn't want to believe Reginald would do such a thing. "He seemed so...so...*taken* with her, like he saw something special in her."

She dipped the dishrag in the soapy water and wrung it out and gave the plate one last going over before placing it on the dry towel she'd spread out on the counter. She'd never washed one single dish so tediously. "Get ahold of yourself, Washie. It's only breakfast dishes. You've done it at least a thousand times." She turned her attention to the simple task before her.

She'd learned last night that the sheriff and his posse were somewhere on the surrounding mountains tirelessly searching for Reginald. She'd fallen to her knees in front of the fire and wept when Alfred shared the news. Seeing her in a heap on the floor moved Alfred to join her. They beseeched the heavens for just an ounce more of hope to carry them through until the search was finished. As they sat by the fire holding each other, Washie recalled a story she'd heard when she was a little girl about ancient travelers searching for a safe place to rest at the end of a long day's journey. Before hotels, people often looked to the kindness of strangers when in need of food and lodging, sometimes traveling late into the night searching for the symbol of a safe place, a single candle in a window. After sharing the tale with Alfred, he went to the kitchen, took a candle from a drawer and placed it in a brass holder. Then he lit it and set it in the front window.

She folded the dishrag and placed it in the sink. The dishes were finally done; she couldn't remember a time when one plate, a cup and a saucer, three utensils and a fry pan ever took almost an hour to clean. "That's what happens when your thoughts are running in so many different directions."

The morning passed quickly. Her chores kept her mind occupied and before long it was time for a bite of lunch. She made a hefty ham sandwich with all the trimmings, just the way Sandy liked. She told herself if she concentrated hard enough and managed to think only good thoughts about Sandy, ate her favorite foods, sang her favorite songs, then maybe, just maybe, it might help make the time apart more bearable. She held on to the belief that Sandy was out there somewhere thinking of and wishing for home.

She placed her sandwich along with a glass of milk on the table and sat down. She bowed her head, offered thanks, and then stared at the plate, a huge lump growing in her throat. She must think of something Sandy had done which made her smile and she must think of it quickly before she went on another crying jag. She noticed Sunflower, an enormous orange tabby, curled up by the fire. She remembered Sandy scooping up the larg-er-than-life cat and swearing she must weigh about twenty pounds. She'd held Sunflower close and waltzed around the room. The cat had gazed into Sandy's eyes as if she were the only person in the world to whom she owed any allegiance, her purring loud enough to wake the dead. From that day on, Sandy and Sunflower routinely enjoyed the Kitty Waltz. Washie closed her eyes and conjured up visions of Sandy and the cat as they spun around the room. The lump in her throat was slowly replaced by a smile as memories flooded her mind. She took a big bite of the sandwich and chewed, determined to enjoy it just as Sandy would have.

Soon, she thought. *Soon we'll eat ham sandwiches together, my darling daughter.*

******

John awoke with a start. It was dark. He wondered how long he'd been sleeping. All he wanted to do was sleep. When he was awake Reginald took every opportunity to torture him. He heard the sound of someone tak-ing a deep breath and then letting it out.

"Sandy," he whispered, pulling himself up and inching over to the wall, "is 'at you?"

"Yes," she answered in full voice. "You've been sleeping for a long time. It must be about nine or ten. Reginald left your supper on the table. Rabbit stew, his specialty."

He grimaced in the dark. "It ain't s' bad, I guess." He tried to stretch his neck muscles but the pain was agonizing. "My neck's right pained. He got me good." Then: "Did 'e take th' lamps with 'im? And where'd 'e go?"

"He left the lamps but didn't leave us any way to light them. He thinks we'll set this palace on fire. Can you imagine?" she laughed and then be-came sullen and dark. "I can't believe it. After all this time, the only thing

I can find to laugh about is his stupid paranoia." Then: "He didn't say where he was going, but I'm sure it was Reginald who spoke to me. He wasn't rude or disgusting or mean. He was just…I don't know…almost *nice*, like when I first met him."

John rubbed his neck, wincing from the pain. "Listen, Sandy, try not t' rub old Luke the wrong way, why don't you. Ever' time you aggervate 'im, he takes it out on me. M'neck might never be th' same. Whoever heard tell o' kickin' somebody in th' neck, anyways?"

"If I thought it'd do any good, I'd try talking to him. But don't you think it would make matters worse? Besides, nothing about this makes any sense. When I make him angry he goes after you. But the strangest thing is that we're beginning to recognize his Voices. I don't know about you but it makes me feel like he isn't the only crazy one around here." She stood and leaned against the wall.

"I know whutcha mean," John agreed. "If'n we don't git away real soon like, th' Good Lord only knows whut'll happen t' us. I don't even wanna think 'bout it." He shuddered with dread.

With her arms extended in front of her, she felt her way across the dark, tiny room. She spooned a generous helping of stew from a cast iron pot hanging over the fire into a tin plate and brought it to John. "Here's your supper. It isn't much but at least it's still warm."

"Ye'r too kind," he said sarcastically. "When we git outta here, I ain't never gonna shoot another rabbit. Heck fire, I don' even wanna *see* one."

She held the plate out and waited for him to find it in the darkness. "Eat," she ordered. "I have a feeling we're both going to need our strength."

"I have a feelin' ye'r right!"

******

In a flash the cabin door flew open and Luke began to rant. "Get up, the both o' you. We're moving." He stumbled in the dark, stepping on John's leg. "Get…out…of…my…*way*!" He grabbed John by the arm and pulled him up with brute force and smacked him across the face. "We're outta here as of right now…this minute!"

John and Sandy did as they were told, grabbing only what they could. She untied the yellow ribbon from her hair and dropped it on the floor as they left the cabin. Out into the cold, dark night they bounded, the host and his minions leading the way.

Chapter Three

Being brave isn't the absence of fear.
Being brave is having that fear but finding a way through it.
~ Bear Grylls

Marcus stepped off the train and pulled his coat collar snugly around his neck. The strong, fierce winds on the mountain were enough to blow a lesser man right off a cliff, sending him flying through the skies like a bird on the wing. He put his head down and began the short trek to his office. Hopefully someone had a pot a coffee brewing. He desperately needed a cup. It had been a long, slow ride this morning without the benefit of Fred's usual banter. He was home nursing a nasty cold. The two of them were preparing for a business trip to the Front Range in a few weeks and it was imperative they both be in tiptop shape.

Just as he approached the administration building he noticed several men, including Sheriff Johnson, exiting the canteen. He waved at the sheriff and then turned to enter the office. A few minutes later, the sheriff wandered in and dropped into a chair and tossed his hat on the edge of Marcus' deck. They shared pleasantries and then got on to the business at hand.

"Sure do 'ppreciate how ya arranged fer th' men t' take meals here, Marcus. It was a right nice thing t' do."

"It's the least we could do under the circumstances. Besides, what's a few more eggs and bacon or pancakes among friends?" said Marcus.

"Last night we found the old cabin the hermit told us about. It was empty, but somebody's been there. The house was warm and a small fire was still burnin'. There was some kinda stew in a pot. Must've left in a hurry. Oh…and we found this." He dug in his coat pocket and pulled out a yellow ribbon.

Marcus's eyes fixed on it as the sheriff dangled it like a carrot before a rabbit. "That's Sandy's. I know it is," he exclaimed. "She was wearing a yellow dress with matching ribbons in her hair that night. I remember it specifically because Faerie mentioned how the color complimented her hair." Then: "Do you think she left it to let you know you're on the right track?"

"Don't know, but if she's as smart as ever'body says, she left it on purpose. On t'other han', she might've left it on accident." He shrugged his shoulders. "Either way, it's a clue jest th' same."

Marcus felt a glimmer of hope for his dear friends. Still, he was leery of becoming too optimistic. He prided himself on being a realist, but there was a place for hope nonetheless. The Somers and Archers needed hope, even if it was just a glimmer. Perhaps it was Divine Providence that there was no way to communicate with them from the mine. It would never do to pass the sheriff's findings on to them only to have their hopes dashed when it turned out to be nothing. Or worse, what if they found the children… No! He wouldn't allow himself to finish the thought. He simply must believe…must hope…must have faith.

Sheriff Johnson knew that far off look in Marcus's eyes. "We'll find 'em," he said, reassuringly. "I know we'll find 'em."

Marcus abruptly glanced down at the ledgers on his desk and scratched his chin. "I want to believe it, I really do. But even if you do find the kids it doesn't mean Reginald will be with them. And…if he isn't, who'll be his next victim? It sickens me to even think about it." He sighed resignedly.

"Listen, Marcus. I understan' what ye'r sayin'. I don' mind tellin' ya that I go t' bed ever' night thinkin' 'bout that no account varmint. When I wake up of a mornin' I can't help wonderin' where he's a'hidin'. Heck, he's even in m' dreams." He chewed on his lower lip then said, "I'm honor bound t' catch that man. Heck, I might even retire when I find 'im. It'd be like I dotted the last 'i' and crossed the last 't' of my life's work."

Marcus half-smiled from one corner of his mouth. "I doubt that. But I know lots of folks who would petition the county to get you a big fat raise."

"I could live with that!" The sheriff rose from the chair with a chuckle and promised one last time to bring the kids home, then bid Marcus a fond farewell.

Marcus watched as the lawman moseyed out of his office and down the hall, nodding to those he passed. He sat fixated on nothing in particular, lost in his thoughts. His mother loved Reginald. She called him Lonesome Rabbit. As a child, Marcus never understood the name; now he did. A rabbit scurried from one place to another, hiding under bushes, not moving, barely breathing, waiting for its predator to pass by. As a child, Reginald was scorned and treated badly by his adoptive family. He was lonely and scared and often ran to the Wright house, straight into the safe and protective embrace of Mother Wright's arms.

"Lonesome Rabbit," he said aloud. "I haven't thought of that in years. It still fits." He turned his attention once more to the ledgers. "Why can't life be like numbers? Numbers don't lie." He hummed as he ran his index finger down a column of figures. He frowned and sat back in his chair. It was no good; no matter how he tried, he couldn't concentrate. He kept thinking about what a captive Reginald was to the life he'd chosen. *If only he'd turn himself in. Perhaps then he'd receive the help he so desperately needs.*

"The truth shall set you free!" he said thoughtfully. "On the other hand, truth can also be devastating. My dad always said, 'once it's out there, it's up to us to decide what to do with it'. I suppose he's right. We can either be totally destroyed by the truth, or we can sort it out and deal with its implications."

He rolled his eyes and ran his fingers through his hair. Why was he so philosophical today? Why was he talking to himself? He was rationalizing about the truth as if it always carried negative connotations. He'd become very pessimistic since Reginald's rain of fire began and he didn't like it one bit. He stood, backing his chair out of the way, left his office and headed to the canteen. He desperately needed a new perspective and a strong cup of Cook's coffee.

******

The deputies mounted their rides and impatiently waited for Sheriff Johnson's signal to start the hunt. It was a cold morning on Red Mountain. The deputies were restless and itching to catch their man. From the entrance of the canteen, Marcus watched as the sheriff waved them into motion. The horses began moving slowly into the stands of spruce and aspen trees, then out of sight. He turned and headed straight to the kitchen for a visit with his old friend, Cook.

Cook Leonard was an old cowpoke who'd joined the ranks of this mine after years of service at a ranch in Montana. He'd grown tired of sleeping out under the stars in all kinds of weather and cooking for a bunch of gnarly cowpokes half his age. He'd left after fifteen years of devoted service to his employers with a letter of recommendation that practically guaranteed him any position he desired. And now he was the chief cook and bottle washer for what he considered to be the finest mining operation in the West.

He was a tall, gangly man dressed in Western garb with a big white industrial-sized apron tied at his waist. His bushy eyebrows reminded Marcus of a hoot owl. At the sight of the old man, Marcus broke into a wide toothy grin. He was glad he made the short jaunt to the canteen. Something about Cook made folks smile.

"Good morning, my friend," Marcus said, warmly.

"Right back atcha," said the wiry old man. "Don't see much of ya these days. Gettin' ready fer a trip?"

Marcus nodded. "I am. Fred and I will be traveling to Colorado Springs in a couple of weeks. We'll be visiting a man who recently struck gold and hasn't a clue how to mine it."

"Speakin' of Fred, where is 'e? I ain't seen 'im this mornin'. That young man must have a hollow leg. Eats a cinnamon roll most ever' mornin' with his coffee. I know Miss Lydia feeds him a hearty breakfast, so I don't know whar he puts it."

Marcus wagged his head as he reached for the coffee pot. "I recall the days when I could eat like that. Don't worry. It'll catch up to him one of these days." Then: "I ran off and left my lunch sitting on the kitchen counter. D'you think maybe you could fix me a bacon and egg sandwich a little before noon? Say about a quarter to twelve?"

"I think I kin handle it. Anythin' else?"

"No. That should do it." Marcus breathed in the aroma from the mug. "I wanted to say thanks for taking care of the sheriff and his men. I know it's an imposition."

"Naw sir, it ain't a problem a'tall." Cook lifted the bottom of his apron and mopped dots of perspiration from his brow. "I jest wish it was fer any other reason than what it is. 'Tis hard t' b'lieve how our boy Reginald has turned out."

"It is indeed." Marcus gulped his coffee and then wished he hadn't. He set the mug down on a nearby table and rubbed his throat with one hand. "Boy howdy! Not exactly the smartest thing I've ever done."

Cook's expression turned pained. "Ouch!"

Marcus laughed. "Some days you just have to laugh at yourself. That was really dumb." Then: "So I'll see you in a couple of hours."

Marcus turned and walked briskly across the grounds toward the office. He thought of Cook. In all the time they'd known each other, Marcus had never asked his real name. He made a mental note to do that when he returned for lunch.

Back at his desk, he took a deep breath and dove into the ledgers. Funny how he'd never worried about the mine's numbers until things didn't match up during Reginald's employment. He chastised himself for letting his mind wander again and poured everything he had into checks and balances.

******

Edward Savage dismounted his chestnut gelding and stretched. He surveyed the grounds looking for just the right place to enjoy a bite. Thanks to Cook the lawmen had hearty lunches of sausage biscuits and fruit. He led his horse to a nearby stream and tied him to a branch so he might have his fill of water. Edward grabbed his lunch from the back of the saddle and sat down on a rock next to the water. Just as he bit into a biscuit he heard the sound of hooves approaching. He looked over his shoulder just as the horse and its rider stopped a few feet away.

"Sam Parker, as I live and breathe." Edward said, full of angst.

"Edward," Sam offered in greeting. He could think of no one he'd enjoy breaking bread with less than Edward Savage. "Mind if I rest a spell while I eat?"

"Free country," Edward said flatly, staring at the stream.

Sam tied his horse next to Edward's. He grabbed his lunch and plopped down on a log by the water. The two men ate in an awkward silence. Finally Sam said, "Edward, I know I'm not your favorite person, but I don't really know why. Won't you at least tell my why?"

Edward pretended to be very interested in his second bacon biscuit, never taking his eyes off it.

"Come on, Edward," pleaded Sam.

"All right, but it's really nothing."

"That doesn't make sense. If it's nothing then why can't we move on?"

"I'm ashamed of myself. I've been carrying this thing so long that I've been hesitant to talk to you about it." Edward took a bite and chewed slowly. "I was the sheriff back home. When I moved here I had no desire to ever be a sheriff again, but thought I might like to be a deputy. Instead of picking me, Sheriff Johnson chose you, a man with no law experience at all. Then to make matters worse, I found out you're his cousin and I got…jealous. *Very* jealous! I began to find fault in you, looking for the least little thing, and my anger grew and grew until…well, until I couldn't stand the sight of you. I made you into a villain. So you see, you did nothing wrong." He dropped his head.

The men spoke not a word for quite a while. The only sounds were a black squirrel on a nearby branch chirping down at them and rushing water tumbling over rocks in the stream. Finally, Sam burst out in riotous laughter.

Edward looked at him in stunned curiosity. "What is so gall-darned funny?"

"You are! You're mad at me because you believed me to be Sheriff Johnson's cousin?" He wiped tears from his eyes with the backs of his hands. "I'm not his cousin, Deputy Dan is!"

"Wh-what?" Edward stammered. He thought back to the day in question. Sheriff Johnson and a young man were standing with their backs to him when the sheriff put his arm around the boy and said, "Glad to have you aboard, Cuz!" He looked over at Sam. "From the back Dan looks a lot like you."

"So I've been told!" Sam snickered. "Edward, you could've saved yourself a world of trouble if you'd just gotten your facts straight."

Edward's face reddened. "I can't believe it. I am so… I don't even know what I am. I can't find the words. I'm so sorry. What a fool I've been!"

Sam moved closer to the stream and dipped his cupped hands in the water for a nice cool drink. He turned and said, "We've got a job to do here, Edward. These kids are in trouble and we've been chosen to find them. Do you think we can patch things up and get a move on?"

"What I've done to you is so petty and childish. Please forgive me."

"It's already done."

The two shook on it and finished their biscuits and fruit as they talked about how they'd take the enemy down and rescue the two young victims.

******

Another workday was ended and darkness was setting in. Marcus pushed his chair away from the desk and stretched. The last time he'd checked the time it was just a little after two. The clerical employees were clearing their desks and gathering their belongings. His secretary hurried into his office and asked if he needed anything before she called it a day. He smiled, assured her there was nothing that couldn't wait until the morrow and waved her on. She wished him a good night and went on her way, leaving him the last soul in the building.

He checked his pocket watch: a quarter past five. He'd have to hurry to catch the train. He definitely didn't plan on spending the night on the mountain. He wanted to be home with Faerie and the girls. He wanted to partake in the lively banter around the supper table and play Chinese checkers in the parlor with George. He wanted to enjoy a glass of sherry with Faerie before they went to bed. He lived for the mundane nightly routine of home. He donned his hat and coat and scurried out of the building and caught the train just as the last whistle blew. He took the first available seat and plopped down unceremoniously.

"Whew!" He watched out the window as the train began its slow departure. In an hour he'd be home. Oh, how he longed to be there after this tiresome day. His eyes were tired from a long day of crunching numbers. His head ached from desperately trying not to think of the posse and wondering about any further progress. He supposed it was a good thing no one had reported any gunshots ringing through the mountains. At least that was one thing for which he could be thankful. Still, it was discouraging to wait on pins and needles for an update and receive not a single one.

He settled in for the ride finding solace in thoughts of his precious baby girls. What a gift Faerie bestowed on him with those two little treasures. He must plan on having a professional family photograph taken soon before they grew and changed too much. He shook his head. What was he thinking? They grew and changed every day. He stared out the window with visions of his girls in his head. Mattie Sue was like him with dark straight hair, olive skin and brown eyes. Hattie Mae was so very like her mother with strawberry blonde curls, hazel eyes and fair skin. No one would ever guess them twins. He thought that a blessing for them as they could be individuals instead of one half of the other. Faerie had already decided they'd never dress alike unless they chose to do so. She never wanted them to be gawked at or the subject of people's curiosity, no matter how well-meaning…or not.

He rested his head against the window and closed his eyes. A short catnap would serve him well and make for a more enjoyable evening at home. Faerie would never stand for him coming home ill-tempered and out of sorts, especially since she made a habit of greeting him every night with a kiss and a smile. He must forget about the posse for sanity's sake and the harmony of his household.

When the train arrived at the station he quickly disembarked and made the short trek to 4th Avenue. Though energized by a walk in the brisk evening air, he wanted nothing more than a quiet evening at home with his family. As he gripped the doorknob, he was suddenly taken with the notion that he was the luckiest…no…the most *blessed* of men. He had a wife who loved him, two children who made his heart so full he thought at times it might explode, a home most people would give their eye teeth for, and friends that money couldn't buy. Oh, yes, he was a blessed man indeed!

Faerie stood at the bottom of the staircase in a high-waisted, long-sleeved azure blue dress. An ivory comb held her long, thick curls loosely atop her head with loose ringlets cascading down the sides and back. He thought her the most welcoming, stunning creature he'd ever seen. As she stood there totally unaware of her effect on him, he basked in her radiance. Their eyes locked as he moved steadily toward her. He took her in his arms and passionately kissed her lips and then cupped her face in his hands.

"You, my dear, are ravishing. You've no idea how the very sight of you thrills me. I fear I've been preoccupied with other matters that we shall not give place to this night. I only have eyes and ears for you, my love."

Coyly, she lowered her gaze. "You and I are taking supper alone this evening. I've set up a table in the arboretum next to the grand window. There's been enough worrying and sulking in this house over things we cannot control. Tonight is ours. Annie has the girls. They're fed, bathed and in the nursery having a grand old time. Supper will be ready in about thirty minutes. A change of clothes is laid out for you on the bed. I'll see you in half an hour."

He was…stunned; there was no other word for it. He watched as she turned on her heels and went straightaway to the kitchen. Evidently he wasn't the only one who'd grown tired of the whole… What was the word? Nonsense? No, that wasn't it. Fiasco? Closer, definitely closer. State of affairs? Shenanigans? He harrumphed and shrugged his shoulders. The only thing that mattered was that he and Faerie were on the same page. A romantic dinner for two in the arboretum: it was the perfect way to relax and take their minds off…the *situation*. He grunted. That's what he'd call it: the situation.

He looked up to the landing at the top of the stairs. The only thing he equally loved and despised about this house was that blasted staircase. It was equally grand and torturous, but mostly the latter at the end of a grueling day. He moaned as he put one foot in front of the other and slowly climbed the steps. He stopped on the landing and stood at the window. He gazed out into the darkness and tried to imagine exactly how the evening might unfold.

******

Susan lay awake listening to the sounds of the night. The wind howled outside the bedroom window, rattling the panes. Simon lay next to her in a deep sleep. She was so relieved he wasn't a snorer. Her father was a snorer; her mother compared him to a locomotive. Thinking about her father's thunderous snoring led to a bout of the giggles that shook her body and took her breath away. She placed a hand over her mouth lest she disturb Simon. She found human nature to be a curious thing. Oftentimes laughter to be most intolerable when in situations where it is untimely or unwelcome, such as in church or when others are sleeping. She tried to stifle her snickering but the more she thought about it the more out of control it became. The thought that triggered it wasn't even that funny, except here she was in the middle of the night, wide awake, and given to a serious case of uncontrollable laughter.

Finally, as with most humor, the moment passed and she was left again in the dark, her mind flitting from one thing to another. She thought of the posse and wondered how the search was progressing. Sheriff Johnson said they would not return empty-handed. That statement held many connotations; however, the only scenario she was interested in was the one in which the sheriff returned with John and Sandy, and Reginald was forced to answer for his crimes.

Crimes. Why did no one ever use that word when referring to O'Keefe's actions? He was a criminal, plain and simple. Perhaps no one wanted to admit they had been friends with, or been married to and conceived a child with a criminal. Then again, she and Simon had never been friends with Reginald. Their connection was much different. He and Simon had shared a common interest in a…lady of the evening. Now there was a juicy tidbit to liven up conversation at a dinner party. She grimaced and carefully sat up in bed lest she awaken Simon.

She stewed on their predicament as she sat in the dark. Reginald wanted to get even with Simon because of a woman. She'd never understand as long as she lived. That woman…Augusta…married Reginald. He got the girl. Still, after all this time, he continued on with his vendetta. Enough was enough. She slid out of bed, donned her robe and slippers and wandered downstairs to the kitchen. Perhaps a glass of warm milk would relax her.

The kitchen was as dark as pitch. She struck a match and lit a kerosene lamp that sat on the countertop. The soft, amber glow of the lamp illuminated the room and transformed it into a cozy, inviting space. She sighed contentedly. Before long, Susan was sitting at the kitchen table with a warm glass of milk and a busy mind. She wanted to turn it off but she might as well face facts. Unless the milk did the trick she'd get no sleep this night.

Then it struck her! She hurried to her favorite chair by the fireplace and dug under the cushion for her journal and pencil. Back to the kitchen she padded, resigned with the notion of spending the rest of the night with her thoughts. She slowly finished the milk but found she was still wide awake. She opened the journal and began to read.

The story she'd been working on was beginning to take shape, its heroine fighting the good fight, struggling to make sense of a life without her husband, who'd vanished on a journey to parts unknown. True, it was her story and she wrote it strictly for her own benefit. Nevertheless, she received a great deal of satisfaction when she read and reread the completed pages. Might Clara's comments concerning her talent as a writer have some merit? Was she gifted in something other than gardening? She stared at the blank page in front of her and chewed on her bottom lip, sup-

45

posing whether or not she possessed such a gift didn't really matter since the possibility of anyone other than family ever reading her stories was remote at best.

The clock struck three. She smacked her lips playfully making a popping sound. She grinned, recalling how Timmy loved to make that sound. It was going to be a long night; she hoped her heroine was up for it. The words began to fly furiously from her head to the pencil and onto the page. She was barely able to keep up with the story as it unfolded. She wrote and wrote and before she knew it the clock struck four. Pages of previously blank paper were now filled with her flawless handwriting. She wondered if anyone would believe such a tale. She closed the journal and set it aside. Resting her arms on the table, she laid her head on them to rest her eyes…only for a moment.

******

Simon awoke to find he was alone. "Susan?" he called. He climbed out of bed and went down the hall to check the time on the grandfather clock. "Five-thirty." He leaned over the banister to see what he could see. There was a pale light coming from the kitchen. "What in the world?" he asked. Barefooted, he padded down the stairs and found Susan hunched over the kitchen table fast asleep. His heart skipped a beat. Oh, how he loved this woman!

He leaned over and kissed the top of her head. Her hair smelled of heather. She *always* smelled of heather. He gently placed his hand on her back. Susan stirred and then opened her eyes. She sat up and sleepily smiled at the sight of him and then yawned.

"Come on, sleepyhead. Let's get you back to bed," he said. "You can sleep in this morning."

******

"Get up, you two!" Luke bellowed. "We need to get a move on. I've found a spot where nobody'll ever think to look for us." Luke didn't know the meaning of the word whisper. "I said get up!" He kicked at the dirt.

In the distance was the faint sound of men's voices. Reginald paced back and forth. The fire was long gone. Sleeping under the stars wasn't his idea of a good time, but there was no arguing with Luke these days. It was just easier to do as he wished.

"Get up!" John received a swift kick to the ribs. "I ain't tellin' you again!"

Chapter Four

Life is 10 percent what happens to me and 90 percent how I react to it.
~ Charles Swindoll

The trio inched cautiously through the pitch black cave, their only light coming from the lone kerosene lamp Reginald used to guide them. From somewhere ahead came the echoing drip, drip, drip of liquid into what sounded like a deep pool. Luke became more and more agitated with the constant dripping. Sandy and John held back a little to avoid the eruption that was bound to burst forth, believing he couldn't restrain himself much longer. John was especially leery of an outburst; he'd been the brunt of Luke's angst since the beginning of their time together.

It seemed they'd been walking for hours when Reginald finally decided to stop for a rest. He held up the lamp and craned his neck and squinted into the darkness in an effort to locate a suitable place where John might lie down and rest. He noticed the boy had been struggling to catch his breath since Luke's kick to his ribs. Against the cave wall just a few yards ahead was a large boulder with a flattened surface.

"There," he said, pointing. "John, that boulder ahead is plenty long enough for you to stretch out on. We'll rest here for a while." He cautioned them to only drink the water they'd brought with them and avoid any water from the cave.

Sandy recalled her grandmother giving her the same warning once when she was little and they'd gone out herb hunting one morning, ending up in a mossy cave. Once John was settled on the rock, she offered him a drink from her Mason jar. "Drink up, John. You've not had near enough water today."

With a little help from Sandy, John climbed up onto the rock and lay on the hard flat surface and turned his head toward her. In the dim lamplight, she saw a tear trickle down his cheek. She wiped it away.

"You're in awful pain, aren't you?"

He nodded. "Let's keep that b'tween us, please."

She held his head while he drank from the jar. "Men are out there," she whispered. "I pray they are looking for us." Then: "You must rest. I'll be close by if you need me."

"How's he doing?" Reginald asked, sounding genuinely concerned.

Sandy sat on the ground. "He's holding his own." She wasn't about to trust him with the truth.

"Oh, is he now?" It was Luke.

She shuddered and refused to speak.

"I'm sick and tired of your attitude, Missy." Luke was now in control. He took a few steps closer to the boulder and kicked it. He swore and grabbed John's right arm and slammed it against the rocks. John screamed in pain and begged for mercy which only heightened Luke's resolve to torture the boy. He began to howl in violent, crazed laughter. Sandy stood and grabbed him by the shirt trying desperately to pull him away from John. He pushed her, sending her reeling into the wall on the other side of the narrow cave.

"Dear Lord, please save us!" she cried, no longer caring what Luke thought.

Luke turned and bellowed, "Stop talking to God! He can't help you now!"

"That's where you're wrong, Luke!" she cried. "He is a very present help in time of trouble!"

The host's hands flew to his ears as he let go a loud wail into the darkness that echoed throughout the cave and out onto the mountainside.

******

Edward and Sam spoke not a word as they followed a deer trail that ended at the opening of a cave. Sam searched the ground before dismounting his horse. "I see tracks. Boot prints. Look there!" He pointed to Edward's left.

Edward spotted them and said, "Well, I'll be." He dismounted his horse and carefully moved around inspecting the prints. "Here's another set of smaller prints. It'd be safe to say this is the print of a young woman."

They stood at the entrance looking in. "It's mighty dark in there," Edward said flatly.

"It is a cave, after all," Sam said with a hint of sarcasm. Then: "What d'ya say we take a look around?"

Edward took a deep breath and blew it out. "I can't say as we have any other choice."

"All right, then…"

Suddenly there was a screech from inside that echoed, bouncing back and forth against the cave walls.

"Holy cow!" Sam exclaimed. "That sounded like a demon straight from the pit of hell."

Edward raised one brow. "Sam, you have no idea." He swallowed as an ominous feeling rattled his nerves. "This O'Keefe fellow…do you know anything about him?"

"Only what the rest of the town knows." There was that sarcasm again.

"Listen, I know he's not right in the head, Edward. I also know that what he's done is pure evil." He looked away and then said, "Let's go get this son of a gun. What d'ya say?"

Edward went back to his horse and retrieved his shotgun. "Let's go."

They tied their horses to a tree and Sam lit a small lamp from his camping gear. They entered the cave and began the slow trek down its narrow path. It was damp and dark and more than a little scary. "I guess now wouldn't be the best time to tell you I don't like closed in places." Sam chuckled nervously.

"Yeah…not the best time. I'd say close your eyes but you'd see about the same thing open or closed. Either way it's a tight fit in here." Then: "So try not to think about it."

"Easy for you to say," Sam kidded.

They had walked in silence for the longest time when all of a sudden the sound of someone whimpering brought them to an abrupt halt.

"That ain't no animal," said Edward. "That's a young'un. Hard to tell how far away."

Just then Sam put out his hand and waved it ever-so-slightly. He turned his head and whispered, "Up ahead. There's light…and shadows. Look!"

Edward squinted. "Whew! So how do we do this?"

They quickly and quietly devised a plan and went with it before they had time to chicken out. It might not have been the best plan, but it certainly wasn't the worst thing either of them ever heard tell. They extinguished their lamp and got down on their hands and knees and crawled to a boulder just their side of the shadows. Barely breathing, they listened to O'Keefe's rantings and the soft whimpering of one of the kids. Edward put his hand on Sam's sleeve as the signal to go.

"Hand's up, O'Keefe." Sam said in his most commanding voice.

Reginald ran in the other direction, disappearing from sight. Sam started after him.

"Sam…let him go," Edward called out. "Our orders are to save the children, even if it means letting O'Keefe go. We'll get him. Right now we gotta get these kiddos outta here."

O'Keefe left behind two very tired teen-agers, one lying atop a boulder, obviously injured, the other trembling in fear and rubbing a spot on her back. In the soft lamplight, Edward held out his arms to Sandy and said, "He's gone now. You're going home." She flew into his open arms and clung to him as if her very life depended on it. He was suddenly relieved they were surrounded by darkness as tears began to spill down his face.

******

John's injuries were far worse than either Sam or Edward anticipated at first glance. He could walk but only at a turtle's pace. Both teens were tired, hungry, and thirsty and getting them out of the cave took some time. The deputies noticed that Sandy held a hand to her lower back and rubbed her shoulders. Edward decided to get them out of the cave before asking any questions. He wasn't certain if Sandy was injured or was perhaps sore from sleeping on the ground.

Once outside in the open air, Sandy took a deep breath and raised her face to the warmth of the sun's rays. She closed her eyes hoping this wasn't just a dream. Even if it was, she didn't wish to awaken. It seemed like a miracle. One minute she and John were doing all they could to survive and then out of the darkness appeared two heroic men to save the day.

Edward came to her side. "Miss Sandy, it'll be dark soon. We'd best find the others and get on back to camp. You can ride with me." He thought of his daughter, Liza, who was the same age as Sandy. Perhaps having a daughter the same age was what triggered Edward's need to protect Sandy and ensure she was out of harm's way. He couldn't imagine the agony Sandy's parents had been through.

John's injuries made it difficult for him to mount Sam's horse so Edward helped him up and then they were off to find the others. He wasn't surprised that neither of the kids had much to say. Not only were they dirty, hungry and tired, but severely traumatized and wanted to get as far away from this place as possible. He'd heard tell of folks being in shock after a life-altering event; this must be what that looked like. He caught a glimpse of John as they rode along: the boy stared straight ahead with glazed over eyes, expressionless, holding his right arm against his torso. He figured Sandy must be about the same. He felt a twinge of something akin to empathy, which quickly turned to anger. He wanted more than anything to take care of O'Keefe. He wanted to be the one to end this.

They came to a clearing and stopped. Edward dismounted, grabbed his rifle, and walked a few feet away from the group. "I'll fire a warning shot. That'll tell Sheriff Johnson and the others where we are. We'll wait for them here." He cocked his rifle and shot into the blue sky. "It'll be dark in a couple of hours. Hope they find us."

Sandy and John stayed on the horses, both too exhausted to move. The men offered them some biscuits and fruit left over from Cook's bounty and allowed them to drain their water jugs. Edward wanted to hide in a corner and cry. He pondered how anyone could do such a thing to such innocents.

A little while later Sam heard the snapping of a twig. He arose from the log upon which he sat and listened intently. He heard another snap and then the sound of men's voices. One by one, the members of the posse found their way to the clearing. Before long they all gathered around, equally excited and relieved to see Sandy and John alive, albeit worse for the wear.

Sheriff Johnson pulled the two men aside to hear their account of the day's events. Sheriff wasn't surprised that Reginald found a way to escape. "It's one o' his better talents," he said, sarcastically. "Don't ya worry none, fellas. We'll git 'im. If'n it takes me th' rest o' my life, I'll see to it."

******

The posse began the slow and tedious journey back up the mountain to the mine. Edward took up the rear, watching and listening, scarcely breathing. Did he make the right choice letting O'Keefe get away? He'd heard stories about him…lots of them. Still, he'd been brought up to believe that everybody deserved the benefit of the doubt, and up until now he would have gladly given it to O'Keefe as well. On the other hand, if even half of what he'd heard was true, and after what he did to these two kids, he'd be willing to let his lifetime philosophy of live and let live slide right on out the back door. O'Keefe acted plum loco, and was as mean as a snake…in his own humble opinion, of course.

The ride back to the mine was long and monotonous. Sandy and John were dazed and quiet. After what seemed like hours, Edward was relieved to see the mine up ahead. He heaved a big sigh and wiped his brow on his coat sleeve. Sandy had leaned against his back and he could feel the deep, even breaths that told him she was sleeping. What he wouldn't give to personally deliver her to her mother.

More than anything, he wanted to go home to his family. Waiting at home, where supper was probably already on the table, was his beautiful wife, two young sons, both as fierce as the day is long, and sixteen-year–old Liza. She was a fragile wisp of a girl, strong in spirit and wise beyond her years, but weak in body after a bout of influenza last winter. She survived; many didn't.

The family doctor back in Illinois had advised the Savages to move west to a higher altitude where the air was thinner and the climate drier. He assured them the move would do wonders for Liza's recovery. They packed up what they could carry in their Conestoga and set out for Colorado, never imagining in their wildest dreams the wonder and beauty that lay ahead.

Liza took to the new climate like duck to water and in practically no time at all there was color in her cheeks and a little meat on her bones. And thanks to a benevolent woman they met at church, a tutor came to their house weekly to help Liza catch up with her studies.

Edward stared blankly ahead thinking of his precious daughter. How would he react if someone…*anyone*…whisked her away in a fit of rage, as O'Keefe had with Sandy Somers? To even entertain the notion sent chills up his spine and a stabbing pain in his chest. The first thing he wanted to do when he got home with give Liza a big old bear hug and tell her how much he loved her.

Chapter Five

There's nothing that makes you more insane than family.
Or more happy. Or more exasperated. Or more… secure.
– Jim Butcher

Fred Thompson was the first to see the posse trudge steadily up the steep incline.

"They're here!" He pushed aside all formality and propriety and high-tailed it to Marcus's office. "Marcus!" They're back! And the kids are with them!" He was short of breath; his words came in spurts of excitement and shallow breathing.

Marcus closed the ledger book and tapped the cover playfully before sliding it to the corner of his desk. He rubbed his eyes and then his temples, relieved that a day of numbers was finally ended.

"It's somehow very surreal, Fred." He smiled. "Let's go! It's time to see those kids back home."

"Amen to that!" echoed Fred.

******

Darkness was closing in. The train had a tight schedule to keep and Marcus figured the engineer wouldn't bow to the needs of a few stragglers. He spotted Sheriff Johnson and motioned him over.

"Would you be willing to allow Fred and me the privilege of accompanying John and Sandy on the train?" Marcus asked.

The sheriff thought for a minute and said, "Take 'em directly to the hospital."

"Consider it done." Marcus extended a hand of gratitude to the sheriff and said, "Thank you, sir. Thank you for everything. You and your men will have made a lot of people very happy before the night is through."

The sheriff tipped his hat then reined his horse to the right, yielding way to the others.

Edward helped Sandy down from the gelding. Pale, hungry, thin, and in desperate need of a bath, she fell into his arms and laid her head on his shoulder. She winced when he wrapped his arms about her in a fatherly embrace. He knew then there was definitely some kind of injury to her back.

Marcus's chin began to tremble as he watched the touching moment. He turned away, tormented by the image and angered to know it all could have been avoided. He felt shame, guilt, and reprehension all rolled up into one. An overwhelming sense of sorrow enveloped him. Reginald's victims deserved some kind of retribution. But how could anything ever erase the memory of what happened to them?

Over the course of time, his mind was often filled with questions of what went wrong between him and Reginald. Had he done something that triggered Reginald's bizarre behavior? Had he simply been so wrapped up in his own life that he missed obvious signs of trouble? Or was it all part of the mental disorder that Doc Fisher had described? Did he suffer with these demons as a child? Did the problem come upon him gradually or all at once, like a rushing tornado, destroying all reason? Was he no longer able to decipher right from wrong? Good from evil? There were so many questions and so few answers.

Marcus recalled the letter he'd posted to his mother after it all came to a head. She held a special place in her heart for Reginald. Their bond had always been so tight and unbreakable that Marcus sometimes felt twinges of jealousy; however, he tried to bury those feelings because Reginald's own home life was tumultuous and abusive. As a child, he might as well have been a slave for all the love and care the O'Keefes showed him.

"Mr. Wright?"

A tired-sounding, youthful voice spoke, ushering him back from his reverie. He swallowed, removed his hat and ran nervous fingers through his dark, straight hair. He was so moved by the sudden turn of events that he was overcome with emotion.

"Mr. Wright, I'm ready to leave this place. Can we please go now? I *need* to leave this place." Sandy's chin quivered as tears made their way down her unwashed face.

He managed a smile. "Let's go," he said softly. He searched the small group for Fred and John. He spotted them standing under a great Ponderosa pine and waved them over. The foursome made their way to the train, boarded, and took seats together. Fred and Marcus shared ominous glances. Neither knew what to say or even if they *should* say anything.

"All aboard," called the conductor from just outside the car window.

"It won't be long now, Miss Sandy." Fred offered a comforting glance as the train began its descent down the mountain to the little town of Ouray.

******

Seventeen-year-old John Archer was a wise young man, though still a child in oh, so many ways. As the train chugged down the tracks, the click-clack of iron against iron mesmerized him. He rested his head on the back of the seat and soon drifted into a kind of restful state, in a world before O'Keefe and his intrusive, nonsensical Voices entered the picture.

Only a brief time before, his father had gone missing. Another of O'Keefe's disastrous missions foiled…or so everyone thought. O'Keefe abducted John for no other reason than to hurt Simon. Even one of the Voices urged him to leave John out of it. Amid O'Keefe's ranting and pacing, another Voice said John must leave with them or they didn't stand a chance of escaping the basement of the house O'Keefe once called his own.

Click clack. Click clack. John opened his eyes, laid a hand to his sore ribs and moaned. Was the ordeal truly over? Had the nightmare ended? He and Sandy were on their way home but their captor was still on the loose somewhere out there on that mountain, most likely planning his next move. Would he come back to finish them off?

The train slowed as it began its final descent into the sleepy little town. As it slowed to a crawl, he felt the jolts of the brakes hard against his battered body. He turned to the window and took in all the familiar sites. His heart skipped a beat knowing he'd soon be home on the ranch with his family. He'd see his beloved palomino, Taffy. He smiled at the very thought of her, reliving times they'd spent together riding in the pastures along the Uncomphagre River, stopping to let her drink her fill of the cold, snowmelt runoff. He shared his problems and secrets with her and confessed his conflicting emotions during his father's long absence. He thought of the way she shifted her weight from one back leg to the other as he brushed her coat and stroked her long, strong neck. She was his best friend. There was nothing he'd rather do than sit on the fence at the corral and watch her prance around and show off for him. Funny how the very thought of her erased unpleasant thoughts and feelings. He wondered what his family would think to learn he'd missed Taffy above all else. He decided to keep that his little secret. The train came to a gradual stop and he turned to face Fred.

Fred said, "Well, my young friend, it's off to St. Joe's for you and Sandy."

John nodded slightly and did his best to return Fred's toothy grin, but could only manage a pained expression. He stood…bone tired…burdened…and anxious for home.

******

Susan and Simon strolled along the path in the indoor garden. All at once she held her fist to her breast and gasped. Something had changed.

Something was different. Not something in her surroundings or relationships or demeanor…not even in her physical being. It was a shift in her spirit, a sort of release. The shackles of worry and doubt seemed to fall down around her feet. It was almost as if God Himself had taken them from her. A cleansing sigh of relief suddenly came from somewhere deep within. She sat on the bench opposite the wall with the wooden cross and fixed her gaze upon it.

Simon sat down next to her. Puzzled, he asked, "What is it, Love? Something's troubling you." He took her hand in his.

She gazed down at their hands which were locked together in her lap. "Nothing's wrong." She paused and met his gaze. "In fact, everything's right. John's coming home."

Simon looked deep into Susan's eyes, which were gleaming with hope, confident and sure. He admired her so. He found her quiet, unwavering faith to be astounding. Sure, he'd grown closer to his Maker over the last year, but he still struggled with matters of faith, the unknown. Trust seldom came easy for Simon. He wished he could be more like Susan, but it seemed he was forever waiting for the ball to drop. Inch by inch, foot only foot, every day was a struggle for him. Not so with his winsome wife; she was the true definition of faith in action.

"What do you mean?" Simon asked tentatively, uncertain he really wanted to hear the answer. He squinted and tipped his head to one side.

Susan mimicked his actions and offered him a sidelong glance. "I can't explain it, really. I just *know*. As we were walking just now I felt my worry just slip away. It was like the Father was telling me that all is well." She pursed her lips. "I know I often use that phrase, but this time is different. I really can't explain it."

He wrapped her in a warm, loving embrace. Simply hearing those words pass her lips gave him the smallest measure of hope. "Our boy is coming home."

******

Doc chose to examine Sandy first. *So pale and thin,* he thought. *Fragile.* That was the word to best describe her. She was as fragile as a rose petal. With good nutritious meals and rest, her physical condition would turn around in no time. As he started to examine her back and neck, he noticed bruising along the thoracic and lumbar spine and learned she'd been thrown against a wall earlier in the day. There appeared to be no breaks, only contusions. He thought of a few choice names to call her abductor, none of which was appropriate to verbalize in front of a young lady.

Sandy's mental wellbeing was another matter altogether. It remained to be seen how the poor girl would adjust now that she was out of harm's way. No matter her physical surroundings, it could take months, perhaps years, to recover from the ordeal.

"Well, Miss Sandy, I believe we shall keep you overnight. I'll send one of the deputies to alert your parents that you've been found. Word has it they're at the Wright's awaiting word of today's search." He gave her hand a little squeeze. "Rest tonight; visit with your parents tomorrow." He gave her a look that reminded her of her dad's stern do-as-I-say expression, except with Doc it was more of a this-is-for-your-own-good look.

She offered a little nod and the faintest of smiles in response and then bit her lower lip. "I'm so very tired." She spoke scarcely above a whisper.

"I'll see about getting you a room and a nice hot bath. How about some supper? You must have a hankering for something special." He wondered how anyone could mistreat such a sweet young lady.

She laced her fingers together and began to swing her legs a bit as she sat on the edge of the examining table. With a lopsided grin she said, "I'd love a ham sandwich with lettuce and a big slice of tomato."

"Well, I think that's simple enough. I'll see what I can do." He smiled. "Anything else?"

"A glass of milk, maybe?" she added.

Doc swallowed down a lump that was forming in his throat. Crossing his arms at his chest and taking a wide-legged stance, he let out a big sigh. "Young lady, I cannot tell you how happy…and relieved I am to have you back where you belong. Stay put and I'll have one of the nurses escort you to a room."

Sandy nodded slowly. She then curled up in a fetal position on the table and closed her eyes. Doc quietly exited the room and gently closed the door behind him. He seriously doubted if Sandy's life would ever return to the way it was before.

******

The good doctor found John's exam to be much different than Sandy's. He, too, suffered from dehydration and weight loss. His eyes were sunken and listless; his cheekbones protruded and his coloring was a peculiar shade of grey. Doc noted the caution with which John moved about, holding his ribs and wincing in pain.

"John."

"Y-yes, sir?" John's voice was strained and weak.

"I was just telling Sandy how pleased I am to see the both of you." Doc paused awaiting a response that didn't come. "Well, now," he continued, "I don't need to tell you what a horrifying experience you and Sandy survived. And I won't ask you to relive even one second of it. At least until you're good 'n ready." Doc sat in a chair beside the examining table.

John sucked in some air, immediately followed by a pained facial expression and "dag nab it".

"So…obviously your ribs hurt. One side or both?"

John placed a hand on the left side. "I think O'Keefe got me good about right here. Hurts front an' back."

"Was it a blow or kick or…."

"He threw me agin a tree then kicked me 'til I passed out. Don't know how long I'se out."

"Nice guy," Doc offered with monotone sarcasm.

"You kin say that agin," John added.

"All I can offer you by way of help for the ribs is to apply some adhesive plaster to keep them stable. We wouldn't want you to puncture a lung. You really *would* have a problem if that happened."

John made a face and replied, "N'more problums, please sir." Then: "M'wrist hurts. It's all swolled up, too, Doc. And the purtiest shade of purple y'ever seen." He held out his left arm.

"I'd have to be blind not to notice!" Doc exclaimed as he gingerly held the boy's hand in his own. "How did this happen? Can you tell me about it?"

"Happened day b'fore yesterdee." John cleared his throat. Doc poured a glass of water and John downed it in one long draw and wiped his mouth with the back of his hand. "O'Keefe was conversatin' w'is 'mag'nary friends. One of 'em he calls Luke was eggin' 'im on 'bout bein' too nice t'Sandy 'n me. Next thing I knowed he grabbed me by th' elbow and smashed m' hand agin the cabin wall, then starts hittin' it over 'n over w' th' butt end of a rifle. Said he wouldn't stop' till I begged." John paused. "Doc, what'd we do wrong? Why us?"

Doc's heart practically burst. "Listen, son. You did nothing wrong. You and Sandy are innocent pawns in O'Keefe's game. He's got it out for lots of folks. If he can't get to them, who better than their family? By tormenting you, he figured your dad would be miserable, and he was right." He shrugged his shoulders. "At least that's my theory."

"Doc…" John looked past the doctor and stared long and hard at the door. "Doc, it wuz awful. Other'n not feedin' 'er, he never laid a hand on Sandy. I guess not feedin' 'er kept 'er under his control. " He dropped his head and was silent for a moment. "Then: "I fergot somethin'. Earlier t'day he threw 'er agin the rock wall in the cave when she tried t' hep me." He wagged his head. "Luke did that. When Reginald was actin' right, he never let Luke lay a hand on 'er. He'd look at her an' his whole bein' seemed t' change. I think he *loves* 'er, really loves 'er in some sick way. When she said or did anythin' that upset 'im he'd hit me er push me, even threatened t' shoot me a time er two. An' he'd say 'this is fer that worthless piece o'trash you call Pa'. Then he'd cackle out 'n laughter and keep right on hittin' me."

Doc was dumbfounded. Rarely was he at a loss for words; however they simply wouldn't come. But *why*? He didn't understand his own reaction…or lack of it. He'd treated O'Keefe's victims before. He'd even delivered words of warning to Augusta. So why the stunned silence? Perhaps because now the victims were innocent children. Making Sandy watch while he punished John was a sick way of exacting two punishments for the price of one. O'Keefe and his imaginary buddies probably reveled in their pain. Not to mention the guilt Sandy likely felt at the beatings John endured when O'Keefe was miffed at her. *Two birds with one stone.*

"I'm going to take care of you. You'll be safe here. I give you my word, son."

Deep down inside, an uneasy mix of emotions was brewing. It frightened Doc; he'd never experienced these kinds of feelings before. A part of him was overwhelmed at the role he was forced to play in O'Keefe's game. Another part felt empty. He was unable to rationalize anything about the situation other than from a purely medical standpoint. Aside from treating the victim's injuries, he was at a complete loss. Never in his wildest dreams did he entertain the notion of caring for victims of a madman when he accepted the position of chief medical officer of this tiny hospital.

Before long, John's ribs were secure in a plaster wrap and his wrist in a cast. There was a gash on the side of his head that required several stitches. The poor lad bit his lower lip and clutched the sheet with his good hand until his knuckles turned white, wincing through the entire procedure. Doc praised him for his bravery and commented when he finished that John resembled a wounded soldier returning from battle. In a manner of speaking, he was.

"Doc, when kin I see m' folks?" John asked, sounding like a homesick child.

"Sheriff Johnson sent a deputy out to the ranch. Despite the late hour, he wanted them to know the good news as soon as possible. I imagine they'll be here first thing in the morning."

John forced a smile and dropped his head. "I'm *so* tired," he mumbled.

Doc sat next to him on the exam table. "Let's get you settled. Sandy's probably in a hot bath even as we speak. We'll do our best to get you cleaned up. It'll be a chore, but we've handled worse. You must be starving. Is there anything you'd particularly like for supper? Sandy ordered a ham sandwich with all the fixings."

John snickered at that. "She tol' me over 'n over that she had a hankerin' fer a ham sammich an' would have herself one as soon as we got outta there."

Doc joined him. Laughter was indeed the best medicine. It was the first sign of true life he'd seen in John since he entered the room.

"I want bacon 'n eggs 'n biscuits with lotsa butter an' jam. Don't matter what kinda jam. Jest jam."

"Now that's what I like, breakfast for supper." Doc stood and stretched his arms over his head and then headed toward the door. "Nurse Bailey will see to you in a few minutes. We'll get you situated in a room close to Sandy. Sit tight." With that, he exited the room. He leaned against the corridor wall, the energy sucked right out of him. *If ever there were any brave souls, it would have to be these two teenagers.*

******

Knowing the Somers were having supper at their house, Marcus happily volunteered for the job of bringing them the news of Sandy's rescue. That would free at least one deputy for other duties. He hurried home from the train station as fast as his legs would move. His pulse quickened more from the excitement and anticipation of delivering such good news than from the brisk pace and cool evening air.

By the time he reached the house he was so out of breath that he thought it best to stay out on the porch until his respirations slowed. He leaned against the brick wall and tried to imagine the expressions on everyone's faces when he shared the news. Marcus chuckled as he turned the knob and opened the front door. The house was unusually quiet for suppertime, especially with guests.

"Where is everybody?" he called.

Annie appeared from the parlor where she was entertaining the twins on a quilt spread out on the floor. "Everyone's in the kitchen except me. Lydia said they all needed to help with supper if they intended to partake."

He shook his head and rolled his eyes. "Good old Lydia."

Marcus followed Annie to the parlor. His face lit up at the sight of the two sweet cherubs playing on the floor: Mattie, who was his spitting image, and Hattie, who favored her mother more with each passing day. The proud papa marveled at the difference in the two little ones. They'd never be mistaken or be able to pull the wool over anybody's eyes like some twins, and there'd never be any doubt who their parents were.

"These girls are mirror images of their parents." He squatted down beside the quilt. "Annie, you're a wonder with the girls."

She blushed at the unexpected praise. "It's my pleasure, Marcus. They're a joy."

Standing, Marcus smiled as he continued to watch the girls. Annie thought she noticed a sparkle in his eyes that hadn't been there for quite a while.

"What's up? You seem especially chipper tonight," she asked curiously.

Reaching down to pick up Hattie, he said, "Grab Mattie and we'll mosey to the kitchen. I have news that can't wait one more minute."

Annie scooped up the dark-haired baby and followed Marcus to the kitchen. There was only one piece of news that could light such a fire in his eyes.

"Marcus, Love!" Faerie jumped to her feet and hurried to his side. "I didn't hear you come in." She brushed his cheek with a kiss.

The Somers were busy slicing bread and emptying a jar of freshly made applesauce into a bowl. He watched in amazement as everyone bowed to Lydia's wishes. Marcus placed a loving arm around Faerie's waist and pulled her close. He cleared his throat and said, "Could you all stop what you're doing for a minute? There's a bit of news I'd like to share."

All the hustle and bustle in the kitchen came to a screeching halt as all eyes turned to him. Lydia dried her hands on her apron. Washie held the jar of bread and butter pickles she was about to empty into a serving dish. Faerie looked deep into her husband's eyes trying to read them.

"Land sakes, Mr. Marcus, don't keep us a-waitin'!" Lydia exclaimed in her faux Irish brogue. She wiped her brow on the sleeve of her dress.

"Well, now, just hold your horses, Lydia." Marcus let go a belly laugh that brought snickers and smiles around the room. "Oh, that felt good!" he exclaimed, gaining composure. "Let's get everything on the table and sit down together. That's a better plan. I promise it'll be worth the wait."

A few minutes later the group was seated around the large kitchen table. After Marcus asked the blessing over the meal, the food began its way around the table, as each person anxiously waited to hear what Marcus had to say.

It was Faerie who finally broke the silence. "Honey, my curiosity is getting the best of me. *Please*...spill the beans!" she begged.

Marcus glanced at the faces around the table and then rested his fork on the rim of his plate. "As you all know, there was a posse today near the mine." There was electricity in the air. It was so quiet you could have heard a pin drop. "Anyway, I'm sorry to say Reginald is still on the loose."

"I thought ye said this was good news," chided Lydia.

"I don't mean to correct you, Lydia, but what I said was that there was a *bit* of news!" He smiled and took an extra deep breath. "I never said it was good." He spooned a generous helping of mashed potatoes on his plate. "But," he continued, dragging out the word, "it's not just *good* news; it's *incredible* news!"

"Then out with it, Love! The suspense is killing me!" Faerie teased.

"A couple of the deputies found the kids!" he exclaimed. "They're safe and sound and resting at the hospital even now."

Washie's hands few to her mouth. Her eyes welled with tears. She wanted to ask questions but the words wouldn't come.

With hands raised to the heavens, Lydia cried, "Praise Be."

Fred gazed at Annie and reached for her hand under the table and gave it an energetic squeeze. Annie smiled as she gazed into his eyes.

Faerie beamed. "Thank the Lord." She paused. "Details, please. Surely Washie and Alfred would love to hear every little detail."

Alfred's chin quivered. A stoic man, it wasn't in his nature to show his feelings; however, tonight all pretenses were cast aside. "You…they… *found* her? Our Sandy?" he asked, swallowing back his emotions. Washie took hold of his hand atop the table.

Marcus was moved beyond words. "Y-Yes" was all he could muster. He picked up his water glass and took a long draw. He was grateful to be the bearer of such news. At the same time he could only imagine what Alfred must be thinking and feeling. How might he have reacted if the shoe had been on the other foot?

"Are they all right?" Annie tentatively asked the question on everybody's mind.

Washie wiped her teary eyes and nodded. "Y-yes, Marcus. Tell me the truth. I want to know before I see her, you know, in case there's something wrong. I don't want to overreact when I…when *we*… see her." Her words were slow, deliberate.

"They're safe and sound in rooms at the hospital. I'm sure Doc Fisher is taking good care of them. Sandy's pale and thin, and was very quiet on the way down the mountain. She's said very little thus far. I'm sure that's to be expected in these kinds of situations. She's tired and hungry. But mostly, she's missing you." He nodded reassuringly.

Washie slowly set down her fork. "I have to go to my girl. She needs me."

Alfred was the voice of reason. "Honey, I know you want to be there. So do I. But let's think this through. If she came down on the train, she got here the same time as Marcus. Right?"

She frowned and nodded slowly.

"She's probably being examined by Doc Fisher and getting cleaned up, maybe having some supper. Let's give her a little time to get situated. In the meantime, let's enjoy our supper. Then we can go and stay as long as you like."

Washie bit her bottom lip and nodded again as she moved food around the plate with her fork. She knew Alfred was right. She hated that he was right. But he was reason in the midst of chaos. Alfred nudged her playfully and winked. She smiled feeling foolish for pouting so.

Fred said, "It it's any comfort to you, Miss Washie, she seems to be fine. She said O'Keefe never laid a hand on her. We can be most thankful for that." He paused feeling guilty for having just told a half-truth, only he wasn't sure Luke's actions counted as Reginald's. It was all so confusing. "And she's ready to see you both. She told me you're all she's thought about." He chuckled. "That and a big ham sandwich."

Everyone laughed.

Alfred glanced sternly, yet playfully at Washie. "Eat, young lady. We may have a long row to hoe with Sandy and I can't have you puny to boot." He winked. Then: "Sandy's wounds will be deep inside. It may take a long time to help her through all this."

"Alfred's right!" Faerie exclaimed. "I'm so excited to see the kids that I can barely contain myself. That being said, they've been through an awful lot. We must all be mindful to treat them with kid gloves. Love on them, give them plenty of room for healing."

Annie leaned over and wiped Mattie's little face and hands. "Goodness me, little girl, you've got taters all over you *and* the high chair. Did any of it actually make it into your mouth?"

"I wish I could protect Sandy from the world just as these babies are." Washie grimaced and thought back to the days when they were still in Arkansas with family who loved Sandy and doted on her. If she and Alfred knew then what they did now, perhaps they'd never have made the move halfway across the country.

Alfred watched Washie through the eyes of a husband with no clue of how to help his wife. He feared the moment was turning solemn instead of joyful, as Marcus had intended. He must do something to ease Washie's mind. He raised a glass. "I propose a toast. Come now, everyone. Raise your glasses with me." He waited. Then: "For their tenacity and strength, but most of all, their courage, I raise a glass to John and Sandy."

"To John and Sandy," was the echoed response from around the table.

The moment was sweet. Any negative thoughts Washie entertained were dispelled with the toast. These people, though they could never replace blood, were family. This was home. This is where they belonged. She felt silly for doubting it for a single minute. She smiled and held Alfred's hand under the table.

Chapter Six

Anger is cruel and fury overwhelming, but who can stand before jealousy.
Proverbs 27:4, NIV

The host's skin crawled; he furiously clawed at his arms. Night had set in and he looked up to the sky. There was no moon, no stars. The darkness enveloped him like a tomb. The still of the night was somehow claustrophobic. He was anxious and paranoid. His chest was tight; it was a chore just to breathe in and out. There was no wind, no sounds of the night. In his paranoia, he entertained the notion that the forest and its inhabitants knew of his dark, anxious mood and had taken a symbolic step back, so that he might wallow in self-loathing and anger.

"They got away!" Luke shouted, his booming voice bounced off the canyon walls.

Reginald began to beat his head again and again with his fists. He crouched down beside a lichen-covered boulder.

"Keep on beating that hard head of yours. You deserve it, you pathetic excuse of a…"

"Shut up, Luke. Shut up!" Reginald's cries were piercing and full of anguish. He cried out in desperation. He shouted and repeatedly beat the sides of his head. He would do anything to stop the Voices.

How he wished he could just go to sleep and never wake. Taking his life would be easy enough. One too many doses of laudanum would do the trick, only he didn't have the nerve to do it. Even though it would put an end to the Voices, Luke chastised him for being too big of a coward to end it all.

Those two kids had been more trouble than they were worth. All that whining! And, for what? Just to have them whisked away by a couple of do-gooders? If he'd had his way, the Archer kid would have disappeared permanently. He wanted to see Simon Archer suffer; he *needed* to see him suffer. Then there was Sandy. She was an angel. She was kind to him, so tender and compassionate. Just like Mother Wright.

"Will you quit your bellyachin'?" Luke's patience was weakening by the minute.

"Now, now. Hollerin' won't get us nowhars," offered Frank, in his quiet, soothing voice.

"You again! When will you ever keep that goody-goody mouth of yours shut! You make me sick!" Luke hissed.

"Quiet!" Reginald laid his head on his knees and put his hands over his ears. "I can't think! Please, Luke. Hush!"

For once Luke did as he was told. The others were appreciative, but none so relieved as the host. "I need rest. We can't go back to the cabin, but I have an idea. Let's go!"

As if they had any choice.

Chapter Seven

I sought the Lord, and he answered me. Psalm 34:4, NIV

Simon settled in front of the fire with a good book. Both he and Susan were avid readers and their expansive library was something he'd missed during his year in hiding. John had long ago finished the Sherlock Holmes series Simon picked up in Jerome, Arizona. When Simon came across the series on the bookshelf, he picked one of them up and decided to give it a try and see what John's fascination was. He'd do almost anything to gain a keener perspective of what made his boy tick.

Susan eased over to him. Catching a glimpse of the book on Simon's lap she smiled and gave his shoulder a little rub and playful tap before settling into her own chair next to his.

It was a few minutes past dusk, the time of evening when things began to settle down on the ranch. The house was quiet, almost too quiet. Simon flipped open the book and read the inscription. "To my son, John, May your quest for learning and adventure follow you wherever you go…for the whole of your life. Dad." His eyes brimmed over. He sniffed and dug for a handkerchief in the back pocket of his dungarees.

"Susan," he said, choking back the tears, "what if…"

"Shh. Don't even think it. Have faith." She too swallowed back emotions.

He pursed his lips, nodded, and stared blankly into the fire, watching the flames spit and sputter. He loved a good fire with its crackling sounds. He prayed John and Sandy were warm tonight. He lazily turned the page and settled in for a good night's read. He loved these times when the house was quiet and no one else was around but the two of them. He glanced over and admired her beauty. She was as lovely today as she was when they met back in school. He watched as she furiously wrote in that infernal journal of hers. All of a sudden his reverie was invaded by the unmistakable sound of horse's hooves, followed by the muffled sound of footsteps and three shorts raps on the front door. The couple looked at each other in surprise.

"Who'd be coming this time of night?" Susan asked.

Simon opened the door to find Deputy Dan standing on the porch, hat in hand, sporting an ear-to-ear grin. "Dan, come in, won't you?" Simon offered, extending a hand of welcome.

Susan's pulse quickened. She knew before Dan spoke why he'd ventured out in the dark, cold autumn night. "You found them," she uttered in an uncertain voice.

"Yes'm, we did. We didn't get Mr. O'Keefe, but we got the kids." Dan nervously rubbed his chin with the index finger and thumb of one hand.

Susan noticed what she could only imagine was anxiousness. "Come in and sit. I'll put the kettle on and we'll have tea. Surely you must be cold and tired. Sit here by the fire and warm yourself."

"Thank you, Miss Susan. It's been a long day."

After a few minutes by the fire, Dan was warmed and enjoying a cup of hot peppermint tea, a treat he'd never before experienced. The Archers were excited and ecstatic over John's heroic rescue, although terribly dismayed over his physical state. It was decided Dan would stay the night and then escort the Archers into town after breakfast in the morning.

Sherlock Holmes himself couldn't have done a finer job of detective work, Simon mused as he readied for bed a little while later.

******

Susan was a bundle of nerves. When she was certain Simon was sleeping, she donned her robe and slipped back downstairs and knocked on Clara's apartment door. When Clara answered, Susan instantly knew she'd awakened her from a deep, restful sleep.

"Is everything all right?" Clara asked with a yawn.

"Everything is perfect. Our boy has been found," Susan said quietly.

Clara eyes popped wide open. She took Susan by the arm and dragged her into the quaint sitting room. "You don't mean it!"

"I *do* mean it! Deputy Dan rode out with the news. He's staying the night and will escort us to the hospital in the morning."

"Thank the Lord!" Clara closed her eyes and raised her hands and face heavenward.

******

With Nurse Bailey leading the way, Washie and Alfred tip-toed down the hospital corridor to Sandy's room. Washie nervously wrung her hands. Her stomach was tied in knots. Her mind was reeling from the quick turn of events and the anticipation of finally seeing Sandy alive and well. She couldn't wait to hold her baby girl close and tell her everything was going to be fine.

"Well, folks, here we are." Nurse Bailey opened the door and stepped to one side, a broad smile planted on her face.

The couple inched into the room to find Sandy sleeping. Washie's motherly instinct took over. Slipping closer to the bed, she leaned over and kissed Sandy ever–so–gently on the forehead. Alfred moved to the opposite side and sank into a chair next to the bed.

"Look at her, honey. She's sleeping so peacefully." Alfred sat as still as could be, his respirations shallow and slow.

"L-Like an a-angel," came Washie's broken response.

Nurse Bailey watched from the door. *What I wouldn't say to that awful man if I had the chance.*

Sandy stretched and moaned and slowly opened her eyes to see the stark white ceiling above. As she shifted her gaze, she saw her dad. She gasped. She turned and there sat her mother. She prayed it wasn't a dream. But how could it be if she was still in the hospital bed? Her chin began to quiver. Then the floodgates opened.

"I tr-tried to believe! I pr-prayed all the time! John kept telling me to h-have f-faith. 'Have faith,' he'd say, but I was st-starting to think I'd never s-see you again…until heaven."

"We prayed, too, honey," Alfred said, softly. "Probably more than we ever have."

Washie was so overtaken with emotion she was unable to speak. She wondered how a body could feel so many things at once. More than anything, she was relieved and thankful. Many times, she'd found herself pondering what life would look like if God's answer to their prayers had been no to Sandy's return home. She stood at the bedside admiring her beautiful daughter. As she did, she offered a silent word of gratitude. Near brokenness, she was eternally grateful for the Father's mercy.

"Mom, I'm all right. Just a lot skinnier than before, is all." Sandy managed a reassuring smile.

"Oh, I was just sending thoughts to God," said Washie softly.

"Doc Fisher said I can go home tomorrow," Sandy offered, passing glances back and forth between her folks.

"Really?" Alfred asked, surprised at the news. "Are you strong enough?"

"Doc said tonight was mainly for observation and rest. I'm fine… and mighty hungry. I've got a few bruises on my back, but nothing to be concerned about." Then: "Oh, wait! I have to talk to the sheriff first." She smirked. "I can't wait for all of this to finally be over."

"Of course," Washie replied, barely above a whisper.

Sandy often felt the need to keep things light where her mother was concerned. Her mother and grandmother had lived in the shadow of the Trail of Tears. Although Washie was one generation past the tragic event, she'd heard the stories and lived with parents and grandparents who lived the journey and its aftermath. Because of it, Washie's fear of loss often clouded her judgment and emotions. Sandy worried how the events of the past few weeks might have affected her mother. Time would tell.

"Guess what I had for dinner, Mama?" she teased.

"I couldn't."

"Oh, come on. Give it a try."

Albert burst in with, "I'll bet I know. It wouldn't be a big old ham sandwich with lots of tomato, would it?"

"It would!" She giggled. "And it was almost as good as yours, Daddy. Not quite, but almost."

"You sure 'bout that?" he teased.

She smiled and her eyes lit up the room.

Alfred thought back to the day Sandy was born. When she was placed in his waiting arms, she instantly owned a piece of his heart, a piece she'd never let go of all these years later.

A yawn from the tired young lady reminded them all of the reality of the situation. "Mom, Dad, I'm awfully tired. Do you think…"

"Oh, that reminds me," interrupted Washie. "Miss Faerie sent a nightgown and some toiletries for you. You know that lemon verbena she wears? Well, she sent some of that, too." Washie picked up the basket and placed it in Sandy's lap. "Go on. Open it."

Sandy peeked inside the basket. Inside was a lovely cotton nightgown with lace across the bodice. She unfolded it and held the fabric against her cheek and then set it aside. She reached into the basket and retrieved a bottle of lemon verbena toilet water. She inhaled the clean, citrusy scent. "Lovely," she whispered. "This is all so nice. It's like Christmas." As she continued to explore her bounty, she discovered a few peppermint candies wrapped in one of Faerie's lace handkerchiefs and Lydia's brownies wrapped in a napkin, as well as two generous slices of zucchini bread. She was like a little girl in a toy store, each item seemingly more special than the last.

"Faerie said to tell you she will pick out a special dress for you to wear home. She also wants to help you with your hair." Washie ran a hand over her daughter's long, strawberry blonde hair. "She said she understands your hair. It's just like hers."

This brought a smile to Sandy's lips. She pulled a lock of hair to her face and studied it. "Come to think of it, I'll just bet I could learn lots about what to do with this from Miss Faerie. We both have Irish hair." She yawned. "I'm happy you're staying with the Wrights tonight. I'm so tired and tomorrow's a big day for me."

"Say no more." Alfred stood, hat in hand, and stretched. "I'm pooped, too. Your old man can't take this much excitement." He winked, which brought a sweet smile to Sandy's lips.

All Washie could do was nod and brush Sandy's cheek with the tips of her fingers. Sandy rolled over on her left side and pulled the covers up to her chin. Before her folks left the room, her breathing became deep and restful. Washie looked up into Alfred's deep green eyes and whispered, "She's sleeping. Our baby's sleeping."

The Somers quietly wandered out into the cold, autumn night. As they crossed the street and stood under the awning of their little café, Alfred took Washie by the arm and pulled her into an embrace. "She's got a long way to go before this nightmare ends," Alfred said somberly.

"She'll be fine," Washie said flatly.

"Will she?" Alfred responded, holding Washie even tighter. He began to sob uncontrollably and when he did Washie could hold it in no longer. They held each other in the dark and wept, neither one able to console the other.

******

"You'd think I'd sleep like a baby tonight. But no! I'm as nervous as a cat on a hot tin roof!" Susan leaned back in the kitchen chair and gazed at the ceiling.

"You're excited. It's to be expected." Clara rubbed her eyes and stifled a yawn.

Susan felt a twinge of guilt. "Just because I can't sleep doesn't mean you shouldn't. Go on back to bed. I'll heat up some milk and sit in my chair and write. Surely I'll doze off at some point."

"Say, while you're writing in that diary of yours, jot down a list of things for the harvest party. We're behind in planning." Clara shot her a plaintive glance.

"Guess I've had other things on my mind." Susan paused and breathed a heavy sigh. Then: "Now off to bed with you."

******

Susan wrapped up in a quilt her mother had sewn for her many years ago for her hope chest. She ran her fingers over the stitching. The needlework was meticulous, a mother's love in each pull of the needle. If she closed her eyes, she could almost see her mother sitting in her rocker, a thimble on her finger, making stitch after stitch, chewing on her bottom lip and humming nonsensical melodies. She smiled as she recalled all those made up ditties. Susan wondered how her mother would have handled this mess. She pulled her legs up under her and nestled into the comfort of the mighty big chair, as Timmy called it.

When Simon was missing, Susan chose not to burden her parents until she reached her breaking point. Around Thanksgiving her heart ached so for him that she didn't know what to do. She knew no one could help and comfort her like her mother. Then this tragedy happened just when life seemed to be moving in a more positive direction. Her mother sent a wire offering to make the journey to Colorado. Susan declined the offer and asked her to wait until John's safe return. She insisted there would be a huge family reunion in the near future to celebrate his homecoming. Disappointed, Susan's mother sent a wire urging her to keep her abreast of every detail, no matter how good or bad, big or little. And, of course, Susan, being the ever dutiful daughter, agreed. Now she and Simon would begin the arduous, yet exhilarating, plans for the family reunion.

Opening the journal, Susan began to write, continuing the story she began many months ago. While Simon was gone, she spent many long evenings in front of the fire, pencil in hand. Her heroine evolved over time into a strong, feisty woman, a combination of herself and Clara. With all that had happened, the story was turning into something she was both possessive and proud of. Writing excited her. Though her pencil moved fluidly over the pages, she couldn't write fast enough to keep up with her thoughts. Just then the upstairs clock struck two.

"This is ridiculous. It's two in the morning." Stretching her neck to first one side and then the other, she began to massage her temples. "I…want… *sleep*."

"Then you should come…to…*bed*, Love."

She jumped with a start. "Simon Archer, you scared the wits out of me. I didn't hear you."

"I expect not. You were too busy talking to yourself." Then: "Have you tried warm milk?"

"A half hour ago."

"Maybe a bite of Clara's apple pie?" he hinted with a playful wiggle of the brow and twitch of the nose.

******

Up with the dawn: that's the way each day began for Washie and Alfred. Today was no different. Washie hurried through her morning routine, ending with braiding her long, dark hair. Her dark green skirt and cream blouse hung loose. She winced as she stared at the reflection in the mirror. Always thin, the recent pressures of life had taken their toll. This morning, however, she was famished. Rested and famished…a good combination. She turned to Alfred, who sat on the edge of the bed pulling on his boots.

"I think I'll head downstairs and see if Lydia needs any help in the kitchen."

He chuckled. "Good luck with that. She's only a *little possessive* about what goes on in her domain."

Washie rolled her eyes. "Oh, really? I hadn't noticed." She grinned lopsidedly. "Myra told me it took months before she felt comfortable around Lydia."

"Because she's so…" He stopped what he was doing and searched for a word that never came. He scrunched his shoulders and turned his attention back to his boots.

"Exactly." Washed kissed her husband on the cheek and gently placed her hand there as if to seal it. "I love you, you know."

A soft, caring expression washed over Alfred's face. He pulled her close. "I have to open the café. We need to keep things as normal as possible."

"I know." She sat down beside him. "I'll bring Sandy by to see you before we come back here."

"Run along now. I'm sure Lydia's waiting with baited breath for you to help with breakfast." This time it was he who rolled his eyes and wagged his head.

"See you soon." She blew a kiss in his direction and hurried down the hallway.

******

The tantalizing aroma of ham sizzling in a cast iron skillet wafted through the house. Susan awoke feeling oddly rested for someone who'd stayed up most of the night.

"Up and at 'em, pretty lady. We've got a big day ahead." Simon was dressed and ready to go.

Susan yawned and stretched, then sat up and pushed back against the headboard. "Morning." Then: "My, don't you look handsome." Suddenly life felt right, *very* right indeed. "I sought the Lord and he answered me." It was but a hint of a whisper.

"What was that?" Simon closed the wardrobe after choosing a jacket for the trip to town.

"Nothing really. I was just reminding myself of God's faithfulness." She hopped out of bed as she thought about what to wear. "Nothing but the best for my men. All of them. What shall I wear today?"

"I like the tan skirt that you wear with the silver belt and brown suede vest and white cotton blouse."

She eyed him suspiciously. "When have you *ever* seen me wear anything like that?"

"Never. That's why I bought it in Los Angeles on my way home. I was saving it for Christmas, but now's better." He stooped down and reached under the bed and retrieved a large parcel wrapped in brown paper and tied with string.

Her eyes were as big as saucers. "Has that been there all this time?" she asked.

"Nope. Clara's my partner in crime. She's been hiding it for me." He sat down on the edge of the bed and extended his arm. "Come and sit." He held the box on his lap.

Susan was flushed. He held the box as she untied the string. Inside the box was a lovely camel-colored riding skirt, a long-sleeved button-down white cotton blouse and a brown suede leather vest with polished leather buttons. A smaller box held a handmade silver belt. She was flabbergasted. "It's beautiful!"

"And you don't have to wear it only when riding. You'll be a knockout. Every lady in town will want an outfit just like it."

She blushed with delight. Today promised to be one of the best of her life. Simon was pleased with her reaction. "I'm going on down now. Take your time." Then: "Or don't take your time. I realize you must be a bundle of nerves." He kissed the top of her head and strutted out of the room like a proud peacock.

Simon closed the door and headed for the staircase. He braced against the strong, sturdy pine bannister and dropped his head as anxiety set in. A dull ache grabbed at his chest forcing him to move to the wall for support. His breathing was shallow and fitful; his head began to spin. He closed his eyes and tried to focus on breathing in and out…in and out. The chatter in his head warred against his ability to concentrate. Would he be able to keep his composure once he saw John? Would life ever be normal for them? He didn't really need to ask; he already knew the answer. *Breathe in. Breathe out*. Life would never even be close to normal until O'Keefe was apprehended or completely lost interest in revenge. And revenge for what exactly? He stood as still as a statue. Breaths were coming easier; the spinning stopped. He opened his eyes and stared at the ceiling. *Breathe in. Breathe out.* He refused to allow negativity to rule the day. He forced himself to shake it off. He silently asked God for strength…and an end to the chaos.

He felt better, more in control. The tightness in his chest steadily dissipated. He'd never experienced anything like that before. Thank goodness it vanished almost as fast as it came. *Must be nerves,* he reasoned.

Downstairs in the kitchen Clara was humming a favorite hymn. *She sounds chipper enough,* he thought. Quietly moving down the stairs and into the kitchen, he snuck up behind her and said, "Something sure smells good. Where'd the ham come from?"

"Bartered with the Whites down the road. They killed that big old pig of theirs and had it butchered. The missus wanted some starter plants for the hot house they just built and since Susan has every plant known to man, everybody figured it was a good trade."

"Wait." Simon put his hands out in front of him. "My wife...lover of all things growing and green...parted with some plants? I can't believe it."

"Well, believe it, Simon. She gave up all kinds of bulbs and ferns and herbs. Not to mention all sorts of seeds and starters. Guess the hankerin' for ham hocks and beans got the better of her."

"I haven't had ham since I don't know when. My mouth is watering."

"If'n you'd set the table, it'd be most helpful."

Simon grabbed plates from the cabinet. Clara had already set out cups, saucers, glasses and flatware, so all he had to do was put them around the table and grab some napkins.

"Is Susan up? What about Timmy?"

"Both are up. Tim's in his room. Last time I checked he was making his bed."

"Good boy. If he keeps that up, he'll make some young lady a right nice husband." Clara loved that boy like her own right arm. "He's really something else, Simon."

"I want time to slow down, Clara. I've missed so much." He set out the flatware and stood back to examine his handiwork. "Not bad for an old clipper ship runner." Then: "I've got a lot to make up for. My boys don't really know me at all."

Clara pursed her lips and leaned against the counter. "Your boys will be fine. Timmy's warmed up to you like nobody's business. He's *crazy* about you."

"Think so?" he asked hopefully.

"Know so."

"You know what?" Susan had managed to slip into the kitchen without being noticed.

"Goodness gracious! Look at you!" Clara smile. "New duds!"

"Like them?" Susan ran her hands over the fabric of her skirt.

"It's...*stunning*," Clara raved.

"*You're* stunning." Simon moved in Susan's direction, smiling and gazing warmly into her eyes.

"Clara," Susan began, never taking her eyes from Simon, "you never answered my question."

"What?" she asked. "Oh, yes. I was just trying to convince your man here that Timmy's crazy for him."

Susan puttered around the kitchen as she pondered Clara's response. She poured a glass of milk and put it at Timmy's favorite place at the table. Turning, she said, "He adores you, Simon. And you'll see soon enough how people reunited from tragedy join together like never before. When *you* came home John was elated. You'll notice something stronger now that he's lived through his own nightmare at the hands of the same man who tormented you." Her eyes welled; her chin began to quiver. Then: "No." She waved her hands in front and stuck out her chin. "I am *not* doing this today. Our son has been spared. This is a day for celebration."

"Mornin' ever'body." Dan flashed a toothy grin as he found his way to the stove. "May I, Miss Clara?" He pointed at the coffeepot.

"Help yourself."

"Well, Glory Be!" Simon used one of Clara's expressions. "You're so quiet we forgot all about you."

"No need for frettin', sir. No need at all." Dan poured a cup and stepped out of Clara's space.

"Where's Timmy? Breakfast is ready," Clara said in mock frustration.

"I'll go get him." Simon scooted from the room as the others sat down at the table.

"So tell me, Deputy Dan. How is that pretty little Nora these days?" Clara asked, catching him off guard. The look on his face told her she'd surprised him. "Well, well, well," she said with a lilt, "I see you weren't expecting an old lady like me to know about your *friendship* with Augusta O'Keefe's nanny."

Dan sipped his coffee. "Nice spread, Miss Clara."

Chapter Eight

Your love, O Lord, reaches to the heavens, your faithfulness to the skies.
~ Psalm 36:5, NIV

A chilly morning greeted the travelers from S & S Ranch. The day was a special one and much too cold for Susan and Timmy to ride in the open buckboard so the Brougham was hitched and waiting for them when they were ready to leave. With Simon driving the carriage, Dan rode alongside on his horse. The journey seemed to take forever. Susan found herself squirming and fidgeting almost as much as Timmy. Simon was glad he remembered a warm pair of leather gloves or surely he'd be frostbitten.

When at last the team led the carriage and its passengers into town, they went straightaway to St. Joseph's. Susan's heart pounded so that she thought her chest would surely burst. "We're here!" She was beaming, excitement coursing through her body from head to toe.

Clara reached over and gave Susan's hand a little squeeze. "Take a few deep breaths. And remember, John might not be up to much excitement."

Susan closed her eyes, took a deep cleansing breath and let it out. When she opened her eyes, she saw that Timmy was fighting back tears of his own. "Oh, honey, what's the matter?" She moved to the other side of the carriage and sat next to him. Brushing his unruly little boy hair from his eyes, she took him into a big bear hug.

"Is John gonna be all right, Mommy?"

Seeing him this way and hearing his sweet voice made her realize for the first time how troubled he was over his big brother's situation, whether he truly understood it or not. She and Clara shared heartsick looks.

"He's going to be just fine. Don't you worry about a thing, Timmy." Susan gave him another little hug and said in her most upbeat, reassuring voice, "Now…what's say we march right on in that hospital and get your brother and take him home?"

With a pouty face, Timmy nodded and nuzzled into his mother's arm.

"Then what are we waiting for? Let's go get 'im!"

******

As the Archer family entered the hospital, they were both surprised and relieved to see several familiar faces. Marcus, Faerie, Lydia, Myra, George, and Washie were all huddled together in a corner chatting in hushed tones. The teens' parents greeted each other excitedly with hugs, pats on the backs, and thank-the-Lords. In the midst of the morning's excitement was a collective sigh of relief.

Faerie and Marcus stood back and watched the interaction between Washie and the Archers. "Too bad Alfred couldn't get away," Faerie whispered.

"He's just across the street. The minute Sandy's released you can bet she'll want to see her daddy. She seems to be a real daddy's girl," Marcus replied.

She snickered. "She *is* a daddy's girl. I've never seen a young lady who loves her father more."

Faerie was secretly envious of the special bond between Sandy and Alfred. She'd never experienced anything like it. Her own father was distant and aloof, often withdrawing from family life to the degree that Faerie's siblings turned to her, the eldest sibling, for guidance. They were all malnourished from their father's irrational need to hoard food. He tormented his children with promises of grand meals and decadent treats and then laughed as the light in their expectant eyes vanished at the sight of a bare table. On more nights than she cared to remember, they were sent to bed without supper.

The sad truth was that there was no shortage of food in McConnell house. Faerie's parents, Jack and Emma, grew up in Ireland during The Great Famine. They survived the famine, but horrific memories of it lived on in Jack's mind. After the youngest baby was born, he suddenly became pre-occupied with saving his family from what he feared the most. He began stockpiling food, saving it for emergencies. He ranted and raved about the starvation he believed to be all around them. He was obsessed with the idea of protecting his children from what he and his wife experienced when they were young. Ironically, Faerie and her siblings suffered exactly as their parents had, sadly, at the hand of their own father. As time went on, he became more and more irrational, resulting in the bizarre pleasure he received at watching his children go to bed hungry.

Eventually Jack was admitted to a psychiatric facility in Boston, where he lived for three years. Once he was institutionalized, family life began to look and feel much different. Faerie's mother managed to expand her sewing and alterations business. Faerie took on the responsibility of caring for her siblings. Feeding them nutritious meals became priority. Though it took time to retrain their thinking and expectations, Faerie singlehandedly steered the McConnell house back on course. Her siblings became used to helping with chores, despite initial resistance. School was five days a week instead of whenever, or if, they chose to go. And lessons were begun promptly upon arrival home from school before darkness set in. Faerie despised seeing them do their homework by candlelight, straining their eyes.

Her mother was dedicated to growing her business. In no time at all, through nothing more than good sewing skills and word of mouth, Boston's most prestigious socialites sought her out to create their ball and wedding gowns. She worked long and hard, sometimes into the wee hours. To save her mother's sanity, Faerie joined the business fresh out of high school, splitting her time between the shop and the home front.

"You seem a million miles away, Love." Marcus brushed a strand of hair from her eyes.

"Not that far. I was thinking of Boston." She offered the tiniest hint of a smile.

"Those days are gone."

"Oh, how I wish my family had the closeness that the Somers seem to enjoy."

"We have it. We're building a life together with our girls that is a blessing from God. The way you are with them is a beautiful thing to see."

She tilted her head to the side. "Really? Do you really think so?"

"I *know* so." Then: "Why don't we join our friends for a minute before they go to their children?"

******

Sandy enjoyed the basket of goodies and toiletries Faerie sent. It felt good to wash her hair. Even though she was in a hospital, she felt like she was experiencing a pampering like no other. Washing her hair and using Faerie's good-smelling oils and creams, soaking in a porcelain tub instead of the galvanized steel tub she was used to, sleeping in a bed she didn't have to make, and having someone check on her through the night…it might as well be heaven. As she combed her long, wiry locks, she wondered what Faerie would send for her to wear home. It felt good to be safe and warm; it was nice to be pampered. Nonetheless, she wasn't fooled by it all. She knew that sooner or later people would forget about what happened to her and John and things would return to normal. And that was just fine with her.

John. She hadn't seen him since they arrived at the train station. He was whisked away to the hospital as soon as his feet hit the ground. Then again, his injuries were much more severe. She found it odd that the doctor examined her first, as he said, but perhaps it was because she would take less time. She wanted to check on him but predicted he didn't much feel like visitors. She worried about his ride home in the family carriage. With all his injuries, the bumpy ride would be most uncomfortable. She thought perhaps the Wrights might offer to put him up until he felt better.

Or, knowing him as she thought she did, he'd probably grit his teeth and brace himself for a most unenjoyable ride. Either way, they were truly blessed to be out of the hands of Mr. O'Keefe and his *buddies.* She doubted she would ever come to terms with all she'd seen and heard up on Red Mountain.

"Shake it off, little girl," she said. The last thing she wanted was to spoil this day for herself or her parents. She'd have to push the memories aside for now. She was safe. She was going home. She was going to get better and stronger and return to school. Thoughts of O'Keefe and his Voices held no place in today's reunion. Whether he was still on the mountain or close by spying on them, she was out of reach. The sheriff promised no harm would come to either of them. Surely O'Keefe wasn't so brazen or foolish to try anything so soon after their rescue. She'd watched as he ran like a scared child when the posse closed in. It was a cowardly move, to be sure. Her daddy always told her that owning up to mistakes, come what may, was a sure sign of bravery.

Faerie had offered to help her with her hair today but she had another idea. She sat cross-legged on the bed and gave her hair one last comb through. Today she would honor her mother by wearing her hair in one long single braid. She loved when her mother wore her hair that way. Sometimes she wished she had her mother's hair, straight, black and silky. She closed her eyes and tried to picture her mother's hair. Once she had the image in her mind she smiled. Sandy had never worn her own hair like that; she didn't want anyone to call her half-breed. Suddenly it didn't seem to matter what others thought of her or her family. She'd had a lot of time over the last month to think about the truly important things in life. Worrying what people said about her or her folks never made the list.

Slowly she began braiding her hair. She vowed never to take such a small pleasure for granted ever again. For a month she'd not washed her hair or been allowed to bathe. Last night Nurse Bailey ran a tub and poured lavender bath salts in the water. It was a gift from heaven. Never had a bath been more luxurious; she relaxed in the warm water until her fingers looked like prunes. She washed her hair, and then washed it again this morning. Each time she thought of Mr. O'Keefe running his fingers through her hair she was repulsed. Knowing it was ridiculous to believe some remnant of his evilness remained there, she wondered how long she'd feel the need to scrub her scalp. She imagined Luke encouraging O'Keefe to take her and shuddered.

She quickly said a prayer thanking God for protecting her from what might have happened had the deputies not found them. She discovered a pretty peach-colored satin ribbon in the basket and tied it to the end of her braid. She pinched her cheeks then stared at her reflection in the mirror. A pretty young lady with rosy cheeks with the saddest, most contemplative eyes she'd ever seen stared back at her. She feared her carefree days were over. Nevertheless, she was happy to be alive…happy to be *clean*. She recalled childhood days when her mother had to practically bribe her to bathe. Well, no more. After a month without a bath, never again would she take such a luxury for granted. For that matter, she hoped to never take *any* of life's simple pleasures for granted.

There was a knock at the door. Sandy smiled when she saw that it was her mother with Faerie bringing up the rear, carrying a small tote.

"Morning, my girl." Washie placed a cupped hand under Sandy's chin. "Did you sleep all right?"

"Like a baby!" she exclaimed cheerfully. "This isn't the most comfortable bed, but it sure beats the floor of a dusty old cabin…or worse yet, the rocky, damp floor of a cave."

Faerie knit her brows together, struggling with the picture Sandy's words painted.

"Miss Faerie, what's in the bag? I fixed my hair. I hope you don't mind." She was babbling nervously.

Faerie moved around the side of the bed and placed the bag on the bed. She smiled coyly and said, "I have no doubt that what's in the bag will turn the head of every young man in Ouray, especially with the way you've done your hair. I adore the braid."

Sandy blushed and dropped her gaze.

Faerie opened the bag and removed a long-sleeved, high-necked, peach-colored cotton blouse with lots of ivory lace and pearl buttons. Next she retrieved a wool riding skirt in the softest of blues and a tan leather belt with a silver buckle. Just when Sandy thought it couldn't get any better, Faerie offered her a new pair of tan riding boots and a cream-colored shawl.

Sandy's eyes were as big as saucers. "This is too much." She looked first to her mother, then Faerie, then back to her mother. The excitement on her face told the women they'd hit the jackpot with this offering.

Faerie sat on the corner of the bed and took Sandy's hand in her own. "Nothing is too much for you, Sandy. You and John are miracles and the only concern any of us have had since the day you were taken. We've been petitioning God on your behalf day and night. There is nothing big or special enough to show you how much you are loved, nothing worthy enough to show our thanks for your return. These tokens are but a small way of welcoming you home, baby girl."

"Oh, Miss Faerie," Sandy cried. She laid her head on Faerie's shoulder and wept tears of relief.

With her arms around the girl like a protective cocoon, Faerie said, "There, there, sweet child." She kissed the top of Sandy's head. Then, with Sandy's chin cupped in her hand, Faerie heaved a heavy sigh. "Now," she began, "let's transform you from a hospital patient to a lovely young woman about town."

******

Susan and Simon shared worried, hopeful glances before opening the door to John's hospital room.

"Here we go," said Simon. He dropped his head and took a few deep breaths and then looked at Susan trying to read what he saw in her eyes. He pushed the door open.

Susan wasn't prepared for what she saw. "Oh, son," she whispered, choking back tears. She cautiously eased his way, wanting desperately to take John in a motherly embrace, but resisted thinking it would only serve to cause him pain. She silently scolded herself for gasping and for the expression that caused John to turn his smiling face into a blank stare.

"I'm sorry, John. I kn-knew you were injured; I g-guess I just w-wasn't prepared as I thought. That's all." She tentatively placed a hand on his uninjured arm.

"Ah, Mom. It's all right. I jest hate t' see ya sad, is all." He forced a grin from one side of his mouth. Then: "Dad, it's s' good t' see ya."

Simon let out a long staggering breath he hadn't realized he was holding. "I'm so glad you…" He couldn't finish. He too was choking on tears. He pulled a handkerchief from his coat pocket and blew his nose.

"B'lieve me, I understan', Dad. I've done cried a river, m'self." John's words were just above a whisper.

"So tell us, son. Are you in much pain?" Simon asked, eyeing his son's sling.

Their reunion was interrupted by a tap on the door. Doc Fisher waltzed in, all smiles. "Morning folks." Then: "John! Good to see you looking a little more chipper than last night." He maneuvered to the bed the best way he could without interrupting the reunion. "How's the pain?"

"Dad jest asked me th' same thing. M' shoulder's something else!" he exclaimed, wincing as if on cue. "It didn't hurt that bad when I fell off ole Taffy." For Doc's sake, he said, "She's m' horse, m' best girl, really." He laughed and quickly offered, "Ooh, that smarts. Now I understand what it

82

means when a body says they died laughin'.'"

Chuckles erupted in the small room. "It's good to have a sense of humor. Just don't ignore pain. It warns us when things aren't as they should be. I'm sending home laudanum with your folks. Don't underuse it; don't overuse it. This stuff is potent, in case you haven't already noticed." Doc gave his patient a serious look before breaking out in a big smile.

"Doc, John looks pretty rough. What's the story?" Simon queried.

"I don't need to tell you he's been through a gruesome ordeal. Only I do think the details should be left up to John…and only when he's ready." Doc raised a brow. He crossed his arms and leaned against the wall. "John's suffering from a number of injuries and ailments, the greatest being dehydration. I can't stress enough the need to drink lots and lots of water." He shot John a look. "Even when you think you can't drink anymore…drink some more. Understand?" John nodded with a smirk. Focusing his attention back on the parents, Doc continued. "Not knowing John's weight beforehand, I don't have any way of knowing how much he's lost. I'm guessing at least ten pounds."

"Looks like more," Simon remarked.

"Probably," agreed Doc. "His left scapula is fractured. That's his shoulder bone, for those who don't speak doctor. That'll take about six weeks to heal. He's got two broken ribs, also on the left. Oh…and a fractured wrist. That's the newest injury." Doc smirked and added, "One last thing to remember him by. Right, John?"

"Nice guy," John said sarcastically. "How could I ever forget 'im?"

Susan exhaled. "Any special advice on how long before John can begin life again?"

Doc dug deep inside himself searching for the answer. He realized she wasn't addressing physical ailments. She was fishing for guarantees that he wasn't able to give. "Susan, a lot of John's healing will be up to him. Knowing he has your support will help. Try not to rush things." He paused, looking down at the floor. "Look, the best advice I can give is to take it slow. John's broken bones will mend. His bruises and scrapes will disappear without a trace." He pursed his lips. Then: "The memories and trauma? That's a horse of a different color. Time is a great healer, except it would be foolish for me to say he'll ever forget what happened."

"Mom," John interrupted, "right now all I really wanna do is go home. You know me. I can't wait t' sleep in my own bed." He gazed at her reassuringly. "I'm gonna be jest fine now that all that other nonsense is b'hind me. When I'm ready, I'll tell ya anything' ya wanna know. Deal?"

"Deal!" Simon said pointedly. He understood precisely what John meant.

"Doc," John began, "when can I bust outta this place? Ever'body's been real nice, the bed's almost tol'rable, but I wanna go home."

Doc feigned hurt feelings. Placing a hand against his chest, he said, "I'm so disappointed you aren't happy with our accommodations. The Sisters are the best at hospital corners. The nurses give the best bed baths in three counties. Why, we have the best medical facility this side of Denver." Everyone laughed. "Ah…now that's what I like to hear. There's nothing like a little levity to cure a case or two of melancholy." Then: "All right, then, young man. Let's get you checked out of here since I can't convince you to stay one more minute." Doc handed Susan written instructions and a packet of laudanum.

Doc filled Simon in on John's discharge instructions as they strolled together down the corridor. The two shook hands and Simon thanked him for taking care of his son. He then made his way to the business office to square things away. When he returned to the room, John was dressed in fresh jeans and a cotton shirt. The clothes that fit John so well only a month before now hung loosely on his battered and bruised body. Simon was shocked…and angry. *What kind of animal are we dealing with?* He turned away before John caught him staring.

"What time is it, Dad?" John asked.

Simon checked his pocket watch. "No wonder I'm hungry. It's time to eat. John, would you like to go across the street for a bite? I'm sure Sandy's dad would love to see you." He had to keep up the charade for John's sake. He kept repeating the same word over and over in his mind. *Celebration! Celebration! Celebration!* "I'll bet Mr. Somers will fix you anything your heart desires." *Take it easy, Simon. Remember this is a Celebration!* He waited for John's answer. *If I ever get my hands on O'Keefe…*

John gave up the slightest hint of a smile. "Sure." Only it wasn't Mr. Somers he wanted to see.

John's smile wasn't lost on Susan. Her eyes lit up as she said, "Maybe Sandy will be there." She knew she'd hit the nail on the head when John's face turned scarlet. Dropping her head to hide a smile, she elbowed Simon in the ribs.

Not wishing John to feel more awkward that he already did, Simon cleared his throat and announced, "We're out of here! Let's go grab a sandwich!" *Celebration! Celebration! Celebration!*

Chapter Nine

If you dwell on the wrong things long enough, you will adopt a fear reaction.
~Bill Johnson

Augusta O'Keefe had settled into a relaxed, carefree existence in the small mountain haven of Pagosa Springs. That's not to say she planned on making it her forever home. Even though certain aspects of her life back in Ouray had turned nightmarish, she felt a twinge of homesickness for her friends. A telegram from Deputy Dan had kindled an overwhelming desire deep within her to return home, despite all logic to the contrary.

For one thing, Reginald was on the loose and the Good Lord only knew where he was or what he was capable of doing. Just thinking about the possibility of a confrontation with him sent shivers down her spine. She worried that he might take Baby Derrick, as he had John and Sandy. Once he had vengeance on the brain there was no stopping him, and Heaven help anyone in his way.

Secondly, there was the issue she had with the town gossips. No matter what she did to help women and children in abusive situations, the tongue-wagging continued. They looked down their noses at her, calling her a busybody for helping those less fortunate. She couldn't win for losing. Whatever their motivation, it seemed odd they'd refer to *her* as a busybody when they were the ones dishing out the gossip. What logic defined anyone as being intrusive when they were only trying to help? No one understood better than she the fear women faced at the hands of their abusers. The problem was, these proper Victorian women took the stance that no one would get hurt if the wife knew her place…and never stepped over the line. Unfortunately, nothing was further from the truth.

One other thing got under her skin more than she cared to admit. Augusta was a favorite topic of conversation at ladies' teas around town because she was a divorcee…a marked woman. To hear those old biddies tell it, she might as well have a scarlet letter on her chest. Yes, this fell under a subcategory of gossiping, but the tea drinkers took their tale-telling to another level altogether. She broke into a grin and stretched out on the bed and laid quietly, her arms folded behind her head, her legs crossed at the ankles. *Those old bats'll start talking about me the minute I arrive in town.* She giggled. *Like my mother always said, 'if they're talking about me, they're leaving somebody else alone'.*

She had taken Nora and Derrick with her when she met with her attorney to finalize the divorce papers. Though she was obviously the primary subject of the whispers in the café, it abruptly changed once the solicitor took charge of Baby Derrick. All the whisperings and sidelong glances became oohs and ah's and "I wish my husband was like that" as he coddled the infant. For once, she left a public place without feeling hurt or embarrassed, holding her head high until she reached the sanctuary of home.

Nora was an angel. She never complained. She cared for Derrick as if he was her reason for living. Augusta wasn't so naïve as to believe for one minute the girl was content with the idea of staying in Pagosa Springs indefinitely. Her beau was on the other side of the mountains. She'd have been blind not to notice the twinkle in Nora's eyes when today's telegram arrived. That settled it. Nora's reaction was the deciding factor in Augusta's decision to cut the trip short. Though she could really use a nap, it would have to wait. She sat up, ran fingers through her curls and smoothed her dress. Just then the clock in the hallway struck two.

"It's too late to leave today. Tomorrow will just have to do," she muttered to herself. She hurried down the hall to Nora's room and knocked on the door.

A sleepy Nora answered. "Sorry Augusta. I fell asleep."

"I suppose you're allowed." She stood tall and straight and feigned an air of authority. Then she snorted as she began to laugh. Though confused, Nora smiled. As excited as a child on Christmas morning, Augusta asked, "What's say we go home tomorrow?"

******

Faerie and Marcus bowed out of lunch to allow the two families time together. Although the Wrights considered the Somers and Archers family, this wasn't the time for interference. Leaving the Brougham with Washie and Sandy, they made their excuses outside the café and strolled down the street arm in arm, deciding to stop at The Bon Ton for a bite.

Once they were seated and their order taken, they spoke of how frenzied life had become. "Now that all the excitement is over, whatever will we do with our spare time?" Marcus teased with a raised brow.

"What spare time? And who says all the excitement is *passed*?" Faerie shot him a sly look from the corners of her eyes.

"I see a twinkle in your eyes, Love. You aren't looking for more intrigue and adventure, are you?"

"Whatever do you mean?" she asked, innocently. Truth be told, even though Reginald's antics scared the wits out of her, she somehow found it most exhilarating at times.

"I wonder." Marcus gave her a playful wink.

"Honey, I absolutely adore trying to solve life's little mysteries, finding and putting the pieces together like a puzzle." She studied Marcus's ruggedly handsome face. "No one knows better than I how outrageous it is, but trying to get inside Reginald's brain gives me a challenge."

"I see," he said, knitting his brows together. "Faerie, Reginald is out of his mind. And I don't need to remind you that he's still out there somewhere." He motioned to the mountains just outside the window. "Please promise me you won't go looking for him. He isn't one of your *little mysteries.*"

She gazed at him solemnly. He winked. She grinned. "Oh, you!" She playfully tapped his chest. "I promise never to go looking for him." Then: "But pray tell, what do I do if he comes looking for me?"

******

Later that day a knock came to the front door of Monstrosity Manor. When Myra opened the door she was not too terribly surprised to find Deputy Dan standing on the porch.

"Afternoon, Miss Myra."

"Come on in. Would you care for a cup of coffee?"

"That'd be mighty nice. I received a telegram from Miss Augusta and Nora. Are the Wrights t' home?"

She nodded and led him to the kitchen where he was greeted warmly by not only the Wrights, but the Somers and Archers as well.

"Well, if this ain't a sight for sore eyes." He grinned from ear to ear. He removed his hat and placed it on the coat rack in the pantry.

"Come on in. We'll pull up another chair." Marcus excused himself to retrieve a chair from the formal dining room.

"What brings you by, Dan?" Faerie asked, bouncing Mattie on one knee.

"There's news from Pagosa Springs, ma'am. Miss Augusta and Nora will be on tomorrow's afternoon train." He grinned sheepishly.

"How sweet of Augusta to give us such advanced notice," Faerie scoffed. Myra snickered. Faerie smirked and continued, "Dan, I expect you'll be most pleased to see Nora."

"Yes'm. I surely miss spending time with 'er." He felt the heat rise from his neck to the top of his head as his face turned crimson.

"Well, Mr. Deputy," interjected Lydia, "would ye be a'wantin' t 'stay fer supper? Sounds t' me like a bit of celebratin' is in order."

"Oh, I couldn't. I…" Dan, usually cool under pressure, was now flustered.

"Of course you can," Marcus said. "Take this chair, Dan." Marcus set the chair down at the end of the table. "Relax. Take a load off."

As Dan lowered into the fancy mahogany chair, he said, "If it ain't too much trouble, I'd be much obliged. I'm awful tired of my own cookin'."

"Since Augusta's coming home, I suspect you'll be moving back home. Your ma's a pretty good cook. She brought a plate of brownies over when the twins were born. I ate most of them myself." Marcus patted his mid-section and grinned.

"Yes sir, my ma sure knows her way 'round a kitchen. Stayin' at Miss Augusta's has given me a taste of livin' on my own. I'm not sure how long I'll stay with m' folks. If I could find a little place about the size of the carriage house out back, I think I'd like to give bachelorhood a shot."

"If you're serious, I'll keep my eyes and ears open." Alfred heard most of the town business at the cafe. "Every now and then customers mention places for sale or rent."

"At the mine, too. I'll keep an eye on the bulletin board. Something's bound to turn up," Marcus added.

Dan smiled. "Thanks, guys. That'd be nice." Dan glanced around the table, his attention focusing on John. The boy looked tuckered out. And so pale and thin. "Say, John, how's that shoulder?"

John's voice was weak. "Not bad. It's the ribs that bother me most. I try not t' cough. Or laugh. It hurts somethin' fierce t' laugh." Everyone including John snickered. He braced his chest with a pillow from one of the bedrooms. "Ow!"

Simon grimaced. "Sorry son. Guess you won't be riding Taffy for a while."

John wagged his head. "I'm glad we're stayin' here t' night, Miss Faerie. I sorta wanted t' go home but I'm mighty tired. And I ain't lookin' forward t' that bumpy ride in the carriage."

"We're pleased to have you. You're welcome anytime." Faerie smiled warmly. Then: "Annie, let's get the twins cleaned up for supper."

"Washie, you and I can help Lydia." Susan stood and stretched her neck. "Maybe Sandy will be up from her nap by suppertime."

With that, the men excused themselves to the parlor for a visit and John headed upstairs to lie down.

In military style, Lydia assigned kitchen duties to her new inductees. Inwardly, she was smiling and thanking her lucky stars that for once all was right within the walls of Monstrosity Manor.

******

Fred Thompson was in the market for a place of his own. He'd heard tell of a quaint three-bedroom house for sale two blocks over from the

Wright's. He wanted to take Annie with him when he went to see it since her opinion would play an important part in his decision of whether or not to sign on the dotted line. If all worked out as he hoped, the couple would soon be setting up housekeeping together.

"You look far, far away," Annie whispered. She ran her fingers through his bangs, brushing them from his eyes.

"Not really. I was just thinking." He moved closer to her on the sofa and took her hand in his. "Your hand is so small. Mine completely envelopes it."

"Hmm." She moaned. "It's as if your hand shields mine from harm."

Placing his free hand on her cheek, Fred gently turned her face to his. "I wish it were that easy, Annie. I fear O'Keefe will never leave us be. He still has a bone to pick with me."

"Perhaps he's gotten the message that he isn't welcome here. Maybe he won't come back," she replied. "No one's seen him since…"

"Since he took the kids." He completed the sentence. "Just because we don't see him doesn't mean he isn't around. I don't want to obsess over him, but I also don't want any of us to let our guards down because we haven't seen him recently. We can't afford to become complacent. Believe me, he's still out there."

She studied his strong, chiseled face and tried to read his thoughts.

"Annie, I want more than anything to protect you and make a good life for us. I just don't know if we do that here…or somewhere else."

"I don't understand."

"Annie, it's no secret how I feel about you. I was going to wait until a more romantic setting, but there never seems to be one." He swallowed. "I love you so much it hurts. I know I'm not nearly good enough for you, but I can only pray you'd love me just a little."

"Oh, Fred," she said softly, "I love you more than you know. I've been so afraid to say it. After my…well, after what happened with my last beau…I tried not to fall for you, but all my efforts were futile. You've taken my heart." She looked down and fiddled with the cuff of her blouse.

"Oh, my dear one, I feel the same. Whatever happened between you and the other fellow, I sincerely thank him for stepping aside. His loss is my good fortune." He stood and reached out to take her hand. "Come with me. Supper's long past. Let's go to the kitchen for a cup of tea."

Once in the kitchen, the couple busied themselves gathering cups and saucers, sugar and milk, spoons and a little something sweet to munch on as they sipped their tea. A few minutes later the kettle sang.

"Lydia makes a fine pumpkin cookie." Fred munched on the tasty morsel.

"Oh, she does, does she?" Annie asked with a lilt in her voice and a raised brow.

He slowed his chewing to a turtle's pace. Swallowing, he asked, "She didn't make them?"

Annie wagged her head and giggled. "I made them. My dream is to be a chef, or maybe have my very own eatery."

"Don't suppose you'd consider being my permanent live-in chef?"

"Wh-what are you saying, Fred?"

"I'm saying I love you and want you to be my wife. Will you marry me?" He reached over and squeezed her hand. "Please." He sighed. "I've already spoken with your dad." He chuckled. "He told me it was about time."

"He did?" She was her daddy's little girl, so she was both surprised and pleased to learn he wanted to marry her off. "So he wants to get rid of me?" she teased.

"No. No, he didn't say that. On the contrary, he got a little teary-eyed when we spoke. And he promised to skin me alive if I don't take proper care of you."

She chuckled. "That sounds more like Daddy." She held the warm cup in both hands. "So I suppose you'll want an answer soon."

"Please don't make me wait too long."

Annie thought he looked like a pleading little boy. "How can I say no? Of course I'll marry you."

"I promise to do my very best to take care of you and make you happy." He arose from his chair and held her hand as she did the same. He took her in his arms and kissed her. Still holding her close, he whispered, "Shall we tell the others?"

She pulled away and looked soberly into his eyes. "Fred, if Faerie doesn't mind, can we marry here at the manor?"

He pulled her close again and held her. "Anything you want. It's getting late. Let's share our news before everyone retires for the night."

"Fred," she whispered, "can we keep it our secret just for a little while? I like having something that's only ours…at least for now."

"Anything you want. But I'll have a hard time hiding it."

Chapter Ten

Loneliness and the feeling of being unwanted is the most terrible poverty.
~ Mother Teresa

So this is where she sleeps.

Reginald wanted nothing more than a hot bath and a warm bed. He missed the opulent lifestyle he once lived. Sitting on the edge of Augusta's bed, he was acutely aware of every sound. He heard the eerie whistling of the wind as it traveled through the pines and the brushing of tree limbs against the house. He heard a dog barking somewhere off in the distance and a coyote howling from even further away. The house had its own creaks and moans. With the exception of the coyote, he missed these sounds. He missed the comforts of home.

He knew he shouldn't be here. Surely that nosy deputy would return any time. He'd have to hurry if he was going to bathe. In the attic was a trunk filled with his clothes and other belongings. He'd sleep up there on a pallet of quilts and slip out before sunrise.

He was curious about Augusta's whereabouts and when she might return. Sure, he knew she was across the mountains in Pagosa Springs. He found that most curious. Why on earth Pagosa? People talk, but even her closest friends were extremely closemouthed about her departure. One thing was certain: she was running from him. His Voices provoked him, made him angry and mean. She'd run from him without a clear understanding that he had no control over them. But who was he kidding? She'd have run anyway. At the time, that's exactly what he'd wanted, to be free from her and the bonds of matrimony.

He was aware of his misdeeds. No, not misdeeds. Misdeeds sounded like a childish schoolyard prank that forced a teacher to make a student stand in the corner or stay after school and write a hundred times on his slate, 'I will not pull Cindy's braids', or 'I promise not to throw rotten eggs at the schoolhouse'. His behavior was ruthless, evil. If he were a wise man, he'd turn himself in, except any moment of clarity was clouded by threats from Luke. Even considering such a move would send Luke over the edge.

Luke was the clear alpha of the pack inside Reginald's head. More and more Voices emerged as time passed, and Luke used ruthless intimidation to keep them in line. Reginald often wondered if his alters could read his mind. He shook his head realizing how crazy it all sounded. If he had a problem understanding what was happening to him how did he expect anybody else to?

He put his head in his hands and whispered, "Is this what happens when people lose their minds?" Sadly, he already knew the answer. He was rapidly slipping into a world of delusion. During brief moments of sanity he planned for the future. His money was well hidden. He'd removed his belongings little by little from the attic on 4th Avenue, and tonight he'd finish gathering up what little was stored in Augusta's attic to take with him in the morning.

He and Luke frequently butted heads over the manor. Luke argued that the house still belonged to Reginald. He accused Marcus of plotting to take it all along. He claimed that Marcus had manipulated Augusta into naming him her financial advisor, thus making her completely reliant on him. This only served to fuel Reginald's out of control jealousy. He couldn't make head or tails of it. No matter what Marcus's endeavors, he seemed to prosper. Then, instead of taking credit for his own accomplishments, he gave it all to God.

The very thought of a Higher Power incensed him. The Great Puppeteer, he called him. *What has God ever done for me?* Anger rose up inside making his blood boil. The only god he believed in was the god of paybacks. When delusional, Reginald was his most humble servant. Retribution was his name and the Voices served him fervently. Reginald followed Luke's orders, and detested his actions after. It made no sense but there seemed no way to stop it. Nothing short of death would break the cycle.

He stood and walked over to the wardrobe and took stock of its contents. He inhaled the scent of her clothes and thought for a moment of how seductive she was back in the early days of their time together and cursed himself for treating her so badly. He ran his fingers over the secretary, and picked up a book left on the desk. *Jane Austen. She always loved Jane Austen.* He touched the drapes and relished the lush fabric. "One thing about Augusta, she has expensive taste." He harrumphed and told himself it was too late to think about her now. He had made choices that could not be taken back

He left the bedroom and wandered about, eventually ending up in the nursery. "My, my, what have we here? This must be where *Junior* resides," Luke seethed. The words dripped with sarcasm and angst. "Sorry, kid. It's no big secret I never wanted you. Nothing personal, but your dad and I had other plans."

Luke was right about one thing. A baby was never a part of the plan. He figured he had about zero chance of being a good parent. Reginald never knew his biological father and his adoptive one used him as a whipping post, so to say not wanting a child wasn't personal was a lie. He never wanted children and would have done almost anything to escape fatherhood, just like his father before him.

Tonight would be the last time Reginald would enter this house. He would defend his position to stay away from Augusta and the baby. The Voices would not win this fight. Baby and mother were off limits.

He wasn't sure how long he would continue to think clearly. Decisions needed to be made quickly. The Voices were alarmingly silent. It frightened him a little; it was also a welcome reprieve. Any minute they could come alive and crowd his head with so much confusion and chaos and noise. There was always lots of noise. And don't forget about Luke's gigantic ego. *Where did Luke's lofty opinion of himself come from anyway?* By comparison, the others were quite docile.

The clock down the hall struck eight. It was time to settle in for the night. Weary, he ran his bath water and relaxed in the tub and then climbed the stairs to the attic. The hour wasn't late, but he was exhausted, mind, body and soul. Besides, the deputy was expected any time.

He scrounged around in trunks searching for blankets and maybe a pillow or two. In the corner was a sofa from the other house. He smirked and thought it odd how things change. A few months ago he lived in the lap of luxury. Now he was thankful for a dusty sofa and a quilt. It sure beat a pallet on the floor, or, for that matter, the damp floor of a cave. For one night he'd enjoy the warmth and safety of four walls.

The fumes from the kerosene lamp filled the attic. All he needed was for the deputy to get a whiff of it and act like a detective. He filled a travel bag to overflowing and sat it next to the sofa. He blew out the lamp and kicked off his shoes and settled in for a good night's rest. He laid in the dark and listened to the quiet. Tonight there'd be no sleeping with one eye open. No big cats or bears roaming about in search of a good catch; no one traipsing around the forest looking for him.

He needed to find a cabin off the beaten path, or better yet, move further up the mountain to an old deserted mining village. He thought that a perfect idea and decided he'd go up around Ironton and find a place. Not many folks were still up in those parts. Maybe he'd grow a beard, let his hair grow: a simple, yet effective disguise until he finalized some plans.

******

Reginald awoke feeling rested for the first time in….he couldn't *remember* the last time he'd slept through the night. With the Voices on holiday, his mind was clear and fluid. It was early, *very early.* No sign of first light. *That's the thing about these blasted mountains. We never see the*

97

sunrise! He sat up and stretched.

Creeping around in the dark, he dressed in fresh clothes he'd found in one of the trunks. The clock struck five. *Dad blasted clock. I remember when that ugly monstrosity was delivered.* He smiled. He'd given Augusta carte blanche when it came to decorating the house. His biggest mistake was allowing her to make a two week shopping jaunt to Denver with Faerie. She came home excited to share what she'd bought. When the deliveries were made, he bit his tongue to keep from hurting her feelings. Most of the pieces were so ornate they practically screamed of money. He'd chosen to live with the gaudy furnishings and accents to give the illusion of wealth. *After all,* he'd thought at the time, *money is power...even if it's only an illusion.*

He quietly padded down the stairs to the kitchen. Careful not to disturb anything, he rummaged through the pantry for food, filling a bag and disappearing out the back door and into the darkness.

Chapter Eleven

Though we travel the world over to find the beautiful,
we must carry it with us or we find it not.
~ Ralph Waldo Emerson

"Travel should be fun, an experience to remember." Augusta pouted. "Don't get me wrong. I've enjoyed our time away, but let's face it. It's wasn't a pleasure trip." The train moved steadily down the tracks, leaving puffy clouds of smoke in its wake.

Nora gave a subtle nod of the head. She watched as Augusta ran a hand over Derrick's thick, black curls. "This may not have been a pleasure trip, only you must admit there's been a big change in you. I don't know quite how to explain it, except to say you seem more serene. And the way you've bonded with Derrick is sweet. It's a perfect picture of mother and child. Say what you will, but it seems to have been more than a journey for safety's sake. It's been a sojourn, a spiritual quest."

"Life is all about growth." Then, with a glint of mischief in her eyes, Augusta added, "Next trip we'll go someplace spectacular. Have you ever been to California?"

Nora shook her head and said, "Never." She got a far off look in her eyes. "I've always wanted to go to San Francisco." She turned to catch a glimpse out the window. "We should be getting close to Durango."

"Don't change the subject, dearie," Augusta teased. "San Francisco is a beautiful place with lots of things to do and see. Oh, and lots of building going on, too. It's a boom town, for sure. Very exciting." She animatedly filled Nora in on the honeymoon trip to northern California. "You should see the hotel where we stayed. The suite was as big as….as…" she searched for a word. "As big as our whole upstairs. And there were restaurants and lounges and a spa with strawberries and champagne and all kinds of goodies for munching. That's where I met Myra." She went on and on, completing her monologue with, "That settles it. We're making a trip to San Francisco this coming summer."

"Are you serious? 'Cause if you are, I'll start planning my wardrobe now."

"Of course, I'm serious. I can't think of anyone who's as fine a traveling companion as you. Not to mention how much Derrick adores you. If for no other reason, you must come. He'd miss you too much if you didn't."

"You can't be serious," Nora responded coyly. "He'd be fine without me."

"Nonsense," Augusta said as she waved off the comment. "And I can attest to the fact that it's also a great place for a honeymoon." She lifted one brow and grinned slyly. "Just a little something to think about for later."

Nora blushed. "Oh, really, Augusta," she said, exasperated. "You know my relationship with Dan is nowhere near a proposal."

"Come now. I've seen the way you smile and sneak away when his letters arrive. You are so deep in love you'll never dig your way out."

"I can't say as I've ever heard it put quite like that before." Nora shook her head, grinning. She looked down at Derrick wrapped in a blanket and sleeping in her arms. "Look, Augusta. There's something about a sleeping baby that makes me feel all snug inside."

Augusta filled up with a mother's love. "Let me hold him."

They carefully transferred Derrick to Augusta's waiting arms. She cradled his head against her bosom. "Nora, this trip has been good for me. You're right about that. I desperately needed to get away. I'm stronger and more sure of myself now, and ready to get on with life."

Nora listened, her brows knit together. Then: "You know, Augusta, *some* people would say you're *already* strong…and *very* self-assured."

"Pshaw." She waved off the comment. "It's all been an act. Why, if the town gossips knew how I felt, how scared I really was, they'd have eaten me alive." She scoffed and proudly stuck out her chin. "You know, it isn't easy to be the subject of everyone's supper conversation. You have to leave them with a little sample of things to come."

"There's more?" Nora was amused at Augusta's quick wit.

"Oh, my dear, I'm only getting started. When I die my epitaph will read 'she always left them wanting more'." They covered their mouths to stifle giggles just as the train's whistle announced its arrival in Durango.

******

"Just a little while longer and we'll be home, Derrick. When we reach the top of this mountain it's all downhill from there." Augusta sat next to the window with the baby on her lap. He held his favorite blanket next to his cheek with one hand and tightly to one of Augusta's gloves with the other. He giggled as the train inched up the tracks toward Silverton. Outside the window scenes of the majestic San Juan Mountains lay before them. Towering blue spruce, quaking aspens afire with golden leaves, a clear mountain stream and occasional deer made the journey a picturesque tapestry of beauty and wonder. Derrick took it all in. Augusta held him close as she, too, was awed by their surroundings. What a marvelous place to call home.

When finally she spoke, she said, "Life is a wonder at his age. Too bad reality slaps them in the face so early on. I want him to enjoy life. I want to protect him from…." Augusta stopped midsentence and stroked Derrick's hair, gazing at him in awe.

"He's a miracle from God. I want a whole houseful of them," Nora said softly.

"How many do you think?" Augusta was thankful for a friend with the ability to bring her out of herself.

"Well…" She stretched out the word as she pondered the response. "Maybe…four…or five."

"You're a braver woman than I," Augusta teased. "I can barely stand the thought of raising this one only to have him leave me when he's grown. Imagine living through those emotions four…or five…times."

"Silly, girl. That's our job…our calling as mothers. The book of Proverbs says if we raise our children up in the way they should go, they won't depart from it when they're older."

"Really?" Augusta asked, quite taken with the idea that the Good Book dealt with childrearing.

"The Book of Proverbs."

"Again with Proverbs," Augusta commented blithely. "Me thinks I must investigate. Show it to me later?"

"Sure," Nora said sweetly. "I remember my mother quoting that verse to Daddy every time I bat my eyes at the poor man, turning his heart to mush. He was never able to chastise me."

"Chastise. What a fancy word for tongue lashing."

"And my mom's favorite Biblical disciplinary verb."

"Heavens to Betsy!" Augusta said under her breath. Then: "My mother was too busy entertaining her gentlemen friends to teach me right from wrong. The only tool I learned was survival…at any cost!" She frowned. "I bat my eyes for a whole other reason, Nora. It pretty much got me what I wanted at every turn back in the day."

"That's all behind you now." They shared a brief silence, the click-clack of the wheels against the tracks filling in the gap.

"Nora, would it be all right if I accompanied you to church on Sunday?" Augusta asked shyly.

Nora's eyes lit up like the stars on a clear night. "I'd be delighted." Then in a more subdued voice, "You know, Dan will be with us."

"I think I can handle it. The question is, can he?"

******

101

The train's whistle sounded alerting one and all of its approach into Silverton. There'd be one more stop to pick up workers at the mine, then onward to Ouray. Augusta was anxious to see the familiar sights of home. After what seemed like an eternity, she was relieved to hear to the conductor's all board. The girls were weary from the day's journey. Nora held the baby, allowing Augusta the luxury of resting during the final jaunt of the trip.

"What do you think? Another hour?" Augusta supposed.

"Probably. We should be home around dusk, maybe a little after."

"I almost wish Faerie was greeting us. She'd be sure to invite us to supper."

"Don't fret about it. She's your closest friend. I doubt she'll disappoint."

Just as Nora predicted, the train made the final descent into town just as the sun was setting. Augusta gazed out the window and marveled at the brilliant shades of orange, yellow, blue, pink and purple that colored the western skies like many brush strokes on a canvas. Nothing could have been a more welcome sight than the silhouette of mountains against such a spectacular backdrop, mere seconds before darkness blanketed the earth. She barely noticed as the train slowed to a turtle's pace, then stopped. Nora gently touched her arm.

"What did I tell you? Look who's out there waiting." She smiled sweetly and pointed, prompting Augusta to look out the window.

"Faerie!" Augusta's face lit up like so many candles on a birthday cake. "I can't wait to give her a big old hug." She suddenly felt very emotional. She tried to hold back the tears but it was no use. "Goodness, no," she said. "I'm a blithering fool."

"Ah, it's perfectly natural. For such a long time you've had to be strong. It was bound to happen sooner or later. Your heart is tender, Augusta. All that bitterness you had is slowly being replaced with compassion."

Augusta knew it to be true. Things that once caused her to roll her eyes, or lash out, or judge others too harshly didn't seem to bother her so much these days. She was a new creature; old ways had been put aside. *Such a transformation,* she thought, thanking God for working a miracle in her life.

******

Dan spied Nora the instant she stepped off the train. He sprinted to her and literally swept her off her feet and then twirled her around until they were both laughing hysterically and just a wee bit dizzy. After they stopped and caught their breath, he sighed and said, "It's so good to see you. If I'd have known how much I would miss you, I'd have done everything in my power to keep you here. I was lost without you." He pulled her into an embrace and kissed her passionately, suddenly unconcerned with their surroundings.

When they came up for air, Nora was flushed and breathless. "If I'd have known I'd receive such a greeting, I'd have come back long before now," she teased.

Dan dropped his head and shuffled his feet in the dirt. "I lost my head there for a minute."

"Oh, no, you don't. So help me, if you apologize for that kiss I'll never speak to you again."

"In that case…" He pulled her to him once more and kissed her so tenderly, so passionately that all the women at the station were swooning… despite their pretense to be mortified at such a public display.

Faerie and Augusta watched the couple from a distance. "By the look of things, I would have to say that absence *does* make the heart grow fonder…at least in *their* case." Faerie admired Dan's tenacity. He loved his girl and obviously didn't care who knew it. Then: "So…are you as glad to see me as Nora to see Dan?" she asked jokingly.

"In a whole different way," Augusta responded. "Let's separate them before every tongue in town starts a-waggin'. We can't allow sweet Nora to take my place as the town's favorite subject of gossip."

Chapter Twelve

When we lose one blessing, another is often most
unexpectedly given in its place.
~ C.S. Lewis

Lydia scurried about the kitchen like a chicken with its head cut off. "Goodness me, I'll never finish in time!" If there was one thing she didn't want to do, it was disappoint Augusta. She was the closest thing to a daughter Lydia would ever have. What she didn't understand was that she held a permanent place in Augusta's heart as well.

"What are you fretting about?" Myra asked, hands on her hips, and a most curious observer of the cook's disorderly conduct.

Lydia wrung her hands and paced. "Miss Augusta's comin' t' break bread with us t'night. With all the excitement of the young people's return, and ever'body stayin' over, I'm runnin' b'hind. I dunno what's the matter wi'me." She wiped her forehead on her arm.

"Not to worry. Here I am to save the day," Myra said with a wink. "Don't get yourself so worked up." She opened a jar of the applesauce that Faerie and Lydia had just put up and poured it into a lead crystal compote bowl. "Good choice, applesauce. Augusta loves it, eats it with everything. Do you remember when she was in the family way? She ate so much applesauce I thought she'd surely grow sick of it, but Nora says she still puts it on the table almost every night."

Having Myra to help took some of the pressure off Lydia's shoulders. She said, "Me ole mother always said that the food an expectant mother craves will often be the wee one's favorite as it grows."

"I hope that's an old wives' tale because I ate enough pumpkin pie to sink a battleship when I was carrying Patricia." Myra wiggled her brows and smiled impishly.

The gals entertained each other with tales of family and friends and before they knew it, the welcome home feast for Augusta and Nora was ready to be served. All that was missing was someone to eat it.

******

In only a matter of minutes, echoes of laugher rang throughout the manor. "They're here!" Lydia and Myra chimed in unison. Myra filled the glasses with iced water. All that remained to complete the table was the platter of roast chicken which sat on the counter. As the ladies congratulated each other on a job well done, Faerie burst forth into the kitchen.

"Well, *however* did you do this? How did you manage to get such a huge meal on the table the precise moment we arrived?" Faerie asked, pleasantly surprised. She half expected to see Lydia in a tizzy with Myra doting over the Irish whirlwind, and trying to calm her down.

******

Supper was served in the formal dining room. Augusta sat at the table taking visual inventory of the room. This was where Reginald sulked by candlelight in the middle of the night with his decanter of bourbon. She'd left the dining table and chairs with the house when she moved. He hated the table; she loved the table. He called it ornate and ridiculous. She thought it grand and most elegant. He'd said a table like this spoke of money. How he had humored her and bowed to her every whim. Why? Was it because he loved her? Or was it because he knew she'd choose the most expensive, grandiose things she could find. Above all, he wished the town to think him rich. And this house and its contents reeked of money.

"Augusta…"

She looked around the table, embarrassed. She'd been caught daydreaming again. She smiled demurely. "Just reminiscing." Then: "This is quite a spread, Lydia. Everything looks and smells delicious." For the time being she forgot all about Reginald and his mood swings and quirks. Everyone she loved and cherished was here in this room. Marcus and Faerie certainly knew how to throw a dinner party at the drop of a hat. Augusta was tired but quite pleased to be here enjoying the friendly banter and laughter. She sat back in her chair in a comfortable silence, more than pleased to be back where she belonged, and finally at peace about so many things.

When she gave up the manor, she sank into a deep depression. It felt as if a part of her had died. In those not-so-long-ago days, she was unsure how to put words to her feelings. She didn't know whether to define them as loss, greed, resentment or a combination thereof, so she bottled them up and pretended to be truly relieved about the situation. Now, after a brief sabbatical, she could honestly say she was happy with how this part of her life had turned out. She was content in her own skin for the very first time. She'd longed for love and acceptance from just one someone and was blessed instead with many.

As far as she was concerned, these folks were the very best this world had to offer. Annie, who was seated directly across from her, was a quiet, gentle soul, never spewing on about anything. Day in, day out, she cared for Hattie and Mattie as if they were her own. Never had she heard the young lady utter an unkind word about anyone – not even about Reginald.

Myra, Augusta's former house manager – had been a steadfast confidante and friend from the time they met. Many a night they sat in the kitchen, both very pregnant, gorging themselves on Lydia's mouthwatering desserts. When she thought about it, she marveled she didn't gain a hundred pounds. Myra was protective, trustworthy, and not just because Augusta had been her employer. It was a part of her very nature. Myra's character spoke volumes about her upbringing. Her mother raised her right! For that, Augusta would forever be in her debt.

George, Myra's strong, yet dutiful husband, was nothing but a big old soft-hearted sweetheart of a man. He'd come to Augusta's rescue on more than one occasion, all of them having to do with Reginald. If not for George's quiet strength and gentle nature, she'd have been mortified for him to witness Reginald's outbursts. He appeared to take it all in stride and behaved as a knight to a maiden in distress. Perhaps one day a man like him might fancy her. She could only hope for such good fortune.

Then there was Lydia, her Georgetown friend with a love of all things Irish. Even the brogue she'd polished into a fine art form was endearing. Augusta thought her feisty, energetic, matronly, and protective, and adored that about her. She'd wager Lydia to be the finest kitchen manager in these parts. No one crossed her; everyone loved her.

What could she say about Nora? That she is young and beautiful, smart as a whip, a good listener and a wonderful caretaker? That she could play the piano like nobody's business? Yes, she supposed so, but above all else, she'd been a lifesaver for Augusta and Baby Derrick. And she owed it all to Marcus. If not for him, she'd never have met the girl who charmed Derrick so. Her child was putty in the young lady's hands.

As for Marcus, she considered him a prince among men. Strange, the extreme differences between him and Reginald. By their own admission they'd practically been joined at the hips when they were younger and had gotten into all kinds of mischief. Now they were estranged because of Reginald's jealousy and maliciousness. She knew for a fact that Marcus grieved the lost relationship and would rekindle it at the snap of a finger, should the opportunity present itself. They'd been closer than brothers for most of their lives. Come to think of it, they could pass for brothers. They favored one another with their dark hair and eyes and olive skin. She knit her brows together as the mashed potatoes made their way to her. Doling out a spoonful, she pondered Reginald's lineage. *What if the two* are *brothers?* She immediately dismissed the idea as ludicrous.

Faerie spoke, interrupting her reverie. "So tell us about Pagosa Springs, Augusta. The name sounds like paradise."

"I suppose it is. It's Ouray with a different name. There are beautiful mountains everywhere and lots of hot springs. The ranch where we stayed had a beautiful, sparkling river rushing through the property. It felt like a little slice of heaven."

Faerie nodded, thinking Augusta looked tired. "Is this a bit much for you tonight? You've been very quiet since you arrived. I must say, you look exhausted."

Seeing the forlorn expression on Faerie's face, Augusta replied, "Don't be a silly goose, Faerie. Any fatigue I feel is far outweighed by this fine meal and the company of good friends. I've just been thinking how very blessed I am. Each of you has a very special place in my life. I don't know what I'd do without you. I – *we've* missed you so much." Augusta cast a look at Nora, who nodded in agreement as she swallowed and dabbed delicately at her mouth with a napkin.

"Here, here!" Marcus raised his glass. "Everyone, lift your glasses." He paused. "Here's to the finest group of folks I know. May we never take for granted the true gift of friendship." Glasses clinked around the table in response to the impromptu toast.

"M'lady," Lydia broke in, "please tell us o' the land o' Pagosa."

Giggles erupted around the table.

Augusta covered her mouth, but the crinkle lines around her eyes gave away her amusement. "Sounds like a mystical place when you say it like that." She laid her fork on the rim of her plate. "Pagosa is a fine place. The hot springs that I mentioned before are sacred to the Utes, just like our springs. Sadly, there are no Utes to be found around Pagosa Springs. They've all been relocated." She paused for a sip of water. Then: "The friends we stayed with have a ranch just outside of town, right on the San Juan River. They're sheep ranchers, and they recruited Nora and me to help once in a while when the herd wandered out too far. I was hesitant at first, but it was great fun. It's safe to say I no longer have a fear of riding a horse like a man. No more side saddle for me. I even wore a pair of dunga-rees."

"How scandalous!" Faerie teased.

Augusta's eyes brightened as she regaled the group with tales of life on a ranch far on the other side of the mountains. The weariness she experienced earlier was replaced by a renewed vim and vigor as she animatedly recounted their adventures to the captive audience around the table.

Dan sat next to Nora. He was fascinated by the new Augusta. She was the life of the party. Gone was the opinionated, proud woman he'd come to know. This Augusta was a breath of fresh air, like mountains in springtime. In her letters, Nora often mentioned a contemplative Augusta. She wrote how Augusta spent hours alone, and often took Derrick for long walks along the river bank. In the midst of it all, Augusta began to ask questions about scripture. It appears the family who took them in did more than provide a place of refuge; they helped bring Augusta out of herself. Nora reported that their hosts had simply continued what Faerie began: to love and accept Augusta despite her imperfections. Love without judgment, Nora had written.

By the end of the evening, everyone had enjoyed their fill of roast chicken, mashed potatoes and gravy, green beans, applesauce and buttermilk biscuits with peach preserves. Augusta called it an early evening and called upon Dan to deliver the weary travelers home. Neither took the time to unpack, heading straight to bed where Augusta slept soundly, Derrick nestled by her side.

Chapter Thirteen

Don't judge each day by the harvest you reap
but by the seeds that you plant.
~ Robert Louis Stevenson

Susan wrapped a shawl around her shoulders, grabbed her walking stick, and headed out the back door. The air was clean and crisp, the sky, a bright turquoise. The golden aspen leaves quaked in the autumn breeze. Closing her eyes, she lifted her face to the sun, soaking in its warm rays. All was right with the world. John was safe and sound and sleeping in his own bed. Unable to completely grasp the reality of it all, she'd checked on him to make sure he was really there.

At last, the family could begin the task of rebuilding trust and respect. Though she despised conflict, Susan believed there was to be plenty of it as John worked through his own personal demons. He'd been plenty angry with Simon and those feelings hadn't been dealt with before he and Sandy were taken. His tendency was to saddle up Taffy and hightail it down to the river and confide in his four-legged friend; however, that was out of the question for now. His riding days had come to a grinding halt. She wondered what he would do instead, how he would deal with his feelings. Since his return, he spent a lot of time alone. He hadn't mentioned anything about the past month except to say he was glad it was over. But was it? Susan brushed it from her thoughts. She would not allow anything to spoil this splendid morning.

The palominos were grazing in the pasture. Taffy caught a glimpse of Susan and reared on her hind legs and whinnied. "Hello, girl," Susan called back, heading in her direction. She wasn't exactly sure how horses processed emotions, but didn't for one second believe the change in Taffy's demeanor was her imagination. She seemed more vibrant and playful. Susan braced her arms against the fence. Taffy moseyed over and Susan reached out and gently stroked the horse's velvety snout. "You're a mighty pretty girl, Taffy." Taffy snorted and reared her head. "Yes, I know. You want to see your boy. Well, he's still sleeping. Seems he needs to catch up on some sleep. Be patient. He'll take you out riding before you know it." Susan stroked the horse's neck and ran her fingers through its thick mane. "What a glorious creature you are!"

"Yes, she is!" John slipped up behind his mother, giving her a start.

"You about scared the life out of me!" Oh, how she longed to hug him but his cast and bandages kept her at arm's length.

"Ya look sad, Mom."

"Do I?" she asked. Then: "I'm just so relieved to see you standing here. I sometimes feel the urge to pinch myself to make sure it isn't a dream. I'd love to wrap you in my arms and never let you go."

He chuckled, followed by the grimace. "Laughin's the worst thing ever. It pains me somethin' fierce."

She placed a hand against his cheek. "So…Taffy's excited to see you. Why don't I take my walk and you spend time with her?"

"Sounds mighty fine. Can't wait t' get back in the saddle."

"Don't rush things, son. Take it easy…one day at a time. Why, when I think…"

"Shh. Please don't, Mom. I ain't ready t' talk about it yet." He turned sullen and dark. "Heck! I might never be ready."

Susan looked across the meadow and watched as a few of the palominos galloped off into the distance. She hesitated to speak. John was as fragile as a china teacup and needed to be handled with kid gloves. She took the look in his eyes as a request for leniency. "I understand." She paused. "John, we won't press you, but there's still a matter of giving a statement to Sheriff Johnson. That can't wait."

"They said they'd contact me. I don't want t' hurt your feelins' or nothin', but I'd rather Dad go with me when the time comes. I jest thought ya ought t' know. There's jest some things I can't say with a lady present."

She swallowed, nodding and avoiding eye contact. For the first time in their lives, something had come between them, a secret of someone else's making. "I understand," she responded quietly. "Now, off with you. Taffy's literally chomping at the bit!" She forced a smile, and then turned to walk away hoping John hadn't noticed she was hurt.

******

Susan walked the perimeter of the fenced-in yard admiring the fall foliage and flowers. Bright orange, red, yellow, and purple mums bordered the whitewashed picket fence. A sea of zinnias in the deepest of reds lined the walk and the front of the house. *Pretty as a picture.* Blessed with a green thumb, Susan's love of gardening made the ranch a stunning sight for all fortunate enough to walk the grounds. Soon the snow would fly transforming the colorful ranch into a wonderland of white with a stand of blue spruce and Ponderosa pines as backdrops. Until then, the vibrantly beautiful autumn flowers served as vivid reminders of the importance of caring for her family with the same gentle, yet persistent care.

Thinking the dining table would benefit from an arrangement of freshly cut flowers, she went to the arboretum to retrieve a pair of cutting shears and a basket. She wandered around the indoor garden, eventually coming to the wrought iron bench which sat next to a bed of orange and yellow tiger lilies. On the bench sat her Bible, worn from use. She sat and opened the Book to First Peter. She settled in for a much needed read. *Cast all your cares on him for he cares for you.* "A verse tried and true. Even so, seems I often snatch my troubles back, as if I were as wise as you, Lord. Perhaps I don't trust you enough. I know it's true what your Word says. Worrying can't add another minute to my life. Thanks for the reminder."

She mulled Peter's words over in her mind. If any of the characters in the Bible could vouch for the faithfulness of God, it was Peter. A fisherman by trade, destined to be a member of Christ's inner circle, he was privy to every word the man spoke, every miracle he performed. Susan looked long and hard at the wooden cross mounted on the far wall. It was Peter who lost his temper on the night Jesus was arrested, becoming so enraged that he cut an ear off the servant of the Jewish High Priest. Jesus calmly rebuked him and mended the soldier's ear. She wondered whatever happened with that servant. Did he just except the miracle and go on as usual or did he become a follower? Did he share the story or hide it away out of fear? She shrugged her shoulders. Later, when Peter was asked if he was one of the Twelve, he denied even knowing Jesus. Three times he denied the Christ. Yet despite his short temper and gruff exterior, and the many mistakes he made, God chose him to carry the message to all who would listen. *If God was able to use a rough and tumble man like Peter, he can use anybody,* she thought.

Susan identified with Peter. She figured most Christians did. He spoke his mind when he would have been better served by holding his tongue. Even though he said he understood who Jesus was and why he came, he clearly didn't. When Jesus warned Peter that before sunrise the following morning he would deny even knowing him, Peter scoffed and vowed he'd follow Jesus to the death. Yet, only a few hours later, frightened and unable to process all that was happening, he turned his back on the One he'd proclaimed to be the Son of God. In her own way, she'd done the same. She was doing it now by trying to own John's situation when she needed to lay it at the foot of the cross. If God cared for a man like Peter, then it stood to reason that he cared for her and her family.

He even cared for Reginald, and that was something she'd never given thought to before. Still, she was frightened of the man and what he might do. She was afraid he might find John or Simon and do more than taunt them. He'd planned Simon's demise and very nearly carried it off. He more than likely took John for no other reason than to torment Simon.

Susan knew O'Keefe was mentally ill. She also knew she despised him. Nevertheless, she wanted to do the right thing. She wanted to put aside her dislike for him, but something inside, something raw and selfish, wanted to hang on to it. She rationalized about it more than she cared to admit, always having the same conversation with herself. She even confided with Clara, who reminded her that the Good Book said to forgive, and without taking a breath, added that it didn't tell us to be blind and stupid. Leave it to Clara to say exactly what she meant. No holds barred. "Everybody needs a friend like Clara. It tends to keep a body honest," Susan said as she set Bible down next to her on the bench.

She stood and waded through the floral maze that led to the door, amazed that a mere five minutes of solitude with nothing but a Bible and an open heart could soothe her nerves and calm her fears. She exited the arboretum, gardening tools and basket in hand, ready to set about the business of cutting and pruning.

Knowing that the S & S Harvest Festival was a week from Saturday, she focused on painting a mental picture of how it should look this year. Every year many folks from both Ridgway and Ouray set aside the weekend, coming together in droves to celebrate family, friends, harvest, and lots of good food. Susan vowed she would never disappoint.

This year was extra special. Simon was home to enjoy the festival for the first time in years. In Susan's opinion, selling the clipper ship was the best decision Simon ever made. She wanted desperately to make the festival something he'd never forget. Each year she looked forward to the festival, but was even more excited than usual when Simon recently began to show some interest in it. He even asked if he might help with the hayrides, which had always been Troy's usual job. When she spoke with Troy, he said he'd been "dying" to try his hand at some of the games, so Susan put him in charge of the ring toss and apple dunking station, as well as the three-legged race. Simon was ecstatic about the upcoming festivities and promised to be on his best behavior when the ladies came on Wednesday to help with baking and decorations.

A cold gust of wind sent a chill up Susan's spine. Deciding she'd best get inside and help with lunch preparations, she sat up and stretched and looked into the basket, which was full of beautiful offerings for the dining table. Snatching a tiger lily from the bunch, she brought it to her nose, inhaling its sweet, organic scent, and then brushed it against her cheek.

"There you are." Simon stepped off the back porch and moved in her direction. "Everything all right?"

"Uh-huh. Everything's fine. Feeling a bit tentative is all. We've been living on pins and needles for so long, I just keep waiting for another ball to drop." She pulled her shawl closer. "Is it getting colder?"

Simon took the basket and held her hand as she came from her sitting position on the ground. "You're shivering. Let's get you in the house." The couple hurried hand in hand through the yard as the biting wind suddenly picked up.

Around the corner of the house appeared John. "Oo-wee. It's some kinda cold out here. Should we bring the horses in from the pasture?"

"Maybe after we've had ourselves something to eat." Simon held the back door open for Susan and John, and then took up the rear, closing the door behind him.

"Well, now. Aren't the three of you a sight for sore eyes?" Clara leaned against the counter with her hands on her hips. "Glad you came in before the wind carried you away."

"It's really something, all right." Simon removed his hat and hung it on the rack by the kitchen door. When he turned, Susan was standing at the counter, her hair windblown and standing on end. With a sheepish grin, Simon bit his bottom lip and snickered. "Susan, love. Your hair…"

Her eyes became as big as saucers. She frantically shot glances from one face to the other. "What? What is it?"

"It's…*everywhere!*" Simon exclaimed through what was now raucous, contagious laughter.

"Heh, heh," Clara chuckled. "Why'd you think I said you're a sight for sore eyes?"

Susan hands flew to her head. She ran up the stairs and to the washroom. "Oh, my goodness." She pulled hairpin after hairpin from what was left of the bun at the nape of her neck, then brushed her long tresses and settled for a long braid down her back. Back in the kitchen she coyly asked, "Better?"

Simon took her into an embrace and kissed the top of her head as he tugged on the braid. "You look like the girl I knew back in school. I adore when you wear your hair down."

Susan blushed but secretly delighted in the compliment. She nestled into the safety of his strong arms before remembering there were others in the room. Looking into his eyes she winked and backed away.

Clara busied herself and stirred whatever it was on the stove. Susan thought she spied an ever-so-slight smile, her dimples deepening. "You can giggle, if you like, Clara. It's all right. I admit it! I was mortified for everybody to see my hair looking like Medusa's.

"First time in all these years I've ever seen you look any way but perfect." Clara wiggled her brows playfully.

"What can I say? I have very high standards." Susan stuck out her chin and offered a most proper look before she rolled her eyes and laughed.

"Oh, brother!" John interjected with a smirk and a long roll of his own eyes.

"You fellas might offer to help me get things ready for lunch. Susan and I could use a couple of extra bodies. There'll be some mighty hungry hands here b'fore long." Clara opened the ice box and took out leftover roast beef she'd saved for hot sandwiches.

"Simon, if you would slice the meat? Susan, the bread? John, you up to setting the plates on the buffet?"

"Yes,m."

Everyone stepped it up and before they knew it, Clara was out on the back porch ringing the dinner bell for the ranch hands. Less than five minutes later ten cowpokes lined up at the kitchen sink to wash their hands and faces.

Clara peeked out the back door to make certain the men had lined their boots up against the wall. There'd be no dusty, dirty, grimy or muddy tracks left on the kitchen floor if she had anything to say about it.

"Clara, you've really outdid yerself t'day." A new fellow by the name of Andy Gentry spoke up.

"Outdone," corrected Clara.

"'Scuse me, ma'am?"

"The word's outdone. You've really outdone yourself is the proper way to say it." Clara blushed noticing for the first time the man's classic good looks.

"Yes, ma'am." Andy dried his hands and face and went to the buffet. "Whatever the word, it smells mighty tasty and I'm much obliged."

"Don't mind her none, Andy." John placed his uninjured hand on the man's shoulder. "She's jest s' dad-blamed happy I'm home, she's full o' spit 'n vinegar…an' a whole lot bossier 'n usual." John made sure Clara caught the wink he sent her way. She grinned and waved him off.

As the group crowded around the table, more chairs were added to accommodate new faces and familiar ones that hadn't joined them in a while.

"I swear our little family keeps growing. We'll soon need a bigger table," Susan said, most cheerfully.

"I'd like nothing better." Simon sipped from his water glass and then carefully set it down. "With all my travels, and the unfortunate year apart from my loved ones, I grew to miss times like this. The harvest gathering

116

can't come soon enough to suit me."

"Here! Here!" cheered Troy. "This'll be the first one for you in many a year, my friend."

For several minutes the only sounds around the table were the clinking of utensils against plates and the occasional request to have something passed followed by a quick thank you. Susan wasn't all that familiar with Andy but thought he seemed nice enough. Troy thought he hung the moon, and since she trusted their foreman implicitly, his word was good enough. He and Troy appeared to be about the same age, early forties.

"Andy," she said politely, "please share with us a little about yourself. Have you family nearby?"

"I growed...*grew*...up in a little town in the Smokies over'n Eastern Tennessee. Johnson City. Anybody ever heard of it?" Andy paused but when he only saw wagging heads, he continued. "Perty little place up in the hills. These'n here makes 'em look like God's little footstools."

Simon chuckled. "I've never heard that before. Sounds like a pretty good analogy." Then: "Any family?"

"Two sisters, both older'n me an' a twin brother. My ma an' pa an' both sets of grands still live there. Home sweet home." He smiled. "They'd never leave unless God Almighty Hisself yanked 'em up an' dropped 'em somewhars else."

"Whatever took you away from such a big family?" Clara asked, trying not to sound nosy or overly cautious. Clara was tormented with a suspicious nature. Hearing Andy say his entire family was living and doing well in the old stomping grounds while he wandered about aimlessly set off all kinds of bells and whistles.

"Kinda per'snal, Miss Clara. But since ya asked real nice-like, I reckon I don' mind sharin'. I had me a fine wife. Dolly was 'er name. She bore me the finest son a man ever laid eyes on. Then one Sunday mornin' we was walkin' t' church when a man in a buckboard rounded a corner up th' road from our house and hit m' precious wife an' baby. And..." Andy dropped his head.

The men around the table stopped eating and passed uncomfortable glances amongst themselves. The room was so quiet you could've heard a pin drop. Finally, Troy spoke up. "Glory Be, Clara!" he declared. "You and your old suspicions. Now you've gone and done it."

"No. No. You mustn't blame 'er." Andy's chin trembled. "It's only natural t' be curious. Maybe even wary." Andy set his fork down and grabbed hold of his water glass and forced himself to drink. "I reckon it's 'bout right fer a body t' be suspicious when another'n jest shows up on yer

117

doorstep th' way I done....*did*...the way I did."

Ashamed, Clara fought to urge to smile as Andy corrected his own grammar. She stared blankly at her lap. Susan reached over and squeezed her balled up hands.

"Andy, please continue your story," Susan prompted. "If you don't mind, that is."

He breathed in; he breathed out. "Dolly's neck was broke...*broken*. Doctor said she never knew what hit 'er. My baby boy lived through th' day and into th' night. Old Doc Emory never left 'is side. Said Benny... Benjamin was 'is name...suffered sev'ral broken ribs some a'which punctured 'is lungs. Can ya believe it? I lost both of 'em at th' same time. Dangest thing I ever heard tell." A tear trickled down his cheek and splashed onto his plate.

"So you left everything and everyone you ever loved and headed West." Clara spoke compassionately.

"We married late. I'm wuz almost forty when we wed; Dolly wuz in 'er early thirties. Ever'body was thrilled when we found each other. We'uns wuz hitched six months after we met and Benny came along less than a year after." He smiled. "My brothers wuz so convinced I wuz a confirmed bach'ler that they made bets 'bout whether 'r not we'd actually git hitched. They thought I'd chicken out. Guess I proved 'em wrong."

There were chuckles all around the table.

"Seriously?" Susan asked through her own snickers.

"As a heart attack," Andy answered as deadpan as anything Susan had ever witnessed.

"Well, I'll be." She wagged her head. Picking up her knife, she sliced a generous piece of roast and stabbed it with her fork.

"Ma, what did that piece a' meat ever do t' ya?" John teased.

She choked on the bite as she swallowed. Simon tapped her a few times on the back and then reached for her water glass. "Drink," he ordered. Soon she was better and enjoying the levity that reigned over the mid-day meal. It did her spirit a world of good to hear so much laughter and see so many smiles. For now, life was sweet.

"Andy," Clara said, "do you plan on going home to Tennessee one of these days?"

"T' be honest, I can't go back. Ever' time I hear from th' family it seems t' pour salt in m' wounds. Jest as things start t' settle down an' I think I can handle a letter from home, one of 'em writes somethin' 'bout Dolly and it all comes crashin' down 'round me agin. I always find m'self wonderin' if it's this hard from s' far away, how bad would it be if'n I'se

118

there livin' it day after day." He paused and took a drink of water. "Maybe someday things'll be diff'rnt. At least fer now, this is home. Besides, I kinda like it here. The people are nice an' friendly-like. Ever'body's been right hospitable."

"Glad to hear it." Simon pushed his plate away. "Just a warning, though. If you don't exercise a little restraint, you'll need to loosen your belt a notch or two. Clara's aim is to feed us until we pop!"

"So I noticed." Andy gave Clara an impish sidelong glance accompanied by a nod and grin.

"Good thing we work so hard." Troy shoveled in a huge bite of the savory hot sandwich. "Speaking of which, men, we have to go out on the north end of the ranch and check the fences and round up any stray cattle before the snow flies. By the feel of it, that could be any time now."

"When were you thinking?" Simon asked.

"Tomorrow morning, right after breakfast would be best."

"Mind if I tag along? I'd love to spend a day out on the range with you. It's time I started getting my hands dirty." Simon looked hopeful.

"Sure thing, Boss," Troy grinned from ear to ear. "I believe I'm speaking for all the men when I say it's been too long."

John dropped his head and heaved a sigh.

Susan elbowed Clara and nodded in John's direction.

"John," Clara began, her heart saddened that the boy obviously felt left out, "what do you say we stick around here tomorrow and go through the harvest decorations and what not?"

John was unable to hide the disappointment on his face. "Sure, Clara," he answered forlornly." Then, addressing Troy, he said, "Don't ferget 'bout me, guys. I'll be back in th' saddle soon."

"Of course you will, son." Simon felt so sorry for him. "Taffy is counting the days." John's countenance was more than grim. "Look, John, please don't fret over this. Let's just revel in the joy of your safe return. When you're better, you'll be able join Troy and the others whenever you wish."

As Susan watched the dynamic between father and son, she thought she could just kick Reginald's behind for this.

******

While Simon left in the buckboard to pick up Timmy and the other children who lived on the ranch from school, Clara and Susan started making lists of necessary supplies for the harvest gathering.

"I hope the weather holds out. We're a couple of weeks later than usual.

All we need is to get everything ready and then have a snowstorm come through. Most folks will hunker down and stay home in front of the fire." Susan leaned back against the cellar wall, taking a breather.

"I don't know about that. No matter what the weather there'll always be diehard regulars who'll make the trip out. What else do the locals have to do on a Saturday during the school year? It's the last hurrah before the snow flies and the dark winter sets in. Well," she backtracked, "assuming the weather isn't a *blizzard*, that is. That would be the only thing that might keep them away." Clara wiped her damp brow on the sleeve of her blouse. "Who knew it would be so hot down here! And so dusty!"

Susan let go a chortle. Even by the light of the kerosene lamp she saw a smudge on Clara's forehead. "We must look a fright," she teased. "You've got quite a spot there right above your eyebrow."

"My ma always said I looked like a street urchin." She wiped the dusty patch off her forehead with her apron. "Better?"

Susan nodded. "Yes, much better. Almost good enough to ask a certain ranch hand to supper." She pretended to make notes on her writing pad.

"I'm sure I don't know what you mean," Clara responded innocently.

"Of course you don't."

Clara cleared a frog from her throat. "Looks like we're in mighty fine shape to bake lots of pumpkin cookies and bread…apple, too. Apple butter would be a right nice thing to finish tomorrow."

Susan jotted down some actual notes. "You know," she said, slowly, "John is so disappointed he won't be joining the men out on the day trip tomorrow."

"Well, he won't miss it too much if we make it sound like a chain gang instead of a day trip," Clara said, planting a fist on each hip.

"Say, that's a right smart idea. He will forget all about the others if we make the day all about him and how lucky for him to be inside with us womenfolk." She stopped and grimaced. "Wait. How is this supposed to make him feel better?"

Clara sat on an empty crate. She shrugged her shoulders and then rubbed a tight spot on her neck. "Land sakes, woman, must I explain everything to you? We put John in charge and run every little detail or idea by him before putting action behind our words. We emphasize over and over that the gathering is all about celebrating his safe return. Give him ideas about how to get Simon and all the other gents 'round here to fall in line and follow his orders come next Saturday." She paused. Then: "You just tend to your gardening and writing and let me teach John how to be a boss."

Susan placed a hand over her mouth, but the crinkles around her eyes gave away her amusement. "Yes ma'am," she said, trying her best not to guffaw.

Clara turned back to the shelves in a huff and began counting jars of pear honey. "Must I do *everything* around here?" she grunted under her breath.

Susan made one last note and closed the tablet. "I think you have this covered. I'll just be upstairs checking the spices and other baking supplies."

"Susan, I didn't mean nothin'…"

Susan inched over to Clara careful to dodge haphazard crates and boxes. "Do you think after all these years, and everything we've been through, that you could ever do anything I'd question?"

Clara dropped her head, ashamed of her outburst. "Susan, sometimes I get testy, 'cept I don't mean any harm by it. I've got to learn to bite my tongue. You must know there's no place I'd rather be."

Susan locked eyes with Clara but spoke not a word. Clara understood Susan's silence. She chose not to speak when tempted to reply with hurtful comebacks.

"You know, Susan, when John's more like his old self, maybe he should give this old cellar a good straightening."

"That'd be nice," Susan replied in a tone she realized sounded strained. She knew something uncharacteristic had passed between them, only she wasn't able to sort it out just yet. So many emotions ran just below the surface these days that the slightest word or facial expression often led to hurt feelings and unwarranted retorts.

Maybe Clara was simply worn out. After all, for more than a year she'd worked nonstop on the ranch, taking on more and more responsibility, which enabled Susan to concentrate on her family. Perhaps the momentary tension between them was Clara's way of dealing with the enormity of the situation. Perhaps something that was said was the one thing that broke the proverbial camel's back.

"How insensitive I've been." Susan tightly pursed her lips. While she'd been wallowing in self-pity, Clara hid behind sarcasm and a self-assured façade. *That's it,* she thought. *It's all a façade.*

Slowly climbing the stairs to the kitchen, she decided it was high time the family did something special for Clara for a change. Today's tiff in the cellar was proof positive that things were far too tense on the ranch. What they all needed was a celebration with Clara as the guest of honor. *As soon as the harvest gathering is over, that's exactly what we'll do. Lord willing and the creek don't rise.*

＊＊＊＊＊＊

Clara plopped down hard on a crate of canned goods. Frustrated and annoyed at her own inability to communicate without a bite of sarcasm, she fished for the hankie in her skirt pocket. She sniffed and blew her runny nose.

"Tarnation!" she huffed. Clara despised weakness. She told herself crying wouldn't change things. Despite her argument against them and her efforts to stop them, the tears kept falling.

She hid her feelings pretty well most of the time; however, there were days like today when she came undone. All she had ever wanted was to be a strong buttress for Susan to lean on when she buckled under the load. Instead she became snippy and irritable at the first sign of strain.

Wasn't it just like Susan to walk away without spewing words that could never be taken back, much less forgotten? Clara couldn't remember a time when she'd been witness to Susan behaving any other way than that of a lady. Susan's abrupt exit from the cellar left Clara with the conclusion that she'd crossed a very personal line. Should she bring it up and lay everything out on the table or simply brush the whole business under the rug and pretend nothing ever happened?

"Dag-nab-it, you know the right answer, you old fossil," she chastised. She clinched her jaw in aggravation. "It's not too late to say sorry. Get up off your substantial backside and march up those stairs and do right by Susan." She stood, brushed off the back of her skirt, picked up a box of canned goods and stomped up the stairs.

Simon and Timmy were at the kitchen table enjoying oatmeal raisin cookies and cold milk. Clara put the crate on the counter and then wiped her brow on the skirt of her apron. She looked around the kitchen, even stepping into the parlor, craning her neck.

"Lookin' for someone?" Simon asked innocently, knowing full well she was.

"No. I mean, yes. Where's Susan?" she asked with a furrowed brow.

"She said she was tired and wanted to go upstairs and lie down."

"I see," Clara muttered, folding her arms.

"Anything the matter?" Simon munched on a cookie, watching Clara's mannerisms. "You seem...*bothered*." He smirked. "Not at all like you."

"I...hurt...Susan's feelings. Right bad, I fear."

"How so?" Simon placed what was left of his cookie on a napkin and brushed the crumbs from his hands.

122

"By being *myself*. You know how I am."

"Let me tell you something, Clara. The way you are is why we love you. You're family. Susan is…*emotionally spent*. I believe that's how she put it. Makes sense. Let's face it. She feels like she's had the weight of the world on her shoulders." He coughed. "And she pretty much has, hasn't she?"

She wagged her head. "And what do I do to help? Not a blasted thing except moan and groan all day…*every day.*"

Simon stood and pushed his chair to the table. "Clara, we wouldn't have it any other way. We'd be all thumbs without you." He chugged the rest of his milk and wiped his mouth on his shirt sleeve like all heavy-handed drinkers, then added, "By the way… you, my lady, are her dearest friend." With a sly grin, he added, "Not counting me."

She gazed at Simon, then at Timmy and crinkled up her nose at them. "You know," she said, dragging out the words, "if you two misfits eat too many of them there cookies, you won't eat supper. And I can't abide wasted food."

"Tim, my man," Simon laughed out loud, "there's that opinionated, overbearing, nagging woman we all know and love."

"Huh?" Timmy looked confused.

"Nothing, son. Eat up." Simon playfully tousled Timmy's hair and pinched his cheek. He turned to Clara and placed his hands on her shoulders and looked her in the eye. "Don't ever change. Are we clear?"

A tear trickled down her cheek as she watched him ease out the kitchen door onto the porch and around the corner, disappearing from sight.

"Timmy, John's out with Taffy. You want to take him some cookies?"

He nodded. "Clara, I love you. Pleath don't leave uth."

His sweet, lispy, little boy voice grabbed at her heart. "I would never." Then she sat down next to him and pulled her chair closer. "Timmy, let me tell you a secret. Should there ever come a time when I need to go, they'll have to drag me outta here kicking and screaming." She leaned over and brushed his cheek with a kiss and ran her fingers through his silky, thick, hair.

Chapter Fourteen

You may not control all the events that happen to you,
but you can decide not to be reduced by them.
~ Maya Angelou

A howling wind whipped around the old cabin like a thundering tornado, shaking the rafters and bending the trees just outside the back window. Reginald was fairly certain there were no tornadoes in these parts, but the memory of Oklahoma twisters was as fresh as if he'd recently survived one.

He watched out the window as branches from a nearby spruce snapped like so many tiny matchsticks. He hunkered down with a book he'd taken from a trunk in Augusta's attic, Charles Dickens' *Oliver Twist*. Mother Wright had given it to him upon his high school graduation. All the more reason he must hang on to it. Having even such a small token as this kept the memory of her fresh in his mind, giving him a ration of hope.

In his dreams, she often came, encouraging and comforting him, listening and counseling. Never judging or ridiculing. She quoted scripture from First Corinthians. *Love is patient. Love is kind.* He struggled to remember the verses but recalled something about love never being rude or boastful and proud.

He tensed. "Love is all the things I'm not."

He gazed around the sparsely furnished room. At least the bed was comfortable. Heck…at least there *was* a bed. No more sleeping on the floor or worse still, in cold, dark, wet caves. He'd found a nice vacant miners' cabin just outside Ironton. It was far enough out of the way that no one would waste their time hunting for him, or even pass by on their way to who knows where. Unless Luke resurfaced there was no cause for worry…at least for the time being. The very thought of it sent chills down his spine. He sat down at the knobby pine table and poured a cup of coffee. For a man who'd become used to the finer things in life, he certainly had taken a deep dive.

Life on the run came with its own challenges, one of which was disguise. For more than a month he'd not shaved and his hair was past his collar. The gentlemen's clothes he took such great pride in were replaced by such lifeless rags as he'd seen old mining hermits wear. But even with the scraggly beard and unkempt hair he believed he still fared better than most of the uneducated, toothless wonders who worked the mines.

Gone were the days of fancy dinners followed by brandy and cigars with the gents while the ladies gossiped amongst themselves. Life no longer revolved around his whimsical desires; life was now all about survival. Blending in with the other folks on the mountain was crucial. He was dismayed that it had come to this. Keeping up outward appearances, both physically and materially, had bocome extremely important to him once he moved to Ouray. He found it hard to admit his lavish lifestyle was gone.

Lots of miners, some with families, had come to these mountains hoping to strike it rich. Many soon realized their hopes were nothing but pipe dreams. Discouraged and penniless, they left, heading for greener pastures. Fortunately for him, lots of belongings stayed behind. He found an old buckboard, still in right good condition. All it needed was a few minor repairs and it was as good as new. Searching here and there, he came upon a bed, a kitchen table and chairs, a rocker, and a couple of parlor chairs. The former occupants of the cabin left the curtains on the windows, and he was thankful for at least a bit of privacy.

He set traps all over the mountain. One thing was for sure. He made pretty good cornbread and a tasty rabbit stew. He trapped a raccoon once. He let it go. Something about its bandit face and leathery paws was disturbing…perhaps a bit of a kindred spirit. Odd that he haad mercy on a four-legged creature but detested most of the two-legged kind.

A branch brushed against the window. He eased over to the window and peeked outside. Pitch black. He lit another lantern. The fire spit and sputtered and warmed the cabin. It reminded him of the quaint coziness of the Wright's home back in Tahlequah.

Ham and beans simmered in a cast iron pot over the fire. Reginald was famished and the heavenly aroma was tormenting him. He was thin. In his fits of delusion, he rarely ate, choosing to survive on coffee and bourbon. Luke was a miser except when it came to bourbon. He had to have his bourbon. No matter how hard things became, how he and the others complained of hunger, the only money spent was for Luke's wants and desires. Well, things were different now. Reginald's pantry was well stocked and he planned on eating hearty.

"So I heard you've been feeling sorry about…*things*?"

"Luke." Reginald suddenly had a sinking feeling in the pit of his stomach.

"So glad to know you haven't forgotten about me." Luke's voice dripped with sarcasm.

"How could I?"

A seething chortle followed.

Reginald felt like he might wretch. He ran outside and leaned over the porch railing and vomited the coffee he'd enjoyed just minutes before. The

Voices inside his head rang with laughter. He turned facing the door and leaned against the railing while pushing his hands against his temples.

"Say, Reggie boy, I have the perfect nickname for you. Try this on for size. Reggie the Ridiculous. Or how about Reginald Wrong? Then there's always O'Keefe the Thief." Luke roared with sadistic laughter.

"Ahh…" Reginald bellowed. "Stop it. Leave me alone. Just leave me! For God's sake, leave!"

All was quiet. He stopped breathing, listening, waiting for some kind of response. He strained his ears waiting for the Voices to return.

Nothing.

"It worked. Mother Wright always told me evil would flee at the name."

******

Reginald awoke the next morning surprisingly clearheaded and alert. He snuggled under the covers where it was warm and comfortable. Nice eiderdown quilts from Augusta's attic. "Thanks for sharing, my dear. As I recall, this quilt was a souvenir of our wedding trip, so it really was half mine to take. Not like stealing at all."

"You can tell yourself whatever you want, but you took it without asking."

A female Voice. Reginald sat up and pushed back against the wrought iron headboard. "Who are you?"

"Violet. Don't you remember me?"

The Voice was young and tender like that of a small child.

"Should I?"

"We were in the Mrs. Butler's Sunday School class. Remember?"

He closed his eyes and thought. *Who was Mrs. Butler? Who was Violet?*

"I can read your mind, you know."

"Yeah, I sort of figured that. I guess you and all your *buddies* hear everything I say and think."

"Reggie, one thing you don't understand is that all of us are a part of you. Not all of us are nice. There's only two of us who want what's best for you."

"I'm not sure about you, but the other guy who's supposed to care so much? Seems he doesn't show up very often. He's kind of yellow."

"No, he isn't. He's kind…and nice. And he's always looking out for you. He told me so."

"Really?" he asked sarcastically. "Where is he when Luke berates me?

127

Did you hear the things he said last night?"

"He's a meanie. But you gotta understand, Reggie, I hafta be careful too 'cause he might thump me on the head. He's always pullin' my braids."

He gasped. He suddenly remembered Violet. "Braids with pink ribbons."

"That's me." She giggled playfully.

"Little Violet from down the road. I remember now." He was practically giddy with delight. "We played hide-and-go-seek and jump rope. Oh…and I recall how good you were at Sword Drills."

"I loved Sword Drills. That's how my mommy taught me the books of the Bible."

"Your mother didn't teach you. Mine did."

"I was just testing you to see if you really remembered."

It all fell into place. He vaguely recalled late night talks with his little friend, Violet. His mother even set a place for her at the supper table until Reginald was around eleven, when Violet stopped visiting. His mother had called her his imaginary friend. He wrinkled his brow in confusion.

Reginald's mother was a no-nonsense, stoic woman, yet when it came to Violet she brightened up like so many candles on a Christmas tree. He wagged his head knowing full well that never in his life would he be granted the ability to understand his mother's behavior. Maybe she had been as scared of her husband as Reginald was. Violet brought out the child in her. He actually liked her when Violet came around.

"Reg-gie," Violet sang, "get up. It's time to get up. I wanna go out and play."

This can't be real. Unlike the other Voices, he was comfortable with Violet. She was a harmless little girl, a trusted childhood friend. Last night he'd banished Luke because of his insolent behavior. Violet was different, sweet, innocent, forever full of joy. Only one thing troubled him. If he sent one Voice packing, shouldn't they all go? Probably so. Except for one thing: he couldn't bear the thought of being alone. Perhaps he might allow just one to stay.

All of a sudden, a rude reality hit him right between the eyes. What if Violet wasn't really a nice little girl? What if she only pretended? What if her purpose was to win his trust, and then, when he least expected, turned into some kind of child monster.

He threw back the covers. As he put his feet to the floor, he recalled a night many years ago when his father released his wrath with a leather belt. The welts on Reginald's legs burned like fire and throbbed like the

Dickens. Afterward, he lay across the bed in his tiny bedroom, sobbing. Violet came to him and before long the two had concocted a plan of retribution. At the time, it felt satisfying. Letting the horses go from the barn and watching as they ran into the night was a payment far overdue for all the beatings he'd suffered. Only it wasn't Reginald and Violet who were punished for the act. It was just Reginald who went to bed without supper every night for a week. That was the beginning of the end of the friendship between Reginald and Violet. She was replaced by others more capable of holding their weight and keeping him out of trouble. Or so he thought.

He filled the coffee pot with water and grounds and placed it on the grill over the fire. As much as he pretended to enjoy cooking on the open fire of the hearth, he longed to find a decent stove…and soon. Cracking first one egg then another into a cast iron skillet, he spoke. "Violet, as much as I enjoyed our childhood antics, I can't do this. You have to go."

"No!" she said emphatically.

He dropped his head, halfway expecting a full blown temper tantrum, but heard only a slight whimper. He spoke gently but with authority. "Yes, Violet, you must go. In the Name of all that's holy, leave."

There was silence. Would it last?

Chapter Fifteen

Turn your face to the sun and the shadows fall behind you.
~ Charlotte Whitton

Sandy stretched, yawned and brushed the long curls from her face. "It's cold!" She decided to forget about reality…and the cold…for a while. She pulled the covers up to her nose and held them there, peeking out, before rolling over on her way back to Dreamland.

******

Washie returned from the chicken coop with a fine basket of fresh eggs. She felt carefree and happy as she practically skipped across the yard back to the house. Now that Sandy was home everything was different. Food tasted better, her chores seemed less burdensome, her mood less crabby. *Even the hens are laying more eggs since Sandy came home.* She rolled her eyes, realizing how ridiculous *that* sounded. *But, heavens to Betsy, everything is better. Life is sweeter. The sky seems bluer. The birds…* "Lord have mercy, I'm being so silly." She offered quick thanks for their blessings as she stepped onto the back porch and hummed a little ditty her grandmother taught her years before.

By now Alfred was well into his breakfast rush at the café. Last night at the supper table, Sandy had practically begged him to let her ride into town with him this morning. Alfred informed Sandy that if she was strong enough to work the breakfast and lunch shifts, then she was strong enough to return to school. She understood Sandy's need to keep busy without being around her school friends and all their questions, but supposed Alfred didn't quite see it that way. Washie's heart ached for her daughter. She'd held her tongue but intended to speak to him about it later. They were walking in unchartered territory, neither knowing what to do or how to respond.

She cracked four eggs into a bowl. Leftover biscuits from supper were halved, buttered and placed in a skillet to grill. This was one of Sandy's favorite breakfast treats…grilled buttered biscuits and plum jelly. As she scrambled the eggs, she pondered how to address the subject of Sandy's return to school. Rehearsing her less than convincing argument, she finally muttered, "How can I talk her into it when I don't even believe what I'm saying?"

"What's that, Mom?"

Startled, Washie whisked around and tried to act nonchalant. "Oh, nothing, sweetheart; I was just talking to myself." She offered up a pleasant enough grin. "You look nice. I didn't know you were up and at it. Somehow I thought you'd sleep in since it's so cold out."

Sandy followed the enticing smell of breakfast over to the stove. "You made it! I *love* you!" she exclaimed. "Grilled biscuits!"

"It's been a long time. *Too* long."

"While I was…*away*…I daydreamed about these practically every morning. I even told John about them." Sandy lifted her head and stared out the window. Washie braced herself, expecting Sandy to burst into tears. Instead, she smiled brightly and turned around, backing into the counter. "I'm so happy to be home."

Washie breathed a sigh of relief and spooned the eggs onto their breakfast plates. "Here, hon. Take these to the table. Coffee?"

"Yes…please." Sandy sighed. "Just think. A year ago you told me drinking coffee would turn the bottoms of my feet black."

Washie placed two cups and saucers on the table and quickly inventoried its offerings before they sat down. "Looks like all that's missing are the biscuits."

When Washie turned, Sandy was holding a plate full of golden brown biscuit halves, their aroma wafting through the kitchen.

Sitting at the table, mother and daughter held hands and offered up thanks for the food and for their precious time together. Sandy meticulously slathered her first biscuit with plum jelly, her jowls tingling in anticipation. Washie sat, amused at the care with which her girl spread such a generous dollop of the sweet, fruity goodness. Sandy very gently rested her knife on the edge of the plate. She closed her eyes and slowly bit into the treat she'd dreamed of for so long. She slowly chewed, savoring the biscuit's crunchy outer coating which was grilled to perfection and topped with a sweet and tangy fruity topping. When at last Sandy swallowed, the corners of her mouth lifted in the slightest hint of a smile. She opened her eyes and said, "Thank you, Mom. This is heavenly."

"Goodness, girl. I can't think of one thing in my life that's given me that kind of pleasure." She abruptly bit her lip and blushed. "Well…maybe *one* thing."

Sandy tilted her head to one side with a horrified look and gasped, "*Mother*!"

"You'll find out for yourself soon enough." Washie nodded and lifted her coffee cup. "Yes, you will," she said with a twinkle in her eyes. She giggled like a schoolgirl with a scandalous secret.

Sandy was mortified and wished the floor would open and swallow her up. "Can we change the subject? Please?" Her face was beet red.

"I'm sorry, honey. I don't know what came over me." She paused and sipped coffee. "Well, I do, but…"

"Mother…*please!*" Sandy voiced in typical teen-aged angst.

"All right! All right!"

They ate in silence for a few minutes. Washie knew something was troubling Sandy, but waited it out. Finally, Sandy lay her fork down and said, "Mom, I've been thinking."

Washie waited for whatever was coming.

"When John and I were away, we spent a lot of time talking about God whenever Mr. O'Keefe and all his buddies weren't around."

"Really?" This was of no surprise to Washie but felt the need to respond and didn't know what else to say.

Sandy nodded. "I know you and Daddy want me get better in my own time and that's sweet. Would you like to know what I want?"

Washie nodded. "Absolutely."

Sandy gazed up at the ceiling. She placed her hands in her lap and leaned forward. "I prayed. John prayed. We've both been taught that God is in control, and that nothing is a surprise to him. It's up to us what we do with that information. Do we accept it? Do we dismiss it as some silly fairytale that couldn't possibly be true?" She sipped her coffee. "I believe it's true, but more than once I had to remind myself. That's why I never lashed out. Well, partly, anyway. Honestly, I was so frightened Reginald was going to hurt John for something I did that I kept reminding myself to keep quiet. Anyway, we both vowed that if we were found…*alive*… we wouldn't hide away. Or whine and cry or feel sorry for ourselves. We decided that we wanted to do the honorable thing, whatever that is. We wanted to survive but not just for survival's sake. We asked God to give us wisdom to make the right choices, and strength to keep our mouths shut. It would have been so easy to get into a war of words with Reginald. But how do you argue with a crazy man? He's *mad*, Mama. So many times it would have been easy to hate him. The way I figure, hating him would have been easier than choosing to forgive him. The hardest lesson I learned was about forgiveness."

"Forgiveness," Washie uttered breathlessly.

Sandy pushed her empty plate aside and set her cup and saucer in its place and sipped. "I have to forgive…and not for Reginald's sake. For my own. Anger and bitterness was threatening to be our undoing up there, until we made a pact to forgive. I can't speak for John, but I'm certain he's working out his own issues. Forgiveness is hard for him, but he'll get there. As for me, forgiveness may take some time, but it will happen."

Washie dabbed at the corners of her eyes.

"Even though I want to forgive doesn't mean I don't think he shouldn't be punished, because he should." Sandy took a deep breath and continued. "Mama, I want to go back to school as soon as I'm rested and feeling stronger. I only asked Daddy to let me go to town because I didn't want to be a bother to you."

Washie sat up straighter. "How could you *ever* be a bother to me?" Washie nervously chewed the inside of her mouth, trying to ward off tears.

"I don't know. Maybe because you're here all day, waiting on me and treating me like some withering flower. Mama, you can't stop living because you're worried I'll break or something."

Silence. The two just stared at each other, close to tears. Washie was the first to speak. "Now listen here, little girl. You just get that nonsense right on outta your head." She watched for any reaction. When a blank stare was all she got, she continued. "You are a joy and I've been lost without you. I'm so proud of the way you and John persevered. You're both very brave."

"Not really, Mama. Whenever the Luke person got angry, he almost always took it out on John. They…*Reginald*…kicked him and punched him and stuck the barrel of a rifle in his face. I was *terrified*." She shuddered and an awkward silence fell over the room.

As if on cue, the silence was broken by the sound of muffled purring which drew ever closer.

"Morning, Sunflower," Washie said as the gigantic orange tabby cat found its way to her side of the table. Before eventually resting at Washie's feet, Sunflower circled around her legs, rubbing and purring, which Washie found comforting. She pulled her shawl snugly around her shoulders and took in all Sandy had said.

Sandy was so grown up. What was meant for evil had strengthened and matured her adolescent heart. Still, Washie knew how troubled Mr. O'Keefe was. She stiffened. Then again, perhaps she *didn't* know. He was so handsome. Women probably fell at his feet, hoping for just a tiny fraction of his attention, swooning over his dark eyes and winsome smile.

How did he woo Miss Augusta? Did he sweet talk her? Shower her with trinkets? Tell her she was the most ravishing creature he'd ever seen? Was she merely a conquest? And if she was, did he treat her as a possession once he'd won her heart? Did he mistreat her? Ignore her? Was he controlling? Yes, that was more than likely the case. Control was definitely a weapon he frequently retrieved from his arsenal.

Washie suddenly felt an obsession to know the truth. She was resigned to the notion, come hell or high water, that she'd learn everything she could about him. Not for the sake of revenge. No, never that. It was personal. More like her own weapon of protection against any further contact with the scoundrel....or anyone like him.

"What are you thinkin' about, Mom?" Sandy asked with a raised brow and smirk.

"Miss Sandy, a woman's got a right to her private thoughts." Washie shot her a playful grin. "Especially when she's following the example Mary set with Jesus by pondering the wonders of her child, and hiding it in her heart...for later pondering, mind you."

"Of course," Sandy mimicked. "I'll clean the breakfast dishes."

"And I didn't even ask! My, you *have* grown up."

Chapter Sixteen

I'm so glad I live in a world where there are Octobers.
~ L.M. Montgomery, *Anne of Green Gables*

Faerie's bad leg was aching…way down deep inside. Ever since the carriage accident a few years before that caused the injury, her leg spoke often, and loudly. Only one thing would give her any relief. She hunted Myra down and handed her a shawl.

"You. Me. Shawls. Walk."

Myra scrunched up her face, curiosity written all over it.

"Don't look at me that way. I'm not daft."

"Could've fooled me." Myra giggled.

"Sorry, Myra. It's just that…well, look outside. It's a gorgeous morning. October is in full bloom. The aspens are afire with color. The sky… why, it's like a magnificent sapphire."

Myra understood the urgency. "Faerie, are you sure you want me? Why not Annie?"

"Because…" Faerie dragged out the word. "I want to spend some time with you. With all the craziness, I fear I've neglected our friendship." Then: "Besides, my leg is paining me something awful. The weather is changing; there'll be snow soon. Then I won't be able to go out and walk."

"That settles it. Grab a hat and your walking stick and let's be off."

"Annie and the girls will be fine. Lydia's just a holler away if she needs anything. Want to drop by and see if Augusta would like to join us?"

"The more the merrier."

******

The ladies veered from Faerie's usual walking path and headed straight for the mercantile. "I've got a little craving, Myra. It'll be my treat."

They stepped up on the wooden walkway and crossed the threshold into the store. A bell attached to the top of the door jingled, which alerted the proprietor of their presence.

"Mornin', Miz Wright, Miz Owens."

"Good morning, Mr. Henry," they responded in unison.

Old Man Henry's store was a local gathering place and Faerie loved the snug feeling it gave her. It reminded her of Goldwater Mercantile in Prescott, Arizona…everything under the sun and then some with a small serving of local gossip on the side. She stood in the center aisle and took in the smells of the inviting, community store. Leather, lavender and lemon: three distinct smells blending into an heady aroma she associated only with the old gentlemanly storekeeper.

"What can I do ya for, ladies? Anything special?" he asked, stepping from behind the long wood and glass counter.

"Mr. Henry, I've got a real hankering for peanuts. Do you have any salted?" Faerie asked.

"Right this way, Miz Wright. You see that old barrel over there? It's full o' peanuts, still in the shells, soaked in briny water and dried."

Faerie gave Myra a quick glance and tapped the fingertips of her gloved hands together. "Wonderful. We just need enough to snack on while we stroll around town."

Myra added, "Old Man, might you have any lemon drops?"

"Well, now, Miss Myra, ya know I do. Want the usual bag?"

"Oh, yes, please." She beamed.

They soon offered up their fare-thee-wells to Old Man and departed the store, each with their own delectable treasures. Myra popped a tart lemon drop in her mouth. "Ooh, so sour! It makes my jaws tingle." She crinkled up her nose and then shook her head. "I love lemon candies!"

Faerie dropped a peanut hull on the ground. "I don't know how you eat those things." Then: "Say, Myra, do you know Old Man's real name?"

Myra smiled coyly, leading Faerie to believe she knew the man's name. The ladies slowed down to a turtle's pace as they chatted. "He doesn't like anybody teasing him about it. Promise to keep it secret?"

"I promise. Do tell." Faerie moved in closer, feeling scandalous. It reminded her of sharing secrets with friends when she was a young girl back in Boston. She waited with baited breath to learn Old Man's secret.

Myra peeked over her shoulder to make certain no one was in hearing distance and moved the lemon drop from one side of her mouth to the other. She whispered, "He won't tell anybody. Says it's so awful he'd never live it down." Then she said, "Wouldn't it be hilarious if it was something like Gustavus Percival Washington Henry?"

Faerie snorted in laughter until her sides were splitting. "How about Horatio Pluto Winston Henry?"

Myra wiped tears from her eyes. "Let's see. Maybe Napoleon Homer Spurgeon Henry."

The ladies were laughing so hard that passersby on the street began to stare. They stopped and rested on a bench outside the Somer's café. "Myra," Faerie said amid her giggles, "are we terrible? Are we making fun of a nice old man?"

"Heavens no! We were just putting silly names together. Besides, if Old Man wants to be called Old Man, who are we to question him? He's a dear, but very set in his ways." Then: "This is morbid to say, but I wonder what will be on headstone."

Faerie looked serious, then said, "Old Man Henry." Serious snorts and giggles broke out again. "Morbid humor…why is it always so funny?" She offered Myra her bag of peanuts.

Gladly dipping her hand in the bag, she dropped a handful into her lap and started snacking. She looked across the street at the hospital. "Mr. Henry will never be anything but a fine old gentleman to me. He prays for the sick and needy, gives a peppermint stick to a child when the mother isn't watching, never gives anyone any guff, but offers a kind word and smile instead." She paused. "Lydia told me she was in the mercantile the day Reginald was released from jail. She said Mr. Henry was right neighborly to him. And listen to this, Faerie. Lydia said Reginald responded in kind….and without hesitation or suspicion. I've often thought about that. It tells me he's still in there somewhere."

"He wasn't sour or rude?" Faerie asked.

"Not according to Lydia. She said he was as meek as a lamb."

"Pardon me for not being able to imagine Reginald ever being *meek*."

Myra's eyes glazed over. She sat up tall and stared straight ahead.

"Myra, what's wrong? Did he hurt you?"

Myra dropped her head and nodded. "Only the one time, on the night he went on his rampage. It started with me, then Augusta, then on to Mr. Marcus."

"Why didn't you ever tell me?" Faerie asked gently.

She shrugged. "He pushed me against the wall and pinned me in and threatened me. He was angry with Augusta for sending Lydia and me to your house. He told me *I* was disgusting, that *Augusta* was disgusting, that *all* expectant mothers were…*disgusting*." Myra had a catch in her throat. Struggling to speak, she said, "I ran home when I got loose. George locked the doors and we stayed hunkered down until Augusta came knocking, begging to be let in."

Faerie looked around. The street was oddly quiet for midmorning. "Myra, I'm so glad you…and your precious baby…are safe. Thankfully, Reginald's left you alone since that one incident. When he's confused or angry, or whatever he feels that puts him in a rage, Heaven help anyone unfortunate enough to be in his path. The good news is that he doesn't seem particularly interested in either of us." She paused. Then: "The Lord only knows where he is these days. I always find myself looking over my shoulder when I'm out and about."

Myra heard nothing after Faerie's comment about Reginald supposedly losing interest in the two of them. "And h-how do you know th-that?" H-How can you b-be so sure? Th-That he isn't after us, I m-mean?" Myra asked, sounding like a frightened child, and suddenly weeping uncontrollably.

Faerie frowned, feeling sorry for Myra. As sincerely as she was able, she said, "Honestly, there's no way to be completely certain. It just seems to me that he's had ample opportunity to come and get us, yet he leaves the women in the manor alone."

"Yes, that seems right," Myra agreed, composing herself. She hadn't really thought of that before.

"And Myra, George would never let him near you again. I can't imagine what you're feeling, or what ghastly memories you have of that day. Just know that you're safe…and loved."

Myra took in a long, labored breath mixed with the hiccoughs of tears. She pulled a hankie from inside her sleeve and dabbed her nose.

"Come on, sweet Myra. No more tears. Let's enjoy our morning." Faerie stood and held out a hand to Myra, inviting her to do the same.

"Is my face red? Can you tell I've been crying?" Myra asked meekly.

"You look fine. Besides, who's going to notice? The streets are empty." Faerie waved her right arm about for emphasis.

"All right, then. Thank you, Faerie."

"For what?" Faerie asked.

"For being honest…and sincere. For helping me see things in a different light."

Faerie turned and with a mischievous smile said, "Let's go. Augusta doesn't even know we've kept her waiting."

The ladies giggled and walked arm in arm down Main Street.

******

Augusta noticed a definite chill in the air as she lay stretched out on the chaise that took up an inordinate amount of space on the back porch. She grabbed the quilt she'd brought out and wrapped up in it and thought anybody seeing her would think her very cocoon-like. Snug and warm, she nestled in for a few minutes of late morning reverie.

She sat mesmerized by the quaking of the aspens in the backyard. The golden leaves shimmered in the sunlight as a heavy gust of wind stole them from the trees, sending them whirling through the air. There was something about this time of year, the season when aspens transitioned from complete wakefulness to sleeping giants. She thought it a marvel of nature how things entering a dormant season appeared more brilliant and

140

alive than ever. She recalled a comment Nora made about what a marvel-ous mystery it was for leaves to become more beautifully radiant at the end of their season than when they are in their prime. The leaves reach the height of their beauty at the appropriate time and then fall away, leaving us with only their memory. The trees then sleep until springtime and the cycle begins again.

"You are entirely lost in your thoughts." Faerie nudged her friend.

Augusta gasped and practically jumped out of her skin. "Lord above, Faerie. How long have you been here?"

"About twenty minutes," she teased. Faerie remained as deadpan as possible for as long as possible before finally grinning and confessing the truth. "Tarnation!" Faerie said to Myra. "I just can't quite pull that off, can I?"

Myra tsk'd then said, "You mean lying? Not so much."

Augusta looked around for Nora. "Did you let yourselves in?"

"No." Myra nodded in the direction of the kitchen. "Nora and Derrick let us in. He's growing like a weed, Augusta."

Augusta beamed with pride. Sheepishly, she replied, "He is, isn't he?" Then: "What brings you by today?" She motioned for them to have a seat at the table as she stood, quilt and all, and inched in the same direction.

"Faerie kidnapped me from the house for a walk, and we ended up here." Myra pulled her shawl closer, tossing one end of it over her shoul-der.

"Very stylish!" Augusta teased.

"This old thing? Made it myself when we first moved here."

"Whenever did you find the time?" Augusta was forever in awe of Myra's never-ending resourcefulness.

"Once I started, it didn't take long. I was done in a jiffy. Crocheting takes a lot less time than your knitting."

"Or my sewing, I suppose," Faerie added.

"Probably." Then: "Say, didn't I catch you spying one of those new Singer sewing machines in the Sears and Roebuck wish book?"

"Guilty," Faerie admitted. "The next time we take a trip to Denver, I'd like to try one out. I've got to keep up with the times."

"Faerie, are you thinking about designing again?" Augusta asked, sounding hopeful.

She blushed. "Maybe, except not so much gowns, but something practi-cal for women who want to look nice but still need to be able to function day-to-day."

Augusta said, "Well, you can start with me. I need a few dresses to

141

squash my reputation as town vixen."

Nora appeared at the door with a tray filled with tea and cakes.

"You're a love, Nora." Augusta smiled warmly. "Where's our young man?"

"Out like a light on a pallet on the kitchen floor, his favorite spot." She clasped her hands together in front of her. "If you don't need anything, I'll get back to it. I'm giving the kitchen a good cleaning today."

"Is Dan coming over for the noon meal?" Augusta asked.

"Same time as usual." Nora blushed, dropping her head.

"Sparks, Nora?" Myra teased.

Without answering, Nora grinned and blushed and headed back into the house.

"Ah...true love!" Augusta proclaimed in her best sing-song voice.

Faerie tilted her head as she poured and served the tea.

"You look puzzled." Myra knew she'd never let the vixen comment pass without addressing it.

Augusta knew it, too. She wished she could reel the words right back into her mouth, chew them up and spit them into the backyard. Better yet, learn to watch her mouth. With a pouty look, she asked, "Is it the vixen thing?"

"You know it is." Faerie put a spoonful of sugar in her tea and stirred. "When did you start caring about what those old gossips have to say?"

"Since I began to think about my son and how special he is. He deserves one parent who's somewhat reputable. If I have to caudle every old bitty in this town until they think I'm as sweet as honey...well, by gum, I'll do it. I'll go to church. I'll work as a volunteer at the hospital. I'll smile...and try to mean it."

"Goodness, girl, what's come over you?" Faerie was taken aback. She couldn't believe her ears.

Augusta poured a splash of milk into her cup and watched the liquids swirl into a velvety caramel color. She stirred the blend and tapped the spoon lightly on the rim of the cup.

Myra and Faerie shared a quizzical look and shrugged their shoulders.

"I've had a lot of free time the last month or so, as Nora can attest. When I first boarded the train to Pagosa Springs, I was nervous and agitated. More than anything I was afraid for my life and the lives of everyone in my circle. Nora and I had a conversation about trust. Not just trusting people, but trusting Someone greater than myself. Both of you know I've been less than open to the idea of a loving God." She sipped her tea. "Or any God, for that matter."

Faerie's expression softened as she began to understand.

Augusta held her cup with both hands. She sipped and then gingerly returned the cup to its saucer. With her shoulders back, she lifted her head and stuck out her chin.

Myra elbowed Faerie and rolled her eyes.

Faerie silently mouthed, "So dramatic".

Augusta said, "I saw that. You're lucky I'm a changed woman or else I might have slugged you, Faerie Wright."

They giggled like silly schoolgirls at the feisty comment. Augusta picked up her cup and slurped noisily. "Is that more to your liking, Miss Smarty Pants?" she asked Faerie.

"Sounds just like Lydia," Faerie spewed.

"I won't tell her you said that," Augusta said, snickering. "As I was saying before the two of you so rudely sidetracked me, I'm happy to do or be whatever I must to salvage my reputation. Derrick deserves a fair shot at life."

Faerie realized better than most how the gossip had morphed into something distorted and hurtful. Some of the women were so taken with the handsome, genteel version of Reginald O'Keefe that they were blind to his instability and ruthless behavior. She'd even heard a young woman at church say that the allegations of his criminal behavior surely must be overstated and that the bearers of such malicious talk should be silenced.

"Augusta, even though your reputation is tarnished, those who truly know you and have a clear understanding of what happened aren't judging you. Don't compromise your integrity for the sake of a few misguided, overzealous busybodies. If the naysayers want to naysay, they will." Faerie wished there was some way to stop the talk, but it was as old as time.

"That's absolutely true," Myra interjected. "Why, if those women you're referring to didn't have you to gossip about, they'd move on to somebody else. Just the other day I was walking down Main Street and a young woman was frantically trying to rein in her young boys. It was nothing really, only energetic young'uns. She wasn't mean or loud. She didn't threaten them. She simply told them to sit down on the bench. That's it. Down at the corner stood Louise Shaw and Ruth Davidson."

"Oh, my! The two most arduous storytellers in Ouray County!" Faerie exclaimed.

"Uh-huh. Anyway, when the young mother sat down on the bench with her boys, the women walked by and Louise said, 'Can you believe it? She practically shamed them into submission right here on the street'. Ruth added, 'She might as well have taken the strap to them'. I watched

143

the two of them walk by with their noses in the air. I swear if I'd had daggers in my eyes, they'd both have been hit. That poor young woman really tried not to cry, but the tears fell like rain. Well, I couldn't help myself. I marched myself over to her and said, 'you're in good company, you know. Anybody who's anybody has been the target of those two busybodies. One day they'll get what's coming to them. I just hope I can be a fly on the wall to hear it.'

"She perked up and thanked me. Before we parted company, she said something that stuck with me. She said that people like that are lonely and bitter, and she felt sorry for them. She told me the Bible says we all will be judged in the same way we judge others. I wasn't sure if she was talking about Louise and Ruth or me or all of us."

Augusta bit her lower lip and resisted the temptation to rattle off all manner of opinions about Louise Shaw and Ruth Davidson. Instead she replied, "So what you're saying is that I need to live my life, avoid gossip, don't listen to or spread it. Let God be the judge and live honorably."

"Impressive!" Faerie beamed, pleased as punch with Augusta's insight and newly acquired maturity. "In the end, each one of us is responsible for how we react when we are injured by others. We can retaliate…or we can walk away, especially when it comes to Louise Shaw and her ladies' circle. I, for one, refuse to give her the upper hand. That's not to say I'll stoop to her level, or the level of anyone like her. That kind of behavior is atrocious."

"In that case, scratch all that other stuff I said. Being kind for the wrong reasons is the same as living a lie." Augusta wagged her head. "I've got a lot to learn."

"Good girl," Myra said, as she gave Augusta's hand a squeeze.

******

An hour of chatting quickly passed. Myra and Faerie coaxed Augusta into joining them for a walk that was topped off with a bite of lunch at The Bon Ton. The waitress sat them at a cozy table by the fireplace, which was perfect for three ladies who'd been walking around in the cool October air.

"I must admit there's a reason I suggested we eat here." Faerie slowly removed her gloves in ladylike fashion.

Myra and Augusta exchanged coy looks and blurted out in unison, "Peach tarts."

"What?" Faerie feigned innocence.

"You know good and well that you can't walk past this place without stopping for a peach tart." Augusta teased her friend mercilessly about her undying passion for peaches.

The noon meal passed far too quickly and before they knew it their visit came to an end. Hugs and well wishes were shared and then the friends parted. Augusta strolled lightheartedly down the street, humming.

"What a fine day!" she exclaimed.

"Never seen better," came a familiar voice from behind.

Smiling, she turned. "Doc Fisher, how very nice to see you!"

Chapter Seventeen

If you could kick the person in the pants responsible for most of your troubles,
you wouldn't sit for a month.
~ Theodore Roosevelt

Fred backed up to the nearest spruce and leaned against it. Crossing his arms, he admired the expanse of mountains and canyons beyond. He marveled at the breathtaking crags with splashes of evergreens, and aspens ablaze in golden yellows and oranges as far as the eye could see.

His thoughts turned to Annie. Life before her had been chaotic and disjointed. Now he was blessed with a kind of peaceful easiness that only comes with contentment. With Annie, every day was filled with wonder and anticipation. He marveled how even the most mundane of tasks seemed important to her. Unlike some young women, she never put on airs. She was Annie: genuine, honest, caring and devoted. Time spent with her was comfortable and fun in a way only she could deliver. He'd never known anyone like her. Her smile could fill his heart with joy; her tears, rip it apart.

He never wanted to be away from her; nevertheless, duty called. He and Marcus were leaving in less than a week on a trip to Cripple Creek and Victor. The Pikes Peak Gold Rush was in full swing and mines were popping up everywhere in the shadow of the grand mountain the Utes called Tava, Sun Mountain.

In 1878, a ranch hand by the name of Robert Miller Womack dug up a chunk of gold, but nobody took him seriously. With the passage of time, a couple of men joined his venture, all clearly novices in need of help. Womack believed he was literally sitting on top of a gold mine, so to speak, and finally reached out to the professionals for assistance.

A telegram from Womack precipitated the upcoming trip across the mountains. There would be no exchange of goods or money. They were strictly seeking guidance from a company that had honed its mining skills and making money hand over fist. Come this time next week, Marcus and Fred would be well on their way to Colorado Springs, where they'd be bunking at Glen Eyrie, General William Jackson Palmer's estate.

Oh, how he wished Annie might accompany him on the trip, but it wouldn't be proper. Tongues would wag and her reputation would be in shambles. She often said she lived vicariously through the travel of others. Since her return from New England two years earlier, she'd stayed within the confines of Ouray County, except for the trip they'd taken with the Wrights into the Arizona Territory a few months earlier.

Overhead an eagle soared on the wind, its cry piercing the sky. He watched its graceful, fluid movements, as it hunted for food far below. He admired birds of prey. So majestic, they seemed to sail above the earth, gliding on the wind with ease and grace, undoubtedly, the most respected of the winged creatures in the mountains. They built their nests in the tops of the tallest trees, deep in the forests, and kept watch over their domain as a ruler over his subjects. Fred lifted the corners of his mouth in amusement. The golden eagle had found its prey. Fred watched as the bird began his descent, his talons like sharpened iron, ready for attack. He screamed again as he snatched the poor creature up and flew away. *To be free to soar like one of these incredible creatures*, he thought. He'd snatch Annie up and take her to the top of Mount Sneffels and look down upon the earth below.

His heart pounded within his chest. Annie had agreed to be his bride; he could hardly believe his good fortune. Her family had welcomed him with open arms. Despite the glowing accolades of Annie's success as a professional nanny, her mother seemed incredibly relieved at the prospect of marriage. Annie was quite lovely, desirable, and smart, and with a quick wit to boot. Even though she could've had her pick of any number of suitors, she fell in love with him.

With the roles of the Victorian woman so clearly defined, he loved that she was refined and polite, yet full of playfulness and curious optimism. He found it delightful that those who knew her best looked the other way when she sometimes stepped over the lines of polite society. It was probably because she did it with a wink and a smile. He chuckled. None of the ladies in her circle exactly followed society's unwritten rules for the fairer sex. Furthermore, none of the men in their lives seemed to mind. He certainly didn't. He could hardly wait for the day when the two of them set up housekeeping. He had a feeling their home would be far from traditional.

The upcoming trip to Colorado Springs was important to him, not so much from a business standpoint, but because he hoped to find a jeweler with the perfect engagement ring for Annie. She didn't expect one. In fact, she'd said often enough that she didn't need a token to prove his love and devotion. Perhaps she truly felt that way, but he had a sneaking suspicion she was only being polite. Perhaps she was saving him an extra expense since he was about to add a mortgage to his monthly bills.

Annie dressed with an understated elegance. From head to toe, her conservative upbringing combined with a little East Coast flair defined her personal style. She wanted none of the glitz that Queen Victoria had brought to fashion. Not his Annie. She was fresh, clean and subdued, yet something about her made everyone gravitate to her. He loved the way she wore her hair down with combs on the sides. She used the excuse of tending to babies all day as the reason for her no frills attire. No matter what she wore she was beautiful. She was definitely no Plain Jane. He admired her casual, no nonsense approach to clothing. When she hiked in the woods she wore a loose-fitting pair of dungarees and a large plaid flannel shirt tucked into them, and a tall wide-brimmed hat that resembled one he saw in a picture of a lawman up north in Canada. She wore a pair of boots similar to those many of the miners wore. When he asked her about them, she said they were her father's. She stuffed the toes with socks so she wouldn't step right out of them. She was a sight for sore eyes in that get up. One of these days he was going to buy himself one of the new Kodak cameras like Faerie had in Arizona. He'd love to take some photographs of her in that garb to show their future children. He laughed out loud picturing it. While the other ladies went for their constitutionals, Annie hiked like a seasoned veteran of the sport.

"There you are." Marcus crept up behind him, giving him a start.

"I was enjoying my reverie. Thinking about much; thinking about nothing."

"As strange as that sounds, I know just what you mean." Marcus bit into a juicy apple.

"Crunchy. Sounds good." Then: "Annie says we're going to miss quite a party at the Archer's place next weekend."

Marcus reached into his coat pocket and pulled out another apple and tossed it to Fred.

"Thanks. I skipped breakfast and I've been drinking coffee all morning."

"Any reason for not eating? That's not like you at all."

"Lots on my mind. Not to mention I got up late and ran out without grabbing my sack lunch."

"Eat up, then." Marcus backed up to a boulder and munched on the apple.

"I haven't been sleeping well, Marcus." Fred twisted the stem off the apple and took a generous bite. Juice dripped down his chin. Speaking with a mouthful, he said, "Land sakes! This thing tastes as good as the crunch."

"Mother Nature's perfect food." Then: "Wanna shed some light on your sleeplessness?"

Fred squinted. "Just can't seem to turn off my brain. I lie there in the dark and watch the shadows creep across the ceiling. I plan my next day.

I concentrate on not thinking. I think about Annie and hope I can make her happy. I wonder what kind of shenanigans O'Keefe will pull next. It just never ends." Then: "You and I are in the same boat. O'Keefe hates us both. You for purely selfish reasons. And me: because I know too much."

Marcus dropped his head and inventoried the ground below. Everywhere he looked was black dirt, tree roots, lichen-covered rocks and tree roots, boulders large and small, and every size in between. He kicked at a rock…granite…pink and slate in color.

"Fred, I think Reg isn't finished with Simon. I'm less worried for us than for the Archers. Reg has never been one to let sleeping dogs lie. And in his present state of mind, it's safe to say we've only begun to see a glimpse of his viciousness."

"I spend a lot of time worrying about the women in our lives. None of them are safe." Fred took another bite of the apple.

Marcus shrugged his shoulders. "They're strong. You have to give them that." He threw the apple core over the side of the mountain. "Faerie and Augusta are trying their best to live normal lives. No hiding behind four walls. Washie appears to be struggling. Being Cherokee, she's seen much sorrow, been mistreated. Trust probably doesn't come easily for her."

"Do you think O'Keefe will go after Sandy again?"

"I want to say no, but I can't, at least not with any certainty."

"Annie said she's afraid he'll show up here at the mine and try to kill us both at the same time."

Marcus furrowed his brow. A chill went up and down his spine. "I sincerely hope your girl isn't a soothsayer."

Fred slowly nibbled on the apple and silently echoed Marcus's hope.

Chapter Eighteen

Things never happen the same way twice.
~ C.S. Lewis

All that stood between the two miners and Reginald was a tall stand of aspens and a great big rock. He watched, focusing on their body language and facial expressions. He was close enough to hear most of the conversation. All the same, he knew he must be very still and as quiet as a mouse, and block out all else to be positive he got it all.

"Tsk, tsk." Luke refused to be squashed. He spoke in a mocking tone. "Poor Marcus. Still confused about us after all this time."

Reginald spoke not a word as he glared intently at his nemesis through the trees.

Luke chuckled maliciously. "I'll give you this one. We can talk later. I can hardly wait to decide who is next."

Reginald smirked as evil made its home in his cold dark eyes.

******

Dusk gave way to darkness as Nora and Dan sat on the porch swing, snuggled under a blanket. The crisp night air bit at their noses and cheeks. It was almost suppertime and they had two promised to cook Augusta a tasty stick-to-your-ribs meal guaranteed to satisfy. From the window above them, the young couple heard Derrick's sweet squeals of laughter.

"Isn't that just the sweetest sound you ever heard?" Nora asked with a lilt in her voice.

The lamplight on the table brought a soft golden beam to her long dark hair. Dan was falling more in love with Nora every day. She was smart, talented, kind and respectful…and clearly far too good for him. His heart warmed to know she adored children and hoped for a whole passel of them.

"You're very quiet, Dan. Speak to me." She elbowed him playfully.

"Honestly, I was thinking about how good you are with children. The kids at church literally cling to you." He slipped an arm around her and pulled her close, tucking the blanket in around them.

She shivered.

"Cold?" he asked.

"A little."

"Just a few more minutes and we'll go in. Then I'll start a fire."

"Ooh, I'd really like that. So would Augusta. She's so cold-natured, she's probably up in her room with one of those eiderdown quilts pulled up to her eyeballs."

He laughed at the word picture she painted. He could see Augusta with her long black hair and big dark eyes peeking out from under the covers, looking like a frightened little girl. "Hmm…" He shook his head.

"What is it?"

"Augusta. She's like a scared child. She presents a good face. What if it's all just an act to guard her heart?"

Nora studied on that for a moment. Then: "She's told me things about her past that turned my stomach. She's had to fight for almost everything she's ever had, beginning when she was little." Nora paused. "Dan, some of us don't understand how blessed we really are."

He nodded. "You're right. When I was little, we ate cornbread and milk for supper more'n I care to remember. And we moved around a lot before settling down here. It wasn't till we came here that things started looking up for us. It was tough for a while." He cleared his throat. "We aren't rich by any stretch. Still I count my blessings every day."

Nora shivered as a gust swept through the porch. "I hate to say this out loud, because saying it makes it so. Anyway, here goes. I fear the cold weather is settling in. Snow is just around the corner. "

"Now you've gone and done it," he teased and then stood and offered his hand. "I'd say it's time to start that fire," he said, then brushed her cheek with a kiss.

******

Augusta was comfy propped against the headboard of her spacious feather bed. She contentedly read from a Jane Austen book while Derrick lay in the middle on top of the comforter unaware of anything around him but his fingers and toes. She listened to the wind as it whipped around the side of the house. The sun had set and the air had an autumn chill to it. A door shut downstairs followed by the muffled sound of giggles. Nora and Dan's chatty Voices carried up the stairs. She put the book aside and listened. Before long she could smell supper wafting up from the kitchen. This was home: joyful, carefree chatter, creaking floorboards, logs on the fire and the heavenly aroma of supper on the stove.

Young love was in the air. Nora and Dan were mad for each other. She so enjoyed watching Nora these days. Her heart was an open book and Augusta couldn't resist living vicariously through her. Oh, how she longed for that kind of love. Not a man who showered her with gifts and empty promises of forever love or one so devastatingly handsome that she became mere putty in his hands. She wanted true love, the kind that was strong enough to weather life's storms. She wanted to cherish and be cherished. She fantasized about greeting her man with a kiss every day when he got home from work. She'd take his hat and coat and have supper on the table the minute he walked through the door. She longed for a man who would care for and love Derrick as his own, and stand by his side as he grew, nudging him in the right direction.

Augusta was hungry for what Myra and George had, or the love and respect between Marcus and Faerie. Those couples were happy. They lived for each other and their children. She'd never had that with Reginald. In the beginning of their marriage they behaved like spoiled brats, spending money like there was no tomorrow, throwing lavish parties, buying on a whim, and staffing their house like it was a luxury hotel. She was the first to admit it was all for show.

All she wanted now was a simple, comfortable home, and a good man with whom to share it. She took a deep breath and took in the aroma of bacon. Nora and Dan were cooking breakfast. That's what she wanted…a man who liked breakfast for supper.

One important fact stood out in her mind. Derrick was dependent upon her. She was responsible for his welfare. Above all else, she needed to make sure he grew up knowing he was loved. For now, the most important thing she could do for either one of them was to be content. Nevertheless, she was preparing her heart for love, if…or when…it knocked on her heart's door.

She adored Nora. She was in awe of how she connected with Derrick, the way he cooed and laughed as he reached for her the second she came into sight. Augusta felt a twinge of something akin to pride when she thought of the budding romance between Nora and Deputy Dan. Seeing them together, the way they looked into each other's eyes, the correspondence that passed between them during their time apart, the color in Nora's cheeks when she opened the front door and found him waiting there, the way Dan hung on every word that passed her lips: Augusta felt a sense of accomplishment for encouraging their friendship in the beginning. She also recognized how very envious she was of what they shared.

She smoothed the quilts and gave Derrick's hand a little squeeze. There was a word for the way she was feeling. She was *melancholy.* Yes, that's what it was. She supposed it was better than living in fear or disappointment. It was definitely better than feeling the need to get even with people the way Reginald did. Yes, she knew the emotion would pass and her mood would change. She chastised herself for the envy she sometimes felt over her friends' happiness. Her time would come. Faerie always told her that our timing was very different from God's. She chuckled. "I can almost hear her now. Be patient, Augusta. Your day will come." She wagged her head and smiled.

How her mind wandered. And when it did she frequently anchored in a place filled with bad memories of poor behavior and life choices. She pondered what might have been as opposed to what actually was. Old ghosts reared their ugly heads, haunting her with visions of a life not so long ago that was futile and filled with self-destruction. Her whole life had been one of pure survival. Those days were long gone and few people in Ouray knew the truth about them. She must keep it that way in order to prosper in such a small town, even if it meant bowing to the idle, malicious gossip that flew off some tongues like so many birds on the wing.

She told herself to brush it off. "A new life has begun. Old things are passed away. I'm not the same person I was even a short month ago."

Derrick rolled over grinning from ear to ear and flashed his big brown eyes at his mother.

"There's my sweet boy. Shall we take a walk downstairs and see what Miss Nora is doing?" The baby smiled and cooed as he reached for her. These were the moments a parent never forgets. "It doesn't get any better than this. Who needs romance when I have you, my precious boy? You've stolen my heart." Augusta picked him up and held him close. He placed a chubby little hand on her cheek and she melted.

******

Doc Fisher nursed a mug of coffee, lost in his thoughts of Augusta. He'd waited impatiently for her return. He now wondered if she might be the tiniest bit unnerved at being back where all her troubles began. He took a swig of the coffee. "Argh!" he scowled and pushed the mug away. "Stone cold."

He checked his pocket-watch and read half-past five. He'd been up all night, which was nothing unusual except for the fact that there'd been one too many all-nighters in a row, and he was beat. One of these days, his shift at the hospital would change. Then there might be a chance at a normal life. Because of his rigorous schedule, he snuck in tiny visits with friends whenever he could. Working nights was a true test of his will… and social life. The two docs on staff were over-worked and exhausted. The Sisters were searching for a third physician, which gave Doc renewed hope that surely help was on its way. If not, he'd be an old man before his time.

Something about that made him think about the widows and orphans both on Red Mountain and Ouray. Mining had proven to be a dangerous way to make a living. He was sorry to say, however, that some of the accidents up there had been because of clumsy or careless behaviors. Many a home had been left widowed and fatherless. He'd been the physician on call on several occasions when the bell tolled at the bottom of the hill alerting the village of an injured miner being brought down. Far too often, family members anxiously awaited news of their injured loved one only to be devastated to hear he hadn't survived the accident. If there was anything about being a doctor he despised, it was informing families and friends of the passing of a loved one.

In a most unusual sense, he thought of Augusta as a widow. Although her former husband was still alive, he was anything but well, and hardly the man she once knew. He chastised and tormented those in his former circle of friends for wrongdoings of his own imagination. Reginald beat and ridiculed Augusta, and filled her head with all kinds of ugly talk. Doc prayed she was doing more than wrapping a bandage around her broken heart. He wished, for the good of all, she'd continue the work she'd begun a few months ago with local abused women and children. He prayed she'd join the ranks of such spirited women as Susan Archer and Faerie Wright, who volunteered their time and money to the support of the less fortunate in the county.

He found her hypnotic. Her dark eyes and thick, silky black hair enhanced her delicate porcelain skin. Even in her everyday dresses she looked like a model in the finest dress shops back East. She turned heads everywhere she went. Even with her magnificent beauty, she was genuine and real, and had a wicked sense of humor. He had to admit he was completely swept away by her.

Might he be so bold as to court her? He wanted to...*very* much. He'd called on her several times, each visit having had something or other to do with Reginald. What would she think if he made a purely social call? That brought up another issue. What if O'Keefe was still stalking her? What if he caught her with another man and lost all reason? What if he went crazy? *Crazy*? He thought perhaps he'd stepped over the line with that one. As a doctor, he figured he might consider using more professional diagnostic terms when it came to such matters. But dag-nab-it, crazy as a June bug described O'Keefe just fine, especially since there was no working diagnosis on the man.

Doc checked his watch again. Time seemed to crawl by in the wee hours. Thank goodness, the sun was beginning to rise. He needed fresh coffee, not the cold, dark sludge in the bottom of his mug. His replacement would be arriving soon. All was quiet on the home front, and had been

155

most of the night. There was nothing to report. Just a passing of the torch and he'd be free as a bird until his next shift.

******

An hour later, rejuvenated by coffee and the fresh mountain air, Doc set out on the street to Augusta's house, whistling a happy tune. He wondered if she would consider him ill-mannered if he showed up for breakfast again. He was itching to see her. He'd never set eyes on a more beautiful woman and was completely taken with her.

He jogged across the bridge connecting her walkway to the street and then onto the porch. He knocked twice on the door and stepped back. He listened to the sound of footsteps scurrying across the wooden floor.

The door opened and Nora, fresh-faced and smiling, greeted him warmly, taking him by the elbow and leading him across the room. She leaned in closer to him and said in a hushed, mischievous voice, "I wondered how long 'til you dropped by." She winked as they stepped into the kitchen.

"Is it that obvious?" he asked.

"Only to me. Augusta's clueless." Then: "Doc, a lot has changed since we last saw you."

"Oh? How so?"

Nora spooned batter into muffin tins. "When we boarded the train to leave here, Augusta was a scared, opinionated, insecure woman. She's returned a much more confident, caring, benevolent one. Still opinionated, but some things are out of our control." She grinned lopsidedly.

"Really?" he mused. "What happened? A life-altering experience?"

Nora stood silent for a moment. Then: "She's searching. She's on a kind of *spiritual* journey. She's studying the Bible, talking about church… you know, attending services."

"Hm." He was pleasantly surprised…and a little stunned. "Why the change?"

"She said she finally just stopped fighting and admitted to herself that God is God. When she did, all else began to fall into place and make sense."

"Well, I'll be," he responded for lack of a better response.

"I'm not kidding. She's a different person, for sure. You'll see." Nora put the muffin tin in the oven and checked the time. "Fifteen minutes for the muffins. Help me keep an eye on them, please." She stacked the bowl and utensils and put them in the sink.

He nodded. "I think I can handle that." Then: "Is she up? It's mighty early." Doc scratched his head.

156

Nora nodded. "She's been up for a couple of hours. Said she woke up ready to get moving, whatever that means. Last time I checked she was dressing Derrick."

He rubbed his hands together. "You've definitely got my curiosity up."

"Stay for breakfast. That way I won't feel guilty asking you to set the table."

"Makin' me work for my breakfast; I see how you are," he teased, heading around to the cabinets to fetch the plates.

"If you're to be a regular around here you have to pull your weight." She busied herself by cracking some eggs into a bowl. "Just ask Dan."

"Yes, ma'am." Doc whistled as he worked. Then: "So...I take it you're all for me calling on the lady of the house?"

"A little male attention is precisely what she needs."

A creaking sound from the direction of the staircase caught their attention. Nora tip-toed to the kitchen door and peeked out into the great room to see what was what. With a flustered face, she scurried back and got to work. She placed a finger to her lips, giving Doc the signal for all quiet.

When Augusta entered the kitchen, she said, "Breakfast smells heavenly. I'm hungry enough to eat a..." It was then she saw the most welcome sight. "Doc Fisher!" she exclaimed. "What a lovely surprise. I see Nora's put you to work."

He beamed with delight at the warm greeting. "Yes, she's a real slave driver. I hope you don't mind I've set myself a place at the table."

"I wouldn't have it any other way. I simply must...or *we* must...Nora and I...tell you all about our little holiday."

Chapter Nineteen

You never lose by loving. You always lose by holding back.
~ Barbara Anglin

Washie and Alfred were grateful for Sandy's quick re-entry into her world. Other than being a little standoffish, she appeared to be pretty much back to her old self. She was hesitant to go to school. She was afraid the students would either shun her out of some misguided fear of hurting her, or worse, bombard her with questions. The prospect of either scenario frightened her. She didn't want to be a spectacle, and she certainly didn't wish to talk about what happened with a bunch of schoolkids.

Tomorrow was the day the ladies had been looking forward to for weeks. The Harvest Gathering was just around the corner and Susan had invited them all out to bake and make decorations, as well as finalize the list of games and prizes. Washie begged Sandy to tag along. She wasn't too keen on the idea, stating she thought it was time to face the music and to return to school, despite her misgivings. Washie bowed to Sandy's wishes even though she believed a day on the ranch would do the girl a world of good.

Washie stretched out on the bed with a book. She read the same paragraph four times before setting it aside. Was Sandy genuinely anxious to return to class? Or was seeing John so soon a painful reminder of a time she'd just as soon forget? As if either of them ever could forget. Sandy had always been an open book. She wasn't one for secrecy; however, Washie sensed there was more to Sandy's request than simply returning to school, especially since just a day earlier she'd been dead set against it.

Alfred assured her that Sandy knew what she was doing. *She's a big girl,* he'd said. *Don't treat her like a baby.* But she *was* Washie's baby and the mother in her was searching for answers. People tiptoed around them and avoided the obvious questions. The ladies in her Sunday school class squeezed her hand and told her Sandy would open up when she was ready. Maybe so, but Washie wanted her to be ready now. She wanted to know what happened that Sandy wasn't telling. Nothing in Sandy's countenance or conversation attested to the fact that she'd been kidnapped and held captive. Nothing, that is, except her rail thin body and the way she isolated herself from others.

Why was Alfred so passive about it? Come to think of it, he went about his business as if nothing had ever happened, while she was desperate to know the whole truth. Washie's hands were tied. She was unable to help because Sandy held her at arm's length.

She closed the book and got out of bed. Why she believed sleep might come easily this night, at such an early hour, was beyond reason. Donning her robe, she padded into the family room where Alfred sat in front of the fire, his head resting on the back of the rocker, his hands, with fingers loosely laced in his lap. She hated to wake him, but bed was where he needed to be. She placed a hand on his shoulder and softly whispered, "Love, bedtime." She brushed her lips across the top of his head. Alfred stirred with the faintest hint of a smile.

"You're pooped!" Washie ran her fingers through his disheveled hair.

"That I am." He stretched his legs out and crossed them at the ankles. "I was dreaming of our life back by the Ouachita River."

She smiled fondly. "I miss it there." Then: "Did we make a mistake? Leaving, I mean? None of this would have happened if we only…"

"Shh. Don't talk like that. We did the right thing coming here. We have this beautiful land and a nice home. We're making it, Washie, really making it. Our families would be so proud to see how far we've come."

Washie crossed her arms and dropped her head. "I just feel so guilty. I wish I'd paid more attention to what was going on around us, that's all."

"What?" he asked pointedly.

"I mean it, Alfred."

"Of course you do," he said, sincerely, "except there's something wrong with what you're saying, Washie. It's just plain silly. You have nothing to feel guilty about. We can't be everywhere all the time." He stood and pulled her close, wrapping his arms around her waist. "Honey, there's no way we could've predicted what would happen that night. How were we to know that O'Keefe would follow our girl from school or hide her in some hidden room in the basement of Monstrosity Manor?" He snickered at the name. "Annie's name for that big old house is perfect, by the way."

Washie sighed and laid her head on his chest.

"Oh, Washie. " He moaned more from sheer exhaustion than from frustration, "I love you more than life." Then: "You've got to find a way to let this go. I'm not suggesting you forget how our lives have been changed; I'm asking you to stop taking the blame."

She nuzzled closer, safe in the arms of her man.

He whispered, "Let's go to bed. Daylight will come before we know it, and you've got a big day ahead."

******

Just as Alfred foretold, a new day rushed in. Even before the sun peeked from behind the mountains, the Somers piled into their trusty buckboard and began their trek to town. The air had a real bite, crisp and cold, *invigorating*. Washie thanked the stars above that their homestead was but a few short miles from town. The three of them rode in silence for a while, each one mustering up courage for the long day ahead. The only sound was the clip-clop of the horses' hooves against the hard dirt road and the chattering of teeth from the cold.

Sandy shivered and snuggled under the quilt she shared with her mother. She sensed her mother's uneasiness and knew it was about many things, most of all, her return to school. She clasped her mother's hand under the covers and held it tight. "Everything will be all right, Mom. Wait and see."

Mother and daughter shared a look that spoke volumes. Washie understood that returning to normal was something the family needed, especially Sandy. She needed to let Sandy do things in her own time…and apparently this was the appointed time.

Alfred was as quiet as a mouse, never shifting his gaze from the dusty road in front of him. Guiding the horses, he listened to the conversation, careful not to comment. He was smart enough to know never to interrupt a serious moment between his wife and daughter. He'd learned long ago that anything he said might very well spark accusations of his taking sides, and he was having none of that.

Gratefully, the moment passed quickly and without the usual mother/daughter angst of who was right and wrong. The remainder of the ride was spent in lively chit chat, nothing important or earth-shattering, just a couple of tales about some of Alfred's more colorful patrons.

One of his favorites was Sister Esther, a nurse at the hospital. He described her as about four foot nothing, big as a minute, and skinny as a rail underneath the costume she called a habit. Every Friday morning she sneaked over to the café and took in the savory aromas of fried bacon and ham. And with each visit she reminded Alfred that just because she couldn't eat meat on Fridays didn't mean she couldn't smell it. Sandy snorted recalling the impish little nun who didn't exactly follow the rules of the Order. Sister Esther was one of her favorite people. She had a wicked sense of humor that no doubt landed her in the Mother Superior's office or the confessional more often than not. Once she confided in Sandy that she was forever in the Father's debt for making the confessional a secret place where nothing was repeated because Father Hamilton often snickered during her visits as she half-heartedly confessed and requested absolution. He was certain God had blessed her with a flair for laughter,

161

love, and levity, and was certain the other sisters would benefit from it, should they be so inclined. However, for the sake of appearance, he felt obligated to give her an occasional Our Father as penance, more for the Mother Superior's sake than Sister Esther's. Alfred and Sandy always looked forward to the sister's weekly visits. Alfred was often tempted to send her on her way with a few slices of bacon, only there was no hiding the smell.

Before long, just as the first signs of the sun teased those fortunate enough to be awake at such an ungodly hour, the horses led the buckboard and its passengers into the final leg of their journey. Sandy and Alfred bid Washie good day, encouraging her to forget about life for a while and have fun with her lady friends. She gathered her belongings and hiked the short distance to 4th Avenue. Lydia, she thought, would be up and about preparing the morning meal.

******

"We're only missin' Augusta an' Nora," Lydia said, bitingly. "George went over to fetch them more than half an hour ago. He's probably chewin' his tongue t' keep from sayin' somethin' ugly t 'er." Faerie shot her a look that told her she'd said enough. She began to stir the oatmeal with a vengeance.

Myra was stunned at the outburst. "She's just on a different timetable than the rest of us. That's all," Myra voiced in Augusta's defense.

Faerie rolled her eyes. "Yeah, that's it." Then: "The truth of the matter is this: Augusta has no concept of time and how being late inconveniences others. I suppose that's one of the many reasons we love and adore her." She sighed. "She's gotten away with it for so long that she probably thinks we don't mind. We either try to tell her nicely how we feel or continue on as is."

Washie didn't know the ladies well enough to join in the conversation. Even so, she felt that if she could awaken at four in the morning to get here on time, then surely Augusta could be ready for a five minute drive across town.

All of a sudden the back door flew open and a carefree Augusta made her grand entrance, oblivious to the agitation of the other women. "It's a *glorious* morning. Sorry we missed breakfast, Lydia. It just couldn't be helped." Lydia kept stirring the oatmeal intended for Marcus and Fred. If she was upset, Augusta didn't seem to notice.

Faerie, on the other hand, noticed the air Augusta was putting on. Something was troubling her. She thought it probably had to do with the

162

prospect of seeing Simon today. "Where's the baby, Augusta?" Faerie asked, trying to remain pleasant.

"Out in the Brougham. We're late and Nora is terribly embarrassed. She's such a stickler for time. Something about if you're on time then everyone's waiting for you?" She shrugged her shoulders and smiled innocently. "I don't pretend to know what that means."

Fighting the urge to lash out, Faerie restrained herself and said, "*She* has no reason to feel badly." Faerie's expression was blank, which prompted shared glances among the other women. "Susan's waiting. We should get a move on."

Augusta's face reddened. She was painfully aware that all eyes were on her, and not because she was dressed in a most stunning burnt orange corduroy skirt with a matching high-collared blouse she purchased from a dressmaker in Pagosa Springs. She was truly a stunning woman and she knew it. On the other hand, the other women were just as pretty without overdoing it, as was her tendency. And today, it was increasingly obvious that she was overdressed and much too primped. She lifted a brow and met the stares.

Before any further banter took place, Lydia proceeded to rush everyone out the door. Washie took up the rear. Lydia leaned over and whispered in her ear. "That one's got a wee bit of a stubborn streak, she does, but God love 'er, she's had a hard life indeed. She means well."

Washie lowered her head and listened intently. *Once married to the most despised man in the county,* she thought. *I should get to know her better.*

******

The Brougham was crowded with the ladies, three infants, and everything, and then some, that babies might possibly need for a day out. Augusta sat next to Myra. The tension in the carriage was so thick it could have been cut with a knife. The babies were giggling and cooing and inspecting each other's fingers, toes, and noses, but the only ones who seemed to take notice and enjoy it were the two nannies. The others were too busy avoiding an awkward conversation and each other's glances. Thankfully, just out the window the scenery was grand. If not for such a welcome diversion, the trip would have been very long indeed.

Finally, Annie said, "This is ridiculous! Augusta was late. Is that a crime? We're going to Mrs. Archer's to help her and *hopefully* have a fun day together. If we keep this up, she'll ask us to leave before we ever set foot in the house."

Myra agreed. "Annie's right. Listen. This is about more than Augusta's tardiness. I'll be the first to admit how insensitive I find it. Augusta, I love you more than I love my fine china, but the world simply doesn't revolve around you, dear."

"What?" Augusta responded defensively, sticking out her bottom lip in a pout.

"Let me finish. Please!" Myra implored. "This is difficult for me. I don't believe you knowingly do it. We're all to blame, really. We've let you get away with it for so long that it's become a part of who you are. And, dearie, it's a part that needs changing. It's rude, whether you mean it to be or not." She sighed. "As for the underlying problem, it's about our not-so-dear friend, Reginald. He's gotten to all of us. That's his intention. If we turn on each other, we're doing exactly what he wants. We're strong. We're friends. Let's not do this to one another. Let's not give him the pleasure."

There was an unsettling silence interrupted only by the cooing of babies and clip-clopping of horses' hoofs. It was Augusta who eventually broke the silence.

"It's no secret I didn't really want to come today. I only decided at the last minute because of something Doc Fisher said. I have to face Simon sometime. Doc told me to face my fears, don't look back, and never give up. I'm sorry for being inconsiderate. Believe me. I'm painfully aware of my many shortcomings. And I'm working on them. Bear with me while I learn how to live my life." She looked imploringly into Faerie's eyes. "Please?"

A smile slowly crept onto Faerie's lips. A brief nod followed. "How can I not?" Then: "I'm sorry, too. My Irish temper almost got the best of me."

Lydia snorted. "At least ye have an excuse. Me Irish attitudes are only wishful thinkin'."

Faerie laughed and said, "One day you and I are going to make a trip to the Emerald Isle together."

"That would be lovely." Lydia's eyes twinkled. "Maybe we should all go."

"I'd love to take a crossing." Nora seemed the most excited.

"Sounds like a nice wedding trip to me," Annie teased.

Nora blushed. "What are you talking about? Dan and I…"

"Are just *friends*." Augusta finished Nora's sentence with a playful wink.

Nora dropped her head as her face turned fifty shades of red.

"Ah…you've *embarrassed* her!" cried Faerie.

"What's a little teasing among friends?" Annie retorted. "Besides… maybe we could make it a double wedding trip."

Astonished glances shot back and forth in the small space. "Do tell," Augusta urged.

"I just said *maybe*. Anyway, that's all I'm saying, for now." Annie closed her eyes and stuck her chin out like a spoiled child.

"Well, that's mature," moaned Nora.

"Here we go again!" chirped Myra. "Can't we just be nice?"

Another long play of silence before Faerie broke it. "What is the *matter* with us? None of us are acting like grownups. The babies are the only ones getting along."

Annie glared out the window. She wanted to blurt out her secret, but had promised Fred she'd wait until he returned from Cripple Creek. Instead of giving her feelings credence, she swallowed her pride. "I was only playing, Nora. Forgive me?"

"Of course I will. Now I need to ask forgiveness for my nasty attitude."

"You did nothing wrong." Annie tilted her head, suddenly looking much younger than her twenty years.

"You didn't know what I was thinking. Trust me, girl. I had an attitude."

"I guess that settles it," Augusta blurted out. "Some things are better left unsaid."

"Amen!" Lydia spoke with such enthusiasm one would have thought she'd just heard a rousing sermon. The other gals couldn't help but giggle.

Faerie glimpsed out the window just as the carriage drove under the familiar S & S archway. She smiled and said, "We're here. I'm so excited to get busy."

Augusta was only able to conjure up a tense half-smile.

Faerie thought she saw worry in her eyes. "Don't worry. Simon is a changed man," she said reassuringly.

"I hope so," Augusta answered, a quiver to her voice.

******

George slowed the horses to a crawl as the carriage turned onto the long drive that led to the house. He loved this spread and looked forward to helping Simon with some chores while the womenfolk gossiped and baked and did whatever it was that gave their get-togethers the name *hen party*. All he knew was that he had hours to kill and he was raring to get started. "Whoa," he called. "Whoa, there." The horses came to a halt.

Faerie's frequent visits to the ranch gave George the opportunity to live out his childhood dream of being a cowboy out on the range. On his first visit, Simon had paired him with a magnificent palomino named Samson. As it turned out, the two were perfect for each other and from that day on Samson was always saddled and waiting when George arrived. When he asked about the horse's name, Simon said it was Susan who named him because of his long, flowing mane and the strong, muscular legs that carried him so effortlessly across the meadow. The animal moved with such grace and fluidity that George never wanted their time together to end. Simon often said that Samson took to George like bees to flowers.

Brushing the dust off from the ride, George jumped down and opened the carriage door. "Ladies, your chariot has arrived at its destination," he said, animatedly bowing at the waist.

Myra smiled. She loved George's sense of humor. Baby Patricia squealed with joy when she saw her papa. He took her in his arms and gave her a big kiss on the top of the head and then both cheeks. "Daddy's going to play cowpoke today." Patricia squealed again as if she understood every word.

One by one the women filed out of the carriage. Simon and John came alongside to help George carry in the bundles of baby necessities, as well as the goodies Lydia had prepared.

"Sure you ladies ain't a-movin' in?" John asked dryly.

"If they did, we'd do our very best to accommodate," said Susan as she and Clara scurried across the lawn. Warm, inviting hugs passed between the ladies as they made their way to the house. Susan was excited to have a day with the girls. It seemed like years since she'd felt strong enough to have company.

From the moment she disembarked the carriage, Augusta had carefully eyed Simon. Instead of the harsh man who'd threatened her at her wedding reception, she saw a friendly, hospitable host who warmly greeted his guests. Perhaps she had gotten worked up over nothing. Perhaps he was a changed man, after all.

"My goodness, it smells wonderful in here," Augusta said, cheerfully, upon entering the house.

"Pumpkin bread," Clara said flatly.

"It's heavenly. Does the bread have nuts?" Annie asked.

"Yes, pecans," Susan replied. "They're from a pecan farm down in Texas. We special ordered them for the gathering." She reached for Hattie, who giggled and gladly leaned into Susan's open arms.

"Faerie, this little one looks so like you." Susan ran her fingers through Hattie's strawberry blond curls.

Faerie smiled proudly. "I hope she doesn't resent me someday for that hair."

Susan chuckled. "Some of the wives here on the ranch will be watching the babies today. They'll be in the next room. That way, all you mommies can enjoy the day, and still have the little ones close by."

Myra smiled. "I hope no one takes this the wrong way. I am *thrilled* to be included today and don't want to miss a thing. I'm also ecstatic that someone else will be minding Patricia so I can enjoy myself. I don't really have much time to socialize or make new friends." Realizing how she sounded, she added, "Not that all of you aren't my friends."

"Not to worry, Myra. We understand. It's hard to be with your employer everyday, all day long." Faerie hoped to put Myra at ease.

"You are the best people I know. *All of you.* I'm going to hush now before I chew my entire foot off." Myra blushed and pretended to fasten a button on her lips.

Clara went to the pantry and returned with enough aprons for everyone. When she handed Augusta one, she said, "You're my pet project today. We can't afford any treats that make a body sick."

Augusta's face quickly turned to a pout.

"Clara," Susan said, hurrying to Augusta's side, "you've hurt her feelings."

Clara knit her brows together and began stuttering and stammering.

"Aha! I got you!" Augusta exclaimed, triumphantly. "Everyone said it couldn't be done."

"Pshaw." Clara put her hands on her hips and guffawed. "Little lady, you and me? We're gonna get along just fine."

Augusta felt a huge weight fall from her shoulders. Acceptance…that's all she'd ever wanted. The greatest joy was that it came from the women of this household. With acceptance also came forgiveness.

******

The ladies split the chores down the middle. While some baked and put together prize baskets for the drawings, Augusta and Clara were on lunch duty for not only the women and children, but the hired hands as well. Susan wanted to include the families in some small way, so she and Clara had planned a ranch potluck. The families and single ranchers were joining them for the midday meal, bringing along a little something to share.

The morning quickly passed and before they knew it, Clara rang the dinner bell. Annie and Nora checked on the babies, but were shooed away and told to get back to the party. Annie was quick to say she needn't be told twice and the two nannies skedaddled to the kitchen.

Both nannies were raised in and around mining families. The closeness of this small, tightly knit ranching community held a fond familiarity for the girls, as they had spent their growing up years in isolated mining communities up on Red Mountain. Potlucks were a regular part of their culture and they discussed among themselves how familiar and comforting it was.

A knock on the back door announced the arrival of the first ranch hand. Josh, a long time hand, was ushered in the back door with his wife, Rebecca, at his side. He was carrying a big cast iron skillet covered by a dish towel. He handed it over to Susan, who sneaked a quick peek.

"Oh, Rebecca, you made peach cobbler. It smells divine," she said, inhaling the aroma of the warm, fruity delight. Turning her head a little to the right and squinting, she playfully asked, "Did Clara ask you to make this?"

Rebecca nodded. "I cannot tell a lie. She handed me a two big jars of peaches she said you'd recently put up and asked me to bake a cobbler. She said one of your guests was… Dear me, just how did she put it? Oh, yes…a *slave* to peaches."

Susan snorted. "So true. So *very* true." She stood on her tip-toes and craned her neck looking for Faerie. When she spotted her, she said, "Come on, you two. I want you to introduce you to the gal who will no doubt be at your beck and call for the rest of her natural life." Susan placed the skillet atop the stove and led the couple to the family room.

Clara took Annie by the elbow and asked her to chop an onion. Lunch smelled like chili and cornbread. As the families arrived, more and more food was added to the buffet table. Annie basked in the gaiety and frivolity, thinking that this was how life should be. Caught up in the moment, she was itching to share the news of her engagement to Fred. Her mother was fit to be tied. Keeping secrets was a true test of her mother's will. Annie smiled as she chopped the onion, almost certain that keeping such a secret must be making her mother crazy as a loon.

"Land sakes, Annie." Clara stood next to her. "That poor onion doesn't stand a chance. Best chopping I've ever seen." She raised a brow and leaned in closer to Annie. "If you don't mind me saying so, you attacked that thing like a woman with a little something on her mind."

Annie stopped chopping and bit the corner of her bottom lip. "I do have a huge secret. *Huge*!" Her eyes were as big as saucers.

"Tell." Clara moved in closer until their shoulders were barely touching.

"I'm simply going to die if I don't share it with someone."

"Then, tell, girl," Clara coaxed. "Don't make me beg."

"I can't. I made a promise."

"Let's see." Clara drummed her fingers against her chin. A big smile flashed across her face. "If I guess, you won't be telling." She leaned back a little and studied Annie's serious expression.

"Hm…" Annie dropped her head and nervously glanced to the right and left and back with a most wicked grin. "Promise not to tell?"

Clara crossed her heart with her pointer finger and then held up her hand palm forward as done when taking a solemn oath. "May my tongue be tied in a knot if I so much as even entertain the idea of breaking my word."

Annie still hesitated, and then said slowly, "All right, then. Ask away."

"Help me put the food out while the others mingle. They'll think we're catching up on the latest while we work."

Annie giggled like a sneaky child who'd taken cookies from a cookie jar without being caught. She put the onions in a bowl and took it to the buffet.

"So this news you're hiding, is it about some*thing* or some*one?*" Clara's voice was hushed.

"Both, I suppose."

"Interesting." Clara poured chilled apple cider into two large pitchers and set them on the kitchen table. "Is it a holiday secret? You know, about a Christmas present?"

"Nope."

"How about…your young man?"

Annie's face reddened. "Could be."

"Not fair. That's a yes or no question."

"All right, then. Yes."

Clara stood up straight and stared off, obviously thinking hard. "Well, he can't be moving away or you wouldn't be so chipper…unless you're a-goin' with 'im. You're getting hitched, aren't you?"

Annie's silence and sudden preoccupation with the food told Clara all she needed to know.

"Oh, honey. Your secret's safe with me. I couldn't be happier for you if I tried."

Annie had no choice but to believe Clara. Fred would be mighty displeased if he learned of this conversation.

"Well, Miss Annie, I believe we can serve these hungry folks." Clara, in her own boisterous way, gathered everyone. Simon asked the blessing and then a bounteous midday meal of chili, cornbread, and more sides than possible to eat at one sitting was served buffet style.

"Yes," Annie said to herself as she enjoyed the organized chaos, "this is the life for me."

******

By four o'clock the ladies decided to call it a day. About that time, George and Simon appeared at the back door asking if it was safe to enter, adding that they desperately needed to wash their faces and hands after a day of mucking stalls and repairing fence posts. "We wouldn't want to cause a disturbance, but we're mighty stinky," teased Simon.

"Ladies, we best get a move on before it gets dark. Don't want to spend too much time on the road at night." George wouldn't say it aloud, but the last thing he wanted was to travel at night with a bunch of women and babies, especially with Mr. O'Keefe still on the loose. "I'll just clean up a bit and then we'll be on our way."

"Faerie…ladies…I can't thank you enough for coming today. We made quite a dent in the baking, for sure. And we had such a good time." Susan was sad to see the day come to an end.

"We certainly did. The hours pass so quickly when we're together." Myra had looked forward to this day for weeks. Now it would live on as a cherished memory.

"We'll be back Friday afternoon." Faerie was excited for the weekend festivities. Being invited back to the ranch for the weekend was icing on the cake.

Simon smiled warmly. "Augusta, will you be joining the party on Friday?"

She swallowed. These were the first words they'd shared since the wedding when he told her she wasn't fooling anybody with her grand party. She offered Faerie a pleading glance.

"She'll be here, Simon. We're all happy to help in any way we can," Faerie said, reassuringly.

"Yes, that's right." Augusta's stomach was doing somersaults. "You and Susan are most kind to open your home to this rowdy bunch."

Simon stood with his arm around Susan's waist. Something about Susan's very presence set Augusta at ease, which she found most peculiar given the past she and Simon shared.

"It's our pleasure," Susan offered, most graciously. "We couldn't think of anyone we'd rather have here with us." She chuckled. "Besides, we'll be putting everybody to work."

"On that note, Miss Faerie, we should go," George offered as he reappeared, refreshed from a good face and hand washing. He opened the door to the Brougham and stepped aside while the ladies and babies boarded. Next, he loaded their gear and then climbed up to his seat, took the reins, clicked his tongue and hollered "yah". The horses moved slowly at first and then picked up speed. And off went the happy but tired group, with Simon, Susan and Clara watching until the carriage disappeared around a bend, far down the drive.

"Did you have a good time, Love?" Simon asked Susan as they turned toward the house.

"Uh-huh. I sure did," she responded. Then: "More importantly, did George have a good time playing cowpoke?"

Chapter Twenty

You make mistakes. Mistakes don't make you.
~ Maxwell Maltz

Dan checked in with Sheriff Johnson around ten, and found him sitting behind his desk, engrossed in a massive amount of paperwork.

"Hard at it, I see."

"Huh?" The expression on the sheriff's face was priceless, like a deer caught off guard by a hunter.

"Your paperwork, sir. Are you getting back on track?"

"Oh. Well, this ain't 'xactly paperwork. Doc Fisher brought me some information about somethin' he called skits-o-free-nee-yah…or somethin' like that."

"Whew!" gasped Dan. "Schizophrenia: now there's a mighty fancy word for touched in the head."

Johnson looked up from the book and chuckled. "I'll let you per'nounce it from now on, if'n ya don' min'." He paused and then solemnly added, "We hafta figure out how t' catch O'Keefe. Doc thought it might help if'n we knew more 'bout his problem." He paused. "Sure can't hurt."

"Sorry, sir. I was only kidding around with that touched in the head comment. I guess some things are better left unsaid." Dan certainly had an opinion about O'Keefe. Even so, it would never do to keep voicing it over and over like he did.

"This is interestin'. Take a load off."

Dan sank into a chair opposite Johnson. "Is Doc leaning toward schizophrenia with our guy?"

"Yep, he is. My old ma would say O'Keefe is full o'the devil."

Dan scowled. "I hafta admit I'd be more inclined to agree with her. How else do you explain all his voices? My folks talk about him at supper most nights. Now that I mention it, he's all they think about. Confound it! Everybody I know talks about him."

"I know what you mean." Sheriff Johnson closed the book. "This thing is full of big words that don't mean squat t' me."

Dan harrumphed.

"Somethin' I read here says that folks what hears Voices may be a'sufferin' from things in their past. Say, for argument's sake, that O'Keefe's pa used th' strap on 'im too much…too *hard*, or just any ole thing that 'e wouldn't even do t' 'is horse. Maybe th' boy couldn't make sense of it. He might've created th' Voices t' take care o' what 'e wasn't able t' do his own self.”

“Too highbrow for me.” Dan shook his head. “I *will* say this, though. When he isn't talkin' to his *friends*, he seems nice enough.”

The sheriff nodded in agreement. “When 'e first moved t' town, ever'body was taken with 'im. Th' ladies liked 'im 'cause he weren't too hard on th' eyes, and he wuz always a'complimentin' em. He had a right good job, an' he wuz friendly. Then 'e bought that house an' married 'im a beautiful young thing. Reginald O'Keefe was th' talk o' th' town.”

“And rightly so, I'd say.” Dan stood. “Everybody still talks about him, only for *very* different reasons. Most of the talk seems to be about not understanding what came over him.”

“I overheard a conversation outside th' mercantile a few days back. Somebody called 'im a wolf in sheep's clothin'. Old Man took up fer 'im like 'e always does. But th 'other men seemed t' think maybe he'd pulled th' wool over ever'body's eyes with 'is gentlemanly act.”

“I don't know.” Dan scratched his chin. “I can't say as I understand any of it. Miss Augusta says he changed overnight. One day he was her Prince Charming and the next he was a monster.”

“She'd be the one to know.”

“She told me he treated her like she was a princess all through their courting. She said he spared no expense, lavishing her with clothes and jewelry and taking her to fancy restaurants.” He smirked. “Well, it was cafes here in town…not exactly the Brown Palace in Denver.”

“Th' what?” Sheriff Johnson screwed up his face.

“Don't you know anything? It's the latest thing in Denver. Everybody's talking about it…when they aren't talking about O'Keefe anyway.”

“Well, ain't that jest dandy,” Johnson replied flatly. Then: “I recollect how well th' two uv'em looked together. You know Augusta was a…”

“Fancy lady.” Dan completed the sheriff's sentence. “Lots of folks gossip about her. If they'd take the time to get to know her, they'd find out that she's changed. She's like a different person. And, sir, she's be most obliged if we kept her past, her past.”

“As long as possible. Unfortunately, it may come out in O'Keefe's trial…if'n there ever is one.”

“Say, Sheriff. What do you imagine triggers his behavior?”

“When things start pilin' up on 'im, when life feels hard. I reckon that's th' reason Doc is studyin' that big long word we'z talkin' 'bout b'fore. It ain't like he can put a bandage on his head and mek it all better.

“An' another thing: Marcus Wright never understood whar all O'Keefe's money come from. His spendin' was out o'control, so 'e started stealin' from th' mine and fixin' th' books. He work real hard an' made an image of hisself that ever' man wishes he could be. I s'pose he thought he had t' do whatev'r it took t' keep up that image an' hide 'is thievin' from th' mine *and* 'is wife at th' same time. He really got in deep."

"So he was hiding all kinds of trouble he brought upon himself."

"That's 'bout th' size of it. And then he broke. Jes' fell apart."

"Mr. Wright told me O'Keefe was adopted. The story goes that his pa regularly beat the stuffing out of him with a belt. Lots of times he was forced to sleep in the barn, and sent to bed without supper. He used to sneak out at night and run over to the Wright's and stay with them."

"If all that's true, an' mind ya, Marcus has no reason t' make up sech a tale, it sounds t' me like his pa needed a taste o' his own medicine. O'Keefe's a troubled soul, an' it's anybody's guess as t' th' best way t' handle 'im."

"You can say that again." Then: "Sheriff, don't you sometimes find yourself wondering if he isn't just around the corner hiding and watching, and probably laughing at us? Feeling like he's just a little bit smarter than the rest of us?"

"Dan, he *is* jest around th' corner. He watches; somehow 'e always knows what's goin' on." Sheriff Johnson stretched his arms up over his head, then stood and grabbed his hat. "Mark m' words, son. One o' these days, he'll git lazy an' let 'is guard down. He's very uppity, an' that'll be 'is undoin'. Th' longer this thing goes on, he'll start t' relax and start t' think maybe he'll never git caught. Jes' you wait 'n see. B'fore long, that know-it-all, pompous, sassy attitude o' his'll be 'is undoin'."

Dan nodded, taking it all in. "You going somewhere?"

"I think it's 'bout time we pay a visit t' Miss Augusta. Judge Lawson wants this guy in 'is courtroom more sooner'n later."

"She doesn't know where he is."

"Maybe not, but she sure as shootin' knows perty much ever'thing thar is t' know 'bout that mangy critter."

"That, she does." Dan's eyes sparkled knowing he'd soon see Nora.

"Now, Dan, don't go gittin' all goggly-eyed. We ain't goin' over there t' visit yer l'il darlin'."

Dan dropped his head as his cheeks began to burn like fire. "Right, sir, this is strictly official business."

Sheriff Johnson took hold of the door handle and said, "Pull it t'gether, Deputy. We can't let yer girl see ya in a tizzy."

"Right, sir."

Amused, the sheriff asked, "Can't ya say anything else?"

175

"Right, sir. I mean, of course, sir." Dan whistled as they walked down the street and turned the corner that led to Nora…his l'il darlin'.

******

Annie wrung her hands nervously as she watched the train pull out from the station. She could have kicked herself over the guessing game she'd played with Clara. Fred would be so disappointed if he knew she'd broken his trust. He and Marcus would be gone for a week…maybe longer. She and Faerie were left to their own devices, yet she was in a self-imposed purgatory until Fred's return. Knowing she should have confessed before he left, she somehow felt the days of waiting were just what she deserved for breaking a promise.

When they returned to the house, she was pleasantly surprised to find that Myra had put the girls down for their midmorning naps. She wrapped a shawl around her shoulders and headed to the back door.

"Going somewhere?" Faerie asked.

She wagged her head. "I thought I'd take a stroll around the grounds. I need to clear my head. I won't be long."

"Is everything all right?" Faerie queried. She was sitting at the kitchen table rifling through a box of dress patterns.

"Uh-huh. Myra's upstairs; she promised to listen for the girls."

"Sure everything's all right?" Faerie didn't know what was going on, but knew Annie was out of sorts.

"Would you walk with me? I need to bare my soul."

Faerie reached behind her and snatched the sweater she'd folded over the back of the chair and then leaned over and grabbed her cane from under it. The cooler weather brought with it a dull ache in her injured leg.

"Let's go. We won't have many more days like this. Snow's just over the horizon, for sure."

Golden aspen leaves sailed on the breeze, dazzling against the turquoise Colorado sky. "The wind is coming from the northwest. I suspect your prediction will come sooner than you know." Annie gazed up to find not one cloud above them. They walked out to the flume and watched the clear mountain water spill over the rocks on its way to parts unknown.

Faerie became mesmerized by the crystal clear water as the two stood silently for a brief moment. Finally, she said, "So, are you going to tell me what's wrong or do I have to guess?"

Annie shot a troubled look at Faerie. "Guess?" she asked tentatively.

"Relax. I'm not the enemy here. Something is obviously bothering you. Guessing would be like pulling teeth, so why don't you just tell me."

176

"Oh, my." She sighed. "I must confess I'm feeling guilty about something. As strange as this may sound, it has to do with a guessing game I played with Clara yesterday."

"Hmm…no wonder you reacted so strongly."

"Yeah, well, it's my own fault. Do something out of character, react out of character." They strolled over to the swing in the garden. "Where to begin…"

A half hour passed as they relaxed on the swing that hung from a sturdy branch of a big cottonwood tree in the backyard. Annie poured her heart out about breaking Fred's confidence. Faerie listened in earnest until she could no longer contain herself.

"My dear, girl," she choked out, stifling a laugh, "everyone knows your secret. We'd all have to be blind not to see it. We've been waiting for one of you to spill the beans."

Annie's back stiffened and her expression turned to disbelief. She managed to screech, "Wh-what? How?"

"Oh, I don't know. Let me see." Faerie thoughtfully tapped a finger on her chin. "All that whispering, the long walks, lots of handholding. Oh, and Fred mentioned to Marcus that he hoped to find a jeweler while they were away."

"That stinker. He let the cat out of the bag before I did. And when I think of how sick to my stomach I've been over this."

" Don't be too hard on Fred. It wasn't intentional."

Annie shook her head and lifted her face to the heavens. "Aren't we a pair?"

"To tell you the truth, Marcus said Fred didn't seem to understand he'd given anything away. He said it was the same as if he'd said he needed to stop by the mercantile. We just drew our own conclusions."

"Why else would he need to see a jeweler?" Annie grinned mischievously.

"Exactly." Faerie snorted with laughter. "We'll just have to let him think he's smarter than the rest of us. I wouldn't want to hurt his feelings."

A gust of wind whipped around the yard. They both drew their wraps tighter and folded their arms to keep them in place. "That wind is *freezing*! Annie squealed. "I'm sure I've enjoyed all the fresh air I can take for now. What about you?"

"Not until you answer one little question," Faerie commented, sheepishly.

Annie shivered as she sat back and waited.

"When did he ask?" Faerie leaned in with curiosity written all over her face.

"The night Augusta first got back from her trip when everybody came over for supper."

"I wondered. You two were awfully cozy that night." Faerie wiggled her brows. "I'm so happy for you."

"My dad is particularly happy. He accused me of being well on my way to Spinster Land."

Faerie smirked and said, "Spinster? You?"

"You know Daddy. He's all talk." Then: "He *adores* Fred."

"So…does that mean you'll set up housekeeping here in town? There's no way your father will let his own son-in-law leave the mine. Fred'll make partner, for sure."

They stood and leisurely walked to the back door of the house. "For now we'll stay in town. Although, Fred has toyed with the idea of getting his teaching certificate, but nothing's set in stone. He'll be looking at houses as soon as he and Marcus return from Colorado Springs."

"That's good. I mean good that you'll stay here, not that he's getting a house." Then: "Well, I suppose that's good, too."

"No matter what you say, it sounds like you might like one of your guest rooms back." Annie nudged Faerie's arm.

"That's not what I meant and you know it." Faerie gasped as another cold wind swept through. "It's cold!"

"*Really* cold. Hope it doesn't snow before the party this weekend."

"That would be awful. Susan and her crew have worked so hard to make it especially nice this year. It'll be the first festival Simon will have attended in years. She said he's really looking forward to it."

"*Her crew!* What a fine choice of words, and so true." Annie opened the back door. Then: "With Clara, everyone jumps when she hollers because she appears so stern. Not so with Susan. People want to help her because she's ever so gracious."

"Even…" Faerie stopped before she started.

"Even what, Faerie?" Annie tilted her head and studied Faerie's face.

"Oh, nothing, really. I was just going to say that even Reginald admired and respected her."

"*Reginald O'Keefe?*" Annie was surprised Reginald admired anybody.

"The one and only. I watched from a distance as he spoke with her at his and Augusta's wedding reception. He seemed quite taken with her. Even so I could tell there was some angst between Simon and him. Sometime later he mentioned to Marcus and me what an exceptional woman she was."

"'Spose that goes to show that even delusional folks can recognize the good in others."

They walked up the steps and into the kitchen. "Wonder what that says about the rest of us." Faerie shrugged her shoulders, then removed her sweater and hung it on the coatrack just inside the pantry.

"Who knows? Don't you think maybe we are guilty by association? What with Fred and Marcus being Reginald's two favorite people and all?" Annie rolled her eyes, her words dripping with sarcasm.

"Probably so. Augusta told me she once overheard Reginald tell Lydia that Susan was just as much a victim of Simon's little escapade as he was."

"Are you serious?" Annie closed the pantry door, leaned against it, and folded her arms. "The way I see it, Susan was definitely a victim, but not Reginald."

"Yes ma'am." Faerie agreed. "Susan, yes, Reginald…*never*!"

"Reginald never *what*?" Myra slowly descended the massive staircase with cleaning supplies bundled in her arms.

"Land sakes, Myra. Let me help you with that." Annie jogged to the bottom step and took some of the supplies. The two co-workers shared a brief smile.

"Are my beautiful cherubs still sleeping?" asked Faerie.

Myra gave a quick nod. "Reginald never what?" she inquired again, continuing in a rather short tone. "Never behaved? Never minded his manners? Never robbed a bank? What?"

Both Annie and Faerie were silenced by the remark, unsure whether or not to laugh.

"Well? What?" Undaunted by the dumbfounded expressions on their faces, Myra continued on to the supply closet.

"All of the above, I suppose," Faerie replied, deadpan. "Mainly, we were discussing how he thinks himself a victim, but really isn't." She decided to let Myra's curt tone pass since she'd been carrying more responsibility than usual around the house, not to mention, having a baby to care for at the end of the day. She was probably just tired.

Myra sighed and sat on the bottom step. "Not these days, he isn't, but I'm certain he was as a boy. He has scars on his back, like when someone gets the strap. I saw them one day when I took a shirt upstairs that I'd just starched for him. I knocked on the door and thought he called out for me to enter. When I saw his back, I realized what I'd heard was a request for me to wait. His back is one big mass of scars." Then: "Annie, are you going to hold that mop and broom all day or do you want to put them in the closet?"

Shocked at the news of Reginald's plight as a child, Annie's jaw had dropped and her mouth hung open. She slowly walked to the closet, just behind the staircase, and returned the mop and broom. After closing the door, she said, "I can't believe it. All of a sudden my heart just aches for him."

The three of them went to the arboretum where they could speak privately. Faerie sat in a wicker chair in the sunlight while Myra and Annie sat on the matching loveseat. Faerie gazed out over the lawn. The wind had picked up in the few minutes since she and Annie were outdoors.

"I love this space. We should use it more." There was a silence. Then: "Children learn from their parents. They mimic the behaviors they witness in the home. All I've ever heard of Reginald's father is that he was a tyrant. Mr. O'Keefe never wanted a son; he wanted a servant, a field hand. When Reginald didn't live up to his father's expectations, the leather belt came out. Instead of coming to Reginald's aid, Mrs. O'Keefe sat by the fire and mended socks while she prayed to the Blessed Mother."

"She just let it happen?" Annie asked quietly.

"What was she to do? Mr. O'Keefe might've hit her, too. Who knows? Besides, from all Marcus has said, she wasn't much better. Reginald was nothing more than someone to take their aggressions out on."

"I feel sorry for the little boy," Myra said tenderly. "Did he hide?"

"According to Marcus and Mother Wright, he ran away many times. Mostly, he ran to Mother Wright. The Wrights offered him a place to stay, but Mr. O'Keefe was selfish when it came to his possessions."

"*Possessions*? How disgusting. No wonder Reginald built up barriers to keep others away." Annie dropped her head.

"Our minds have interesting ways of protecting us. In Reginald's case, it appears he's developed personalities to take over. He's out of control, so they pretty much mind the shop, so to speak." Faerie knit her brows together. "I wish someone could help me understand."

"Unless he's caught or has a moment of clarity and turns himself in, we all need to be very careful." Myra spoke from experience. "When he's out of his mind, anyone in his path is a target."

"I'll never forget the night his rage took over." Faerie's tone was dark as she spoke to Myra. "You and Augusta were his first victims. Then he sought out Marcus while I was upstairs in bed having babies. Since then I've heard he visited an opium den down in the shadier part of town. Strong medicine and drink are a bad combination, especially for someone with a troubled mind."

"I remember that night," Annie interrupted. "I came downstairs just in time to see Reginald punch Mr. Marcus in the nose. The look on Reginald's face was priceless. It was like he didn't know what had just happened."

Myra dropped her head and spoke hesitantly, as if she was ashamed of what was to come out of her mouth. "I hate to say this, and I don't want anyone to misunderstand 'cause I mean it in the most honest and humble way." She cleared her throat and looked first to one friend and then the other. "I sincerely wish Augusta could find someone to love her and that precious baby boy, and take her away from all this…someplace where Mr. Reginald would never find them. She'll never be safe or free to escape the gossip and devastating memories otherwise."

Annie was the first the comment. "For all it's worth, I agree. Only one thing would keep her here. Pride. She's a prideful woman. She doesn't want him to win."

"What she doesn't understand is that what she calls winning is actually losing, and not only for her, but for every one of us." Faerie was reminded of Augusta's life before Reginald…what little she knew of it. "Before they met, she had a *hard* life. A life most of us could never imagine. I understand she doesn't want to give in. Girls, somehow we have to make her see that safety is what she *really needs*. I'd be willing to do almost anything, especially if it meant safety for her and the baby."

"You don't think Mr. Reginald would hurt Derrick, do you?" Annie asked, alternating concerned glances between the ladies.

"He never wanted that baby, Annie." Myra's gaze was about as stone cold as Annie had ever seen. "He was fit to be tied when Augusta told him she was expecting. From that day on, he ridiculed her and called her names, told her she was fat and ugly…and *disgusting*. He told her time and again that he wanted nothing to do with the baby."

Faerie shook her head. "I can't imagine a father not wanting his child. Maybe he was afraid he'd be as bad a father as his was. Still, he was meaner than a snake and became worse as time passed."

Lydia stood in the doorway, drying her hands on her apron. "That he did. All this breaks me ol' heart, it does."

"Lydia, you rarely step out of the kitchen unless you need something. Can I help?" Faerie asked kindly.

"I only wanted t' let ye know that lunch will be in about 20 minutes. That'll give ye slackers time t' get finished with yer talk, or just bring it on t' the table."

"Pshaw. Slackers indeed. We're merely taking a well-deserved break with our employer," Annie teased as Myra and Faerie looked on with amusement. "Why, we can work circles around you."

Lydia put her hands on her hips in mock insolence. "Ye think so? I'll take ye on anytime, anywhere, dearie." She stood stoically with not a hint of a smile, then burst into laughter. "There's no doubt about it…I can't think o' any other place this ol' gal would rather be than right here with the three o' ye. Now go an' get ready. I want t' see them wee ones enjoy their taters."

"Oh my, what would I do without all the banter between the two of you?" Faerie teased. In all honesty, she wouldn't have things any other way. This house would be a tomb if not for all the activity and frivolity of the staff. "Ladies, it appears our secret is out. We are slackers with a capital S. Let's get to it so we can earn our lunch."

Annie sprinted up the stairs in true unladylike fashion. Her keen sense of hearing alerted her that the twins were awake and becoming cranky. She found them sitting up in their beds reaching for each other, one with her chin quivering, clearly about to begin a crying jag, the other bouncing on her bottom.

"Well, let's get you girls washed up and changed for a bite to eat. Sounds like you're having potatoes today. "Or 'taters', as Lydia calls them. I can't wait to see you dive into them. They'll be all over you and the floor in no time flat."

With a little assistance from Faerie the girls were soon dressed in burnt orange play dresses with matching tights, and were being carried in true princess fashion downstairs to the kitchen.

"Miss Faerie, it seems these wee ones get purtier ev'ry day. And, my how they're a'growin'. Seems only yesterday, we…Myra and me, that is… was a-helpin' Mr. Marcus cope while ye was in the throes o' childbirth."

Faerie and Annie situated the twins in their highchairs while Myra excused herself to fetch George and Patricia from the cottage. A few short minutes later the gang was settled around the table spying a smorgasbord of leftovers from the previous two suppers. Roast chicken thinly sliced to perfection, homemade bread, lettuce, sliced tomatoes, bread and butter pickles and freshly churned butter were the perfect ingredients for sandwiches, not to mention mouth-watering home fried potatoes with sautéed peppers and onions.

Faerie was happiest when the family was gathered around the table, and today everyone was present and accounted for, aside from Fred and Marcus. Sure, there were other workers milling about the property, but they lived elsewhere. They chose to eat with their own families, except for special occasions. It reminded her of the Archer's arrangement with their ranch hands.

Speaking of the Archer family, she wondered how Susan and Clara were holding it together during the final preparations for this weekend's bash. The upcoming party was practically the sole topic of conversation around town. Practically the whole town loaded their buckboards and carriages and caravanned to the ranch every year. It was the highlight of autumn in these parts.

"Faerie? Miss Faerie?"

She was brought back from her reverie by Annie waving a hand in front of her face. She blushed as everyone snickered and teased her. "Day-dreaming again?" Annie asked, smiling broadly, and offering a plate of sliced bread.

"Yes. I am so excited about this weekend I can barely see straight." She took two slices and passed the plate on. "I just wish Marcus and Fred..." She stopped midsentence. No useful purpose would be served by wishing for things that could not be.

Annie patted her hand. "I know." She sipped from her coffee cup. "Nonetheless, I'm fit to be tied. I think about it all the time and try to imagine how it might possibly be any better than last year's."

Myra chimed in. "I wholeheartedly agree. All through my chores, I find myself reminiscing about last year's festival and doubt it could be any better."

George dabbed at the corners of his mouth. "I hate to bring down the festive mood, but I thought I ought to mention that Simon hired some men to watch things this weekend, if you know what I mean."

The ladies shared worrisome glances. "Oh?" Lydia asked with a wrinkled brow.

"There were lots of local men deputized to help with the search for Mr. Reginald and the two kids. They're still deputized, seeing how he hasn't been found yet. When we were at the ranch, Simon told me he spoke with the sheriff and asked if he could put the word out for any who might want to make some money working security this weekend."

"I'm sure it's probably a wise thing to do," Faerie said. "I worry they might frighten some folks. After all, the whole town knows Reginald is still out there somewhere. And he probably still wants to take care of Simon."

"Not to worry," George said assuredly. "I think Simon's got it all covered. He thought deputies might frighten some, so he's having three of them come with their families to spend the weekend, just like all of us. They won't wear badges or act like lawmen. They'll wander around with their wives and kids, while keeping their eyes peeled at the same time. Hopefully, no one will suspect a thing."

"I can't speak for the rest of you, but I'm relieved." Myra added. "The thought of that man showing up and causing a raucous is worrisome, to say the least."

"For obvious reasons, Simon stays pretty close to home these days. He and Susan don't want to push John into anything. He mentioned that the family only goes out when absolutely necessary." George reached for the pickles as he continued. "Every day Simon takes Timmy and some of the other kids to and from school. For now, they've made arrangements to pick up and return John's assignments once a week. Susan will tutor him at home for a while."

"Sounds good to me," Faerie said. "Is it what John wants?"

"I don't know about that," George answered. "They talked it over with the sheriff and came to the conclusion that he still isn't safe. None of them are. So until they feel a little more stable or Reginald is caught and taken in, this is how it will be."

Annie shook her head. "The whole thing is ridiculous. Don't misunderstand me. We all need to be wise. On the other hand, we can't hide forever."

Lydia dabbed at the corners of her mouth with her napkin. "I know what ye mean, missy, but none o' us can say how the Archers feel. One day soon, I figure that fam'ly will feel comfortable enough t' go out in public, an' the festival is a start. I say they're takin' a huge step by goin' ahead with it." Lydia shrugged her shoulders. "Maybe this'll be the beginnin' o' some real healin' for 'em." She backed her chair away from the table and went to the stove for the coffeepot and refilled everyone's cups.

Things were quiet for a time while the group enjoyed their sandwiches. "George, did Simon happen to mention how Timmy's handling everything?" Faerie asked.

"He seems to be doing fine. Simon said they were trying to be careful not to speak of things that might scare him or make him worry. He's so young there's no telling where his little mind would go."

"I don't know what I'd do if anything happened to my babies," Faerie said with a catch in her voice. "I can't imagine how the Archers and Somers are dealing with it all. Their children are home now. Even so, the fact remains that they've lived through a terrible ordeal and won't soon forget it."

"All true. Hopefully this weekend will help them forget about it for a little while," Myra offered. She bit into one end of a sandwich half and a tomato slice came out and hung between her teeth and down her chin. She tried unsuccessfully not to laugh. She snickered and turned red. Eventually, she bit the tomato in two and a big piece of it dropped onto her plate. "Well, there you have it. The things I learned in etiquette class." She rolled her eyes and dabbed at her chin with her napkin as laughter peeled around the table, lightening the mood.

George patted her on the back. "My wife: I love her but can't take her anywhere."

Chapter Twenty-One
'You cannot do a kindness too soon,
for you never know how soon it will be too late.
~Ralph Waldo Emerson

The ranch was abuzz with activity. Every available body was about the business of painting game stands, gathering pumpkins from the pumpkin patch, tying cornstalks together, and rummaging through last years' decorations. Several of the ranchers' wives had baked an abundance of apple, pumpkin and sweet potato pies. Under Clara's tutelage, others baked loaf after loaf after loaf of tasty quick-breads. No expense was spared. No shortcut was taken.

Susan found it all very therapeutic. She and John spent hours in the indoor garden pruning, watering and gathering. John seemed more contented than she'd seen since his return from Red Mountain. He even asked if Sandy would be coming out with Washie, and was sincerely disappointed to learn she wouldn't be out until later in the afternoon. It was a good sign. John was ready to see her again. She only hoped the feeling was mutual. Despite returning to school, Sandy might not be ready to face him and be reminded of the thing she was trying so hard to forget.

Over in one corner of the garden sat bushel after bushel of ripe red apples shipped in from Washington State for the festival. Simon's import and export business had yielded many valuable connections, one being an orchard owner in the Pacific Northwest. Simon sent a wire asking the price of apples and the man surprised him by sending several cases of red delicious free of charge. News of the family's troubles had reached him and he wanted to do something to help. The only thing he asked in return was a place for he and his family to stay should they decide to vacation in Colorado. A response was sent by post containing an open invitation to Mr. and Mrs. Herschel P. Gustafson and Family.

Susan had heard tell of Mr. Gustafson for years. She'd heard that his wife, Sharon, suffered from rheumatism something fierce. Susan wondered if the drier climate of Colorado might not be just the ticket to give her some relief. She'd never visited Washington but had heard the weather there was often rainy and dreary. Good for growing; bad for aches and pains.

"Mom, d'ya think we should set up apple bobbing tubs in lotsa diff'rent places?" John stood, a spade in one hand, and stretched. "What d'ya think? The flower beds are right nice."

"Oh, son, they look amazing. I should let you work the gardens more

187

often." Then: "Apple bobbing, huh? Yeah, I think lots of tubs scattered around is good. Heavens knows we've got plenty of apples to spare."

"Awful nice o' Mr. Gustafson."

"Sure is. Such a generous gesture." She glanced around her sanctuary. "Can't you just feel God here? I can't think of another place that sets my heart to peace like this one does."

John swallowed. He and God were at odds. He couldn't understand why somebody like O'Keefe was allowed to roam the earth and others were left to pick up after him. "Whatever ya think, Mom."

She looked at him thoughtfully before ducking her head. "One day it won't hurt so bad, son. I can't fault you your feelings. Just remember, nothing you think about the Father is a surprise to him. He knows your every thought, and he'll still be waiting when you're ready to resume your relationship. He's a gentleman and won't push you. He's patient and kind and ready to handle your cares, should you decide to let him."

John shuffled his feet and stared at the ground. He knew she was right; she was *always* right. Nevertheless, he felt like wallowing in his pity for a while longer. Not particularly wanting to talk about it for the nine hundredth time, he said, "Ready, Mom? There's still lots t' be done."

She decided to let sleeping dogs lie. She'd let God work on John's heart, since it was His area of expertise. "Come on. Let's go see what kind of mischief we can get into." Then, with the slightest giggle, she added, "By the way, son, just a word to the wise. Unless you want kitchen duty, steer clear of Clara. She's drafted her own soldiers, and from what I've heard from a couple of them, she's one tough sergeant."

John harrumphed. "Ya know, all these folks here on the ranch? They've lived here long enough t' understand she's all bark 'n no bite."

"You're probably right about that, but let's allow her the dream of being chief cook and bottle washer for a little longer. We can find something to do outside." She tapped her foot as she thought. Then: "I know! We could brush down the horses, if you like. Taffy would love t' see you."

＊＊＊＊＊＊

Simon whistled as he hammered a large wooden donkey to a cottonwood in the middle of the backyard.

"Perfect!" A familiar voice called from the edge of the drive.

Simon turned. "Troy, get yourself on over here. Do you think the little tykes'll enjoy pinning the tail on this old guy one more time before we retire 'im? He's getting pretty beat up."

"Still looks mighty fine to me." Troy shoved his hands into the back pockets of his work britches. "Say, Simon, I was lookin' for a good place to put the lasso game. What d'you think about over there next to the back fence? There's lots of open space. We can put several bales of hay out there stacked one of top of the other and make a couple of different heights. I can just see it now…some little boy with his pa teaching him how to lasso a bale. They'll have a right good time."

"Sounds like a plan. Just hearing you describe it reminds me of when my dad taught me to shoe a horse. Even though I still despise shoeing, I'll always treasure the time we had. Ah, those were the days. Anyway, that's what this weekend's really all about…creating memories to last a life-time."

Simon was as excited as a child on Christmas Eve night. He wanted all their guests to have a grand time. He wanted them to leave at the end of the day sorry it all had to end. He wanted to ensure their safety and had taken steps along those lines. O'Keefe was to be the least of their worries and he didn't want to waste any time talking about him, but Troy was not to be silenced.

"Simon, what if someone causes a raucous on Saturday?"

"Troy, I've taken care of it. You're my foreman; I should keep you in the loop on what's happening and I haven't done that. Let's take a walk and I'll tell you all about it.

******

Sgt. Clara and her helpers were busy as beavers. It was a marvel to watch Clara's system. And Susan wouldn't even think of interrupting the flow. To Clara, the yearly harvest gathering was not only a great party for the locals, but a way to feed those too proud to visit the soup kitchen in town. Hidden behind a mask of fun and frivolity, the festival was truly a gift of Christian love and charity to the county. Children were given toys and sweet treats and allowed to pick out a pumpkin from the enormous patch on the property. The hayrides took folks out on a section of land where the Uncompahgre River ran. At the end of the trail a blazing camp-fire roared to warm the riders. Tin cups of warm apple cider and slices of pumpkin bread were served as ranch hands strummed their guitars and sang familiar songs like *Home on the Range* and *Clementine.* When every-one had warmed up and had their fill of goodies they embarked on the ride back to the main house. Clara's desire was that all the guests, especially the children, leave the ranch at the end of the day with memories to carry them through the long, dark winter.

So many families in the county struggled to make ends meet, forever robbing Peter to pay Paul. She knew of some who often sent their children to bed without supper. Those who lived on the ranch were blessed beyond measure and the gathering was but a small way to share their bounty. For a little while at least, gifts of food and fun would sustain those who crossed the threshold onto the ranch. Pies, cakes, cookies and breads, apple and pear butter, and baskets laden with fall vegetables were available for the taking.

Clara became a little misty at the laughter and gaiety of the women as they labored in the kitchen and baked untold amounts of goodies. Oddly enough, it reminded her of days gone by when her dearly departed husband helped her bake pies for Sunday socials. A ache tugged at her heart. Even after all these years, the memories still stung…and she wouldn't trade them for anything.

Susan had her all figured out. She never retorted when Clara slipped and made use of her sassy tongue. She recognized pain and the need to put up one's guard. Clara's reputation as that of the *real* boss of the S & S was a ranch-wide joke. Underneath her gruff exterior was a woman whose broken heart was still on the mend. She appeared to be strong and self-assured; however, those who knew her well would say that deep down inside, where it counts, she was as fragile as a china cup.

"Miss Clara, when will the other ladies be here?" one of the girls asked.

 "Not soon enough to suit me, around eleven or so." She harrumphed. "Just in time to fix a little something to eat." She shook her head. "Perfect timing," she scoffed.

The others ladies giggled and went back to their business.

There I go again, she thought. *When will I learn to tame that beast inside my mouth?* Deciding to slough off her own petty opinions, she moved to the kitchen table where a few of the gals were rolling out cookie dough. Tin cutters in the shape of pumpkins sat in a bowl in the middle of the table.

"Maybe I could help cut the dough?" she asked, wanting to help instead of just supervise.

A pleasant young lady handed her a cutter and said, "Miss Clara, tell us about when you came to be at the ranch."

She felt another tug as she thought of laying her beloved to rest. "It all started the day my husband made passage to heaven." The ladies were mesmerized with her story. Before long they all learned a side of her they never knew existed, and came to understand the woman that was Clara.

******

This time Augusta wasn't the last holdout. Augusta, Nora and Derrick were the first to arrive at Monstrosity Manor, much to the delight of Faerie and the others. Soon the Brougham was packed to overflowing with women and babies, travel bags, and goodies baked at the last minute. Donations from the mercantile and a local toymaker were tucked away for safekeeping in the baggage compartment at the back of the carriage. As soon as George was confident all was secure and the travelers were seated inside the Brougham, he took up the reins and gave a cluck, signaling the horses to make tracks.

Excited chatter filled the carriage. Babies cooed and drooled as they watched scenery pass them by outside the windows. Myra remarked how well the babies seemed to travel with Faerie offering frequent jaunts to some place or another being the reason. Annie agreed and then regaled the group with a story about the children in her former position back East. They traveled poorly, preferring to stay home and play or read or nag the hired help. She laughed and said working for the Wrights was not like working at all, which prompted Faerie to surprise her with the offer of allowing Annie to stay at the manor forever and take care of the young ones at no charge. At first, Annie wasn't sure Faerie was joshing, but when Faerie broke out in a big smile she realized the joke was on her. She laughed and said, "That was a close one. I almost talked myself out of a job, ladies."

Laughter erupted. From his perch atop the carriage, George heard the frivolity and wondered what in heaven's name was so gall darned funny. He called out to the horses to hurry on down the road before someone in the coach brought out the peach brandy and the party got out of control.

******

"They're here! The carriage is a-comin' ever'body! They're here!" John's voice echoed across the yard, carrying into the house.

Susan wiped her hands on her apron and brushed a strand of hair from her face. The busyness all around her brought a kind of electric excitement to the air that couldn't be defined with mere words. She made her way down the walk and stood at the gate with her arms folded and watched the big black carriage move slowly up the drive toward the house. Clara joined her and heaved a big sigh.

"Another festival's about to happen, Susan. Can you believe it's already been a year?"

She pondered that for a moment before replying. So much had happened over the last year. "Yes, Clara, I can. In one way, the days have flown. In another, I'll be happy to start a new year. When I think about the events of the past year, I cringe."

Surprised by the response, Clara looked to the heavens. "You know," she began, "life has a way of happening whether we want it to or not. What better way to slap the devil in the face than to throw a party for all our friends and neighbors?"

Clara was right. Susan knew it. She nodded and opened the gate. "Come on. Let's greet our friends."

******

Faerie and Augusta took a leisurely stroll around the property eventually ending up in Susan's sanctuary of greenery. "Why, it's enough to take your breath away." Stunned by the sheer beauty and serenity of the garden, Augusta dared not speak about a whisper. She moseyed slowly along the walk, sensing this was more than just an indoor garden. "This feels like….like…something very *sacred*," she said.

"It is! This is Susan's place of solitude." Faerie stooped down to touch an orchid. "Exquisite. Have you ever seen anything so delicate and beautiful in your life?"

Augusta opened her mouth to speak but was overcome with emotion. Her throat closed up, leaving her incapable of responding.

When Augusta didn't answer, Faerie peered up over her shoulder to see tears running down Augusta's face. "Oh, sweetie, what is it?" She arose and gently touched Augusta's arm.

"N-nothing is wrong. In fact, everything is r-right. It's this *place*." She paused and swallowed. "I don't know how to describe it. Even in San Francisco where everything is new and beautiful and, well, just *wonderful*, I've never seen *anything* like it."

"Come with me. There's something you simply must see." Faerie took hold of Augusta's hand and led her down the winding path. They stopped at a wooden bench. Next to it was a side table with a kerosene lamp, several writing tablets and pencils, and a worn Bible.

"This must be Susan's quiet place," Augusta acknowledged.

"Turn around."

Augusta looked curiously at Faerie who smiled pleasantly and nodded in the direction of the far wall. Augusta turned and looked ahead. Taken aback, she gasped and her hands flew to her mouth. She couldn't take her eyes off the big wooden cross that hung on the wall directly across the room from where they were standing.

Her voice trembled as she spoke. "If I'd seen all of this even six months ago, I'd have written it off, believing Susan to be a poor, misguided woman. Now I know I was the misguided one."

Faerie swallowed the lump in her throat. "Augusta, are you saying what I think?"

"I am," she said quietly. Then: "Oh, Faerie, how could I have been so blind?" She never broke her gaze from the cross. "I've wasted so much time."

"Just remember this: the very second you came to this knowledge all the angels in Heaven rejoiced." Faerie twirled around and danced a little jig, laughing all the while. Then she said, "And *I'm* so happy I can't help but dance."

"So that's what you call it," Augusta replied snidely. "Do me a favor and save it for the festival." Augusta smirked and wiggled her brows playfully. The two of them shared a good laugh and continued down the winding path that led to the door.

Faerie said, "We'd best be moving along. I'm sure the others are calling us slackers by now."

"Slackers?" Augusta queried.

"A new word Lydia taught me," Faerie laughed. They locked arms and strolled out the building just as the midday dinner bell rang.

"Perfect timing," Faerie said.

"Sounds like something Clara would say," Augusta said, with just an appropriate amount of sarcasm.

******

A fresh batch of tomato basil soup and toasted cheese sandwiches was a quick and easy fix, as well as a nutritious, bone-warming midday meal for the helpers. Nora curiously watched Annie down one bowl of soup in no time flat and then head over to the buffet table for a second helping.

"Got a hollow leg today?" she asked when Annie sat down at the table.

"No, I just love tomato soup and this is divine. Best I've ever had." Leaning in, she said softly, "Do you think Clara might share the recipe?"

"We *are* talking about Clara. First she'll tease you and accuse you of trying to pry a secret family recipe out of her. Then she'll tell you she has to think about it because, after all, it has been passed down from generation to generation. After she makes you beg and plead, she'll hem haw around and tell you she needs to think about it. Then, when you think all is lost, she'll write it out and give it to you just as we are loading up for home on Sunday and say something like 'don't you go sharing this with one single soul. You hear?'"

Annie covered her mouth to stifle her snorting laughter. "Sounds like you've got Clara all figured out."

"You think so?" The harsh response sounded from behind the girls.

Slowly, they both looked over their shoulders to see Clara standing there with a grimace and one raised brow. "Here's your recipe. Thought you might like to have it. But I'm warning you, if you make it somebody's going to want the recipe and you have to give it to them. Not *my* rule…. my *grammy's*."

"Grammy?" Nora asked, confused and more than a little surprised.

"My *grandmother*. This is her recipe and her recipes were *never* secret. She shared with everybody." Then: "By the way, Nora, nice imperson-ation. You hit the nail on the head." Then she added sarcastically, "Flat-tery like *that* will get you far in life."

"Sorry, Clara." Nora dropped her head.

""Nothing to be sorry about. Just don't let on that you know I'm all talk and no bite. Folks might try to put one over on me. And we can't have that, now, can we?"

"No, I suppose not," Annie replied with a twinkle in her eye.

Clara sat down next to them. "The only other people who have me figured out are the Archers, and they won't tell a soul."

Annie was touched Clara would share the recipe. She skimmed over the card and then said, "I'll treasure it always. Without question, it's the best tomato soup I ever ate. Your grandmother had the right idea: sharing reci-pes from generation to generation like they're precious gems. What better way to honor those who went before us? And what a legacy!"

"I don't have children to pass them on to. You girls are about the age any child of mine would be. Maybe that's partly why I'm so fond of you." Clara grinned. "Humor me and let me think of you as my own every now and then."

Nora and Annie passed a knowing glance. "I think we can do that," An-nie said as she squeezed Clara's hand,

"Just promise me one thing?" Nora crinkled her nose. "Don't send me to my room without supper if I misbehave. I can't sleep when my stomach rumbles."

Clara placed her elbows on the table and laced her fingers together and tried to look serious. "I'll try to keep that in mind, young lady. But re-member, a little cooperation on your part surely couldn't hurt. Remember, we mothers have eyes in the backs of our heads. It isn't just an old wives' tale."

"Yes, ma'am," Annie and Nora said together.

******

George spent the afternoon with John and Simon and a few of the other cowpokes inspecting and decorating the buckboards for the hay-rides, mucking out the barn, and finishing off Susan's honey-do list for the outside. His childhood dream of being a cowboy was realized whenever he set foot on the ranch. Simon made sure of it. And he always had a great time. He was pretty sure, however, that hanging Chinese lanterns across the backyard was never a part of his dream. He thought the scenario quite droll: lanky cowboys dressed in ranching duds, some with a wad of chewing tobacco stuck in their cheeks, each man doing his very best at one-upping the others' heroic stories of life in the Wild West, all while hanging delicate paper lanterns as the womenfolk looked on with approving smiles and nods, and occasional directions of moving a lamp just a tad to the right or left.

A little before sundown the ranch resembled an autumn county fair with its booths, games, and colorful pumpkins and gourds scattered all around. Bales of hay and friendly-looking scarecrows were placed here and there in the indoor garden and outside the barn, as well as all entrances and exits of the property. The only thing left to do was to place the perishables out first thing in the morning before the crowds began to arrive.

Susan and her lady friends walked about admiring the fruits of their labor. "Magnificent," she said. "It almost takes my breath away. And I love the added touch of the Chinese lanterns. It's not in the least harvest-like but it's *very* festive. Don't you think?"

Faerie nodded enthusiastically. "Oh, yes indeed. I didn't think it was possible to top last year's decorations, but this is truly amazing." Faerie shivered and pulled her shawl closer. "It's awfully chilly once the sun goes behind the mountains. You'd think after living here for so long I'd get used to it."

"Hopefully, the weather will hold out tomorrow. I can't stand the thought of even one child being disappointed. They so look forward to this." Susan gazed up at the sky, relieved there was nothing to see but the stars beginning their watch over the night.

Augusta and Myra were the lone stragglers, choosing not to keep up with the others. The door to the barn stood open, offering full view of George and Simon brushing a couple of the palominos. Myra took Augusta by the elbow and off they went in the direction of the barn. Augusta's stomach did a flip flop, yet she held her head up high.

"Ladies, you'll get your nice clothes dirty if you come in," Simon said, playfully.

"I dropped in to see what my husband is up to." Myra smiled as she watched George brush Taffy.

"That horse belongs to John, but she seems to get along fine with George. I'll tell you one thing. If Marcus and Faerie don't watch out, I might just offer him a job he'll find hard to turn down." Simon winked at Myra. "Of course, he certainly wouldn't consider such a thing without discussing it with *you*, Myra."

Myra smiled demurely thinking her husband knew on which side his bread was buttered. He'd never consider anything of the sort without a nice long sit-down discussion with her. Though she knew he wished for a ranch of his own, for now their time was best spent with the Wrights. Living rent free in the carriage house was most advantageous and enabled them to put back far more money than they'd thought possible. For the most part, she held her tongue on the matter, and George rarely mentioned it. Still and all, she saw the look on his face and the gleam in his eyes whenever they visited the Archers. Perhaps it was time to begin making some long term plans.

Augusta dropped her head and glanced over at Myra from out of the corner of her eyes. She knew that look on Myra's face. It spoke of respect for her husband coupled with dismay over the idea Simon had obviously put in George's head. She remembered Simon's uncanny ability to plant such seeds. She'd been a part of his world long enough to know what a smooth talker he was. On the other hand, Augusta found herself wanting to give him the benefit of the doubt. He seemed to have turned his life around, for which she was both relieved and grateful. Perhaps his words were nothing more than a tease.

"Don't worry, honey. Simon knows we're happy in town. He's perfectly willing to let me tag along when we make the trip out." He read the expression on Myra's face and smiled apologetically.

Myra eyed him seriously and then turned her attention to Simon. "I cannot tell a lie, Mr. Archer. We actually came over to see these beautiful horses. They're quite something."

"Please, call me Simon. No need for formality around here." He continued brushing. "Myra, do you ride? Perhaps you and George would like to come out one day soon and ride with Susan and me."

"Perhaps," she offered, solemnly. "Augusta, the others are probably wondering where we wandered off to. Let's go."

Augusta wagged her head ever-so-slightly and shrugged her shoulders as she waved to the men. "See you later at supper."

******

Simon and George peered out the barn door, watching the ladies stroll arm in arm toward the house. Simon removed his hat and scratched his head.

"George, I hope I didn't get you in trouble with the little lady. I was only joshing. Guess she doesn't know me well enough to make such a joke…not yet, anyway."

"A lot's happened, Simon." George sighed. "I guess you'd know that better than most. She's nervous about practically everything these days. The thought of picking up and moving anywhere, even if it's just down the road a piece, is mighty fearsome to Myra. She wants to stay put. I don't have the heart to uproot her and change her life again."

"I see. Well, you can't blame a man for trying." Simon crossed his arms at his chest and chuckled. "Besides, you can come out and play cowpoke anytime you want, George. I'm happy to have you."

George nodded as he took one final gander in the direction of the house. "Simon," he began, "you and Susan have been through a lot. How do you feel about Augusta being here?"

"I've made some horrible mistakes where my marriage is concerned. At first, when it dawned on me that Augusta was part of this ladies' group and probably always would be, I got physically ill at the prospect of it. Then one day it hit me like a lightning bolt right between the eyes. If my wife could welcome Augusta into our lives, then I should, too. After all, it was my obsession with her that brought about the mess we're in in the first place. If I don't make amends with her it's like saying I did nothing wrong. And, George, nothing could be further from the truth."

"Huh. I guess I never thought about it like that. I just figured all of this was about Mr. Reginald and his inability to take responsibility for his own actions. He could learn a lesson or two from you." George smirked.

"Yeah, well, I don't think that's ever going to happen. I have nightmares about meeting him face to face and fighting to the death. Only I wake up just before the final blow."

George leaned against the stall with his arms folded. "Mind me askin' who's about to get sacked?"

"I wish I knew. I never see faces; I just sort of *know* it's O'Keefe and me. Does that make sense?"

"Do dreams *ever* make sense?"

"Good point." Simon took a quick visual inventory of the barn. "I think we're done here. Let's go get cleaned up before supper. If there's one thing Clara can't abide, it's a filthy ranch hand, even if it is the man who pays her wages."

******

After supper some of the menfolk gathered together and played a few hands of cards while the ladies spent their time chatting and working on various handcrafts. Augusta surprised everyone by pulling out a lamb's wool sweater she was knitting.

"I knew you were a knitter, but goodness me, I didn't know you were *that* good!" Faerie gawked at the beautiful heather-colored yarn. "This is some of that yarn I brought back from Arizona."

Augusta smiled, laying the project in her lap. "I saved this yarn for the perfect project. It had to be something spectacular and one can only have so many shawls or mufflers." She fingered the delicate yarn. "I found this pattern at the house in Pagosa Springs. I was in the attic one day nosing around and came upon a box of old dress patterns. I brought it down to my room and spent an entire evening just going through them. Stuck between some of the papers was a small book of knitting patterns. This one especially caught my eye. I showed it to my hostess and she told me to take it….and anything else I came across in that box that caught my fancy."

"Well, this is beautiful. I'm impressed. I've always wanted to knit, except I'm all thumbs." Annie said.

"Look, if I can do it, anybody can. If you want to learn, I'd be happy to teach you."

"Really?" Annie asked with a crinkled up nose.

"Yes, really." Augusta slipped a stitch from one needle to the other.

"Me, too?" Nora looked hopeful.

"Of course." Augusta felt like one of the girls…*finally*. "I have lots of needles and yarn. I'd be happy to lend you a pair of needles for your first project. We can set up a regular time to meet, if you like. Let's talk about it more after the festival."

Susan smiled, touched that Augusta would be mindful of the real reason everyone had gathered. "Augusta, if you've a mind to, maybe you could knit an afghan or two for the widows and orphans Christmas project," Susan suggested, sounding hopeful.

Augusta beamed. "Are you kidding, Susan? It means a lot that you'd ask. I can't think of a better way to use my free time."

Faerie was proud of Augusta for coming out of her shell where the Archers were concerned. By all appearances, she seemed to be getting along with them just fine.

"Myra, Lydia and I are making a quilt to donate." Faerie added. "We've been having a fantastic time meeting in the evenings. I'm blessed to have a sewing room big enough to accommodate most any project."

"Maybe I might be able to knit a scarf, Miss Susan." Nora smiled sweetly. She gave Augusta a quick look. "If I'm a fast learner, that is."

"Pshaw." Augusta waved her off. "Don't let her fool you, ladies. This girl entertains me with Beethoven and Chopin almost every night after supper. Her fingers move across those piano keys faster than an ant to honey. She'll pick up knitting in no time flat. So will Annie."

"Piano, Nora?" Susan asked, surprised. "I didn't know that. Would you mind playing for our Christmas party this year? Even just a few carols would help to add a touch of class to a cowboy party." She grinned broadly as a few of the ladies snickered.

"I'd be honored. I must admit I've been eyeing your upright grand." She looked around the room. "Would it be all right if I tried it out now?"

"Absolutely. We'd all love to hear you play."

Nora walked over to the piano. She pulled out the bench, sat down and ran her fingers slowly over the ivories and then played a couple of scales to get a feel for its touch. She sat still for a moment and thought of what to play. She closed her eyes as the music began playing in her head. Suddenly the room was filled with the mournful strains of Chopin's *Prelude in C Minor*. She closed her eyes and gave herself over to the sadness of the minor chords and melody. As was always the case when playing this piece, Nora became somber and forlorn. She wondered what Chopin was thinking when he was composing it. Was his suffering from a broken heart? Or was he prone to bouts of melancholy? Whatever it was, this music left Nora aching inside for a man whose life was cut short by consumption. It was no coincidence that the somber *Prelude in C Minor* was played on the organ at his funeral.

What she couldn't see were the women behind her with hankies held to their cheeks, most hearing the piece for the very first time. When she finished the piece, she put her hands in her lap. The women's applause rang throughout the house. Not only had the women been blessed by Nora's interpretation of Chopin's masterpiece, but the men playing cards in the kitchen as well. When she turned to face her small audience, she became overcome with emotion to see that they truly understood the music.

Susan reached over from her seat next to the piano and took Nora's hands in her own. "What was that? I must hear more of it."

"That was *Prelude in C Minor* by Frederic Chopin, my favorite composer. It's often referred to as the Funeral March. I find it heart-wrenching and full of agony. Each time I play it, I'm left with a longing I can't describe."

"It's masterful. It's full of...*yearning.* It's almost painful to listen to, yet when it was finished I wanted to hear more," Susan said, thoughtfully.

"That's it exactly." Nora smiled.

"Please play something else," Annie urged. She looked expectantly at the other women. "Wouldn't you like to hear something else?"

The women begged her to continue.

Nora thought for a second, then said, "I think I'll play Bach's *Jesu, Joy of Man's Desiring.*"

This piece made her daydream of waltzing. She'd dare not admit that to anyone lest they think her blasphemous. Still, she was unable to keep her head from lilting side to side as she played. Bach wasn't her favorite composer, yet there were some works, like this one, that stirred something hopeful deep within. Pleased to hear a few of the women hum along, she smiled.

When she finished the piece, someone said, "My ma used to play that on the piano. My sisters and me….well, we used to practice dancing to it."

Nora grinned sideways. "I'm so glad to hear you say that. This song always makes me want to waltz. I never said so because my mom told me it was blasphemous and folks might get the wrong idea."

"I know your mom," Faerie said. "She just has your best interest at heart." Then : "David danced before God. So should we."

"Tell you what, ladies. I'll play one more song. Any requests?"

Annie piped up. "Would you play something by Beethoven? I particularly like *Moonlight Sonata."*

*"*Then *Moonlight Sonata* it is," Nora chirped, happily. "I love that one, too, Annie. The thing about Beethoven, in case you aren't familiar with his story, is that a good deal of his music was written after he lost his hearing."

"That's amazing," Faerie said. "To be so gifted that he was able to compose complete works and know exactly how they would sound once the instruments came together. He only heard the music in his head."

"That's right. His Ninth Symphony was probably his greatest work. The story is told that when the Ninth debuted Beethoven conducted it. When the last note of the last movement was played, he turned to the audience to see if they were applauding. He was completely deaf. That alone is an incredible feat, but he wrote it as well. I mean, can you imagine?" Nora hesitated a moment. "I've often wondered what it would be like to never hear music again. I can barely stand the thought of it. I suppose that knowing our minds hold memories…and that includes music…might make it more tolerable." She smiled and shrugged her shoulders. "Anyway, Annie, here's your song."

Nora closed her eyes and prepared herself mentally for the piece she was about to play. The room was as quiet as a tomb. She breathed in and out. Then, like a gift from heaven, beautiful music began to flow from Nora's memory to her fingers, sending Beethoven's strong, yet tender melody through the house as on angels' wings. Afterward, Nora entertained the ladies with the tale behind the haunting tune, originally known as Sonata Opus No. 2. It was written for one of Beethoven's students, a 17-year-old countess who stole his heart. He eventually proposed to the countess, but one of her parents wouldn't allow the engagement because Beethoven didn't rank high enough on the social ladder. The piece became known as Moonlight Sonata sometime later when a German music critic said the melody reminded him of moonlight shining on a lake.

Clara and Annie slipped away into the kitchen and returned a few minutes later with trays of pumpkin bread and hot coffee. Nora never knew the joy of the company of women until she came into this circle. She breathed it all in, memorizing the faces of each rancher's wife. Her own mother was so busy tutoring the children up on the mountain that she rarely engaged in any kind of entertaining, except for the occasional party or dinner for the mining executives. It was the only life Nora had ever known, which explained why she poured herself into music and its history.

"Isn't that so, Nora?" Augusta asked.

"What?" She blushed. "I'm afraid I was in another world. Isn't *what* so, Augusta?"

"We're still talking about music. I was telling the ladies that you'd taken on quite a task when you agreed to teach me to play the piano."

Nora snickered. "No worse than you thinking you're patient enough to teach me to knit."

"Touche'!" Augusta offered playfully, with a twinkle in her eye.

Faerie rolled her eyes. "There she goes using that French word again, ladies." She leaned in and said matter-of-factly, "She thinks it makes her sound smart."

Augusta recognized her friend's quick wit. "Are you saying I'm not?"

"Now whose turn is it to use that fancy word?" Annie chirped, followed by hoots of laughter from the others.

Susan was thrilled the evening was unfolding so well. As always, she'd been apprehensive about having Augusta on the ranch. Thankfully, she and Simon seemed to have either called a truce or made amends. She didn't know which. She was just relieved how carefree Augusta seemed. She was like a different person.

Susan stood and stretched her weary back. She wandered into the kitchen to check on John. He'd been especially quiet all day and she was worried. Faerie followed her.

"Too bad Marcus and Fred couldn't be here," Susan commented.

"Yes, but Marcus promised this was the last trip until summer."

"It'll be nice for you to have him for a while, especially with the holidays coming up." Then: "Augusta seems so *different*. She seems carefree and friendly, almost joyful. I can't really describe it. Whatever the reason, I *really* like it!"

"She's found something the rest of us have known about most of our lives. What kind of joy can change a person so drastically? Just think about it." Faerie crossed her arms and leaned against the counter.

Susan's eyes lit up. "The joy of the Lord is my strength."

Faerie nodded. "It's like day and night, Susan. She came back from Pagosa Springs a new creation. "

Chapter Twenty-Two

One thing you can't hide - is when you're crippled inside.
~John Lennon

He didn't want to do it. Chopping wood was definitely not one of Reginald's favorite pastimes. Yet if he didn't, he'd probably freeze to death. His hands ached from the cold, which made gripping the ax handle near to impossible. He willed his frozen fingers to grasp the long wooden handle. He lifted the ax and grimaced at the first contact of ax and wood. Memories came flooding back.

"I'll take ya b'hind the woodpile, boy, and then ya won't be *able* t' use that smart mouth!" Reginald grew up believing that his pa thought anything he had to say was backtalk, and all eye contact was made in defiance.

His pa was a red-haired man with muscles on muscles who would just as soon backhand Reginald as look at him…except on Sunday. On Sunday he'd get all spruced up and pay a visit to the confessional where he'd slide a few measly dollars to the priest, hoping to buy his silence and stay in the good graces of the Church. Or at least that's how Reginald had always imagined it.

The ax flew faster now. He'd never be able to repay his pa for all that tender love and care. He imagined his pa being strung up in the same manner he had always been as a boy. Each swing of the ax represented a belt strap to his back. Slowly Reginald's neck and shoulder muscles began to relax, relieving the headache that traveled up the base of his neck to his temples.

Maybe there was some truth in what Marcus had to say about an honest day's work. "An honest day's work acts on a man just like a tonic," he'd said. "He doesn't have time to think about his troubles." Reginald always smiled and nodded when Marcus rattled on, thinking it to be some highbrow nonsense he'd learned at that school back in Boston. But gall darn-it, if it wasn't true. As he chopped, he felt the shackles fall from his shoulders and the nonsense that crowded his head was quiet for a change. As much as he hated to admit it, Marcus had been right all along. He smirked. *I'll admit it to myself, but never to anybody else. After all, I've still got my pride…and a bunch of nuisances that chatter nonstop day and night.*

"Watch out, old man, we can read your mind, you know." Luke's overbearing, sarcastic voice boomed loud and clear.

"Why don't you just take a nap, Luke? I'm not in the mood for any of your silliness today. Allow me one day…just one day!"

"Whatever you say, old man." He was quiet for a moment, then: "If I hear anything that might be a problem for us, I *will* let you know. You can take that to the bank."

"Would you ever do it any other way?" Reginald responded, sarcastically.

The wind whistled through the spruce. He loved that sound: eerie, mysterious and haunting. For now, the Voices in his head were honoring the request for silence. He backed up to a towering aspen and leaned against it, still holding the ax, his only physical weapon against the anxiety that ate away at his soul. With his head resting against the smooth, white bark, he relaxed. He breathed in; he breathed out. Never able to anticipate when the others might begin their incessant chattering, he cherished these brief respites of clarity and peace.

There were times when he tried so hard to be strong. Times when he wrestled with the demons. Most of them yielded to his will; nevertheless, Luke would not be silenced for long. When Luke bowed to Reginald's requests for solitude, it always came with a warning. Like today, he often threatened his swift return at the first sign of discord. Oftentimes, he made some nasty remark about how stupid and weak Reginald truly was, reminding him of his red-headed, poor excuse of a father. In any case, Luke's silence came with a price.

He'd worked up quite a sweat chopping the devil out of the woodpile. Most people viewed a woodpile as a sign of security and warmth against the cold of the dark winter months. To the naked eye, this stash was no different. Only Reginald knew the significance of it. Standing back and observing the finished product, a nice stack of logs for the fire, gave him an extreme amount of satisfaction, replacing his usual angst and sullenness. Nevertheless, he was nobody's fool. He was well aware his clarity of mind came only in brief snippets. Typically, he was plagued with anger, stress, and a feeling of uneasiness associated with the Voices. He was sweaty and dirty, his hair needed grooming, and he probably smelled like an old black bear, but he didn't care. He wasn't thinking about peeking in Augusta's windows or slugging Marcus in the nose. He wasn't even imagining what it would be like to finally put Simon out of his misery. He was thinking about how satisfying it was to lean against a tree just for the sake of leaning against a tree, and knowing he'd just finished a grueling task.

His old cabin had none of the comforts he'd come to enjoy. Even so, he appreciated being on his own with nobody watching or breathing down his neck. If he didn't want to bathe, then so be it. No wife to tell him he'd not slip between her sheets unless he was clean as a whistle and smelling good. If he wanted to eat biscuits and gravy for supper, then biscuits and gravy it was. No Lydia, even though he respected her more than life, to tell him he needed three squares a day, at least one of them being a stick-to-your-ribs, sit-down-at-the-table-and-take-your-time kind of meal.

A fierce wind whipped about, giving Reginald a whiff of his gamey self. He remembered his ma saying if a person could smell himself, everybody else had smelled him for about three days. Just one more whiff of his earthy fragrance was all it took to convince him that bathing now rather than later was a most brilliant idea. He trekked the short distance back to the cabin and propped the ax against the front porch railing. He pumped water into a pot and placed it over the fire. Before long he had enough hot water to pamper himself with a proper bath in the galvanized steel tub he'd found in the shed out back.

When finally he emerged from the bath, he chose his clothes carefully. He was a wanted man. He chose a pair of brown dungarees and a plaid flannel shirt and a wide-brimmed felt hat. He'd recently found a pair of gold-rimmed glasses in an old abandoned cabin and thought them a great addition to his disguise. The lenses were weak, practically just glass. They fit on the end of his nose, like so many old gents used when reading, and disguised his dark, brooding eyes enough to be passable. Growing out his hair had done a lot to change his appearance. Discarding his fancy duds had been a difficult, but necessary and wise choice. He'd taken his cues from the old hermit over on the other side of Red Mountain by steering clear of people who wandered in and out of the abandoned camp, never using his real name, and only venturing into town when absolutely necessary. He believed he was well on his way to mastering the art of survival.

The locals he'd met knew him only as Leon. No last name. He was careful never to offer any personal information or participate in long conversations. For the sake of anonymity, he re-invented himself as a widower from Kansas who left family and friends to begin a new life away from everything that reminded him of his dearly departed wife, Mae. He spun the tale so well that women's heartstrings were plucked and men found themselves offering to help him clear his small plot of land and patch his roof before winter. For about two seconds he felt bad about misleading these folks, then waved it off, convincing himself he wasn't really lying but creating a new reality. What they didn't know couldn't hurt them. They were better off not knowing the truth. In his mind, it was a simple as that. He hadn't planned on making friends with any of them. So as long as he stuck with the same story he didn't foresee any problems. After all, these were mountain folk, most of whom had lived in these parts all their lives and didn't really keep up on the news from down in the valley. They probably had no idea there was a killer on the loose. And they sure didn't think he was anything but what he professed to be.

******

He followed a path that led through the woods to the train stop. He was glad he brought along a jacket; the temperature seemed to be steadily dropping. No matter; this outing wasn't intended to be an all-day affair. The sooner he made his purchases and returned home the better. He fancied himself a good actor. He'd never been on a stage, but he did a fine job of lying and leading folks to his way of thinking. As long as no one recognized him he should be fine. Still, it was important to keep on his toes and not let his guard down.

Far off in the distance, he heard the lonesome sound of the train whistle. He picked up the pace by jogging down the footpath. Soon he saw a cloud of gray and white smoke swirling above. For a moment, he thought he felt Luke trying to rise to the surface, but he kept moving, running now, to the stop in Ironton.

He arrived just as the train came to a stop, a thick rush of smoky steam billowed up from the undercarriage. When finally the smoke cleared, he was none too surprised to see that no one exited the train, and that he was the lone passenger to board at the Ironton stop. Soon the train began its journey toward Silverton. He wrestled with his decision to take the train; he could easily have walked the distance in less than an hour. The more he fretted about his decision, the more uncomfortable he became. His skin was clammy; his stomach, tied up in knots. As he stared out the window, he forced himself to breathe slow and deep. When his anxiety began to dissipate, he realized he'd been clenching his fists so intensely that his nails were embedded in the palms of his hands. He loosened the grip and turned his palms upward. *No bleeding.* This would be when Luke would tell him how useless he was. *Shave-tail,* he thought. *Luke actually called me a shave-tail.* Darkness loomed over him, the kind that comes from a brooding temperament. *Who does that guy think he is?*

"I can hear you," was the reply. "Perhaps I was wrong, Reggie-boy. Perhaps you are *worse* than a shave-tail. Worse than a no good, unbroken pack mule."

A few of the passengers turned to him. He snarled and dropped his head. *You can't do that, Luke. You can't just speak out like that.* He looked up quickly and took a quick gander around the car.

One man glared at him with squinted eyes and clamped jaw. He blinked nervously then got up from his seat. He dropped into the seat across the aisle from Reginald.

"Say, don't I know you?" The man turned in his seat with his feet in the aisle. He dropped his head and looked back and forth. "Ain't you that O'Keefe fella ever-body's lookin' for?"

"Naw. That ain't me. Fraid yer mistaken," he responded in a hillbilly twang that surprised even him.

He smirked and gave Reginald a good once over. "Sure y'are. The clothes is diff'ernt. Hair's a little longer. And those glasses…"

"Listen, sir. I don't know nobody named…" He paused for effect. "Reginald, was it? I'm jest a tired man who's lost 'is wife. All I want is fer folks t' let me be whilst I work through m' grief. Understan'?" He fixed his gaze on the back of a man's head straight ahead.

"Anything you say…O'Keefe."

Reginald's heart was beating like nobody's business. He dropped his head and grabbed at his chest, willing his body to relax. He began to tell himself that surely the guy was all bark and no bite. He watched as the man made his way to the front of the car and plopped down, then turned and gave Reginald a knowing glance through piercing green eyes.

By the time the train arrived in Silverton, the snow had begun to fly. Reginald had worked on Red Mountain long enough to know it was wise to be prepared for any kind of weather. He'd experienced blue skies and balmy breezes giving way to freezing temperatures and blizzards with little warning. He pulled a thick wool sweater from the pack on his back and donned a pair of wool gloves. Stepping off the train, he stretched and headed over to the general store to pick up a few supplies.

Music and laughter echoed from the saloons and brothels that made their homes on Notorious Blair Street, just a couple of blocks from the thriving business district. Why one town would need upwards of thirty watering holes was beyond him, but who was he to complain. He'd stop in and have a drink or two before he went back to his home sweet home. Besides, he'd not known the company of a woman in a while and he had an itch that needed scratching. He smirked and harrumphed. *Now there's a place old Marcus would never be caught.* To his recollection, none of the cribs he ever visited had Bibles on their bedside tables.

Silverton's general store reminded him of Old Man's mercantile down in Ouray. He stood in the center aisle and made a sweep of the surroundings. *First things first,* he thought. Meandering over to the counter, he examined a fine display of stick candies. From childhood on, he'd suffered from an insatiable sweet tooth. As luck would have it, he had more than enough money to spend on treats, so instead of weighing his options he took a couple of sticks from each jar. With a peppermint stick in his mouth, he wandered around gathering the items on his mental list. Canned peaches, half dozen apples, a pound of coffee, two pencils, a writing tablet, a few potatoes and a sack of corn meal completed the list. The shopkeeper promised to keep an eye on the items until he returned.

He stood outside the store with the peppermint stick lodged between his right cheek and gums and looked both ways. He finally decided to go to the left and find the livery stable. He needed a good mule and if the liveryman wasn't able to oblige him, he certainly would know who could.

"Got yourself a sweet tooth, do you?"

Coming from a few paces behind him, Reginald heard the voice of the man from the train. He certainly wasn't a stranger. Reginald found him vaguely familiar and tried to recall where they'd met. He kept walking. The steps from behind came faster.

"Go away." Reginald kept walking, never looking back.

"O'Keefe, I ain't got nothin' agin you."

"I already said I'm not…what did you call me?...O'Keefe? Sorry t' put a hitch in yer giddy-up."

"Well, I ain't never heard that'n b'fore." He let go a belly laugh as he trudged on, trying to keep up with Reginald's pace.

"If'n ya don't mind, I've got things t' do. Go find somebody else t' pester."

Reginald found himself sorely annoyed with the hillbilly talk he was using, but it was all a part of the disguise. He'd do whatever it took to get rid of this scoundrel.

"I ain't gonna leave you be 'cause I know who you is."

Reginald's anger was festering. He kept walking, turning south toward the seedier side of things. Mr. Nosy would follow and Reginald would be able to settle the matter between them once and for all. The snow was coming harder now. Reginald turned up his jacket collar and tucked his head down. From the sound of the footsteps behind him, he guessed the man to be but a few paces behind and closing in.

All of a sudden, Reginald decided it was time to pick up the pace. He ran into an alley and hid behind some wooden boxes that were stacked against one of the buildings. Sure enough, only seconds later the grizzly, green-eyed man followed. Reginald was as quiet as a mouse.

"I know you're back here, O'Keefe." The man stepped slowly, stopping a few feet past the barricade of boxes that hid Reginald.

The man listened carefully for any sound that might clue him in as to Reginald's hiding place. He silently wished he'd listened to his more rational side and kept to the original plan of visiting his sister, yet here he was in the middle of something from which his pride would not allow him to back away. The howling wind brought with it swirling gusts of snow, blinding and disorienting him. He swallowed nervously. He turned to find Reginald standing directly behind him wearing a most sinister grin, his dark eyes flashing.

"It took me a while to figure out where we'd met, Tobias." Reginald inched closer, clinching his jaw and squinting. "Then I was reminded of a day when you called my girl …well, it doesn't matter much what you called her. You disrespected her and that's what mattered at that time." The two men glared at one another for a long spell. Finally, Reginald said, "I'll never forget your eyes. I blackened both of them that day. I'd have killed you if…" He stopped. "You owe Augusta a huge debt of gratitude, Tobias. If not for her, you'd probably be dead." His nostrils flared as he grabbed the man by the coat collar. "If you should ever find yourself in Augusta's neck of the woods, it would behoove you to stop by and thank her for having mercy on your worthless hide. It's the least you could do." The words dripped with an ominous sarcasm. He let go of Tobias and chuckled under his breath. "She'd probably faint right there on the spot."

Tobias backed against a wall of the building behind him, never breaking his gaze with Reginald. "Now, I think we could work somethin' out, O'Keefe. I ain't gonna tell nobody. You got my word on that."

Reginald snorted. He pulled a knife from his belt. Inching closer to the man, he whispered, "Beg. Beg for your life. Tell me why I shouldn't gut you right here and now."

The man swallowed. He stuttered. "Ah, c-come on, n-now, Mr. O'Keefe. You don't hafta do somethin' you'll r-regret l-later. I got kids to f-feed and a w-wife what's in the f-family w-way. I'm beggin' you, sir. P-Please."

Reginald stood tall and straight. Still holding the knife, he crossed his arms at his chest. "A wife and kids, you say?"

Tobias quickly nodded as tears began to flow. He wiped his nose on the sleeve of his coat.

"A family. I hafta admit, I never saw that coming, Tobias. And it better be the truth, because if I find out you made that up, I'll come looking for you and you'll have the devil to pay. Understand?"

"Yessir. I swear it's the truth. On my dear mama's grave, I swear." He nervously ran fingers through his hair.

"Get on out of here. But keep your mouth shut. My name is Leon. Do you hear me? Leon."

Tobias shoved his hands in his pockets. "Leon. S-Sure thing, L-Leon. I got it." He nodded, his head nervously bobbing up and down.

"Skedaddle."

Reginald watched Tobias tuck tail and run, disappearing somewhere near the east end of Blair Street. He put the knife back in its holder, slowly made his way back to the end of the alley, looked both ways and headed to the Westminster Saloon to see what mischief he might find.

******

She waited for quite a while. No one else came walking through the alleyway. She peeked out from behind the stack of boxes midway down the alley. Not a soul in sight. She inched out, her stomach feeling queasy. Her hands were shaking, her teeth chattering. When she came out of the saloon, she only intended to get a breath of fresh air. Never in her wildest dreams did she expect to be witness to two men at odds. She pulled her lace shawl close. Her saloon garb wasn't exactly cold weather attire.

"Pearl? You still out there?" sounded the shrill cry of a woman in the doorway of the bordello.

"Yes'm. I'll be right there. Just feeling a bit woozy, is all."

"Stay out too long and you'll catch your death."

Pearl rolled her eyes and silently mimicked the woman's words with a sassy nod of the head. Then: "Coming, ma'am."

Pearl knew she'd just witnessed something she mustn't keep to herself. She knew the man with the knife. She'd seen him many times in Ouray. He paid handsomely for time with Augusta…or Constance, as she was known by her clients. She wondered what happened to Augusta. Word had it she married that varmint. The madam became so frightened of him that she packed up and moved her business to Silverton. *What was his name again? Think, Pearl, think. Reginald something or other. Yes, that's it. Reginald.*

Out the back door came a buxom woman with bright pink feathers in her even brighter orange hair. "You all right, girl?"

"Not really, ma'am. Do you remember that fella what spent time with Augusta way back when? Reginald?"

The madam recoiled as a wave of nausea crippled her. The bitter taste of bile crept up her throat as her salivary glands started to work overtime. She covered her mouth with her hands and forced a swallow. Then: "What made you think of him?"

210

"I just seen him, ma'am." She pointed at the stack of boxes. "I was behind these boxes just takin' a breather, ma'am. It was then I seen he had a knife to another man's throat. I don't know what was said between 'em, ma'am, but that Reginald fella fin'ly turned 'im loose. The man made tracks, runnin' somethin' fierce whilst Reginald stood there a'pickin' 'is fingernails with the knife and laughin' real *crazy* like."

The madam took Pearl by the elbow and pulled the screen door open. "Get yerself on in here, girlie. He ain't nothin' but trouble. Here's hopin' he didn't see you."

******

Tobias hightailed it to the train and took a seat in the front of the car. He should've known better than to confront a man like O'Keefe. It was true what everybody said about him: mean as a snake and as crazy as a pet skunk under a purple calliope. He could've kicked himself.

He thought back to the days when he frequented Second Avenue in Ouray. He knew his wife would take a cast iron skillet to his head if she ever found out he was down in The District. One afternoon he'd had a little too much to drink and mouthed off to the pretty little dark-haired lady on the arm of the man he now knew as O'Keefe. From out of nowhere a fist planted itself against his nose, another to his left cheek, knocking him to the ground. O'Keefe straddled him and commenced pulverizing him, calling him name after name, screaming obscenities at him. The lady with him cried out for him to stop. Then, as if something unseen had latched onto O'Keefe's raised fist, he stopped, looked around, stood up, and ordered Tobias to leave. For whatever or whoever saved him, he'd been eternally grateful, and never visited The District again.

He knew O'Keefe would follow through with his threats. He'd heard talk of O'Keefe's Voices. He'd heard rumors that he was a suspect in the murder of some drifter. Then he heard another man went missing for a year. Rumor had it that O'Keefe was behind that, too. And now he was hiding up in these mountains. Tobias guessed it had to be somewhere about Ironton. He knew what he had to do, even if it meant he must take his family far away.

******

Reginald took a step inside the noisy saloon and scanned the room over the top of his glasses. The place was full of miners who'd obviously just put in a hard day's work and wanted nothing more than a few beers and a flirty girl. No one seemed to notice him…and that was a good thing. He

211

sighed with relief, not recognizing any of the men. Music from a player piano in the far corner filled the establishment with the strains of a lively tune he didn't recognize. He spotted an empty table next to the bar and moved in that direction. He removed his jacket and hung it on the back of a chair that faced the entrance. Again he swept the smoky room with a glance as he slowly inched into the chair.

"A gentleman always removes his hat when he comes inside, sir."

He looked up with a sly grin, which quickly turned to a frown. The woman raised a brow and placed her hands on her hips. "If you know what's good for you, you'll scoot right on outta here."

"Mona, my *dear*, dear Mona. How've you been? It's been far too long."

Reginald motioned to the chair closest to him and asked her to have a seat. She looked over her shoulder, then pulled the chair out and sat stiffly on the end of it.

Mona Goodwin and Reginald O'Keefe shared a history that would cause the members of the Christian Ladies' Guild of Ouray to faint dead away. Until recently, Mona owned the most successful brothel on Second Avenue. She had rarely ventured far from The District because of the disapproving looks she received from the women of the town, some whose husbands paid regular visits to her 'house'. Back then, Reginald was a regular patron. As such, she offered him nothing but the best. He had his eyes on Augusta from the beginning and paid handsomely for her services. In the end, she lost a good customer and one of her best girls. After she learned of his problems, she became leery of him and tried to avoid him at all costs. She closed her doors in Ouray and headed for the hills when he began to show up on her doorstep drunk, mean and talking to himself.

"I wondered how long it'd be before ya showed up here. Listen t' me. We don't want no trouble. Ya hear?" Mona raised a brow. She placed her hands, palms down, on the table. "Why don't ya jest turn yerself in?" She kept her voice low…intense.

"Sounds like a right smart thing to do, but I just can't!" He eyed her with disdain and added, "By the way, call me Leon. All my friends do." He threw her a malicious glance over the top of his glasses. "Like my new look?"

Her skinned crawled. "I need to get back to work…*Leon.* Have one drink…on the house. Then go. And don't come back." She stood and gave him a sober look.

"You'd think I was a wanted man, Mona, the way you're treating me. And I thought we were such good friends. My mistake. "He chuckled, menacingly. "Guess all you ever really wanted from me was my money," he snarled. He stood. She backed away. "Forget about the drink. All of a sudden I'm not so thirsty."

Grabbing his coat, he sneered and stomped toward the swinging doors, pushing chairs out of his way. Mona stood planted to the same spot, trembling with fear and anger, as she watched him leave.

Pearl came up behind her. "Ma'am, that was that fella Augusta married. Ain't so?

"*Is* so." She folded her arms. "The question is what t' do now that we've seen 'im? D'ya think that other guy might go t' the sheriff?"

"Can't rightly say, ma'am. Seems like maybe we should tell somebody." Pearl scrunched up her face as she tilted her head. "It's the right thing t' do."

"Good thing the law 'round here don't hold our *occupation* agin us." Mona went to the bar and whispered something to the bartender. He nodded. She turned to Pearl and motioned for her to follow. They went to Mona's upstairs apartment and changed into more respectable dresses and hats, without the plumes and feathers they generally sported. A little soap and water took off most of the face paint. A few minutes later they were on their way to the Municipal building on the other end of Blair Street.

"Sure hope somebody'll listen to us," Pearl fretted.

"Why wouldn't they, Pearl? We look like nice respectable ladies. Well…except for my *hair*. There are times when I think I oughta get rid of this orange hair, but it's like my….*calling card.*" She fluffed her orange locks playfully.

They stood in front of the Municipal building. "You ready?" Mona asked.

"As I'll ever be," muttered Pearl.

Chapter Twenty-Three

Doing the right thing has power.
~ Laura Linney

Alfred and Sandy loaded the last of the supplies for the festival on the buckboard. Just as they were climbing into their seats, a husky voice called out to them from up the street. Alfred squinted and craned his neck to get a better look.

"It's the sheriff, Pa," Sandy said. Her heart jumped to her throat. Every time she saw him she wondered if there was any news.

"Alfred, wait!" Sheriff Johnson jogged over to them, securing his holster at his side. By the time he reached them, he was completely out of breath. "Well….it's….either the….altitude…or I need to…exercise more…or …both, I s'pose."

They watched him gasp for air in curious silence. Then: "What's up, Sheriff?" Alfred asked.

The sheriff took a deep breath before continuing. "There's news. I don't have all the details, but there's news. O'Keefe's been spotted up in Silverton. He's dressin' jest like ya said, Miss Sandy, like an ol' miner. Seems he got 'isself into a scuffle with a man in an alley. Then he showed up at a saloon an' two o' th' women who work there reco'nized 'im. Seems they both used t' work down here over in…" He stopped short of finishing the sentence and nervously cleared his throat. Then: "Well, I reckon it don't rightly matter where they knew 'im from. Interestin' thing is, one o' them ladies was b'hind some boxes stacked in th' alley an' heard ever'thing. The other'n said she and O'Keefe once had some biz'ness arrangements. I kin almost guess what that might've been, but we kin save that nonsense fer 'nother day." Sheriff Johnson hesitated to give further information about the women out of respect for Sandy.

Sandy's hands flew to her mouth. "I'll bet they knew him from a *bordello* over on Second."

Alfred and Sheriff Johnson gawked at each other in stunned silence. Then: "How'd you know about such things, sweet girl?" Alfred asked, dumbfounded.

"Because," she began, dragging the word out, "he told me all about it. He said he met Augusta when she worked as a….*fancy lady*." She shrugged. "Just because I'm young doesn't mean I don't know about such things."

"Land sakes, girl," her papa replied. "I don't know why I'm surprised. Nothing that man does should surprise me. He probably only told you to

215

try and make her look bad or make you blush."

"Oh, who knows? Who *cares*?" she asked. Then: "So, Sheriff, what happens now?"

Sheriff Johnson marveled at how grownup Sandy seemed. "The deputy up there wired me with th' news. They'll be a'lookin' mighty hard fer 'im." He offered them a big toothy grin. "Miss Sandy, you and yer daddy need t' go have a good time at th' festival this weekend and leave th' worryin' to me. Deal?"

"You got it, sir," she said and jumped down from the buckboard to give him a great big hug. "Thank you, Sheriff."

As she backed away from the embrace, the sheriff thought he noticed a light in her eyes that wasn't there before. Under his tough exterior was the heart of a big old softie. It was moments such as this that made his job worthwhile. He was choked up, that's for sure.

Alfred said, "Sandy, we've got to be off. Don't want to be on the road after dark. Besides, it's gettin' right nippy." Then: "Sheriff, the festival's shaping up nicely and sure to be quite a celebration. Hope t' see you there."

"Wouldn't miss it fer th' world." Sheriff Johnson wished them well and said his goodbyes, feeling like a weight had suddenly been lifted from his substantial shoulders. He stood in the alleyway behind the café and watched as father and daughter climbed onto their seats in the front of the buckboard and then slowly turned onto the street.

For the first time since the whole O'Keefe mess began, he felt confident the man's days were numbered. O'Keefe was getting sloppy. Or maybe he believed himself to be so much smarter than everybody else that he figured he'd never get caught, and let down his guard. Whatever the reason for the slipup in Silverton, it was a costly mistake on his part. The sheriff smirked and started to mosey down the middle of the alley, whistling as he went. A new air of confidence washed over him. His steps seemed lighter, his mind clearer, and his temperament milder. He grinned devilishly and spoke into the wind, "Better enjoy yer freedom whilst ya can, O'Keefe, ol' buddy."

******

Washie checked the clock in the kitchen. "Three o'clock," she said quietly, predicting it wouldn't be much longer before Alfred and Sandy arrived.

Susan sidled up next to her. "What're you thinking about?"

"Not much, just missing my family" She offered Susan a little smile. "I expect they'll be here soon enough. Alfred planned on closing the café

216

just as soon after the lunch rush as possible. And we sent a note to Sandy's teacher asking that she be excused early. Alfred promised me they'd be on their way as soon as Sandy got out of school, and they finished loading the wagon."

Susan put an arm around her and gave a little squeeze. "John's looking forward to seeing Sandy. Hope the feeling is mutual."

"I expect so. Sandy really doesn't talk very much about what happened. But she misses John." Then: "I told you she went back to school, didn't I?"

"I think you mentioned it when you were here the other day. How's she handling things?"

"Fine, I s'pose. I've heard no complaints. It was me that did all the whining about it. I thought it was too soon. I didn't want her to rush into anything."

"I wish John was able to go. Right now I'm schooling him at home. If the decision was left up to him, he might never go back. For the most part, he fares pretty well around here. Even so, it's concerning that he doesn't want to venture away from the ranch. Part of it's his injuries. The rest of it…well, you know what it is."

Washie shook her head. She pursed her lips and drummed her fingers against the counter. "That man! How does he hide so well?" she implored. "Our children have been forever changed because of him. We've all been affected in one way or another by that…that…*monster*." She spied Augusta across the way, sitting at the kitchen table dipping one apple after another into a bowl of caramel sauce. "How does she do it, Susan?"

Susan wrinkled her brow, not following Washie's train of thought. Then realizing her friend's gaze was fixed on the other side of the room, she looked. Augusta was sitting at the table, dipping apples with a group of ladies, talking and appearing to have a grand time.

"She's chosen to let it go. She told me she's tired of wasting her life worrying about Reginald. I believe her exact words were 'he shall not steal my joy'."

"Good for her." Washie's response sounded flippant and trite.

"Don't misunderstand her, Washie. She's been dealing with Reginald and the aftermath of his behavior for a lot longer than the rest of us." She waited for a response. There was none. "He's a sick man. Augusta said that Doc Fisher called him *criminally ill.*"

"Hmm. So what does that mean, exactly? That because he's mental, he doesn't have to pay for his crimes?"

Susan wagged her head. "I don't know much about the law. I do, however, know the difference between right and wrong…even if the person in question isn't right in the head. And in this case, I've heard tell that's what the doctor believes. What are they calling that these days? Mentally ill? Disturbed? Whatever it is, when Reginald's caught, he must pay. There has to be consequences for his actions. Why, I heard of a man back home who began hearing voices, similar to what Reginald seems to be experiencing. The difference was that he claimed it was God speaking to him. He bludgeoned his wife in a fit of rage, claiming God told him she was a demon and had to die. His attorney used an insanity defense and he was sent to the state asylum. The stories of what goes on in those places makes my skin crawl. I don't know what's worse, life in prison or an asylum." She shuddered.

Washie knit her brows together. "You don't think Reginald will get away with it, do you? Or try to escape the charges by getting as far away from here as possible? He's got lots of money. He could very well leave and start over someplace new."

"If he goes away, he'll still be the same man with the same problems. One way or another, his days of freedom are numbered. I'm counting on it." Susan paused. Then: "Washie, we must rely on our faith. I don't mean to make light of the situation. People don't realize how much power there is in faith." She harrumphed. "Sometimes it's called *simple* faith. And it should be simple to trust our Creator, except it's anything *but*. Putting all our eggs in one basket and leaving them there? I suppose it sounds foolish to most folks." She paused, then solemnly added, "I learned about faith the hard way. When Simon was gone for such a long time, with no word, no nothing, I worried my head off. I had very little appetite and was up many nights pacing the floors, wondering where he could be. Then one day as I was out working in one of the flowerbeds, it hit me like a bolt of lightning, right between the eyes. I was either going to trust God or I wasn't. I was either going to live my faith or walk away from it. I stopped digging in the dirt and started to pray. Right then and there I decided faith was more than just talk and decided to turn everything over to God." She grasped Washie's hand. "Washie, listen to me. None of us can fix the problems we have with Reginald. They're too big. The good news is, God is bigger. He can handle it. Let him!"

Washie lifted her head and thought on Susan's words. "You're right. My people have been through great turmoil. When our family heard about the White Man's God, we chose him because of the great gift of his Son. What father would give up his son for mankind? None I know. What greater love is there?" The corners of her mouth turned up ever-so-slightly.

"Thank you, Susan. I needed to be reminded of the Father's great love for us. It's a gift beyond measure."

They hugged. Suddenly, someone in the living room said, "Another buckboard just pulled up." Susan and Washie strolled out the back door to greet them. Washie's face beamed when she spotted Alfred and Sandy.

Alfred watched Washie as she scurried across the lawn to the wagon, a smile plastered on her face. He jumped down from his seat and gave her a big hug. "Such a warm greeting, Love. I haven't seen you smile like this in such a long time."

"I'm so happy to see my family." Then she noticed there was something different in Sandy's countenance. She was sitting taller, smiling broader. "Sandy, you look...*radiant*."

"We have something to tell you that will make your day. Shoot, it'll make everybody's day." She hopped down from her seat and went to the back of the wagon to help Alfred with unloading.

Susan and Washie waited for the big announcement. When it didn't come, they gave each other puzzled glances, shrugged their shoulders, and joined in the task before them.

"Looks like you cleared out the café. Is there anything left in the kitchen?" Washie grabbed a big box of groceries and skittered quickly to the back door.

Alfred heehawed and said, "She can really move when she has to. Look at her go."

With everyone helping they were able to empty to wagon in one trip. Alfred had previously volunteered to fix supper for everyone on the night before the festival. His specialty was navy bean soup and ham sandwiches. The soup was in a big pot he carried into the house and placed on the stove.

Clara couldn't resist taking a peek under the lid. "I do declare, Alfred. The soup smells heavenly. Secret recipe?"

Alfred furrowed his brow and wagged his head playfully. "It's navy bean soup. *Southern* style. That's no secret at all."

"Southern style," Clara tapped her pointer finger against the side of her face and gazed up to the ceiling thoughtfully. "That means, ham hock, pepper, salt, a little bit of cream for taste and thickening."

He winked. "That's about it. Oh, one more thing: lots of time to cook." He stirred the soup and leaned in slightly. Closing his eyes, he took in the heavenly aroma. "I'm glad it's almost time to eat. I can't take it much longer."

"Are the sandwiches build-your-own style?" she asked, backing into the counter and crossing her arms at the waist.

"I thought that would be best. Keeps the bread from getting too soggy." He cringed. "If there's one thing I can't abide, it would definitely be soggy bread." He shrugged and moaned, "Ugh."

Clara curled one side of her upper lip and scowled. "I know what you mean. Kind of gags me." She laughed out loud. "I know that isn't very ladylike, but it's true."

"You should hear my wife and girl make gagging sounds when they're doing dishes and they come across soggy bread. It sounds like a couple of folks plagued with the grip."

She snorted and half the ladies in the kitchen turned around. She and Alfred both guffawed. With tears streaming down her face, she picked up a wooden spoon and shook it at the crowd and said, "What're you lookin' at? Get back to work."

Susan said, "You heard her, gals. The boss has spoken." A few of the girls shared coy glances and snickers. Despite their playfulness, they'd been hard at it since early morning and were tired and hungry, and ready to call it a day.

After supper, the ranch families disappeared into the night with nothing but the light of the harvest moon to guide their way to Cowboy Village, the group of cabins which housed the men and their families. Susan stood at the back door and watched them go, little ones holding the hands of their moms and dads. When the last of the group was out of sight, she went back in the house and hung her shawl on the hook by the door.

Clara brought in a tray filled with empty cups and saucers and set it in the sink. "What a day!" Susan heard the tiredness in her voice.

"Why don't you go on to bed now? I'll take care of whatever needs tending."

"For once, I won't argue with you. I'm so tired I can hardly put one foot in front of the other." Clara yawned.

Susan nodded and said, "Off to bed, now. See you bright and early in the morning." She turned to the sink and stacked the cups and saucers. About that time, Sandy wandered into the kitchen.

"So, are you enjoying yourself tonight, Sandy?" Susan asked as she poured a kettle of hot water into the sink.

"Yes ma'am. I like it here on the ranch. Kind of reminds me of home, only there's a lot more to it." She snagged a cookie from a plate on the table. "Can I help with anything?"

"As a matter of fact, there *is* something. I'll wash the dishes, if you'll dry and stack. I'll help you put them away after." Susan reached in a drawer and grabbed a dishtowel. "Here you go." She smiled sweetly at the girl.

"Miss Susan, may I ask you a question?" Sandy timidly dropped her eyes to the floor.

Susan furrowed her brow. "Anything Sandy."

Sandy cleared her throat. "Is John all right?" She paused. "I mean, he seems so distant."

Susan chewed on her bottom lip as she pondered the best response. "He's...having a hard time adjusting. He doesn't eat much, sleeps even less. The only time he seems anything like his old self is when he's with Taffy."

Sandy fiddled with the edges of the dishtowel. "He sure does love that horse." She had a far off look in her eyes. "Maybe he should talk to somebody. Maybe Pastor Duncan?"

"He doesn't want to. Not yet, anyway. He tells me not to worry, that he'll be better soon. I thought seeing you would help." Susan set a cup in the dish drainer. "Has he even *attempted* a conversation with you?" Susan already knew the answer.

Sandy picked up the cup and commenced drying it...slowly...contemplatively. "No'm. He's barely spoken to me. I wanted to sit with him at supper but he went straight to Troy."

"I saw that." Then: "In Troy's defense, he's been a good friend to John. For some reason, John doesn't really to want to talk with anyone *but* Troy these days."

They worked in silence for a few minutes both pondering John's understandable withdrawal, the only sounds being the splashing of water and the clinking of dishes.

Finally, Susan said, "Don't let John's distance put you off. He told me he was anxious to see you again. Maybe *you* should start the conversation."

Sandy shrugged her shoulders and said, "I'll sleep on that tonight." She slowly dried a glass and set in on the counter. "It might seem to you that I've moved on, that I'm doing better, but it isn't so. I think about what happened all the time." Then: "I'll sit by John at breakfast. He'll have to talk to me then." She gazed at Susan shyly. "Promise not to let anybody else sit by him?"

"I promise." She winked, giving Sandy a reason to smile. Before they knew it, the dishes were done and the kitchen was as clean as a whistle.

******

The clock on the second floor landing struck ten, signaling the women to begin their nightly beauty routines. The men laughed and said there was definitely a certain advantage to being a man. Undressing, slipping into their nightclothes and robes, and brushing their teeth took only a matter of a few minutes. They were amused that getting ready for bed took the ladies as much time as their morning rituals.

The sleeping arrangements reminded a few of the ladies of the slee-povers they'd had when they were young girls. Annie, Nora and Sandy shared a room on the far end of the second floor, away from the couples.

Faerie and Augusta were in the guest room which had been decorated and furnished with Susan's parents in mind. As they rarely visited because of the great distance, the room was seldom used, and was as nice as any luxury suite in a fancy hotel. A huge mahogany four-poster bed waited to carry them into Dreamland. There were pillows on top of pillows and an eiderdown quilt in the vibrant colors of fall covering a down mattress. Even Augusta was impressed with the lavishness of the room. She went from one side of the bed to the other searching for steps to help them climb into the huge bed.

Just when the two of them finally decided that the room was the fan-ciest either of them had ever seen outside of Monstrosity Manor, they discovered the full bath that was hidden behind a closed door. Thinking it was just another closet Faerie opened the door to discover a sink, a toilet and a porcelain claw foot tub. When Augusta eyed the tub, she exclaimed that surely she must have died and gone to heaven. A lively discussion fol-lowed about which one should be the first to use it.

Tonight Hattie and Mattie would join their mommy in the bath, each taking a turn, with Augusta following suit with Baby Derrick. Annie and Nora were jealous and pouted so much that Faerie and Augusta finally gave in and let them each enjoy a turn. When Sandy got word of it, she timidly asked if she might have a turn as well. The only right thing to do at that point was make a schedule so that each of them might enjoy a hot bath, while not using all the hot water.

By midnight everyone was nestled and snug in their beds. Faerie and Augusta lay in the dark, chatting like teenagers. For one night, there was no talk of Reginald. Thoughts of him were as far as the east is from the west.

Faerie was having such a good time that she didn't want the night to end. "It's been a long time since I've laughed so hard and so much," she said between giggles.

"I know what you mean," Augusta offered. "I never had friends over

222

when I was growing up. We were so poor, and my mother…well, you *know* about her. Even if she'd allowed me to have friends over, I wouldn't have. I was so ashamed of her." She paused. Darkness consumed the room. "Faerie…is that a terrible thing to say? That I was ashamed of my own mother?"

Faerie turned onto her side. "Augusta, you were a child. And living that way wasn't fair to you…or to her." She took a deep breath. "I don't think it's so awful for you to feel ashamed of a shameful situation." She harrumphed. "Now *that* was terrible. What I just said was *terrible*." She took a deep, cleansing breath. "Our situations weren't so different, you know. My dad was *confused*. He was disturbed and treated us badly. I've never been sure if he understood how awful he truly was.

"As for your mother, she was trying to survive. What I find so aggravating about her situation was that she was the one who had her reputation ruined, not the men who frequented your house. Such a double standard." She bit her lower lip and thought for a minute. Then: "You and I were deprived of our childhoods. All the more reason for us to shake the dust from our feet and make certain our babies have the best life has to offer. I'm not talking about material possessions. I talking about joy-filled lives that come from loving parents."

"When you're right, you're right, Faerie." Augusta wore a wicked grin that was lost in the darkness. "Now that we've established the fact that our children will have the childhoods we *never had*, I suggest we go to sleep and dream about it. The morning will come sooner than we expect."

Faerie yawned and said, "G'night, Augusta. Sweet dreams."

Chapter Twenty-Four

Truth exists; only lies are invented.
~ George Braque

John lit the kerosene lamp on the bedside table. The clock in the hallway had just chimed three. *Three o'clock in the morning.* He moaned. Every night was the same. When he returned home he figured being in his own bed was the remedy to sleepless nights. He was sadly mistaken. He went to sleep as soon as his head hit the pillow but never stayed that way for long. He awoke in a cold sweat from dreams of a crazed man relentlessly kicking him while he lay helpless on the ground. He groaned and shook his head in frustration. Any hope of sleep was but wishful thinking.

He sat up in bed and leaned against the headboard. His mind turned to thoughts of Sandy. He always had a clear picture of her in his mind; long strawberry blonde hair, soulful eyes, that cute Southern accent. At least Reginald hadn't taken away her sweetness…her kindness. He had been foolish for avoiding her since she arrived. She'd even tried to sit with him at supper and he left lickety-split. *She probably thinks I'm a worthless varmint.* In truth, whenever she was around he went all soft inside.

He knew he'd have to do better by her in the morning, maybe save her a seat at breakfast. Spend the day…well, at least part of the day…with her. He reached over and extinguished the lamp. He scooted back down in the bed, laid his head on the pillow, and then pulled the covers up to his chin. *Close yer eyes and go to sleep. Turn off yer brain; stop thinkin'. Lord, please give me sleep, jest this one night.*

All was still and quiet as a tomb. It was almost suffocating. He felt like he was about to climb the walls. Even his skin felt like it was crawling. He tried not to think about it but after a few minutes of staring into the darkness, he was as restless as a coyote on the prowl. He sat up again and grabbed his robe from the foot of the bed and headed downstairs to the family room to pick out a book. The lights were on. He heard someone milling about. *How strange.* He shrugged his shoulders thinking one of their guests was probably unable to sleep. He continued on to the bookcase and perused the wide variety of choices before him. He smiled at the sight of the Sherlock Holmes collection his dad brought back from Arizona. He eased one of the books from the shelf and gazed at the cover thinking back to the day of his dad's homecoming. A sudden calm settled over him. He clutched the book and turned to go back upstairs.

Just as he began to ascend the stairs a voice said, "Trouble sleeping?"

He turned to see his dad standing across the room, just outside the kitchen, holding a glass of milk.

"I don't know what's wrong w' me, Dad. I jest can't sleep these days."

"Come on in the kitchen. I'll warm some milk for you. My mind is busy tonight, too. I didn't want to keep your mother up, so I came down for something to settle me down."

John nodded, searching his dad's eyes for assurance. He'd seen it there many times since he got home. Still, John kept him at arm's length even though he knew it was harsh and hurt his dad's feelings. He realized how hard Simon was trying to make things right. Be that as it may, there were times John found himself questioning even the smallest things Simon did or said. He was ashamed of his feelings. From all appearances, everybody else seemed to have forgiven Simon and was genuinely thankful he was home again. So what was *his* problem? Why couldn't he let it go and let the past be the past?

"You are definitely not in the moment, son." Simon lit a burner on the big cast iron stove. "This won't take but a minute."

John said, "I don't know what's wrong with me, Dad."

"Yes, you mentioned that before." Simon stirred the milk. "Seems to me you've had more than your share of heartache over the last year or so, and you're still trying to figure out our relationship. Isn't that about the size of it?"

John plopped down in a chair and rested his elbows on the table. He hadn't expected Simon to get right to the heart of the matter. "I'se mad at ya fer the longest time, an' then ya got yerself in harm's way an' I felt awful guilty 'bout how I was feelin'. Spent me a lotta time worryin' an' prayin' an makin' promises t' God an' spillin' m' guts t' Taffy. I want us t' be like other dads 'n boys, but it ain't never been like that with us. All I can r'member is how ya've been gone more'n ya've been here. I think mostly I'm mad at m'self fer always bein' mad at ya. I really want us t'start over, Dad. I'm tired o' bein' mad, an' I'm tired o' not trustin' ya."

Simon poured the milk from the small saucepan into a mug and set it on the table in front of John. "It's hot. Be careful."

"Thanks, Dad." He picked up the mug and cupped it in both hands. "Hot milk ain't all I need t' be careful 'bout these days. Like Mom always says, 'life is fragile'. I need t' be careful in all I do and say. My time away taught me s' much. Mainly that m' family is the most important thing in life t' me. I've jest had a troublesome time figurin' out how t' show it."

Simon felt a tug at his heartstrings. His boy was suffering and he didn't know what to do about it. They sipped their milk in silence for a while, then Simon said, "John, I don't expect you to just forget everything I put you through. And I may never be able to forgive myself for what I did that caused Reginald come after our family the way he has."

"Dad, I didn't…"

Simon waved him off. "Don't, son. Don't try to explain it away. Don't try to make light of it. I was a scoundrel. I know it; you know it; your mama knows it. If I had been an upright man, Reginald O'Keefe would never have been a part of our lives. And it's no secret he only took you to get back at me. I'm so sorry he hurt you. If I could've changed places with you, I would've." He clinched his jaw. "He had no right to hurt you or Sandy. Every single day I regret the hurt I've heaped upon my family." He choked back tears. "Oh, son, I just love you so much. I can't stand this wedge between us. I can't take back everything that's happened, but I can do everything in my power to make sure it doesn't happen again. I wish you could believe me."

John's chin began to quiver as tears poured like rain down Simon's face. In his entire life, he'd only ever seen his dad cry once, the day he came home on the train just a few short months ago. He could no longer hold back his emotions. Cleansing tears began to fall. He wiped them away with a sleeve from his robe. Simon reached across the table and took one of John's hands in his and squeezed. John looked up, gazing at his father through tear-filled eyes. Though his chin and lips quivered, he managed a lop-sided grin.

"I'm sorry, Dad." He wiped the tears again. "I've been…"

"You were dealt a hand no one your age should have to play. No son or daughter should be handed all the family responsibility, no matter what their age. I don't blame you for being hurt and angry, or for being leery of me."

John wiped his eyes once more and took a swig from his mug. He was touched that Simon was opening up so. He stretched his legs out under the table and crossed his feet at the ankles.

Simon continued. "On the Colorado Maiden's final voyage, I spent countless hours in my quarters below deck. Alone in my quarters, I learned a great deal about myself. I realized what a selfish, underhanded, uncaring, opinionated, self-righteous man I had become. Nothing mattered to me as long as I got what I wanted. Life was to be lived on my terms. Period.

"Before I left on that trip, your mother and I had a long talk. I wanted to give our life another shot. Though I didn't know it at the time, she had purchased some journals and put them in my bag. I discovered them when I unpacked. I recalled a conversation when she shared that she wrote down her thoughts in a journal and that it had really helped put things into perspective for her. Well, in case you aren't aware of it, your mother can be very persuasive."

John nodded and grinned. "That she can," he agreed.

Simon paused and chugged the last of his milk. Then: "I had a lot of free time on that voyage. One afternoon early on in the trip, I was sitting on my bunk flipping through the pages of one of those empty journals. Your mother's voice kept echoing in my brain, 'Just give it a try, Simon. Just give it a try.' So I did. I began to write. In the beginning, I only decided to do it just so I could honestly tell her I'd given it a try." He chuckled. "As it turned out, I had a lot to say. There were times I wrote until my hand was so cramped I thought it might never be the same again. Then one night something wonderful happened. I'd never been one to pray, but I knelt by my bunk and had a chat with God. It was a real breakthrough for me.

"Over the course of that voyage, the walls of my arrogance slowly began to crumble. The blinders fell from my eyes and I began to see myself as I really was. I can't explain it really, except to say God changed my heart. The only thing that seemed to matter was my family and making things right. I couldn't wait to get home. I wasn't fool enough to think you'd forgive me right away. I completely understood that the healing between us would take time, and I was willing to wait. I was willing to give you the time and space you needed to work it all out and learn to trust me again.

"I learned of O'Keefe's plan to have me killed soon after I boarded the train home. I was fairly certain I'd never make it home alive. I was heartbroken that you'd never see the changes God brought to my life. I hid in that quiet little town of Prescott and pretended to be someone else. I prayed for your mother and Timmy…and for you, too, son. However, I must confess that I mostly *worried* about *you*. I knew you'd take the world upon your shoulders. I also knew you'd struggle with whether or not to forgive me."

John stared at the table and counted every nick in the wood's grain from years of meals taken here day in, day out. He made circles on the surface with his index finger. "Dad," he said slowly, "I'm sorry. I'm sorry fer bein' s' mean t' ya. I've shied away from ya when all I really wanted wuz t' be by yer side ever' second after ya came home. An' then, that ol' coot took Sandy and me away an' I didn't know if I'd ever see ya agin." He dropped his head and stared at the tabletop.

Simon yawned. "The milk is starting to do its work. I can hardly keep my eyes open. How 'bout you?"

John forced a weary smile. "I'll say." There was an amiable silence.

Then: "Thanks, Dad. I…I love ya."

Simon felt that little tugging at his heart again. They stood and backed away from the table. They met in the middle of the kitchen and embraced. When they parted, an unspoken bond had been forged between father and son. They extinguished the lights and headed for the stairs. John held Sherlock Holmes close…he'd read it again, but with renewed fervor…a gift from his father. At the top of the stairs they reluctantly parted.

Lights out. Darkness enveloped the house once more.

Quiet. John soon fell into a sweet, blissful sleep.

Chapter Twenty-Five

There's no fear when you're having fun.
~ Will Thomas

Saturday morning arrived with not a cloud in the sky, promising to be a splendid day for a party. Things were abuzz inside the house as everyone dressed and had a quick bite to eat. Before long, buggies full of excited, happy folks turned from the road onto the long drive that led to the house. Troy greeted each one as they crossed the threshold onto the ranch with a fine howdy-do, while a handful of cowpokes directed the parade of guests to the parking area, where they could water and feed their horses. The excited laughter of children, young and old, filled the air. Haystacks, scarecrows, and colorful balloons were everywhere. Streamers of yellow, red, orange and green were strewn over anything that stood still. Barrels of apples and pears were placed here and there all around the yard.

The palomino's lush manes had been brushed until they were shiny and silky soft. Their tails were braided and adorned with satin ribbons. Soon the trail rides would begin. John was decked out like a range rider, complete with cowboy hat, bolo tie and leather chaps. Sandy, his assistant for the day, wore traditional Cherokee dress and turban.

"Ya sure do look perty, Sandy," John said, shuffling his feet in the dirt. "Yer ma make that dress?"

"My grandmother in Arkansas made it for me. She sent it for my last birthday. My mother's half Cherokee and Choctaw."

"I wondered 'bout that," he remarked. "She's a right handsome woman."

Sandy smiled and leaned against the corral fence. "John," she began, "I'm glad you saved me a seat at breakfast this morning."

He cleared his throat. "'Bout that, Sandy." He screwed up his face when the bright morning sunlight hit his eyes. "I've been actin' mighty strange....an' not jest t'wards you. My dad got the butt end of all m' anger." He wagged his head with his lips tightly pursed. "I've been right pitiful, that's what I've been. I ain't proud o' myself. You hafta know that, Sandy."

"It's all right," she said softly. "You and I...why, we've been through something most people will never experience, much less understand." She smiled sheepishly.

"What's that look?" he quizzed.

"I know a secret. Don't want to get my hopes up, but it's a right smart secret." She paused, looking pleased as a peacock.

"Are ya gonna spill it 'r keep me guessin'?"

"Well…" she dragged out the word. "Promise not to tell?" she begged. He nodded. "Sure, silly."

She leaned in closer to him, and then looked over one shoulder and then the other. "Sheriff Johnson came to see Daddy and me while we were loading the wagon yesterday. Seems somebody in Silverton reported seeing *our friend*. From what the sheriff said, it sounds like whoever it was gave the sheriff up there a pretty good description. He's got himself a disguise these days, pretty much the same as when we were with him, 'cept now he's got himself a pair of spectacles. The good news is that the search is back on."

John's face remained stoic. "Is that the big secret?"

She nodded slowly, disappointed with his reaction.

"Ah, now, don't go gettin' yerself in a tizzy. It's jest that my dad hired a bunch o' the deputies from the last search t' work here t' day. Sheriff Johnson will be here b'fore long, too. Now *there's* a secret for ya."

"I'll say," she sounded chipper again. "So nobody knows?"

"Not a soul. Dad was a-feared ol' Reggie might show up an' raise a raucous."

"Well, wherever he is, he needs to be caught, locked up and the key thrown far, far away." Sandy looked toward the house. "Everything looks so…*festive.*"

"Lotsa folks this year. More'n last, and maybe the year b'fore that." John watched as a young couple approached.

"How much for the trail ride?" A young man with a pretty, petite blond on his arm pulled out a pocketful of coins.

"Yer money's no good here. Everything's on the house." John said, cheerfully.

The couple looked at each other in disbelief. The young man asked, "May we ask you something?"

"Anything," John answered.

"We're new in Ridgway and don't know many folks yet. Who lives here? Any why are they so generous?"

"M' folks own the S & S. Stands fer Susan and Simon. Archer's the last name. I'm John. Mom started doin' this a few years back when lotsa folks in Ouray was havin' a rough time makin' ends meet. It went over like fireworks on the Fourth o' July, so we kept it up an' do it ever' year. Nobody pays fer nothin'. All our friends come from town t' help. And the ranch hands and their families lend a hand, too. It's a great time fer all."

Sandy stepped up and extended a hand to the young lady and introduced herself. "What brings you folks to our neck of the woods?"

"My husband, Seth, is the new pastor of the Baptist church in Ridgway. We come from Colorado Springs."

"Pastor, my mom'd skin me alive if I didn't bring 'er right on over. Stay put whilst I go an' fetch her?"

Seth smiled and nodded.

Sandy and the young couple were lost in conversation when John returned with Susan. John made the introductions and a few pleasantries followed.

Susan asked, "How did you hear about the pastorate in Ridgway?"

"I'm fresh out of seminary, Mrs. Archer. Our families make their homes in Colorado Springs. The last pastor in Ridgway moved to the Front Range after leaving here. We met him at the First Baptist Church in Colorado Springs. My folks mentioned that I had just finished seminary and the next thing I knew he was giving me the names of folks I should talk to at the church here. I sent of letter of inquiry and was surprised to hear back by telegraph in no time. One thing led to another, and in a matter of a month we found ourselves moving from one side of Colorado to the other." He smiled and shrugged his shoulders. "We're happy to be here."

"So glad you've ventured to our part of the country. I think you'll find the folks here warm and welcoming…for the most part, anyway." Susan offered her most amiable smile. Then teasingly, she said, "John, don't make these good people wait all morning for their ride. Give them the grand tour."

He tipped his hat in her direction. "Yes'm. Whatever ya say, Mom."

Soon the pastor and his wife were riding through the meadow with John and Sandy. Susan watched, sensing John seemed more like his old self. The pastor was a young man; perhaps he and John might forge a friendship. It would do him a world of good to have a friend closer to his own age. The pastor looked to be in his mid-twenties. This was definitely something she would encourage.

******

Simon and Alfred wandered here and there over the property visiting with the guests and keeping a watchful eye out for anything suspicious. Simon spotted a few men he recognized as deputies and was impressed with how well they blended in as plain clothes officers. No one would ever guess they were anything other than family men spending a day out with their loved ones. He really must remember to thank Sheriff Johnson again for the loan of a few deputies.

"Simon, I have a piece of information you might just be interested in," Alfred said nonchalantly.

"Is that so? Well, do tell." Simon motioned for Alfred to head toward the barn. When they reached it, they climbed the corral fence and planted themselves on the top wrung.

"When Sandy and I were loading the wagon yesterday, we got a surprise visit from the sheriff. He said he had some mighty good news for us. I didn't share it with you last night because everybody was having such a good time. I didn't want to chance putting a damper on things. Even though it's good news, it's still a painful subject." He removed his hat and ran fingers through his hair, then put it back on. "Somebody spotted Mr. O'Keefe up in Silverton a couple of days ago and reported it to the authorities. There's a new search underway."

An astounded look passed over Simon's face. Alfred waited for a response of one kind or another. Finally, Simon said, "I'd shout for joy if I didn't think it might scare our guests half to death. I'd love to get excited about this. On the other hand, I dare not get my hopes up only to have them knocked down again. He's so shifty." Then: "By the way, thanks for keeping that on the down low last night. You're right about saving it for a private conversation. I wish I could feel a hundred percent confident about catching him."

"I know what you mean. I feel what my ma always called cautiously optimistic."

"Hmm…that's it exactly…cautiously optimistic." Simon hopped down from the fence. He took his hat in his hands and tossed it in the air, caught it, and then ran a finger around the rim. "I never thought I'd hear myself say this, but I don't have the energy to fight this battle anymore. It's all in the Father's hands." He looked to the heavens. "Alfred, one of these days, I'll tell you the long, sordid story of what brought Reginald O'Keefe into our family's life. No matter how hard I try, I doubt I'll ever be able to forget."

"Simon, no amount of talking will ever convince me you deserved what he's given you." Alfred climbed down from the fence and nodded in the direction of the house. "Let's mosey on over to the backyard and see how things are going over there."

As they made their way, a wagon full of excited folks were just beginning a hayride across the meadow over to the site Troy had set up against the ridge on the far side of the ranch. Two of the ranch hands' wives were on board leading the group in a sing-a-long. Alfred said, "Looks like they're having a grand time. What do you say, Simon? Feel like taking a ride out Troy's way with our ladies later in the day?"

"I'm supossed to be charge of the hayrides, but oh well. It's only fair to warn you, my singing may put the horses in a foul mood. Might make them pick up speed and cheat our guests out of a long, leisurely ride." He chuckled.

"Well, to my way of thinking, there's an easy solution, my friend. Don't sing." Alfred nudged Simon in the arm with his elbow. They grinned at each other.

"We'd all be better off for it," Simon added. The two men snickered as they reached the backyard "I need to check on the games. Come on.

Albert smiled and offered up a little wave when he saw Augusta and Faerie and their babies lounging on a pallet on the back porch. They were dressed for the elements as a cool breeze was beginning to come down from the mountains. He poked Simon in the ribs and pointed, who in turn tipped his hat and the two took a detour over to the porch.

"Little ones, say hello to Mr. Simon and Mr. Alfred," Faerie said playfully. With Hattie sitting beside her, and Mattie on the pallet next to Baby Derrick and Augusta, Faerie

"Simon tipped his hat and said, "Good morning again, ladies….and babies. Anything you need?" Augusta was suddenly very attentive to Derrick, which didn't go unnoticed by anyone. "How about you, Augusta? Is there anything I can get for you?"

Her face turned crimson. "N-no. Thank you, S-Simon," she stuttered. "I'll probably take Derrick in soon. The breeze is a getting a little chilly."

"Me, too. Don't want these wee ones to catch a cold." Faerie smiled sweetly. There was a silence as a shout of glee came from one of the apple dunking stations. "Sounds like somebody is having a good time."

Alfred said, "Simon and I have walked the entire grounds and from what we've seen, *everyone* is having a good time. I know I am. And Washie? Why, she's more relaxed than I've seen her in a month of Sundays."

Augusta sat up straight and stretched her back. "I'm not as young as I used to be. My back is paining me something fierce after sitting here on the floor." As pleasantly as she knew how, she said, "Thank you, Simon. I'd like that very much." Then: "For now, I must get this little one back inside." The others watched as she gathered Derrick and his things and slowly disappeared inside the house.

Simon said, "Alfred, remember when I told you that one day I'd share things with you? Well, I'm afraid that fair lady is part of the story. I believe I owe a large portion of my survival to her."

Faerie nodded. "Yes, Simon, you do. Even so, she's trying to move past it, as are we all."

He dropped his head and stared at his boots before repeating the words in agreement, "As are we all."

Alfred chuckled nervously. "I can't say anything about Miss Augusta except she's one strong lady. We've all had our dealings with her husband. And you see, that's the thing that mystifies me the most. He was her *husband*. I can't imagine what her life was must've been like."

Faerie wagged her head and smirked. She thought of how to respond. Pulling her thoughts together, she replied, "Reginald wasn't always the way he is now. He was gentle and kind and sweet. And that's the man she grew to know and love. Somewhere along the way, something inside him snapped. Something none of us will ever understand. I know he's dangerous. I also believe he isn't well. Doc Fisher is working under the assumption that Reginald is mentally ill. Having said that, he still needs to be caught and dealt with. I just hope and pray he gets the help he so desperately needs. And I pray it happens before he has the opportunity to hurt someone else."

Simon moved over to the porch swing and took a load off, laying his hat on his lap. "I'll never understand it as long as I live. Then again, maybe it isn't necessary that I understand. All I know is there's some things worth fighting for and my family is that thing for me. Long before O'Keefe came along I was ready to throw in the towel. I was ready to give up everything I'd ever known…everyone I'd ever loved." He paused. "I'm mortified to think how horribly I treated Susan and the boys. As painful as it was, Augusta's wedding was a turning point in my life. It was a real slap in the face. Seeing the reality of the situation that day forced me to come to my senses." He choked up a bit then continued. "Soon afterward I left on that fateful trip. I promised Susan I would come back and fight for my family. I never expected to be sidetracked for almost a year. More than that, I was desperately afraid they'd written me off long before my return. I certainly never gave them any reason to want me here." He stopped and gave Faerie an appreciative smile. "If not for you, Faerie, I might still be in Prescott, Arizona, working the flower garden at the church, waiting for news that it was safe to come home."

Alfred's eyes became as big as saucers. "You mean to tell me Faerie found you?"

"She sure did. And I am forever in her debt." He gazed at her once again and then smiled from ear to ear, deciding it was time to liven things up. "I'd say that's good enough reason to throw a big old party."

They laughed together. The babies squealed with delight in response. Simon suddenly felt carefree and light. They watched as people milled about, laughing and talking, munching on snacks, gathering baskets of baked goods and jams and jellies. Simon relished the time, thankful to be a part of the thing that gave Susan such joy. For a brief moment, his heart ached as he thought of the many festivals he'd missed while sailing the Colorado Maiden to places these folks would probably never see or hear about. He surrendered that ache to the Father. He was here now, and that was all the really mattered. He felt a happiness all his own. He looked around at all she'd planned and brought to fruition. He was in awe of her. What a fool he'd been; he'd come so close to losing her and the boys forever .He'd been given a second chance with his family. Some might call it fate, others luck, but he knew the truth. He knew it was grace, pure and simple.

During those long months in Prescott he'd spent many hours pondering the meaning of life and the games people play in pursuit of happiness. He reminisced over the life he and Susan had lived together. When he married Susan he loved her, as much as he knew how. Life had been good to them. In every way imaginable they'd been blessed beyond measure. Whatever they touched seemed to prosper. Susan believed everything they had belonged to God. It angered Simon when things they worked so hard for finally fell into place and she turned around and gave God the praise for *their* accomplishments. Oh, sure, she'd loved him and had always been proud of him; of that, there was never any doubt. She'd blessed him with two fine sons. But it wasn't enough; it was *never* enough. He always wanted more. As much as he hated to admit it, more than anything he'd resented her relationship with God…how she talked with him as if he was right next to her.

Over time Simon became a selfish man. He lived only for himself. He took what he wanted when he wanted it. Never had he cared enough for others to think his actions might hurt them and that went double for Susan and the boys. No longer was his dream of ranching enough to keep him satisfied. Before long, wanderlust set in. Leaving his family behind, he took a journey to the California coast and fell in love with clipper ships. He had to have one. Upon his return home, he informed Susan he'd purchased one and planned to sail around the world. He knew she wasn't happy about it. Nevertheless, her job was to keep silent and let him be, which she did all too well.

One particular evening in Prescott, he sat alone in his second story rented room and listened to the booming of thunder as it came over the mountains. Rain fell in torrents. He feared the town might be washed away. The storm continued well into the night and into the wee hours of the morning. Lighting his kerosene lamp, he sat at the tiny desk next to the window and began to write in his journal. He recalled a stormy night much like this one on the Colorado Maiden's final voyage back to California. He had cried out to God asking forgiveness. He wanted to be the kind of man Susan would be proud to have by her side. He was ashamed that he'd actually demanded her silence rather than her opinion. What he didn't know, what he *couldn't* know, was that she'd always been proud of him. She'd kept silent; however, her silence hadn't fallen on deaf ears. It was in those times that she offered unspoken prayers to the Father on his behalf. Alone in Prescott, his wanderlust had morphed into a longing for home and family. A roar of thunder and crack of lightning brought his head down on the desk where he sobbed himself to sleep.

Thinking back, it seemed like a whole other lifetime ago. Had he discovered the meaning of life? He surveyed his surroundings and realized he'd discovered it years ago, but was too blind... or possibly too *arrogant*...to see it. He recalled walking in on a conversation between John and Susan that, at the time, had stunned him. "Dad r'minds me of an ol' rooster, struttin' 'round the place, all puffed up an' actin' all proud o' hisself." Simon chuckled. *Truer words have never been spoken,* he thought.

"What's so funny?" Susan stepped up from behind and wrapped her arms around his neck.

"You'd best be my wife or we're both in trouble!" he teased.

She dropped her arms and he turned to face her. "Where's your sidekick?" she asked.

"George or Alfred?"

"Both, I guess," she replied, giggling. "They admire you so. They're good friends for you, Simon."

"I think so, too. About the friends, I mean." He scratched his cheek. "I'm getting hungry. What time is it?"

"Time for lunch. That's why I came looking for you. There's a roast chicken sandwich with all the fixings in the kitchen with your name on it." She held out her hand. He took it.

"Fair lady, it would be my pleasure to share my sandwich with you." He bent down and gave her a smooch on the mouth right out in front of everybody.

A few of the ranch hands got an eye full and began whooping and hollering. "Yeah, boss," came one very loud voice of encouragement.

"Back to work, you lazy cowpoke!" Simon teased. The air filled with the electric sounds of laughter. He leaned closer to Susan and said, "I'm the most blessed man alive."

She beamed. "I'm glad you didn't say the luckiest man 'cause luck's got nothin' to do with it."

******

The day passed in a flash and before they knew it, darkness was upon them. The Archer's family room was filled to capacity with tired bodies and cranky babies. Annie and Nora took the babies upstairs and put them all in the tub, which acted on them like a tonic. Once fed, bathed, and in their nightclothes, they were soon in their beds fast asleep. Nora volunteered to sit with them while Annie relaxed in the tub. Both were tired and sleepy from an exciting and fun-filled day.

Downstairs in the kitchen, everyone munched on leftovers and hot bread and butter with strawberry jam. Even though everybody seemed worn out, there was lots of chatter around the table about the day's activities. John and Sandy sat by the fireplace with their snacks, talking animatedly. Susan and Washie watched them from the kitchen.

"It wouldn't bother me one iota if those two had feelings for one another." Susan blew on her mug of hot tea and took a tentative sip. "Ooh-wee, that's hot!" She put down the mug and gently put her hand to her mouth.

"Sandy was worried that John was having trouble coming to grips with …*everything*. Good to see him more like his old self." Washie lifted her shoulders, giving her tired muscles a needed stretch.

"He's been moping around, sulking, mostly staying to himself. He didn't talk to anybody but Taffy. Guess it's easy to talk to somebody who can't talk back." Susan stirred a dollup of honey into her tea. "Then suddenly, like a miracle, he's turned the corner and a new and improved John appeared just a day or so ago. Whatever happened, I'll take it and be grateful."

"Sandy got back to normal right away, it seems like. I'm still not there, but I'm working on it." Washie popped a bite of pumpkin bread in her mouth. "Never had anything like this before we came here."

"Pumpkin bread? It's a staple around here." Susan yawned. "I can barely keep my eyes open and it's only a little after seven."

"You should go to bed. Get some rest," Washie said. "I'm not too far behind you. What a day!"

"Did you have a good time? Was it worth all the work?" Susan asked.

"Best day in a long time. I don't know when I've ever had such a good time. Back home we had gatherings, but our community was very small.

We lived on a farm owned by a most benevolent man who loved the native people. Many Cherokee and Choctaw families live there. With such a mix of folks, something's always going on. Everyone shared their culture's celebrations." Then: "I'm the first to leave since our family first settled in the Ouachita Mountains. I miss it terribly."

Susan said, "I'd love to meet your family. I suspect Marcus and Faerie would like to meet them as well. Marcus misses his family. He's begged his parents to come for a visit, but his mother always puts him off. She doesn't stray too far from the reservation."

Washie shrugged. "It's understandable. Marcus has done well for himself in the White Man's world." Then: "Is his father a teacher at the Indian Seminary in Tahlequah?"

"I believe so. That's where he and Mrs. Wright met. He's a few years older than she."

"It would be nice if they would come and see for themselves how well Marcus has done. Maybe someday…"

Susan yawned again. "I'm sorry, Washie. I can't stop yawning. I'm going to call it a night. I don't think anyone will miss me. Some of the younger girls still seem pretty wound up from all the activity. I'll nudge Clara and ask her to solicit their help in straightening up the kitchen."

"Good idea. I believe I'll head upstairs, too. I should find my better half and let him know. He'll more than likely want to stay up awhile and jaw with the menfolk. He seldom gets such an opportunity. We don't have neighbors close by for him to pal around with." Then: "Do you mind if I borrow a book from your library? I doubt I'll get much read before I drift off, but I like to read before lights out."

"Take anything you like. I have some Jane Austen or Charles Dickens. Those are two of my personal favorites."

"I think I'll try Miss Austen. Do you have *Pride and Prejudice?*"

"Yes ma'am," Susan answered cheerfully. "Seems I heard Augusta say she especially loves Miss Austen as well."

"I surely do," a voice chimed from one of the over-stuffed chairs by the fire.

The ladies giggled and made their way past John and Sandy and sat on the hearth. "I wondered where you were." Susan stretched her neck first one way and then the other.

"After I fed Derrick his supper, I drifted off for a little while, but I'm wide awake now." Then: "Susan, I hope you don't mind that I grabbed a book from the shelf." She held up the book, a copy of Herman Melville's *Moby Dick.*

Washie harrumphed. "That's quite an undertaking for one evening, Augusta."

"I suppose. Maybe I can pick it up again the next time I come out, Susan?" she asked, looking hopeful.

The expression on Augusta's face had just the effect she intended. Susan reached over and gave her knee a little pat. "Anytime," she said warmly. "I'm enjoying getting to know you. Maybe you could teach me how to knit?"

"We talked about that before, didn't we?" Augusta tilted her head to one side and scratched an itch.

"Yes, we did, but decided to wait until after the festival." Susan sat up straight. "It's after the festival!" she exclaimed cheerfully.

Augusta smiled broadly, touched that anyone would ask anything of her. She could get used to this friend business.

"You look as pleased as punch, girl. What are you thinking?" Washie asked.

Augusta's face reddened. "I was just thinking how sweet life feels right now. I have *friends, real friends.* I've never had friends before I came to Ouray,"

Susan pursed her lips and felt a lump growing in her throat. She willed it to go away and said, "I know you've had a tough life, Augusta. The good news is that there's a whole houseful of people here who love you. Seems to me that when a person's had a hard life, trust would be a real issue. I can see how it might be difficult for them to believe people could love them without wanting something in return. You know, a *payback.*" She smirked and gazed up to the ceiling thinking about what she said. Then: "Does that make sense to you?"

Augusta dropped her eyes briefly and then said, "I suppose it does. I grew up thinking nobody loved me. Later I went to work as a…well, let's just say, I chose a line of work that pleased others and all I got in return was an occasional black eye from a client, or a nasty comment here and there from folks in town who looked down on me."

"That's all in the past now. You're a special lady, and stunningly *beautiful* to boot, I might add. God sent you our way so we could love you. Let us do it. You hear?" Susan meant every word…and Augusta knew it.

A few minutes of amiable quiet passed. Washie eventually stood and stretched. "Ladies, I have to go to bed." She grinned slyly. "And I'm not even going to find Alfred to let him know. He knows I poop out fairly early most nights." She winked. "See you in the morning." She grabbed *Pride and Prejudice* from the bookshelf and trekked slowly up the stairs.

"Have a good rest." Susan called up after her. She wasn't too far behind. She was dead on her feet and could hardly keep her weary eyes open. Soon she was safe within the confines of the quiet retreat she and Simon shared. Using the bedside steps, she climbed into the enormous feather bed and snuggled between fresh, crisp sheets and a thick eiderdown comforter. Laying in the dark, she listened to the oddly comforting sounds of muffled voices and laughter wafting up from below. This was the life she loved: a houseful of friends, all comfortable and enjoying themselves, and her family safe, happy, and under one roof. Yawning, she pulled the covers up to her chin and quickly drifted into a deep, restful sleep.

Chapter Twenty-Six

Friends and good manners will carry you where money won't go.
~ Margaret Walker

Simon, George and Alfred lingered at the kitchen table long after the others called it a night. Clara put on one last pot of coffee, leaving it with the men to watch. When they were certain everyone was in bed, they ceased idle chit chat and got down to business.

"He wasn't here today. We know that for sure," George stated, emphatically.

"He wasn't on the main property. That's all we really know, George. He's proven himself far too slick for the likes of us. He coulda been anywhere, hiding in plain sight." Alfred lifted one brow and stood to his feet. He walked to the stove and poured a cup. "Anybody else want some?" He held the pot up. Cups lifted around the table. As he circled the table, refilling cups, he said, "I don't want to sound contrary, but this guy's like a…" He snapped his fingers trying to pull the word out of his brain. "What do you call them things? A chameleon….changes all the time." He held the pot up and said, "Empty again. Well, that's that." He set the pot on the back burner and went back to the table.

Simon nodded and said, "Maybe so, but even a leopard can't change its spots. There are some things that never change. He'll always be the same height; he'll always have those dark, brooding eyes and dark skin. Why, any of us could spot him. We just need to pay attention, that's all. If he alters his appearance, it might give us reason enough to second guess whether it's him or not. Heck fire, even if we think we've spotted him but aren't sure…well…the sheriff is open to any and all possible sightings." Simon laced his fingers, resting his hands on the table.

"Alfred, did Sheriff Johnson give any indication when the law up in Silverton might start looking for O'Keefe?" George asked.

"He said they were going to start looking; he didn't say when. Since he's wanted for killing a man, don't you think it would be more sooner than later?"

Simon dropped his head.

"What is it?" George asked.

"Marcus…and Augusta. I can't imagine how all this makes them feel. They're the two who knew him best." Simon said solemnly and then smirked.

"Or thought they did," offered George.

"Or *thought* they did," echoed Simon. He cleared his throat. "Until this is over and done, our families aren't safe. He's unpredictable and reckless and we'd be naïve to think he's over his need to punish us."

George heaved a big sigh. "I've lived with the man. I never found him to be overly friendly, but there were times when he showed a sensitivity I didn't expect. When Myra and I moved to Colorado to work for the O'Keefes, we thought we'd struck gold. That was in July, right after they wed. By Thanksgiving, the house was upside down. He sulked and stayed locked in his office all hours of the night drinking bourbon and talking to himself." He harrumphed with a smirk. "Now we know he was talking to the Voices in his head. By Christmas he was stark-raving mad, lashing out at poor Miss Augusta or Myra or just anybody who got in his way. I've never seen a man treat his wife as poorly as he treated Miss Augusta. There were times I wanted to wring his neck. If it weren't for her, I probably would have. The day he hurt my wife…well, I think his actions speak for themselves. What he did that night ended my association with him." He shook his head in disgust.

Alfred took a big swig of hot coffee and immediately wished he'd been more careful. "My tongue! I burned my tongue!" he moaned. "It'll never be the same."

Simon and George grimaced and moaned in mutual empathy. "Done that a hundred times at least. Myra always calls it drinking with gusto," George added.

Simon chuckled as he mindlessly stirred his own cup of brew.

Alfred pushed the coffee aside and stepped into the kitchen for a cool glass of water. "The problem is the distance between our places," said Alfred. "We aren't in close enough proximity to come to one another's aid quickly, should the need arise. If a situation came up, like what happened when O'Keeffe showed up at our house acting crazier than a stink bug, what would we do? We hafta keep our families safe." He downed his water and put the glass in the sink. Then: "High alert. The best thing is to be on high alert. Back in Arkansas, we lived in a small community of Indians and Whites. Everybody got along and helped each other out. Basically looked out for one another. How in the world can we do that if we're spread out all over the county?"

Simon raised a brow and made a clucking sound. "Well, fellas, all I can say is keep your rifles loaded and at the ready. That old coot has it out for us. I worry about Faerie and her crew. George, I don't need to tell you that it all falls on your shoulders to keep *that* household safe. Marcus is gone so much, I know he'd appreciate the help."

"You got that right!" he agreed, meaning it. Then: "What about Miss

Augusta and the baby? Oh, and Nora? Scares me t' death t' think about what he might do t' *them* should the temptation arise."

"Deputy Dan!" Alfred said flatly.

George livened up at the mention of the name. "That's right! I'll be hogtied. I forgot about Deputy Dan." He stood and stretched before wandering around to the other side of the table and over to the icebox. "I need something for a sweet tooth."

Simon pointed to the bread box. "Clara hid some pumpkin bread in there. Have at it."

George took the loaf from the box and sliced half of it, putting the slices on a plate. He set the plate in the middle of the table and said, "Coffee and sweet bread late at night. We'll never get to sleep now."

"Probably just as well. I've got a feeling in my gut that things aren't as they seem around here." Simon took a swig of his now lukewarm brew. "Something's been eating at me all day. I can't quite put my finger on it." He shrugged. "It might be nothing. Then again, it might be something… something *big.*

"I know what you mean, buddy, 'cept I've been thinking that for more'n a year now." With a smirk, George shrugged his broad shoulders. "Sitting here, right now, I've kinda got the willies." He suddenly broke out in an ear-to-ear grin showing big white teeth.

Alfred and Simon shared a quizzical glance. "What?" Alfred said, trying not to laugh at George's silly expression.

George chuckled. "Did I ever tell you about the night Reginald locked the door to his office and wouldn't come out for beans?"

"No. Do tell," Simon urged.

"He was really fit to be tied that night. I don't recollect what had him so wound up, but it doesn't matter 'cause he was always wound up about *something.* Anyway…Myra and I had just settled in for the evening. She'd been on her feet all day and was dead tired. It was nice and quiet in our little cottage when *bam.* Loud, hard knocking commenced at the door. Scared me so bad I almost left for the Great Beyond without packing my bags."

Simon slapped the table and guffawed.

Alfred spit coffee all over himself and everything else in close proximity. "Good grief," he said and went to the sink for a rag to clean things up.

"Miss Augusta was on the other side of the door looking a fright. 'Please come,' she said. 'He's locked himself in the office and won't come out, won't answer me, won't stop that infernal chatter' she said. So we all trotted through the yard and the kitchen and on to the office. She banged on the door and told him he'd best open the door or we'd take it right off the hinges." He pinched a bite from the sweet bread and popped it in his mouth.

"Did he open the door?" Alfred asked, enthusiastically. He was ready for a good story, especially if it made Reginald look a fool.

"Well, now, Alfred, do you think you can contain yourself? I mean, I don't want another shower right yet." George winked and grinned while the others snickered.

"Sorry about that, guys." Alfred blushed. "Go on, George, tell us. Did he open the door or not?"

"What do you think?" He paused. Then: "Of course not. Nothing's ever that easy with him." He wagged his head back and forth, and then gulped his now cold coffee. "Ugh! Nothin' like cold coffee." He pushed the cup away and folded his arms on the table.

"Anyway," he continued, "Miss Augusta was like a little lost lamb, but she held her ground like a mama cougar. 'Look here,' she said, 'you come right on outta there or we're coming in.' There was no reply. We stayed as quiet as we could and listened for any sign of what might be happening on the other side of the door. It was so quiet you could hear a pin drop. Miss Augusta put her ear to the door and then stepped away just shaking her head, and those big eyes of hers flashing with anger. Myra and I gave each other what-do-we-do-now looks. Well, the three of us were standing there like knots on a log when all of a sudden Myra perked up and whispered for me to go fetch m' toolbox. When I came back, Miss Augusta was standing next to the office door with her hands on her hips and one eyebrow raised…like she does when she's peeved." The men knew all too well about that raised eyebrow thing she did. "Then she said, 'Well, what are you waiting for? Get to it.' So I commenced taking the door off its hinges."

"You actually took the door off its hinges?" Alfred asked, chuckling.

George nodded. "Lord A'mighty, it was tough. Whoever pinned those hinges meant for them to stay put until Kingdom Come…and *then* some. I took a screwdriver and mallet and set my jaw just right, like my pa always did, and took to aiming at the first pin. Nothin'. No, sir, it wouldn't budge. But I wasn't about to let a silly hinge get the best of me. After all, the women folk were there and I didn't want to embarrass myself in front of 'em. So, I told myself to take control of the situation. I took a deep breath and with one quick strike I hit the pin just right and about knocked both the hinge and door facing off. I lost my balance and the ladder went to swaying with me on it. 'Gall-darn-it,' I said out loud. I was thinking much worse but it's not polite to say such nonsense in the presence of ladies."

Alfred lowered his head and snickered. "Did you fall off?"

"Nope. My beloved grabbed hold of the ladder and leaned into my legs and just like that," he said with a finger snap, "the ladder was perfectly still. I peeked down at her and gave her a wink and a nod and went right back to that blasted pin. 'Look here, you stinking pin, I ain't giving up now so you might as well.' I gave it one more knock in the head and out it flew, landing on the floor and rolling so fast that Myra had to trot along to catch it before it landed in the fireplace. I'll tell you what! I thought to myself that if that bullheaded so and so didn't come out of the office like a gentleman after all that trouble, I'd skin him alive. Thank goodness, the other two pins weren't as inclined to put up such a fight. When the last pin was finally out, I turned around to Miss Augusta and I said, 'All right, Miss Augusta, that's it.' We took the door down and what did we see?" He wiggled his brows and started laughing.

"Well? What *did* you see?" asked Simon, amused with Georges' story-telling abilities. "I'm dying to hear how somebody actually got Reginald's goat. Less laughing and more talking, please."

Once George stopped laughing he continued. "You're gonna love this! He was as contrite as a little kid who'd gotten caught playing a game of marbles for keeps on the school yard. He made excuses and said he was only joshing and what was the matter with us anyway that we couldn't take a joke. In the end, he came out and went straight to bed. Miss Augusta told us the next morning that he was truly embarrassed about his behavior. Said his *pride* wouldn't allow him to open the door. I'd have made him put the door back up by himself, except I'd have had to show him how and in the end it was just easier to do it m'self." He laughed and shook his head.

"I wish I could've been a fly on the wall," Simon replied.

"Hard to imagine that snake ever feeling contrite about anything, es-pecially what with all those racket going on in his head." Alfred yawned. "I mean, can you imagine? Hearing that nonstop all day, all night? It's enough to drive you..."

"Crazy?" Simon finished Alfred's thought.

Just then a quick, harsh wind whipped around the house. At the same time they heard the palominos neighing from the barn. "Best go check that," Simon said flatly.

The men grabbed their jackets from the hanger on the back wall and scooted out the door, each carrying a pistol lodged in their belts. About that time, one of the horses went flying down the drive with a rider hun-kered down with his face turned away from them.

"Hey, there!" called out Troy, who'd come running in the direction of the barn. It was too late. One of Simon's prized palominos had been stolen. Even if they did saddle up and ride out, the chance of catching the thief in the middle of the night was next to nothing.

"What are you doing out this time of night?" Simon asked Troy.

"Couldn't sleep. Something just didn't feel right."

"Interesting. We just had that same conversation." Simon rubbed his eyes and said, "Let's go see if anything's missing besides the horse."

After a general search with nothing but a kerosene lamp, the only missing things besides the horse were a saddle and a blanket. Oddly enough, Simon did find something interesting in the missing creature's stall: a pair of wire-rimmed glasses lay in the hay. "I guess there's one thing to be thankful for here. The thief didn't take Taffy. John would've been heartbroken." Simon looked around the barn, feeling violated. He tossed around the idea of whether or not to share with the men the news that O'Keefe's latest disguise included a pair of wire-rimmed glasses.

******

Sunday morning came bright and early. Despite reports of sleeping well, many were still tired, but insisted it was a *good* tired, the kind that comes from a job well done, or a good time being had by all. Most of the cleanup began on Saturday evening as soon as the last guest had passed through the ranch archway on their journey home. Still, there was a good amount left to do. Every last man on the ranch chipped in and worked to set things back in order, while Clara and the ladies were married to the kitchen preparing beef stew and big cakes of cornbread for lunch.

By mid-afternoon, not a hint of anything remained of the fine hoedown that had livened up these grounds less than twenty-four hours before.

Simon, Alfred, and George agreed that for now it was best not to inform the others of the theft. They particularly worried that the women would fret and be unable to enjoy a peaceful ride home for fear of meeting the thief along the way, should the news be shared before their departure. Simon would tell Susan privately after their guests were well on their way back to Ouray. He didn't know for certain the thief's identity, but believed the culprit to be O'Keefe. If it was, his usual habit of behavior was to avoid groups of people at all costs. Even so, Simon found great solace in knowing the group was traveling together, and that the men were armed, if confronted with trouble along the way.

He and Susan sat down at the kitchen table and relaxed after their friends were gone. She took a deep breath and stretched her neck. "Want a cup of tea?" she asked.

He nodded. "Do we have any peppermint?"

She met his gaze and looked into his eyes. Slowly, but surely, the light was returning and she was seeing the man she had loved all these years in a new and different way….through the eyes of forgiveness. "Uh-huh. I picked some up at the mercantile on our last supply run." She wearily padded behind the counter and filled the kettle with water then placed it on the stove. "Won't be but a minute," she said, as she grabbed the tin of tea from the counter and the teapot from the cabinet.

"Come and sit. You look exhausted." Simon smiled faintly, feeling a combination of fatigue and worry. "There's something I need to tell you."

That's never good, she thought. She sat and laced her fingers together, resting her arms on the tabletop. "So…spill it!"

He laughed and reached over and lovingly lay a hand on her cheek. "It's not all that bad. And, no, I haven't done anything wrong…and neither have the boys." He chuckled again. "I just didn't want to say anything while our friends were still here. No sense worrying or frightening anybody."

"Simon, you're killing me. What's wrong?" Her pitch was getting higher and she was twirling a lock of hair like nobody's business.

"Calm down, dear. It's all right." He sighed. "Last night the menfolk stayed up and were talking here at the table when all of a sudden we heard the horses neighing. We decided to go out and check on them and just as we got to the front yard we saw one of the palominos with a rider headed down the drive lickety-split."

Her hands flew to her mouth and her eyes became as big as saucers. "Oh no! Somebody stole one of the horses?"

"And a saddle and blanket. We decided to keep it to ourselves so your lady friends wouldn't be frightened."

"We, being you, Alfred, and George?" she asked.

"And Troy. He was out walking and almost got pummeled by the horse."

"Gracious!" she breathed. "Who would do such a thing?"

"Woman, you are far too trusting. Don't get me wrong. It's just that not everyone is as honest and good as you."

With a pouty look, she waved him off. Then, as if a stout realization hit her smack dab in the face, she sat up straight and said in a low voice, "You don't think…"

He lifted a brow and nodded, biting his lower lip. "I most certainly do." He reached to the center of the table and lay a hand atop his wife's laced fingers. "Don't worry, hon. He's running. We know that. For the first time since all this started he's actually using disguises. And guess what we have? A pair of glasses was found in the stall…just like the ones the sheriff said he was using."

She swallowed and slowly shook her head. "What if he…"

"Stop it. Stop it right now," he chided. "He's panicking. He's made one mistake by being seen by someone who's known him for a long time. He'll make another. He's getting sloppy. Just hide and watch. It won't be long now. I mean, how could it be?"

"I'll tell you how. He's as sly as a fox."

"No, he isn't. Think about it." The kettle on the stove whistled and he got up. "I'll get this. You just sit and let me wait on you for a change."

"You won't get any argument from me," she said, rubbing the back of her neck.

"I know that neck thing of yours. Every time you become stressed you get a little something going on back there. Am I right?"

"You are." She continued to massage the tight muscles as Simon busied himself tea preparations. As he sat the pot and bowl of sugar on the table, she commented playfully, "You're pretty good at that. If we don't make it at this ranching business, you could get a job as a waiter."

"Very funny." He placed cups and saucers on the table and then sat down at his place. "I was just thinking about something. If O'Keefe took our horse and saddle, he might get the noose."

"You're probably right. It's a shame when horse thievery is a greater crime than taking a man's life. I've heard many a tale about that. I've even heard there are times when the ones doing the searching didn't even wait for a judge; they hung the thief right there on the spot where they found him."

"And why are we talking about this?" The very thought of hanging made his skin crawl.

"Hey, you brought it up." Then: "Are you going to tell the sheriff about this?" she asked. "You should, you know. Reginald's taken enough from us already."

He searched his wife's eyes to see what he could see. "Listen to me, Susan. Don't let Reginald steal your joy. There's no denying he's taken a great deal from us. Even so, if we let him steal our joy, we've got nothing inside but an empty heart. You, better than most, know about true joy and from where it comes. Don't let him rob you of it."

She frowned, feeling conviction. "I'm sorry, Simon. I'm just so very tired of it all." She wiped her eyes with the backs of her hands. "Tea?" she managed to croak.

Chapter Twenty-Seven

Complete success alienates a man from his fellows,
but suffering makes kinsmen of us all.
~ Elbert Hubbard

Faerie sat at her dressing table and stared at her reflection in the mirror. She was lonely for Marcus and counting the days, hours, and minutes until his return. She grumbled at the early signs of crow's feet, as if the very sound would cause them to vanish, leaving her face youthful, captivating and the envy of all women of a certain age. In all honesty, she marveled there weren't more lines on her face; the climate was so very dry in these Rocky Mountains.

One by one, she carefully removed the pins that held her hair in place until a pile of them lay in front of her on the vanity. Her hair was thick, natural curly, and past her waist. Most women of the day had long, luxurious locks which they wore piled on the tops of their heads. The only problem with hers was that she'd recently begun to experience headaches and was certain it was because her hair was so thick and heavy. She'd noticed the headaches were worse when she wore her hair up. She scooped up the pile of hairpins and put them in the small velvet-covered box in the top drawer. She began to brush her hair. It felt good to run the brush through her thick mane. The tensions of the day seemed to fall away with each stroke.

Would it be terribly scandalous if she were to cut her hair? Would the ladies in town think her tacky or outrageously disrespectful? She wondered why it mattered so much how women wore their hair. More than that, why was it anybody else's business? Most of the women she knew lived with the notion that a woman's hair was her glory. Did that mean she could never cut it, even if a shorter, less cumbersome style might offer even the tiniest amount of relief from the headaches? Only a few inches off the length might very well make an incredible difference in how she felt. She brushed at a turtle's pace, staring trance-like into the mirror as she tossed the dilemma around in her head. Oh, the woes of being a proper Victorian woman!

Suddenly, she sat up tall and straight as an interesting thought occurred to her. A smile began to take shape, crinkling the lines around her eyes that she'd only just seconds before scrutinized. She said to herself, "Washie's hair is lovely and all she does is wear it in a long braid down her back. Why can't I do the same? I could have a few inches taken off the length and wear a braid." She liked the idea. She giggled mischievously. "No one would even notice my hair had been cut if I wore a braid now and then."

A knock on the door startled her. "Come in."

The door was opened at a crawl by an exhausted-looking Myra. "Anything else, Faerie?"

"No, I think not." Just as Myra was about to leave, Faerie said, "Myra, how do you think my hair would look if I just wore it down in a long braid?"

Myra stepped over to the table. "Like Washie's?"

"Exactly like Washie's. My hair is so thick and heavy that wearing it up has started giving me headaches." She sighed and looked into the mirror, meeting Myra's gaze in the reflection. "I know Marcus wouldn't want me to cut my hair. If I only cut a little and wore a braid, it wouldn't be too noticeable."

"Marcus is a reasonable man. He probably wouldn't mind if you wanted to do something different with your hair. Besides, it's you he loves, not your hair." She took the brush and playfully shook it at Faerie's reflection in the mirror. "And need I remind you that it's *yours* to do with what you want?" Then: "Can you imagine the old chatterboxes around town talking about it behind your back?"

Faerie waved off the comment. "When have I ever cared what those old flour bags have to say?"

Myra laughed out loud as she began brushing Faerie's locks.

Faerie closed her eyes, enjoying the luxury. "What a treat! I feel like a princess."

They enjoyed a moment of quiet as Myra continued to brush.

"Would it be too much to ask if you would braid my hair tomorrow morning?" Faerie eventually asked, pleadingly. "Just to try it out?"

"I'd be glad to. Besides, it will probably take a lot less time than the way you usually style it."

As she smiled at Myra's reflection, Faerie noticed dark circles under Myra's eyes. "Out," she said, playfully. "You're exhausted. Why have I never noticed how tired you are?" She held out her hand and said, "Hand over the brush and then off to bed with you. And tomorrow you must take the day off, after you braid my hair, of course." She winked at Myra's reflection, and then smiled sweetly. "George, too. You both deserve a rest."

"Are you sure?" Myra asked.

"Absolutely. There's nothing going on around here that can't wait a day or two. Marcus and Fred are due back on Thursday afternoon's train. As long as the house is in order by then, I don't see a problem. Besides, you work too hard. Don't think I don't appreciate it, because I do. Nevertheless, seeing you now, with those circles under yours eyes, I can't help but feel a trifle worried about you. I've noticed that you're thin, too."

Myra tried her best to get a word in.

Faerie wasn't having it. She put her hand up in defiance and said, "It's settled. Your bossy old employer has spoken. It won't kill you to stay home and put your feet up for just one day. I'll send lunch and dinner over so you won't have to worry about it. And if you'd like us to watch Patricia, that's fine, too." Faerie winked.

Myra smiled, giving in. "Thank you, Faerie. I'll see you in the morning…just to braid your hair."

Faerie turned in her seat and watched as Myra left the room. Something about her seemed different. Other than looking a little thinner than usual and dead tired, she couldn't put her finger on it. The door closed slowly with barely a sound. She turned back to the task at hand. After a few more brush strokes, she gathered her tresses and tied a ribbon around them at the base of her neck. Her pale blue flannel nightgown billowed as she padded across the Persian rug to bed.

The bed Marcus and Faerie shared was a monstrous thing made of dark mahogany with tall posts, massive head and footboards, and a feather mattress covered with thick, lush eiderdown quilts and white Egyptian cotton sheets. Resting against the headboard were several oversized goose down sleeping pillows. Propped in front of them, was a plethora of decorative pillows purchased on their trip to Arizona, which always ended up stacked one on top of the other at night. When she lay her weary head down at the end of the day, the billowy softness of her goose down pillows was a great comfort. She often became lost in the heavenly bliss. Using the bedside steps, she eased into bed and pulled the covers up to her nose. She snuggled in and savored the moment. The lamp on her bedside table cast a soft, golden glow over the room which she found soothing. Unable to keep her eyes open, she leaned over and extinguished the lamp. The room was instantly black as pitch and as quiet as a tomb.

No amount of wishing would bring Marcus home any faster. She closed her eyes and conjured up an image of him: his dark hair and complexion, the smile that never failed to melt her heart, the way his eyes danced with mischief. Mattie favored him. With each passing day she resembled him more. She was definitely Daddy's little girl.

She yawned and grabbed a pillow from Marcus's side of the bed. She buried her face in it and breathed in the scent of him, and then clutched it to her chest. She tried desperately to stay awake as she said her prayers.

When she awoke later, just as the clock struck one, she guessed she'd been unsuccessful.

She lay in the darkness and had a chat with God. Her head was still groggy from sleep, so she apologized to him and said she hoped he wouldn't mind if she kept it short and sweet. When she and God finished their talk, she lay in the darkness, calm and serene. She faded fast into a deep slumber.

When she awoke in the morning, she was in the same position as when she drifted off. The bed covers were smooth with no rumples or wrinkles, like she'd not moved all night. Perhaps, she thought, her little talk with Jesus in the wee hours was just what she needed.

******

Early Wednesday morning Marcus and Fred bid their final farewells to General Palmer, extending warm invitations for him to visit. Both men left Colorado Springs with more luggage than they'd arrived with, having purchased gifts for friends and loved ones. As they watched their belongings being carted to the baggage car, Fred said, "I suppose one can never have too much luggage."

"Please don't mention that to Faerie," Marcus said, followed by an almost inaudible chuckle.

"All aboard!" The booming voice of the conductor carried across the platform. Promptly travelers rushed to the cars as they waved good-bye. As for Marcus and Fred, they were weary and anxious to return to the comfort of Monstrosity Manor.

When at last the train began the trek across the mountains, Marcus relaxed. He settled in, reading the newspaper he'd picked up at the station, confident in the knowledge that his sweet Irish rose and two cherubs were waiting for him on the other side.

******

Sheriff Johnson was more than a little disgruntled to hear that one of Simon's palominos had been stolen. He too feared it was O'Keefe who'd done the deed. When Simon and Troy came in to make the complaint, he'd just about dropped his jaw on the floor to hear of something so brazen. What troubled him most was the probability of O'Keefe having been on the ranch during the festival, biding his time until he could pull off the theft. And with deputies there to boot! He'd fooled them all with his little get up. Simon brought in the spectacles he'd found in the stall. They were almost a perfect match to the ones in the drawing that was circulating. The sheriff was fit to be tied. *Jest wait 'til I git that no good...*

"Sheriff, have I got news for you!" cried Deputy Dan, red-faced and out of breath, as he burst into the office.

******

Dr. Hughes gently knocked on the examining room door as he gently pushed it open. "Good day, Mr. Walters."

The doctor quickly assessed the situation as he crossed the room. Before him lay a man who appeared to be in a fair amount of distress, his left leg wrapped in a blood-soaked shirt. He put the patient chart down on the end of the bed and introduced himself. He carefully removed the makeshift bandage to find a fresh gunshot wound. "Can you tell me what happened?"

The man grimaced and spoke through clenched teeth. "You can see for yourself I've been shot."

"Yes, well...how did it happen?"

"Never mind how it happened. Just fix it." Then: "You aren't the regular doc." He glared at the doc through dark, piercing eyes.

Statement of the obvious, he thought. "No, I've only been here a week or so. Doc Fisher put a cry out for help and here I am. This is a mighty busy hospital for such a small town." Trying to make light of the situation, he said, "You a friend of Doc Fisher?"

"Not hardly." Then: "I'm not here to make small talk. Just fix my leg and I'll be on my way."

******

Alfred stood at the front window of the café and curiously watched the goings on across the street at St. Joseph's. A man just hobbled into the hospital...a man who looked *very* familiar. Only, it couldn't be. *Could* it?

******

"Well, are ya gonna tell me, 'r what?" croaked the sheriff, not really in the mood for any guessing games.

Not even the sheriff's surly attitude was going to ruin this for Dan. "Put yer hat on, Sheriff. We're takin' a walk."

******

Dr. Timothy Hughes was a graduate of Harvard Medical School. In fact, he and Doc Fisher were only a year apart in their studies and were close friends during those lean years when supper often consisted of cornbread crumbled up in a glass of milk. As he recalled, Doc Fisher was quite gifted in the art of cornbread making. He'd wager he hadn't had any nearly as tasty since they parted ways upon Doc's graduation.

When Doc's telegram came with the offer of a position at St. Joseph's Timothy had laughed, believing it to be another of the practical jokes his friend had been so famous for back in med school. His wired response was brief: "Very funny". After three additional wires from Doc, the last of which was a desperate plea, he was finally convinced the offer was legitimate and accepted with the understanding that the pay would be nothing like what he might earn in Boston.

Since Doc's graduation, the two friends wrote frequently. Doc's letters were filled with tales of life in the Rockies and how fortunate he was to have found his place in the world. He made it sound like paradise, but Dr. Tim wasn't buying it. After one such letter, he wrote back swearing there must be something Doc wasn't telling because no place was as perfect as he made Ouray sound. He thought Doc was handing him a line or trying to butter him up in hopes of getting him on a train to Colorado. In his mind, there were visions of primitive Appalachia, and he'd always vowed he'd never ever practice medicine in such a backward place. And now…here he was…practicing medicine in the Rocky Mountains alongside his buddy. So much for *never ever.*

Unfortunately, he'd not been ready to see anything the likes of what routinely darkened the doors of this hospital. In his letters, Doc had conveniently left out the part about the locals and their sometimes less-than-civilized behaviors and idiosyncrasies, or of doctoral duty payments in the form of chickens and rabbits, or coon and beaver pelts. Once, as payment for an extremely grievous injury, he'd even been paid with the remains of the mountain lion that inflicted said injury. The pelt of that critter now hung in the hospital waiting room…an alarming sight to see in a place of healing.

The culture shock alone kept Timothy on his toes. Just when he thought he'd seen it all, another patient with some bizarre injury wandered into the hospital for treatment. In the few brief time he'd been on staff he'd treated an elderly man who chopped off one of his thumbs with an ax, a knife wound from a hunting accident, a man attacked by a black bear, a broken arm from a riding accident, a "two-timin', no good, snake-in-the-grass" husband with fresh stab wounds who'd been hauled into the emergency room by his wife (yes, she did it!), a man missing two fingers as the result of a mining accident involving a blasting cap, and now this guy…this Mr. Walters…shot in the leg, claiming he'd done it while cleaning his gun. The Wild West certainly lived up to its name.

He figured Mr. Walters took him for city folk, or thought him too young and naïve to know the difference between an accidental shooting and one in which the victim was a target. This one fit the latter category. He'd definitely been someone's target.

"Well, Mr. Walters, the good news is I can fix your leg. The bad news is you aren't going anywhere. I won't allow you to take the chance of getting an infection and having to come back and have that leg sawed off." He waited for the impact of the news to sink in.

"Sawed off?" the man bellowed. "There ain't no way you're gonna saw my leg off." The patient grabbed his coat and tried to sit up."

"Uh-uh-uh. Get yourself right on back down. You're in no shape to be traipsing off in a tither."

A triple rap on the door interrupted the conversation. "Don't move!" ordered the doctor. "I'll be right back."

******

Alfred locked the door and put up the CLOSED sign. The breakfast crowd had been about the same as usual, but the lunch crowd, now that was something to write home about. If his business kept growing, he'd need a bigger place before long. As he stood there, musing over the day's events, he was suddenly taken aback to see the sheriff and his deputy hightailing it into the hospital. Alfred's heart leaped in his chest. *Maybe that was* him *hobbling into the hospital. Only...where's the horse?*

******

Nurse Bailey closed the door to the patient's room. She and Dr. Tim stood nose-to-nose in the hallway, speaking in whispers. "It's him. I know it is."

"Did you find the deputy?" he asked.

She cautiously looked over her shoulder. Then: "Yes. He was just down the street. I suspect he and the sheriff will be here anytime."

"Good. Good job, Nurse Bailey." He swallowed. "I've never been in a situation like this. I've got to convince *Mr. Walters* he needs surgery. Wish me luck." He rolled his eyes, placed his hand on the doorknob, took a deep breath, turned the handle and pushed open the door.

"We have a room ready for you, Mr. Walters. How about this? You allow me to operate. We need to get that bullet out and fix you up. Spend the night here and if things look better in the morning, I'll set you free."

The patient studied on that. "I'll agree on one condition."

"What's that?" Dr. Tim held the chart to his chest and waited for a

259

response.

"Everybody stays out of my room except you and maybe one nurse. No visitors. No priests. Nobody."

The doctor sighed. "I think I can arrange that." *Now if that sheriff will make tracks.*

******

Sandy gathered up her books and scurried across the schoolyard. Since her return to school, she'd taken to walking to and from the café by a different route. Though it was unlikely Mr. Reginald would strike again, especially in the same place, she didn't wish to be reminded of the day her life changed forever. Even though the new route added a couple of extra blocks, she felt safer and more secure. She walked along Main Street and sometimes stopped for a stick of candy and a howdy-do with Old Man, and then past the assay office, the Bon Ton, whose yummy-looking pastries made her mouth water, the dressmaker's shop, and before she knew it, she was safe and sound at the café.

She slipped in the back door and went straight to the ice box. She grabbed a platter of sliced ham and wrapped it in a lettuce leaf.

"Daddy?" she called out, her mouth full.

"Sandy, come quick. I'm in the front."

She hurried past the counter over to where her father stood staring out the window. She nudged him and offered a silly grin to which he winked in response. "What's so interesting?" she asked.

"I've been watching the strangest comings and goings over at the hospital today."

She looked across the street and focused her attention on the entrance to the hospital as she munched. "Do tell."

"I don't know for sure, but I be willing to bet my last nickel somebody's over there a lot of people would love to see behind bars."

Sandy's face grew pale, her gaze frozen.

Alfred put a hand on her shoulder. "Are you all right?"

"I-I don't know. I-I mean, we've been w-wishing for his capture for a long time and now that they're about to catch 'im, I'm kinda nervous."

******

Augusta and Nora sat at the kitchen table discussing possible menus for a dinner party they were planning when out of the blue there was a knock on the door. Augusta took a gander at the watch pinned to her blouse.

"Three o'clock," she mused. "Are you expecting anyone?"

Nora shook her head. "We won't find out who it is unless one of us answers the door." Nora stood, shrugged her shoulders and padded to front door, humming.

As she opened the door, Dan peeked around the jamb, smiling. She giggled and wrapped her arms around his neck and kissed him on the cheek.

"What are you doing here?" she asked. "Not that I mind, of course."

He gave her a quick peck on the lips. "Have I got news for *you!* Is Miss Augusta home?" He craned his neck looking past Nora.

"Come on." She took him by the hand and led him away from the door. "She's in the kitchen."

"Is that Dan I hear?" Augusta pumped water into a kettle and placed it on the stove.

"Afternoon, Miss Augusta. Put your kettle on and have a seat. I've got some news that'll knock your socks off. Or stockings."

******

Sheriff Johnson was escorted to the doctor's lounge where he waited for Dr. Tim or his nurse to return. It would never do for *Mr. Walters* to see the law waiting around in the hallway. Despite a bum leg, the sheriff worried he just might try to crawl out the nearest window.

Several minutes passed before Nurse Bailey poked her head in the door and said, "The coast is clear."

He stood, stretched, and nervously cracked his knuckles, one by one.

She cringed and said, "That'll give you rheumatism, you know."

"Old wives tale, if you ask me…which you didn't." He grinned crossways and gave her a sly wink, which made her blush. "Care t' have a cuppa coffee with an old crotchety lawman?" He thought she was the prettiest gal since Baby Doe married Mr. Tabor over in Denver.

She blushed again, this time dropping her gaze. "That'd be real nice," she answered, barely above a whisper.

"What was that? I can't hear you," he teased. Then: "I'm only joshin' ya, Miss Bailey."

"Please call me Emma."

"Emma," he said thoughtfully. He studied on it for a minute. "I had an aunt by that name. Aunt Emmaline, we called her."

"Emmaline…that's nice."

"Nice, yes…only her name was just plain Emma. No *'line'* to it." He chuckled.

She furrowed her brow as they began to stroll down the hall. "So where did it come from?"

"One of the young'uns called 'er Aunt Emmaline one day and it stuck. Even on the tombstone directly under 'er Christian name is 'Aunt Emmaline' instead of the usual something or t'other. You know, like "singin' with the angels" or "our beloved" or some such nonsense that we never say to 'em when they was a-livin'."

"That's sweet…in an odd sort of way." With a raised brow and smirk, she wagged her head. "Let's have our coffee in there." She motioned to an open door behind the nurse's station. "I'll run down to the kitchen and fetch the coffee. Be right back."

He nodded and wandered into the room, where a couple of nurses sat gossiping in the corner. "Hope I'm not interruptin' anything, ladies."

"Oh no, sir. Come right on in and have a seat."

In no time at all, Nurse Bailey returned, carrying a tray with a carafe, sugar bowl and creamer, and two sets of cups and saucers. There was also a plate with an assortment of cookies. She set the tray and its contents on the table right in front of the sheriff.

"That's a right fancy spread, Nurse…*Emma.*"

There were giggles from the corner, which abruptly stopped when Emma flashed them a look with a raised brow for emphasis, the meaning of which read, "just you wait".

He dropped his head, hiding a smile behind one hand, impressed by her command of the situation. He cleared his throat and said, "Cream an' sugar?"

"Just cream, thank you."

He poured the strong, aromatic brew from the carafe, added a dash of cream and placed it in front of her, then did the same for himself. "How long d'ya reckon the surgery'll take?"

"Hard to say. A lot depends on what the doctor finds once he opens the wound. If it's just the bullet, it'll be quick, in and out, with a few stitches. If there's other damage to repair, like a torn muscle, for example, it could take much longer."

He shuddered. "There's a reason why some folks go into doctorin' and some don't."

She snickered. "I suppose." Then: "I've assisted Doc Fisher with a lot of operations since he's been here." She blew on her coffee and then took a sip. She smiled coyly and said, "I have a confession. I think I'd like to be a doctor, except it seems like most people don't take kindly to lady docs.

"Well, that's jest nonsense!"

"Even so, I've seen it. One of the girls I went to nursing school with decided to go to medical school. She's graduated now…and at the top of her class, I might add…and she's about half starving to death. Nobody in her little town will even darken her doors. Of course, they'll take their horse and buggy clear across the county to a decrepit old man who can't even see to stitch up a cut."

He tsk'd and said, "Don't seem right somehow, does it?"

She wagged her head while mindlessly stirring her coffee. Then: "Say, Sheriff, our patient was wearing quite a disguise. Why, he almost fooled *me*."

He furrowed his brow. "Did he give you anything besides *Mr. Walters?* A first name, maybe?"

"Luke, I believe. Why?"

"We got 'im! Boy howdy, we got 'im." He clasped her hand and gave it a little squeeze, grinning to beat the band. Seeing the confusion in her eyes, he said, "Luke is one of the Voices."

******

By twilight the town was abuzz with the news of Reginald O'Keefe's arrest. Deputy Dan had delivered the news personally to each family in town that had been directly affected by O'Keefe's vendetta.

Dan sighed. He was bone tired. His poor horse was pooped, too. They'd ridden all over the place delivering the news. They both deserved a day off.

He still had a little time before supper. Despite being tired, he was looking forward to it because he and Nora were cooking for Miss Augusta. He decided to clean up and lie down for an hour.

He was proud of the work he'd done this day; however, one question still remained. "Where is the *dadblamed horse?*"

Chapter Twenty-Eight

To what will you look for help if you will not look to that
which is stronger than yourself?
~ C. S. Lewis

"But where's my horse?"

"That's all 'e said?" Sheriff Johnson slapped his knee and took to laughing.

Dan couldn't hold it in and cackled so loud and hard that tears coursed down his face. He wiped them with the backs of his hands and snorted as another round of hysteria began. "Yessir, that's what he said. I mean, he had the funniest look on his face. I said, 'Mr. Simon, it means he's not going to bother you anymore', and he said, 'I got that part, but I want my *horse*.'"

"Well, I'll be hogtied." The sheriff shook his head and sat back in his chair, his hands laced behind his head. "It's a great day, son…a great day indeed!"

"Yessir. You got that right!" The two stood in companionable silence. Then Dan said, "I'm on my way to see, Nora. We're cooking for Miss Augusta night. Looks like there's a lot to celebrate."

"Ye'r darn tootin'!"

******

Lydia busied herself in the kitchen, trying her best not to think about Mr. Reginald being laid up in the hospital like he was. She was a mix of emotions. Yes, she knew he needed to be held accountable for all the bad things he'd done. Yes, she realized the folks around here could finally breathe a sigh of relief. And, yes, she believed he should be in a place where he could get some help. But darn it all, if she didn't feel sorry for him; he reminded her of a wee lad lost in the dark who couldn't find his way back home.

Mr. Marcus was scheduled to arrive home this afternoon and she wanted to fix a welcome home supper fit for a king. *He's a mighty good man, he is.* She knew deep down inside that there wasn't anything he wouldn't do for Mr. Reginald. Sadly, Mr. Reginald didn't want his help…or anyone else's, for that matter. He only listened to those silly Voices in his head.

She'd heard Mr. Marcus tell Miss Faerie that he'd pay for any treatment Mr. Reginald needed. Yes, sir, he was a good man indeed! She'd noticed that whenever there was any sort of news about Mr. Reginald, Mr.

Marcus went straight to his office and wrote a letter to his mother. Lydia found it curious and thought perhaps one day maybe he'd explain what that was all about.

She thought it was a right Christian thing the Wrights did by looking past Mr. Reginald's faults and sending up a prayer now and again for his lost soul. She felt all jittery inside. It made her sick to think about him laid up in St. Joe's, more than likely chained to his bed, or some such nonsense. She took a hankie from her apron pocket and wiped her nose. She had to be awfully careful in *this* house lest she be seen weeping over a man who'd made all their lives miserable in one way or another. Still, she couldn't help but hold to the belief that even Mr. Reginald was a child of God and deserved someone to care about him. He was troubled beyond anything she could imagine. She'd witnessed his sullen moods and outrageous violence. She'd seen him pacing and talking to himself in the middle of the night. She'd even seen him hit Miss Augusta and push Myra out of his way. Why, he'd even scolded her for nothing at all a time or two. But what most folks didn't know was that she and Mr. Reginald had an understanding. For some reason she couldn't make out, she held a special place in his heart, and he in hers. No, they'd never said they liked or even halfway cared about each other. They didn't need to. Their respect for one another was unspoken. Besides, if what her priest always said was true, actions speak louder than words.

She tossed around different ideas about what to fix for supper. It had to be something really special, something she'd not made in a while. She tossed around the idea of fried chicken, then decided against it. If she knew anything about Mr. Marcus's travels, she knew he was fed well, for a hostess always put her best foot forward. He'd been staying in a grand house in Colorado Springs and more than likely had his fill of roast beef and fried chicken. No, he must have something that would warm his innards. *I've got it.* She nodded and knew Mr. Marcus would smack his lips in delight and think he'd died and gone to Heaven.

She wore a lopsided grin as she ambled to the pantry and selected the ingredients for chicken and dumplings. She smacked her lips. *That's what it'll be t'night. Chicken 'n dumplins'. One 'o his fav'rites. Mr. Marcus will have double reason t' celebrate tonight. He'll be home with no more travelin' 'til spring, and Mr. Reginald is safe 'n sound in a place where he canna hurt anybody, nor anybody hurt 'im.*

******

Faerie was a mix of emotions. Marcus and Fred would be home at last in only a few short hours. A feeling of calm washed over her as she imagined resting in his arms again after such a long time. She supposed Annie must be experiencing these same kinds of feelings and having similar thoughts. Two lovesick women in the house might have been a recipe for misery; however, they'd managed to keep busy while their men were away. In some ways, the time had passed like molasses in January, while in others it had flown. The festival had been a great diversion. If not for that, she might have spent many hours wringing her hands and pacing.

She stood at the big window on the landing at the top of the stairs and stared out the window. The aspens stood tall and bare, their leaves like a carpet on the ground, some being carried away to parts unknown by autumn winds. A shiver ran up her spine; she pulled her shawl closer. She was confounded by the news Deputy Dan delivered earlier in the day. Marcus was right. Reginald's fatal flaw was in bowing to the wishes of his Voices. Most likely, at least one of them convinced him he'd never be caught, that they were more cunning than the sheriff was competent.

Today the victims of his crimes had much for which to be thankful. Tonight everyone could rest easy. If that was so, why did she feel so sad? Why was she troubled in her spirit? Why did she feel a dread more crippling than when Reginald roamed the streets?

Myra approached carrying her basket of cleaning supplies. "This should be a happy day, Faerie. Why so glum?"

Faerie clinched her jaws and breathed shallowly as she stared out the window. After a moment, she answered, "Myra, why do I have a feeling this whole thing with Reginald isn't really over? A part of me is petrified. I can't explain it. It's...*crippling.*"

Myra set the basket on the floor and inched over to the window. She folded her arms, glanced out the window and cleared her throat. "I know. I feel it, too."

Faerie quickly turned to face Myra. "You do? Truly?"

Myra pursed her lips. She lay a comforting hand on Faerie's shoulder. "See those trees out there? They're sleeping for the winter. The autumn winds have slowly but surely mesmerized them into a state of rest. So it is with Mr. Reginald. His Voices have wooed him into a state of unreality. We are no longer dealing with the man, but the illness. The winds of his illness have swept through his mind and body and have taken over. Unlike the autumn winds, he won't awaken in the spring to find all things fresh and new. His awakening will be far more severe. Whatever happens to him, it's out of our control."

"I can't help feeling sick over this...and more than a little guilty. I wonder if I could have done something…*anything*…to help him."

"You did."

Faerie cast a baffled look. "How so?"

"You came to Augusta's aid. You and Marcus took over when Augusta was in a state of disbelief, when she couldn't function. If not for you, he might have gotten to her and the baby, and Lord only knows what might've happened then. I shudder to think about it."

"I never thought about that being helpful to *him*," Faerie stated slowly.

"Whether Reginald wants to admit it or not, you saved him a world of hurt by getting Augusta and the baby out of harm's way." Myra scoffed, "Maybe I should say, whether his *Voices* want to admit it or not. I'm so confused about all that I don't know which end is up."

"Well…" Faerie responded. "I'm exhausted from just thinking about it. I'm going to lie down for a bit. Maybe write Mother a letter. I really am the most horrible of correspondents." She noticed that Myra looked tired as well. "Why don't you go home for a little while, Myra? We're all taking supper together tonight. Read a book. Take a nap or a little walk. Do whatever it is that rejuvenates you and we'll meet again at the supper table."

Myra tsk'd. "I'm all right, Faerie." Then: "You mustn't keep giving me time off. I might get used to it," she teased. "Besides, I can't let Lydia do all the work."

Faerie let out a belly laugh. "Now that is *funny*! When was the last time she let you help in the kitchen…other than to set the table or clean up?"

Myra nodded slowly, her bottom lip covering the top, giving her chipmunk cheeks. "When you're right, you're right!" She picked up the basket. "See you at supper."

******

Augusta's back rested against the headboard. She stretched her legs out on the bed and crossed her feet at the ankles. Her knitting needles clicked furiously as she worked on a secret project in the privacy of her room. She took quiet moments when Nora was busy or out of the house to work on a shawl she hoped to give her for Christmas. The color was a rich cranberry, which Augusta thought would be lovely with the color of her hair. She was excited as all get out because she'd never before given anyone a gift she'd made. She didn't want to appear a braggart, but genuinely felt she was gifted in the art of knitting, and was excited to begin giving lessons to a few of her friends. Never in her life had she felt she had anything to offer others, yet here she was with a list of women interested in a knitting class.

Dan and Nora were in the kitchen fixing supper. He'd saved her house for last as he made his rounds with the news of Reginald's capture. She wagged her head thinking about young love as the needles moved with lightning speed. She heard them giggling as they worked, a calm settling over the house.

Tomorrow morning she intended make a visit to the hospital, maybe take some of the cookies she and Nora baked today, and offer her gratitude for a job well done....unless, of course, Doc Fisher made one of his early morning house calls. She snickered and felt her face flush; there was definitely the beginning of a crush developing for him. Flustered, she tried to concentrate on her knitting. Still, she wondered at her reaction. She *was* alone, after all. She thought perhaps he had feelings for her as well. Why else would he show up like a lost puppy on her front porch after a long night at the hospital? If nothing else, they had forged a friendship that brought a smile to her face and warmth to her bones.

Now that Reginald was in the hospital and under the watch of deputies, Doc might show up with more frequency to share updates on her ex-husband's progress. She stretched her neck to the right, holding it in one position for a few seconds to work out a kink that seemed to always pop up whenever she became too engrossed in her knitting. She laid the project in her lap and rubbed her shoulder and neck, and then leaned her head back against the headboard. She gazed at the ceiling as she listened to the gaiety wafting up from the kitchen. She picked up her knitting and held it close. The laughter from downstairs triggered something in her that was missing. For the life of her, she didn't know what it was.

She whispered a prayer asking for love to lend itself to Nora and Dan in a sweet, gentle, and promising way. It certainly had never been that for her. She closed her eyes and replayed images of her life with Reginald. She recalled one episode on their wedding trip when Reginald took off early one morning with no word of when he might return. She kept busy during the day with shopping and a visit to the hotel spa, but when night fell and he had not returned she became anxious. She sat up and waited for him well past bedtime, pacing the floors, worrying and wondering where he might be. She fell asleep sometime after midnight and awoke the following morning to find him sleeping in a chair with his legs propped up on the bed, sporting a black eye and a nasty cut over his brow. Not knowing whether to be concerned or angry or both, she'd opted for both, and decided to let him sleep to postpone an argument she wasn't ready to have. Then there was the day she found out she was expecting. He'd grown sullen and ill-tempered and accused her of trapping him. Later on, he tried baiting her by saying she was getting fat, and ordering Lydia to hide the sweets. He threatened to divorce her if she kept it up. The final straw was broken when he completely lost all sense and hit her, pushed Myra against a wall, flew out of the house on a rampage, and wound up at the Wright's, where he completed his tirade by punching Marcus in the nose. These were just the highlights. "I could write a novel!" she said.

"Then you should!" Nora answered, causing Augusta to practically jump out of her skin.

"Good heavens, girl. You scared me half to death!"

Nora craned her neck to try and catch a glimpse of the project lying on Augusta's lap. "The color is beautiful. What're you making?"

"Oh, this old thing? It's just a little something for Faerie. Thought it would make her eyes stand out. What with her porcelain skin and all those freckles, she needs all the help she can get," she teased.

"Augusta! That's awful!" she said, then snickered under her breath. "She's stunning, don't you think? So refined, so genteel and kind."

Augusta got a faraway look in her eyes. "Kind is right. Benevolent and kind…truly beautiful, inside and out. I don't know how I would have made it through these past months without her."

Gazing over at the project once more, Nora said, "Anyway, she'll love it…whatever it is." Nora shrugged her shoulders. "I came up to tell you supper will be ready in about half an hour. I'm going to feed Derrick now."

"Oh, let me. Go ahead and get it ready and I'll bring him down in a few minutes." Then: "Is he awake? It's been so quiet upstairs I thought surely he was still napping."

"Playing quietly in his crib," Nora answered. "I just changed him. He's dry and happy."

"All right, then, go on back downstairs. You mustn't keep your young man waiting. Derrick and I'll be along in a few minutes."

Augusta felt a real kinship with Nora and hoped she'd stay on forever. Nevertheless, she wasn't blind. The writing was on the wall. Dan would propose before the year was out. She could only hope he would allow Nora to continue on with her.

******

The temperature was dropping. Sandy wrapped up in a blanket they kept stowed away in the back of the wagon. She glanced over at her dad, holding the reins, all decked out in his heavy coat, as well as a hat, scarf, and gloves. One of these days she'd actually listen when her mom told her to bundle up before she went out. Her scarf and gloves were tucked neatly in the bottom drawer of her dresser. She wanted to leave them there until it was absolutely necessary because using them meant the best of the warm days were past and winter had reared its ugly head. She supposed now was the time to admit it was absolutely necessary to bring them out of hiding.

"I'm excited to get home, Daddy. I can't wait to see Mommy's face when we tell her the big news."

"She'll be surprised, all right, but you know your mother. She's a bit of a pessimist. She'll ask lots of questions that we won't know the answers to, so patience is the key." He stole a quick glance followed by a wink and then got back to the business of steering the team.

"She *is* a pessimist. " Then: "Don't you think maybe that's a good thing? Don't you think it probably keeps her from jumping right into something before checking it out? Probably saves her a lot of grief in the long run."

"When did you get to be so smart?" he asked, playfully.

She looked up to the sky. "It'll be dark pretty soon. I don't much like being out at night. Especially since…"

"It's over, sweetheart. He can't hurt you anymore. Not ever."

"I dream about it sometimes. Not as much as when I first got home, but sometimes. My dreams seem so real."

"We can tell when you've had a bad night. You're sweet not to trouble your mother with it." He paused, and then said, "She can *always* tell when you're upset, little girl. There's no hiding it from her."

"Really?" she whined.

"For one thing, those dark circles under your eyes are a telltale sign. Makes you look like that mama raccoon that hangs around the back porch." She giggled. "Then there's the silence at the breakfast table. You barely lift your head. You pick at your food. And you ask for seconds on coffee…which, by the way, you never drink unless you're tired."

"I guess I'm not as good at hiding things as I thought. Sorry Dad." She looked away, partly in shame, partly in regret for worrying her parents. "I'll try to do better."

"Little girl, did I say we were put off with you? I only told you because we want you to know we love you and want to give you all the time you need to work through everything." Then: "Have you talked with anybody about this?"

Taken aback, she sat up straight and replied, "No. Why would I do that?"

"Relax. I only meant that maybe you might to talk to somebody besides us. Your math teacher might be a good listener. You seem to really like her.

271

Or what about Faerie? She's taking a liking to you. It's just something to think about. It might help."

"My math teacher, Dad? Really?" She was mortified at the very thought.

"Well…don't be so quick to dismiss it," he countered.

"Yes….but…goodness, Dad. She's my *teacher*. What if I confided in her and she looked at me different somehow?"

"What about Faerie?" he asked.

"Maybe…I'll just have to wait and see," she said, flatly. "I just don't want to talk about it if I don't have to.

Hearing how put off she sounded, he shrugged his shoulders. "It was only a suggestion. You're a big girl now and can make your own decisions. Your mother and I completely trust your judgment. Promise me that if it all starts to feel like too much to handle, you'll at least consider talking to somebody." He turned his head quickly to the left, thinking he heard a rusting in the bushes.

"Probably just that mama raccoon waiting for us to pass by," she said, elbowing him playfully.

He grinned and elbowed her right back. "Probably so." They rode in silence for a few minutes. Then: "Sandy, I want to say one more thing and then I'll leave it alone. I promise."

"Sure," she said, slowly.

"Mr. O'Keefe may be in custody, but the ordeal is far from over. He'll be charged with multiple offenses; he's got a long history. At some point, you'll have to testify against him. You'll be asked to tell the judge everything that happened." He brought the team to a stop and looked Sandy solemnly in the face. "Hear me. Draw from your faith. Commit this thing to the Lord. You're about to take the rest of a journey you probably never dreamed of taking in the first place. You survived the first leg; you can finish the course. Please don't try to do it alone." He wrapped his arms around her in a fatherly embrace. "Your strength must come from the Lord." He paused. Then: "It's probably safe to say that Mr. O'Keefe's trial…or trials… I'm not sure which…will be something the likes of which this town has never seen before."

"Daddy…" She gnawed on the inside of her cheek. "Would it be all right if I only go to court when it's about John and me?"

He wished there was a way to protect her from what was bound to come. Who knew how she'd react upon seeing O'Keefe again. "Sure, honey. I don't understand how all that court nonsense works, but I think your wishes will be considered. The judge might even consider allowing you to give your testimony in his chambers, avoiding the courtroom altogether."

"Really?" She sat up tall and straight, looking hopeful.

"Yes really. I don't want to get your hopes up, but I've heard of that happening before. When we find out what's what, we can have a chat with the District Attorney." Then: "We'd best get a move on. We're losing daylight."

Before long, they saw the welcoming lights of their humble home illuminating the night. Pulling up to the barn, Alfred said, "Go on in the house, but remember, mum's the word. I'd like for us to share the good news with your mom while we eat. You know, like a real celebration supper."

Sandy stood on her tiptoes and gave her father a peck on the cheek. She walked to the house without fear, secure in the knowledge that for now, all was right in the small corner of the world she called home.

Chapter Twenty-Nine

All we have to decide is what to do with the time that is given us.
~ J. R. R. Tolkien

Simon stood on the landing at the top of the stairs and tucked his shirt in. He grinned lopsidedly as the sound of Clara's off-key singing rang through the house. She was tone deaf; there was no other way to put it. The words she sang were familiar, the melody…not so much. It was awful. Despite that, if it was silenced even for one day, he'd miss it.

He trudged down the staircase, going over the day's schedule in his mind. He needed to ride into town but didn't see how he could. There simply weren't enough hours in the day. He stewed on it for a few minutes and then the solution hit him like a bolt of lightning. *Send one of the hands.* "Simon, you're an absolute genius," he said aloud, facetiously.

Spying him in the family room, Susan tiptoed up behind him and poked him in the ribs, startling him. "I heard you singing your own praises. What's up?"

He rolled his eyes and playfully stuck out his tongue at her. She reciprocated. Shoving his hands in his pockets, he raised his shoulders and rocked back and forth on his heels. He hem hawed around, and eventually said, "You caught me. I was trying to come up with some kind of a plan that might help me find my horse. Then it hit me right between the eyes. Send one of the men on a mercantile run. While he waits for the order to be loaded in the buckboard, he can scoot across the street and enlist the sheriff 's help." He smiled broadly and nodded enthusiastically. "Brilliant idea, huh?"

"Absolutely, Buster, except…who can you spare? Winter's setting in and you said yourself that it's all hands on deck to mend the fences on the far end of the property before the snow flies."

His big toothy grin slowly faded until the corners of his mouth pointed downward. "Darn it! I completely forgot about that."

"Just wait it out, Simon. The sheriff will send somebody out as soon as there's any news."

"Yeah, you're right…as usual. I love that about you: clear head, calm exterior, beautiful, talented." He moved closer and wrapped his arms around her waist and laced his fingers together at the small of her back. "You're a mighty fine woman, Susan. The Lord has given us second chance…and I don't intend on fouling it up." He leaned down and gave her a smooch.

"I love you, Simon Archer. And I believe you'll see your horse again."

275

John finished cleaning Taffy's shoes and gave her a pat on the left hindquarter. He glanced over at the empty stall and sighed. *Where is Dad's horse?* He picked up Taffy's brush and began her favorite part of their morning routine. She would stand still for hours if John would just keep brushing.

"Don't worry, Taff. Gold Dust'll be back soon enough. If he ain't, Dad'll go lookin' fer 'im. You know how 'e loves Gold Dust." He snickered. "Almost as much as I love you, ol' girl."

"You've got me pegged, son. I miss my horse. I'd do almost anything to get him back." Simon moseyed over to Taffy's stall and plopped down on a wooden box that propped open the stall door.

John brushed; Simon watched. For quite some time, they spoke not a word. Just as John finished up with Taffy, the silence was broken by the muffled sound of hooves against the hard ground. They gave each other surprised glances.

"Who'd be a'comin' out here s'early of a mornin'?" John asked.

"Don't know. Sounds like a couple of riders. Let's go see."

Outside the barn they were elated to find their friend and closest neighbor, Joshua Benton, sitting on his horse, and holding Gold Dust by the reins.

"Joshua Benton, how on earth did you end up with my horse?" Simon hurried to his palomino. Gold Dust whinnied and excitedly jerked his head up and down at the sight of Simon. Joshua handed over Gold Dust's reins before dismounting.

"Well, now, that's a tale you'll be a'wantin' to hear. It was early Sunday morning and I'd jest commenced checkin' the fences over by that grove o' cottonwoods on th' south end of m' property when I heard a twig snap and what sounded like a horse a'snortin'. I slipped b'hind one o'them big old trees an' peeked 'round real quiet like, an' jest what d'ya think I seen? Some sidewinder ridin' this here horse. Now I thought t' m'self that I ain't never seen a horse as perty as this'n 'cept here on yer spread, Simon. So's I took m' shotgun an' slipped out from b'hind th' tree an' hollered at 'im t' get down off'n th' horse right slow like. Now I don' know 'bout you, but if'n there wuz a man a'pointin' a shotgun at me, I'd prob'ly do jest 'bout anythin' he asked o' me, an' right quick like to boot. But *naw*. That crazy old coot kicked this perty thing in the belly, let out some kinda Injun soundin' yelp an' headed straight at me. I didn't want t' kill him but I hadta do somethin' fast, so's I waited 'til he got closer an' shot straight up in th' air. Yer horse here took off. I shot again, an' this time I think I must've got

276

th' guy. He kept on a'ridin. I thought t' m'sef, somebody'll find 'im layin' on th' side o' th' road, so's I went 'bout m' bizness. 'Magine m' surprise when a few minutes later, I see th' horse a'headin' back m' way, minus th' rider. I tied 'im up down by the creek an' commenced a'lookin' fer th' guy, 'cept I never did find 'im. Anyhow…that's how I came across yer horse, Simon."

John and Simon looked at each other in stunned disbelief. Then: "Joshua, sounds like you just saved the world."

Joshua removed his hat and gave his head a puzzled scratch. "Well, sir, I don't rightly know 'bout that, s'much. Jest yer horse."

"Did you ever hear of Reginald O'Keefe?" Simon asked.

"Well, now, sure I have. He's that guy what's been a'causin' s' much trouble round 'bout Ouray. Least that's what most folks are a'sayin'."

"I think you just shot him in the leg." Simon rubbed Gold Dust's neck as he pondered the story he'd just heard. "Have you talked to the sheriff yet?"

"Naw, sir. I was a'feared t' tell. Thought I might get m'self in some trouble." He dropped his head and kicked some dirt around with his boot.

"I don't think so. Horse rustling is grounds for hanging around here." He gave Joshua a minute for that little tidbit to sink in "I tell you what I'll do. I'll just run in the house and tell Susan I've an errand to run and then you and me, well, we'll head on into town. In case you haven't heard, O'Keefe's laid up in the hospital recovering from a gunshot wound."

Joshua perked up and exclaimed, "Say what?"

"Joshua, my friend, miracles happen every day. You've done us all a huge favor."

******

He opened his eyes. Disoriented, he blinked a few times as he turned his head this way and that trying to figure out where he was. No matter how hard he tried, he couldn't for the life of him recall what happened. His leg was wrenching in pain. His nose itched. He tried to move his arm but it was trapped somehow. He looked down to see both hands tied to the bed railings.

In a panic, he cried, "Help me! Where am I? Somebody tell me what's going on."

******

Still in her nightgown, Augusta stood at her bedroom window and looked out upon the backyard. She felt perfectly lazy this morning. Nine o'clock and she hadn't even attempted getting dressed. All she wanted to do was stay in, hide from the world and have a private celebration with her son. With the news of Reginald's hospitalization, came freedom. She wanted to pinch herself to make sure she wasn't dreaming.

Dan seemed confident there was nothing to fear. No longer would she sit and wait for Reginald's next act of retribution. His fate was sealed. The courts would decide his punishment. Whether he spent the remainder of his life in the penitentiary or a mental hospital didn't really matter to her. She just wanted peace. And now, it suddenly, and finally, seemed within her grasp.

Reginald's mad rain of fire ended when he hobbled into St. Joe's.

Sometime during the night a heavy fog had rolled in and showed no sign of clearing. Such dreariness inclined her to spend the day relaxing in front of the fire with a nice cup of tea and a good book, or perhaps her knitting. It was a perfect day for finishing Nora's Christmas gift, a perfect day for sitting on the floor with Derrick and playing peek-a-boo, a perfect day for reflection and gratitude. She smiled. It was perfect day to make a batch of oatmeal raisin cookies.

******

Myra sat on the edge of the bed with her head bowed and eyes closed and willed this morning's unwelcome queasiness to abate. She moaned and took the tiniest nibble of a soda cracker.

After quietly suffering through several days of a sick stomach, she shared her suspicions with George and swore him to secrecy with a vow that there would be no spilling of the beans until she was ready. Having had very little sickness with Patricia, she hadn't expected so much this time around. She thought the nausea would ease, but after six weeks of it, she paid a visit to Doc Fisher. He was sympathetic to her plight and told her she might never wish to see another soda cracker again after this pregnancy.

Every morning was the same: peppermint tea and soda crackers to settle a topsy-turvy tummy. She trudged through each morning and typically rallied around lunchtime. Unfortunately, her energy spurts never lasted long. By mid-afternoon, she was done for. She found it worrisome that Faerie had noticed and thought it best to send her home for some rest. Lydia for sure was suspicious, having given Myra a raised eyebrow a time or two when some curious food combinations had been requested for lunch. And then there was Annie, who'd mentioned on more than one occasion how pale she looked.

Since the people they cared about most were obviously concerned about her wellbeing, Myra and George decided to share the news, despite having had little time to absorb the it privately. A toddler *and* a newborn: the thought was overwhelming. Myra tried desperately not to obsess over it, lest she fret through the entire pregnancy.

After downing a handful of crackers, she nursed a cup of peppermint tea. She washed her face, dabbed it dry with a towel, and lay down for a few minutes to wait out the waves of nausea that threatened to send her into another bout of retching.

Concentrating on being as still as possible, she strained to listen as George coaxed Patricia to eat her scrambled egg. She managed to lift the corners of her mouth ever so slightly as he made funny noises and teased the baby, resulting in squeals of delight. She was grateful for such a darling of a husband. *Everyone should have a man like George in their life*, she marveled.

After a half hour bout of morning sickness, the queasiness began to subside. She dressed, grabbed the bag George had put together for Patricia, kissed him on the cheek, picked up her precious baby girl and hurried from the cozy cottage and across the yard to the big house. Once inside the spacious house, she handed Patricia and her bag off to the welcome arms of Lydia, so that she might remove her coat.

"Glory Be! You're as winded as a rabbit bein' chased by a fox." Lydia offered Patricia a soda cracker, which brought forth a high-pitched giggle from Myra while she was still trying to catch her breath. "It's….been… quite a…morning…already!" She tried to take in some deep breaths. "The crackers, Lydia…I've eaten enough of those lately to…"

"I knew it, I knew it, I knew it!" exclaimed Myra, cradling the babe in her arms. "This'n's gonna have a wee one to play with!"

Myra smiled, and then knit her brows and crinkled her nose. She placed a finger against her lips and said, "Shhh! Mum's the word until I tell Faerie."

"Oh, right! O' course you're right!" Lydia beamed. "Lord o' mercy, I don't know if I can handle s' much news in one week. First, Mr. Reginald, and now the blessed news of a babe t' be born! Saints be praised!"

******

"Settle down, Mr. Walters. Are you in pain?" asked Nurse Bailey, biting her tongue.

"Wh-what? Who are you? And why are you calling me Mr. Walters?" His wrists remained cuffed to the bed. He was confused and beginning to lose control. "Why am I cuffed to the bed?" He jerked and pulled, yet no amount of trying would loosen his bonds. He squinted, giving the nurse a long, hard look. "Wait a minute!" he scowled. "You're that nurse…what's your name? Bailey? Am I right?"

She nodded. "That's right. And you're Mr. Walters."

"No…I'm…*not*!" he seethed through clenched teeth. "Let me out of this…this…*contraption*!"

"Not until we settle a few things. When you came in, you told us you were Luke Walters. If you aren't Luke Walters, then who are you?"

A low guttural sound emerged from somewhere deep within the patient. His face contorted. His back arched. He turned his head and looked at her, his eyes dark and sinister.

Nurse Bailey cautiously stepped back and rapped twice on the door. A deputy opened the door and made his way to the end of the bed.

The patient slowly turned his gaze in the deputy's direction. "You want Luke, you've got him!" came a low, growling response.

"Luke?" Nurse Bailey responded.

"Yeah, doll, it's me. I have to take over because our boy Reggie can't handle things anymore. Understand?"

"I believe so, yes." She swallowed. "Luke, are you in pain?"

The host's facial expression softened. "I am. I'd be much obliged if you could do something about it."

"I'll go see what the doctor has ordered and I'll be right back. Just hang on."

A bizarre, crazed-sounding chuckle omitted from the bed. "So what else would I do?"

The deputy remained at the foot of the bed with his arms folded, his weapon in plain sight. The patient and deputy stared at one another, neither uttering a word until Bailey returned with a dose of laudanum, which the patient happily swallowed and drifted off to sleep.

******

About midmorning, Marcus retreated to the family room and relaxed by the fire with a book he'd purchased in Colorado Springs. As if on cue, Lydia appeared with a tray of coffee and oatmeal bars. She thought him far too thin after his visit to the Front Range and told him so. He thanked him and smiled, knowing better than to argue with her. In all honesty, he loved the way she doted on him. And he had to admit his pants *were* a "wee bit saggy", as she had so aptly informed him at breakfast.

The staff was hard at work on this dismal day. Despite the gloominess of the weather, the atmosphere in the house seemed carefree and light. The news of Reginald's capture, if that's what one chose to call it, had spread like wildfire, with the residents of Monstrosity Manor being among the first to receive it.

Marcus poured a splash of milk in his coffee and stirred. He picked up the cup and brought it to his lips. The aroma of the caramel-colored brew aroused his senses. He set the cup back on the tray and rested his head against the back of the large cozy chair. It was good to be home. And he didn't need to report to the office until Monday…three whole days of heaven.

He tried to keep his mind from dwelling on the trials and tribulations of Reginald O'Keefe. Even though his heart ached for the lost friendship, and knew he could never truly understand what went wrong, he wanted nothing more than to sit in this chair, enjoy his coffee and snacks, read his book and hope for snow. He loved snow and couldn't enough of it. He couldn't wait until the girls were old enough to go sledding and build snowmen, or have snowball fights, and then rush into the kitchen for Lydia's delicious hot cocoa.

He downed one cup of coffee and poured a second. As he doctored it, his smile grew broader, thinking how sweet life was for his tidy little family. He picked up his book, which had been open, face down on his lap. He settled in and began reading the second chapter.

"*Great Expectations*?" queried Faerie, as she sauntered into the room.

"Yes, I read it in college. I came across it in a bookstore in Colorado Springs and had a hankering to read it again…without the boring lectures."

She sat in the chair next to him and pulled her legs up under her. "I've never read it. Is it something I'd like?"

"Hmmm…" He thought on it and then said, "Probably so. It's a story about an orphan boy named Pip who was raised by his sister. There are several colorful characters in the book who move in and out of Pip's life, some good, some bad. One of the characters, Magwitch, isn't at all what he seems. What Pip doesn't know is that the two of them are bound by more than friendship. I don't want to tell you too much in case you decide to read it. Let's just say, it's right up your alley, what with your love of intrigue and mystery."

She grinned slyly. "Well, then, pass it along when you're finished. I'll give it a go." She watched the roaring fire. "Marcus, it's hard to believe there are only a few short weeks left before Thanksgiving. You and your buddies will soon be going on your yearly turkey hunt for the big dinner."

"Can't wait," he muttered, his nose stuck in the book.

She gave him a disgruntled look and said, "We'll talk about it later… when an old Dickens' novel isn't so compelling."

******

Fred and Annie sat in the two over-sized chairs in the nursery. "Can you believe it?" she asked. "Mr. O'Keefe finally caught."

"So strange how it happened. Almost like he was being led there by some unseen force," Fred added.

"Maybe he was. I mean, Faerie told me that Mr. O'Keefe doesn't believe in God." She paused and thought about how to say exactly what she meant without fumbling all over her words, losing the meaning altogether. "What a horrible way to live life…separated from The One who knows us best." She slowly shook her head. Then: "No matter how hard mankind tries to ignore him, or deny his existence, God can't and won't be dismissed. He cannot be explained away. He will not be hidden in the dark. My grandma always used to say how odd it seemed to her that the Created were given a choice whether or not to believe in the Creator. I don't find it odd at all. God is a gentleman. He gave us free will. Even so, can you imagine making the choice *not* to believe? If I chose not to believe in God, I think a part of me would feel empty and unfulfilled, and eventually ask the question, what's the point of life."

Fred knit his brows together and pondered her words. He didn't exactly know how to respond, so he chose to be silly. "Whatever you say, Love. *Whatever* you say," he said with a wink. The truth was he'd had a conversation much like this with his mother before he left home, and didn't have a response then, either. God was a mystery to him. A mystery he intended to explore with Annie's help.

"Oh, you!" She waved him off.

"Annie?" he began. "Does your ring sparkle as much as it did last night?"

She held her hand out, gaping at it. "Even more. Oh, Fred, it's so beautiful."

"Annie…" He paused. "I don't want to wait too long. I'm going to see that house again today. Would you like to come with me?"

She blushed and lowered her gaze. "Yes, I'd like that very much."

******

"Doc, how long d'ya think he ought t' stay in th' hospital?" Sheriff Johnson asked, pointedly.

Doc was astonished by the events of the previous day. To think he'd gone weeks without a day off and when he finally took one, look what happened! He was doing his best to remain calm and collected. He nervously tapped his right thigh with O'Keefe's chart as he frantically analyzed the situation.

"If he remains stable and the wound heals quickly and without infection, I'd say a week, maybe a week and a half. Based on the surgical notes, the wound is very serious, Sheriff. O'Keefe's lucky to even *have* that leg. The bullet tore a muscle in the back of his leg and shattered his patella... his kneecap. It also shattered the tibia and fibula...both the leg bones below the knee. The bone injuries are substantial enough to keep him from walking for a very long time...if ever. Only time will tell. And the torn muscle's going to hurt like nobody's business and take a heckuva long time to heal. Something the court will need to consider is that he'll probably need additional surgery somewhere down the line. But that won't be until after he's...well, you know...in prison, or *wherever*."

"I hate t' sound ugly, but it couldn't've happened to a nicer guy." The sheriff shook his head. "Too bad they all can't jest walk in an' give up th' way he did."

"That's not exactly what happened here," Doc Fisher said. Then: "By the way, the District Attorney will be coming by this afternoon around three. I want to find out what I need to do to get our patient an evaluation with a psychiatrist before he goes to trial."

"Good luck with that!" the sheriff scoffed. "They're goin' t' be out fer blood!" Then: "I wish I knew who filled his leg full o' lead. I'd like t' shake 'is hand. Shoot! The mayor'd prob'ly give 'im th' keys to th' city."

"Keys to the city, my eye!" Doc said with a chuckle. "I don't even know who the mayor is."

"Name's Chester Wilson, 'cept it ain't official. It's kind of in-name-only, if'n ya know what I mean. Th' town council voted him in jest so's we could say we got a mayor."

Doc rolled his eyes. "I'll be." What else could he say? "Does he get paid?"

"Not a penny."

"Sounds right since he doesn't really *do* anything." Doc scratched his head. "Say, do you want to be a part of the discussion this afternoon?"

"Well, now, that'd be right nice. Most folks don't think much 'bout keepin' me in th' loop."

"I'm goin' home to rest my weary bones. How about meeting back here around 2:45?"

The sheriff put on his hat and tapped it once for good measure. "Sounds good t' me. See ya then."

******

Fred and Annie arrived at the house on Second Avenue just minutes before the seller. The yard and exterior of the house was neat and clean and well taken care of. A wrought iron fence and gate lined the perimeter of the property with a nice brick walkway leading to the front porch steps.

Annie stared at the house feeling as if she were living a dream. "How did you know?"

"How did I know what, Love?" Fred held her hand and gave her a curious look.

"This house. I've always loved this house. Ever since…"

"Good day, Fred. This must be your bride-to-be." A stout man dressed in tweed britches and a black wool vest and tan shirt clambered toward them. Strands of white hair stuck out from the sides of a black derby hat, and a long, unruly salt-and-pepper beard lay across on his chest.

Annie dropped her head in amusement. She supposed this was probably how Santa Claus might look in regular street clothes.

Fred stuck out his hand in greeting. "Hello, Aaron. Good to see you again. I'd like to introduce you to my fiancé, Annie." He smiled broadly. "I can't quite say that enough. It amazes me every time. I'm the most fortunate of men."

"Indeed." He focused his attention on Annie, now blushing. "Annie, dear, Fred tells me you are employed by the Wrights."

She nodded. "That's right."

"Then I shall allow you the honor of letting the cat out of the bag regarding this house," he said, with a telling grin.

She smiled sweetly and swallowed. "Fred, I have a very special history with this house. This is where Marcus and Faerie lived before they moved to Monstrosity Manor." Fred's eyes lit up in surprise. " I started working for them the last several months they were here and, I must say, I fell in love with this house. It's warm and inviting. There's something very special about it."

"'Scuse me, Annie, but did you say *Monstrosity Manor*?" Aaron asked, curiously.

"Yes," she said with a chuckle. "The first time I went to the house on 4th Avenue was with Faerie. We were to fetch Miss Augusta for a ride out to the Archer's place. Miss Augusta has a tendency toward tardiness, so I volunteered to run in and hurry her along. When the carriage pulled up

284

to the house I gasped. I'd never seen anything like it. I jokingly called it Monstrosity Manor and the name stuck. When the Wrights took possession, they actually gave it the name. In fact, it's on record as such at the Assessor's office."

"Well, I'll be." Aaron ran one hand down the length of his beard. "So, Fred, shall we see the house that has so captured your lady's heart?"

"By all means." Then: "I had no idea." Fred was stunned. "I don't believe in coincidence, so it must be something akin to the scripture you sometimes quote about asking for and receiving the desires of one's heart." He raised one brow and said playfully, "And all that time, you didn't think I was listening when you rambled on and on about your ladies Bible study."

Annie smiled demurely and took Fred's hand as Aaron Bennett lifted the latch on the gate and led them to the lemon yellow house where she'd begun her relationship with the Wrights.

She knew the house well. Fred and Aaron left her to her own devices while they surveyed the house room by room, exploring every nook and cranny, tapping on walls, listening for creaks in the floors, and discussing how well maintained it was. To Fred's delight, an indoor toilet and tub had been installed recently, as well as gas lighting. He was certain Annie would be delighted when she discovered the updates.

Annie prayed for this to be their home. It was just right for a couple just starting out. A three-bedroom, two story home, with a large parlor for lounging or entertaining, a fine kitchen and dining area, a front and back porch…everything she'd always dreamed of in a home. For now, they planned to stay in Ouray, but eventually, Fred truly wanted to study history. Something inside him burned with the desire to teach young minds about the ones who went before. She sighed. On a teacher's salary they'd certainly never be rich, but they'd have an abundance of the things that really mattered.

"So Annie, what d'ya think?" Fred asked, as he climbed down the stairs to find her staring out the parlor window in a daze.

She turned with a start. "You know what I think. I love it. I'd live here forever, if I could. The question is, what do *you* think?"

Aaron roamed into the kitchen so the couple could speak in private. He was surprised to hear Fred calling out to him only a few minutes later.

"Aaron, my friend, let's shake on it. I believe we have ourselves a deal." Fred said, jovially.

Annie squealed in delight, and then quickly placed one hand over her mouth.

Aaron gave a lopsided grin. "Congratulations you two. I'll draw up the paperwork. You can come by my office anytime next week to finalize everything." The men shook on it. A few minutes later, Aaron shuffled down the walk, whistling a happy tune.

"You can almost hear him counting the money now!" Fred commented.

Chapter Thirty

When you believe in a thing, believe in it all the way,
implicitly and unquestionable.
~ Walt Disney

Doc Fisher rubbed his sandpapery eyes. He checked the time on his pocket watch and then laid it on his desk. "Ugh! What have I gotten myself *into*?" he moaned. He stretched his neck to first one side and then the other as he massaged a kink in his right shoulder. He decided he needed coffee or tea or a walk around the block, or perhaps all of the above... whatever it took to revive him. It was half past one on Tuesday morning and he should be home in bed.

"I must be crazy!" he muttered emphatically. The aroma of freshly brewed coffee sent him on a journey down the hospital corridor, past the nurses' station, and into the employee lounge, where a gathering of nurses sat munching on cookies.

"I thought you were taking a few days off," one of the nurses chided.

"I am. Just pretend like you don't see me. I'm working on a project that requires access to more medical journals than I have at home." He poured a mug of coffee and leaned against the counter, cupping it in both hands. "I've been barricaded in my office for hours. Thought a change of scenery might do me some good."

"Why don't you go home and have a rest? You look exhausted." Sister Martha asked. She was new to the St. Joe's nursing team, having recently moved to Colorado from a convent in Philadelphia.

Doc thought he heard a slight accent. "Sister, I know you came from Philadelphia, but where before that? You are definitely not from the States."

"London, sir. I took my vows in London. I was offered the opportunity to take nursing school in Philadelphia and jumped at the chance. Then one o' the doctors there intrigued me with talk of the Rocky Mountains. When I found out the Sisters of Mercy had this hospital, I begged and pleaded t' be sent here."

"And we're mighty glad to have her," Nurse Andrews, the night supervisor added. "Even our most infamous patient seems to have taken a liking to her."

"Be warned, Sister. Don't be too friendly with him. He'll take advantage of you, for sure." Doc said.

"And won't think twice about doing it," Nurse Andrews added from the other side of the table. "He's got quite a reputation, Sister."

287

"Nurse Bailey told me all about him," the young sister responded. "I have no intention of doing anything other than what my vows require."

"Impressive! Your mama raised you right!" teased Andrews. "Keep your eyes on the prize."

Sister Martha giggled and when she did her eyes sparkled, reminding Doc of the lovely dark-eyed lady he planned to see a lot more of in the very near future.

He bid the nurses a fond adieu and moseyed back to his office feeling refreshed and ready for another session with the psychiatric journals that were spread all over his desk. His request before the district attorney, and possibly Judge Lawson, must be compelling in order to win them over to his side. O'Keefe might very well be a monster in the eyes of the community, but he was still a human being. He certainly deserved to be held accountable for his actions and punished accordingly. Believing that with his whole heart, Doc was also convinced that as time went on O'Keefe's Voices took over. If everything Doc read in the journals was true, it stood to reason that O'Keefe's psychosis slowly evolved resulting in violent, outlandish, vile behaviors. If a psychiatrist found this to be the case, his punishment might very well result in him spending the rest of his life in an institution for the criminally insane instead of a penitentiary. Which was worse? It was difficult to say.

His symptoms were characteristic of Multiple Personality Disorder. Doc studied page after page, reading and jotting down notes, flipping through periodicals searching for anything that might lend even a small amount of clarity. To be clear, this task was daunting, but necessary. Judge Lawson, an old country lawyer, presided over the jurisdiction. It didn't help matters that he and O'Keefe had a history. Truth be told, he'd just as soon string O'Keefe up by the nearest tree and call it good. Nevertheless, Doc trudged on, acutely aware that many a tongue would wag at the news of what might well be viewed as an allegiance to a known murderer and kidnapper. Still, Doc had an obligation to his patient. He must intervene on his behalf to ensure the man's well-being…despite his criminal behavior.

To think of the turmoil O'Keefe had caused made his stomach turn. It would take an awful lot of convincing for the Prosecutor to see things his way. Was he up to the challenge? You bet he was! He couldn't wait. From a mental health standpoint, O'Keefe was every psychiatrist's dream in terms of a case study. From a human standpoint, he was a terror. Though he personally despised the man, he knew better than to let any personal opinions cloud his judgment, especially if he wanted the Prosecutor to take him seriously.

Doc was haggard and worn. He needed to be surrounded by the comforts of home. Back in medical school, he'd enjoyed nothing more than hibernating in his room in the middle of his bed, surrounded by a sea of periodicals, books and all manner of notes from class, often working furiously through the night. Some of his best work resulted from those all night sessions. Inspired by his study habits of days gone by, he gathered up the books on his desk and called it a night. There would be no interruptions or distractions. If all went well, he'd have all his ducks in a row by first light.

Energized by a sudden rush of adrenaline, he scurried out the back door of the hospital and whistled as he hit the street for the short jaunt home. He smiled imagining how impressed the District Attorney would be with the wealth of information he'd provide, on a topic from which most people shied away. He'd do his best to convince the Prosecutor to at least consider the benefits of getting to the bottom of O'Keefe's unbalanced behavior. Doc ultimately hoped to win him over with an impassioned plea to avoid a rush to judgment when O'Keefe was clearly a prime candidate for treatment in a mental hospital. All they needed was the diagnosis and testimony of a seasoned psychiatrist.

As he reached the house, he realized how very tired he was of hearing the mentally infirmed referred to as crazy, demented, one shoe shy of a pair, paddling around with one oar, possessed. *Possessed? Really?* The public's view of the mentally ill desperately needed to be changed. He realized such an undertaking would be an uphill battle. He also knew there were those who would never change their minds. Still, he hoped what he had to say would begin a conversation in the right direction.

He put a pot of coffee on the stove. He spread the materials out on his bed, with paper and pencils at the ready. He changed into his favorite pair of pajamas, donned a thick pair of socks and settled in for a long night.

Chapter Thirty-One

Food is a great way of communicating.
~ Jan Karon

Lydia was a hard sell. Though she was an employee of the Wrights, she often behaved as though she owned the kitchen. Even so, everybody had a weakness and Annie knew just what Lydia's was. She despised cleaning up after supper. The other meals were all in a day's work. Supper, on the other hand, was at the end of the workday and she often went on and on about her dogs barking, which Annie translated as tired aching feet.

Annie stood just outside the kitchen and gave herself a pep talk, wary of crossing the threshold into Lydia's domain. No one ever stood up to Lydia. Even Faerie knew all too well the benefits of staying out of her way. She was a tough old bird with a fake, albeit beloved Irish brogue. Finally deciding she had to do this thing, she took the plunge into the inner sanctum of Lydia's domain, her heart in her throat.

Lydia stopped stirring the pot she was so carefully tending and said, "Well, out with it, child. You've been mutterin' on th'other side o' the kitchen door for the longest time. What's on yer mind?"

Annie cleared her throat and took a deep breath, slowly blowing out the air. She feared her face must be beet red based upon how hot her cheeks felt. She bit her lower lip and stared back at the woman, desperately wishing she could disappear. Nevertheless, here she was. It was now or never.

"Well?" Lydia put the spoon on its rest and folded her arms at her chest.

"I suppose I could stand here like this all day, but you wouldn't have it, so here goes." Annie swallowed. "I have a proposition for you."

"I'm lis'nin" Lydia said, relishing the moment. She could smell fear a mile away.

Annie couldn't have been more frightened had she been in a face off with a mad bull instead of a middle-aged foghorn of a woman. "What would you say if I promised to do your after supper duties for, let's say, a month?" Annie asked, tentatively.

"Mah supper dishes n' such, y'say?" Lydia asked, tentatively.

Annie noticed Lydia's brusqueness seem to soften a bit and thought, just for a second, she could see her wheels turning as she imagined such a luxury. Feeling a little more confident, she responded with, "Yes'm, that's what I said. Why don't you turn down the burner on that potato soup and sit with me awhile?"

Lydia agreed and they moved quickly to the table. Annie had her attention. This was going to be a piece of cake. Far sooner than she imagined, Annie was in control. She had Lydia right where she wanted her, a most welcome turn of events.

When they were seated across from each other, Annie laid her arms on the table and laced her fingers together. "It's like this, Lydia…"

******

Faerie could barely contain herself as Annie recounted the conversation she'd had with Lydia only moments before.

Annie was giddy with excitement as she finished the tale. "And then, her eyes became as big as saucers when I told her it was a secret to be kept just between the two of us. I let that sink in for a moment, then added for emphasis that perhaps it wouldn't be right if we didn't include you in our arrangement. She knit her brows together and said 'Saints alive, Missy. O' course, Miss Faerie should know. It's her house, fer sure.'" Annie rolled her eyes at her poor attempt at mimicking Lydia's brogue.

Faerie dabbed at the corners of her eyes with the ever present lace hankie, the true sign of a lady, according to her dear mother. "It went better than we imagined." Then: "Middle-aged foghorn, my eye."

"It would behoove us to keep our plotting and planning to ourselves, so as not to hurt the old girl's feelings," Annie added in a whisper. "I'd never hurt her for the world. She's just a stubborn old gal who's finally found her niche in the world and doesn't want to lose it."

Faerie nodded, still amused by how well the conversation had gone. "Now the planning begins. Do you and Fred have a date set for the wedding, or do you want to celebrate the purchase of your first home?"

"Both!" She exclaimed. Then: "We're going to discuss a date for the wedding tonight after supper." With confidence, she said emphatically, "Both…*definitely* both."

"I know this is perhaps a little premature, but have you thought about where you'd want to have the ceremony?" Faerie asked, sounding hopeful.

Annie lowered her gaze. "Yes, we've talked about it. Fred left it up to me to ask."

"Oh?" Faerie sounded even more hopeful.

"You have to know we want to be married here. It would be grand to say our vows at the bottom of the staircase with lots of flowers and ribbons and bows…oh, and tulle…I just love tulle…all over the banisters and anything else that stands still long enough to be decorated. What do you think?" She met Faerie's gaze, her eyes dancing.

Faerie clapped her hands and stood, and then gasped. "Oh….I forgot about the babies." She turned to see if the girls stirred and when she was certain they were still dreaming, she said, "Me and my big mouth!" She sat back down, but the excitement of the moment sent ideas racing through her head. "Marcus and I were hoping you'd ask. What a party it will be!" Then: "Oh! Listen to me. I sound like I'm running the show. This is *your* big day and we'll do *whatever* you want…*whenever* you want…*however* you want."

"Thank you, Faerie." Annie reached over and took Faerie's hand and gave it a little squeeze. "Back to *this* dinner: I have a few ideas. I want to cook it…and I want Lydia to sit and enjoy it…which is why I wanted the kitchen to myself."

"I suppose the first thing we need to do is make a guest list. This is one time your parents need to come spend some time with us. It isn't everyday their daughter has such big announcements to celebrate."

"Mother and Daddy love Fred, you know. Mother told me I'd better grab hold of him. She knows a good man when she meets him. After all, just look at my dad."

"Your parents are gems. I wish I'd gotten to know them better. Perhaps planning both the dinner party and the wedding together will help remedy my lack of hospitality.

Annie frowned and said, "Faerie, if there's one thing you're not, it's inhospitable. Everything will be all right as far as my parents are concerned." She stood and said, "I'll be right back. I need to grab a couple of things."

Faerie sat with the girls while Annie went to the parlor to get paper, pen, and a calendar. Then the planning began. A list of invitees was jotted down. Faerie was surprised it wasn't more, until she remembered Annie alone would be doing the cooking.

"Do you know what you'd like to serve?" Faerie asked.

"I think so. My dad loves a good pork roast, so...there you are." She shrugged her shoulders. "It's always wise to keep the father of the bride happy since his wallet will be much thinner when all is said and done." They shared a chuckle. "Nothing goes better with pork roast than scalloped potatoes, green beans and baked apples." She paused and grinned mischievously. "Wait until you hear what's for dessert."

"Do tell!" Faerie urged.

"Dessert will be a triple layer coconut cake."

"Annie….good grief…my mouth is watering."

"So, what'd'ya think, Faerie?"

"The sooner we have this dinner party the better, is what I think." Faerie replied exuberantly. Then: "Have you been pondering the menu long? Or is this spur of the moment?"

"Neither. It's just when I thought about Daddy coming, I knew the main course had to be pork roast. The rest just makes perfect sense, especially for a late autumn supper."

Faerie loved to entertain. Oddly enough, until moving to Ouray, she had never entertained at all. She'd been far too busy working with her mother at the dress shop and caring for her siblings. Then she and Marcus married and moved across the country to a community where they were total strangers. With Marcus working on Red Mountain, she knew it was up to her to get out and meet people. She joined the fellowship committee at church and before she knew it she was routinely called upon to organize the monthly socials. As she began to know the townspeople and got a feel for the community, she took notice of the many underprivileged families in the area. Seeing them brought back a flood of memories of the hard times her family had lived endured at the hands of her father. She spoke with Marcus about it and he gave her his blessing to help in any way possible. She met with Susan Archer, who ran the local soup kitchen, and between the two of them they organized several charity benefits, one of which was the yearly Thanksgiving meal for the needy. Over time, she became the most sought after hostess in the county, and most everyone secretly wished to be on her guest list.

Vibrant shades of rose, pink and purple, orange and yellow filled the western sky as the sun sank behind the mountains. "The only thing I don't like about autumn is how early nightfall comes. It's only a little after 4:30 and look how dark it's getting." Annie pulled back the lace curtain and glanced out the window. "But would you look at those colors, Faerie."

Faerie sighed. "I love twilight," she said. Mattie stirred and Faerie craned her neck to peek over the railing. "There's something about the quiet beauty of the sunset that I find…" She pursed her lips. "What's the word I'm looking for? Soothing? Yes, that's it, soothing."

Annie moved to Mattie's crib. She smiled as the baby reached out for her. Annie picked her up and said, "Faerie, will I still be able to work here after I'm married?"

Faerie knit her brows. "Why wouldn't you? We'll just have to make a few adjustments. Nothing will change except that you'll go home to your husband at the end of the day. Don't give it another thought. Besides, what would I ever do without you?"

Annie sighed with one less thing to worry about. She and Fred hadn't discussed whether or not she'd work after they wed, but in her mind the matter was settled. Surely he wouldn't want her to give up something so important to her.

"This one's wet. And she's hot and sweaty." Annie laid Mattie on the dressing table to change her diaper and wet clothes. "She gets so hot in her sleep. Just look at this mop of wet hair."

Faerie smiled and said, "Hattie is the complete opposite. Her little legs and arms get chilly if she isn't covered, just like her dear old mother." She stood over the crib where Hattie lay and watched as the babe began to stir.

These were the moments that made life worth living. Time was running away. Oh, how she wished she could find a way to slow it down. The girls were growing, changing every day, learning, experiencing, discovering, and she didn't want to miss a second of it.

******

Delighted with the outcome of his meeting with the District Attorney, Doc Fisher decided to take a chance and wander over to Augusta's for a visit. Hopefully, he'd not worn out his welcome with all the impromptu early morning knocks on her door. A late afternoon visit would certainly take her by surprise.

The wind was cold and biting. November had flown in with a vengeance, bringing with it the ominous foreboding of things to come. Dark clouds loomed overhead while only minutes before the skies had been clear. *Colorado weather,* he silently mused. Doc buttoned his coat and turned the collar up as he gazed to the sky. *There's snow in those clouds.* He loved the snow. Never would anyone hear the words of dread so often uttered by the locals when the snow began to fly. He trudged on, walking against the wind. When finally he reached the bridge that led to her front door, he smiled. He had a funny feeling in his stomach…*nerves.* He chuckled. He was definitely taken by this dark-haired beauty. Standing at the door, he took a deep breath. Just as he was about to knock, the door opened. Augusta stood there in all her ravishing beauty and he turned to mush, unable to speak a word.

"I was hoping you'd drop by," she said, cheerfully. "It's been a month of Sundays since I last saw you."

She welcomed him inside, trading the coarse wind for the warmth and comfort of the fireplace, and the smell of something chocolatey baking in the kitchen. His stomach did a few flip flops, reminding him that today's visit was much different than the others. Today he came courting.

"It feels so homey in here, Augusta," he exclaimed. "I need homey today." He removed his hat and coat and hung them on the coat rack. He rubbed his hands together to get the circulation moving and said, "It's been a whirlwind since your ex-husband made his way to the hospital."

She scowled with the added emphasis of a lifted brow, and responded in a most surly voice, "I'm sure. How is he, anyway?"

"As cordial as ever," he answered, sarcastically. "Seriously, though, his leg is a mess. He's in for a world of hurt and aggravation with this injury. It'll make that break he had in his hand a while back like child's play."

Augusta crossed her arms and looked up at the ceiling, recalling the night when all hell had broken loose. She cringed and tried to dismiss it with a jerk of the head. There was a long silence as she contemplated Reginald's plight. Her haughtiness suddenly turned to concern, which Doc found most curious.

"He's a tormented soul," she said, quietly. "A few months ago I'd have cursed him and probably stormed out of the room in a huff, not wishing to talk about it. Now I'm at peace, but guarded, mind you. Does that even make sense?"

"Oddly enough, yes. I, too, am torn when it comes to Reginald. I've never known the man you and Marcus speak of so fondly from times past. It must be very bittersweet to have known that man and compare him to the one we now know." He paused. "All I've known is the crazed, angry man who can't seem to get a hold on things." he said, "Which brings me to one of the reasons for my visit."

"Oh?" she queried, with a flirty tilt of the head.

His heart flip-flopped. He swallowed. They moved to the wingback chairs in front of the fire. He stared into the flames and pulled his thoughts together. He felt like a shy schoolboy sitting next to the prettiest girl in the class.

"Sheriff Johnson and I met with the District Attorney this afternoon concerning Reginald's mental status. It's all so very complicated. I explained to them in detail his tentative diagnosis of Schizophrenia with Multiple Personality Disorder. At first, I felt like the Prosecutor wasn't buying it; he just sort of stared blankly back at me. He listened and never interrupted, only I got the feeling he'd already made up his mind about how things should go with Reginald. I thought all was lost. Then, out of the clear blue sky he knocked me for a loop. He began to ask questions and a small glimmer of hope rose up inside me." He paused and then said, "It seems he has a soft spot for you, my dear. He asked if you'd ever been privy to any of Reginald's episodes, other than the one that landed him in court."

"Yes, many times." She bit her lower lip.

"That's what I told him. I also gave him names of some the Alters."

"Alters?" she asked, confused.

"Sorry. That's what the individual Voices are called. Over time I've learned that he has several, including one who is a small girl, about six years of age, I'd wager."

"I don't know what to say. I had no idea."

"To make a long story short, by the end of the meeting, with my documentation and the sheriff's input, the Prosecutor agreed to file a motion with the court to have Reginald evaluated by a psychiatrist." He lifted his brow and shrugged his shoulders. "Take my word for it. This is a *good* thing."

"I suppose so. I trust you completely. Besides, it's out of my hands." Augusta smiled faintly. "You'd think I'd be relieved that I bear no responsibility in this; however, that's not the case. My heart breaks for him. On the other hand, I still tremble at the mention of his name. Two very different emotions that are so often entwined: sorrow and fear."

"Maybe so, Augusta, but I find it perfectly understandable. It shows that you have a good grasp of the reality of the situation, don't you think?"

"I guess I hadn't thought of it that way." Then: "Can we *please* talk about something else? Anything else?" She gazed at him imploringly, the light from the fire dancing in her eyes, bewitching him even more than her mere presence. "You said your meeting with the Prosecutor was *one* of the reasons for your visit. That leaves me to believe there's more?"

He gathered his courage before answering. "I simply wanted to see you. That's it in a nutshell." He looked deep into her eyes. "I cannot tell a lie, Augusta. You have my heart in your hand. I'm quite smitten. I very much enjoy the time we spend together and now that your divorce is final…"

She dropped her gaze and pretended to be very interested in the handkerchief she had twisted around her pointer finger. She was pleased…no… *elated*. She raised her head and studied his face, trying to read what she saw there.

"Have I been a fool, Augusta? Have I overstepped any boundaries?" he asked.

"Quite the contrary. I've never been one to follow the rules of etiquette. I dare say the old biddies in this town look upon me with much chagrin. I don't know how to be anyone other than who I am. I abhor the coy little games women play with their gentlemen friends. I won't do that to you." She took a deep breath. "I, too, am smitten. And have been for the longest time. I think about you day and night." She swallowed as she placed her hands palms down in her lap with her arms straight and shoulders scrunched up. "There! I said it!" She smiled happily and relaxed, sitting back in her chair. She looked into his eyes and found them dancing with joy.

"Augusta, my dear, you've made me the happiest man alive! May I come courting?"

"If you don't, I'll come looking for you!" she teased.

Nora appeared from the kitchen and interrupted what appeared to be an intimate moment. "Augusta, will Doc be staying for supper?" she asked with an I'm-sorry-for-bothering-you face.

"Well?" She waited for his answer.

"Only if that chocolate something-or-other you're baking is for dessert." He smiled and wiggled his brows playfully.

"I'll set another place," Nora said, with a nod and a smile. She spun around and hurried back to the kitchen to check on the something-or-other that had awakened Doc's chocolate senses.

******

Morning light shone through the lace curtains long before Annie was ready to face the day. She yawned and stretched and wished she could pull the covers over her head and give another go at sleep. She'd slept fitfully through the night and hardly felt rested. Her dreams were wildly vivid and filled with pages of guest and to-do lists whirling about over her head, annoyingly just out of reach. A red-haired woman dressed in black, who looked like an outrageous version of her mother, squawked incessantly, insisting Aunt So-and-So and Uncle What's-His-Name must be invited to the dinner party or their feelings would be mighty hurt, reminding her how silly they acted when they were upset. She awoke with a start, relieved to learn it was only a bizarre dream.

Thank goodness this was her day off. She planned on spending most of the day hidden away, working on the invitations to her dinner party since she had insisted they be all written in the same script. Annie had delicately declined Faerie's offer of assistance. She wanted her first dinner party to be something of her own creation from start to finish. The wedding, she told Faerie, would be another story altogether. Lying in bed, staring at the ceiling, she wondered if she'd made a colossal mistake by not taking Faerie up on her offer.

She rolled over and closed her eyes. Her mind was racing; her heart beat faster and harder by the second. *Goodness gracious!* She threw the covers off in frustration and sat on the edge of the bed for a minute and took in some deep breaths, then padded over to the window and opened the curtains. The sun was shining; it was a grand day. Suddenly, the lack of sleep didn't seem so important. "What time is it?" she asked. Then: "Coffee. I need coffee and toast."

Despite feeling like she'd been run over by a stampeding herd of elk, she took the time to make certain every hair was in place and her long-sleeved white blouse was tucked nicely into her tan skirt. She donned a burnt orange sweater and called it good enough for a day off. She stepped into the hallway and checked the clock on the landing. 9:30. She couldn't recall having slept so late since she was....well, she couldn't remember *ever* sleeping so late.

Down in the kitchen she got an earful from Lydia about sleeping the day away. She graciously smiled and nodded, and managed to tune her out, missing what she assumed was nothing but a tirade about time being a precious commodity. There was simply too much to do to get sucked into a battle of words with Lydia. She poured a cup of coffee and added a drop of cream and watched the two liquids blend into a rich caramel color. The smell sent her to heaven. Lydia never allowed Annie to make her own breakfast, but seemed put off by her request for a mere two slices of toast and any kind of jam or jelly that was already open.

Sitting at the table with her back to Lydia, she rolled her eyes and managed a slight grin. She thought Lydia was ridiculous at times. *Some things will never change.* She wondered if Lydia was put off by having to stop what she was doing to make toast or that it wasn't enough to feed a bird, which is what she usually said. Either way, it was the same old same old. She sipped the calming brew and vowed to be as gracious as possible, even if it required biting her tongue.

Myra came strolling through the kitchen on her way to the nursery. She had agreed to watch the little ones on Annie's days off. She'd been coming in a little later than usual for the last couple of weeks. Annie wasn't exactly sure why, and though it wasn't really any of her concern, she hoped everything was all right.

Myra came over to the table, Baby Patricia attached to her hip.

"Well, good morning, Miss Patricia!" Annie said, beaming as she patted her chubby little leg. "Myra, I want to thank you again for doing this for me. I can't tell you what a difference it makes to have a day off every week.

"Believe me, it's my privilege, especially now!" Myra exclaimed.

"What do you mean?"

"Don't tell me you've been so busy with your own plans that you

299

missed the grand announcement."

"I'm afraid you have me at a disadvantage," Annie replied, embarrassed.

"George and I are expecting another baby."

Annie's hands flew to her mouth as she gasped. "Oh, Myra, I'm so happy for you. When did you find out?"

"Very recently. I was only teasing about the grand announcement. We really haven't told anyone but Faerie and Marcus. And Lydia caught me red-handed eating soda crackers and put two and two together."

"That's right, m' friend! I did 'n I kept yer secret, fer sure." Lydia offered, sporting a self-satisfied smirk as she wiped down the counter.

"I must rush, Annie. I'm a little later than I promised. Faerie's probably fit to be tied."

Annie waved them off with a smile. She found herself wondering how long after the wedding she and Fred would have a *grand announcement.*

******

The day passed in a flash. The invitations were all written and the envelopes addressed, and with nary a cramp in her hand. The envelopes were stuffed and sealed with a wax stamp and then carefully placed in a box to be delivered to the post office first thing the following morning.

Annie sat on the edge of her bed, dressed in her favorite flannel nightgown, her hair in a long braid down her back. She was tired, but was as pleased as punch with all she'd accomplished. She and Fred had enjoyed a nice supper with her parents earlier in the evening, and after much discussion and checking of the calendar, had agreed upon a date for the wedding. She yawned, barely able to keep her eyes open. There would be no journaling tonight. She blew out the lamp and snuggled under the covers. She would not be troubled with overactive dreams this night.

Chapter Thirty-Two

Whatever is begun in anger ends in shame.
~ Benjamin Franklin

St. Joseph's Miner's Hospital did not a good jail make. The patient in Room 12 did his utmost to make the nurses miserable. He spewed rubbish night and day and was well-versed in the age old art of sexual innuendo, making lewd comments and outrageous requests whenever a nurse entered his room He cursed and yelled and talked to his imaginary friends all hours of the day and night. What were the nurses to do when even the deputies outside his room couldn't even get a handle on him?

Nurse Bailey was at her wit's end. Never in all her years of nursing had she been dealt such a card. Yes, she'd had difficult patients, and, yes, she'd had some who made her want to rush out the back door of the hospital never to return, but this man…*this* man…was a pistol. He was demented. She backtracked recalling how Doc Fisher despised such cruel, descriptive words. But, if not demented, then what?

The Sisters scurried up and down the corridors tending to the patients' needs, but even they steered clear of Room 12. The only one who voluntarily entered the room was Sister Martha. She was kind and attentive… and she always left the door to his room wide open.

The name on the patient's chart read *Walters*. Nurse Bailey wondered if perhaps Walters was one of the Voices. It didn't really matter; it was his alias and he stuck to it…well, sometimes he did. At other times, he seemed terribly confused about his identity, insisting the only Walters he ever knew was an old man back in Tahlequah.

"Mr. Walters, you must lie still. That leg needs your cooperation." Any number of requests and recommendations were made in Sister Martha's tender, caring way. He responded in kind. She'd smile sweetly and pour a glass of water, or fluff a pillow, or straighten his covers, promising to return, always reminding him to let the guard know if he needed anything.

Nurse Bailey didn't know where Sister Martha's strength came from. She had a sneaking suspicion that if she asked, the response would be something akin to "my strength comes from the Lord, who made heaven and earth". While she couldn't argue the point, she had an unseemly desire to hang Mr. Walters up by his toes until he begged for mercy. She wondered what the kind Sister would think about that. She desperately wished she didn't think such ridiculous thoughts about him. Walters brought out her humanness, the part of her that wanted retribution. Sister Martha was wise, for one so young. Bailey decided to ask her over for tea and a nice long chat, and the sooner the better, before her emotions took over.

Walters kept all three shifts hopping. 'Get me this!' 'Give me that!' 'Why are you staring at me?' 'You're a blasted idiot!' He pushed everyone to their limits, even the ones with no direct contact with him. He screamed, cried out day and night, begged for mercy, and was told by another Voice how weak and useless he was.

Bailey begged the doctors to put their heads together and come up with some way to stop his combativeness and incessant yammering. They decided to increase his laudanum dosage a fracture and that seemed to do the trick. She was aware of the dangers of overmedicating a patient. For the first time in her career, she found herself hoping for a patient to overdose. She was deeply ashamed of these feelings. She'd never say the words out loud. She'd never admit it to anyone, and she certainly would never do such a thing.

Yes, Nurse Bailey needed to have tea with Sister Martha…and soon.

Chapter Thirty-Three

It is not how much we have, but how much we enjoy, that makes happiness.
~ Charles Spurgeon

The day of the dinner party finally arrived. Annie awoke to a bright, sunshiny day with not a hint of snow in sight. More than anything, she'd feared a snowstorm would cripple the town and all of her planning would be for naught. She'd hoped for fair skies, and unless some unforeseen glitch occurred, the weather was cooperating. Storms in these Rocky Mountains could be sudden and severe, unrelenting. She was pleased as punch and mighty grateful for the generosity of a bright sunny day in which to bring all the final touches together.

A luscious triple-layer coconut cake made from her mother's county fair prize-winning recipe was finished and in the ice box. She could hardly wait to see her mother's reaction when the cake made its appearance on the buffet.

She was too excited to simply lie in the bed. She hopped to it, jumping up with a boost of energy not common to her morning routine. Thoughts of everything she still had to do raced through her head like a locomotive. She dressed in no time flat, and with one last look in the mirror rolled her eyes and decided it would just have to do. She supposed it didn't really matter what she looked like. Fred and Marcus were off to work, and George never seemed to notice anyone's appearance but Myra's. Lydia mostly looked like an unmade bed and should keep her comments to herself. *Wait! What was that?* She snickered. *When did Lydia* ever *keep her comments to herself?*

In the kitchen, she took the time to sit down and enjoy a bite of breakfast with Faerie and the girls. Lydia, knowing the day would be long and tiring, had made ham omelets and biscuits, which Annie dove into like she'd not eaten in days. Faerie watched curiously, commenting on her enthusiastic appetite.

"I don't believe I've ever seen you eat with such....*gusto.*" Faerie sliced a biscuit in quarters and handed each twin a piece to gnaw on.

"I'm especially hungry this morning. Some people can't eat when they're nervous; I'm the complete opposite." She sipped her coffee and then took a healthy bite of biscuit slathered with butter and strawberry preserves. "Lydia, this is superb! You've really outdone yourself."

"Why, thank ye, miss. That's something comin' from a fine cook sech as yerself."

Annie lifted her head and raised one brow and then cut a look at Faerie out of the corners of her eyes. "Is she being snippy?" she whispered, with a smirk.

"Of course she is. Just kill her with kindness and she won't know how to respond," Faerie returned quietly.

Mulling that around as she munched on a bite of biscuit, she decided Faerie was right. "Why thank you, Lydia. That's probably the nicest thing you ever said to me," Annie countered, never turning to face her, undoubtedly sending a mixed message. She gave Faerie a wink and the two dropped their heads feigning sudden renewed interest in their plates as their shoulders jerked up and down.

Faerie wiped drool from Hattie's mouth, using it as an excuse to cast a quick glimpse at Lydia, who was muttering under her breath, and looking particularly befuddled. She tapped the table lightly catching Annie's attention, and then whispered, "She's flabbergasted. What did I tell you?"

Annie practically choked on the coffee she'd just gulped. She began to cough. Faerie stood and ran to the sink to fetch a glass of water, and hurriedly brought it back. Handing it to her, she said, "Drink this!" Annie did as she was told and when the coughing fit subsided, she said, "I never understood why drinking something helped stop choking when it was in drinking that the fit began."

"'Tis strange indeed, missy, but 'tis an auld remedy, t' be sure." Lydia sidled up next to Annie and said, "I know ye were foolin' w' me, jest as I was a'foolin' with ye. I'm sorry fer being catty."

Annie's face flushed hot as coals on a fire. "Me, too, Lydia. There has to be a way for us to be friends instead of just tolerating one another. What's say we call a truce?"

"I'll start with brewin' a fresh pot o'coffee for the two o' ya." Lydia lightly pat Annie on the shoulder before stepping away.

Faerie reached across the table and squeezed Annie's hand. "Good job, Annie." She nodded reassuringly.

Annie dabbed at the corners of her mouth. "It's going to be one busy day today. I'm so excited I can barely see straight."

"Just tell me what to do. I'm all yours. Myra and George volunteered to watch the girls today."

"It just so happens I have a list right here in my skirt pocket," she replied. "Mother and Daddy will be here about four. She wants to help set the table. She's made some incredible place cards. Thank goodness you have a big dining table." She hesitated, and chewed on her bottom lip. "It occurred to me that perhaps people won't want to serve themselves at the buffet. What do you think?"

Faerie waved it off and said confidently, "Nonsense. One of the best parties I ever gave was with a buffet table. Don't give it another thought."

The coffee brewing on the stove smelled heavenly and reminded Lydia of the days when she was but a girl back in Georgetown, sitting around the space that served as both kitchen and living room in her family's cabin, enjoying an evening of fiddle playing and dancing with her father's friends from the mine. Although she seldom allowed herself the luxury of reminiscing, when she did it was with both fondness and trepidation. The good times she shared with her Dad and Mam in their cabin had ended in heartbreak. She wiped away a stray tear with the back of her hand and silently chided herself for wasting time with things she couldn't change.

"Lydia, are you all right?" Faerie asked sincerely.

She cleared her throat. "Yes'm. Jest a wee bit of a mem'ry comin' t' me, is all." Her chin quivered. "I've got yer coffee ready. Would ye be ready for a cup?"

Both ladies nodded holding their cups out. Lydia shook her head and harrumphed. "Ye two are a pair if I ever seen one."

******

With one last look in the mirror, Annie checked to make certain nothing was out of place. Though most women of the day wore their hair up for such social gatherings, she had gambled on a long braid resting over one shoulder with a satin ribbon woven into the braiding and tied at the end. A knock on the bedroom door gave her a start.

"Who is it?" she asked, standing with her ear to the door.

"Annie, it's me, Faerie. May I come in?"

Annie cracked open the door and motioned Faerie in.

"Oh, my, don't you look stunning," Faerie said, breathlessly.

"Really? Do you really think so?" She looked down and ran her hands delicately over the lace ruffle on the bodice of her taffeta dinner gown. The emerald dress captured the flecks of green in her hazel eyes. The off-the-shoulder dress which was gathered at the waist with a satin belt, made her tiny waist appear even smaller, and would undoubtedly make her the envy of every woman at the party.

"I don't think so, I *know* so. If that dress doesn't make Fred's jaw drop, nothing will." She sighed, taking in the loveliness of the girls' nanny. "I have a little something that I'd like to offer for the occasion." She held out a small velvet box. "Open it."

Annie gave Faerie a quizzical look and then carefully opened the small box. In it was a single strand garnet necklace laying atop a bed of white satin. "Marcus gave me this necklace the first year we actually had any money to spend on Christmas gifts. We would be honored if you wore it tonight. It would mean so much to the both of us."

Annie was moved beyond words. She whispered, "Will you put it on me?"

The two stood in front of the full length mirror as Faerie clasped the necklace. She stood back, allowing Annie to have a look. Annie's hands went to the necklace, touching it ever so gently, as she met Faerie's gaze in the mirror.

"I don't know what to say. I feel like a princess."

"And tonight you are."

******

Marcus watched from the landing as the guests filtered in one by one, Faerie and Washie greeting them and taking their wraps. Annie was the perfect hostess, mingling with the guests as they enjoyed their appetizers of fresh vegetables, olives, and cheeses from a bountiful table at the foot of the grand staircase. He noticed Fred seemed a bit out of his element and decided to rescue him.

"Annie is stunning this evening, don't you think?" he asked Fred as he walked up behind him.

"I'll say. She's so beautiful, so elegant." Fred spotted the drink table across the room and suggested they mosey over and take a gander. "Would you care for a glass of punch or something stronger?"

"Punch is fine. I'm not much of a drinker. A glass of wine with dinner will be more than enough for me." Marcus glanced about the room, smiling and nodding at those who made eye contact.

"Same here." Fred looked to his right and noticed his future in-laws approaching. He swallowed. "Here we go," he said under his breath.

******

As things turn out, Annie had worried for nothing with regards to the buffet line. A mouthwatering pork roast with potatoes and carrots, baked apples, green beans, and hot yeast rolls left the guests with nothing to complain about. Conversation easily flowed around the table with talk of the upcoming holidays and what a grand undertaking it was for Annie to put together a dinner party one week prior to Thanksgiving. She was the perfect hostess and the guests seemed quite taken with her.

After generous portions of cake and coffee were served, Fred and Annie stood. Fred cleared his throat and asked for everyone's attention. Suddenly all eyes were on the couple. They looked at one another nervously. Fred opened by saying, "Annie and I want to thank you for joining us this evening. I must admit I am a terrible clod at parties." He took Annie's hand and smiled warmly. "As you can see, Annie is a natural. If not for her ease and grace, I would have fallen flat on my face tonight." There were lots of chuckles around the table. "Each of you were invited here tonight simply because we love you and wanted to share an evening with you."

"And," Annie interrupted, "because Fred and I have wonderful news and wanted you all to be the first to hear it."

There were smiles and whispers around the table, most believing they knew what was coming next.

Fred cleared his throat. "A few days ago, I signed papers finalizing the purchase of a house on the north end of Second Street. Interestingly enough, it's the house Marcus and Faerie lived in prior to purchasing this one, which Annie unashamedly named Monstrosity Manor." Again, there were chuckles all around the table.

Annie met Nora's gaze and the two shared an unspoken moment of friendship from across the table.

Fred continued. "Once I learned of Annie's connection to the house and that she has such fond memories of her time there, I had no choice. I simply had to buy it for her." Around the table there were audible gasps from some of the ladies, not to mention a few accolades from the men's section.

Annie saw Faerie wipe a tear from the corner of her eye with her napkin. She smiled as Marcus brought one of Faerie's hands to his lips and delicately kissed it.

"Having said that," Annie continued nervously, her chin and bottom lip quivering, "we have one more thing to share." As she gazed around the table, she was touched by the expectant looks on the faces gazing back at her. She swallowed and said, "Please set aside February 12 of this coming year to celebrate our wedding vows with us." Cheers exploded, greatly surprising the happy couple. Annie waited for the calm. "Marcus and Faerie have generously offered up the use of Monstrosity Manor for the ceremony and reception."

Augusta lowered her head. She too had been wed in this house. It was *her* house then. She lifted her head and stuck out her chin, raising one brow in defiance. *I will not allow that memory to ruin this night. That was then; this is now.* She stood and raised her glass. "Won't you all join me in a toast to the happy couple?"

******

"Where were you last night?" Nurse Bailey asked Doc. "I thought you were working. Imagine my surprise when our young Dr. Hughes showed up instead."

"Young?" Doc chirped. "He was only a year behind me in school."

"Oh, get over it. You know what I mean." She grimaced and shook her head. Then, all smiles, she asked, "So how about this: our *new* Dr. Hughes?"

"I still don't like it, but I'll deal with it." Then: "To answer your question, I was at a dinner party at the Wright's mansion. And what a party it was!" He gave her a sideways grin, as if he carried a great secret.

"What is it? Do tell," Bailey chided. "This is me you're talkin' to."

"I was invited by Augusta O'Keefe."

"I knew it! I just knew it!" she gloated.

He rolled his eyes. "Yeah, well, don't go spreading it around just yet."

Chapter Thirty-Four

A single twig breaks, but the bundle of twigs is strong.
~ Tecumseh

Joshua Benson arrived at Monstrosity Manor right on time. He'd been summoned by Sheriff Johnson, except he had no earthly idea why. All he knew was that it seemed very mysterious and secretive. For the life of him, he couldn't figure out what anybody in this big old house would want with him, unless it had something to do with Simon's horse. He stood, holding his big ten gallon hat, on the street side of the wrought iron fence that surrounded the property. Yes, sir, it was a right big house and whoever named it got it right. It was the fanciest-looking house he'd ever laid eyes on and he couldn't wait to see what it was like on the inside. He'd heard tales, only he wasn't one for listening to idle gossip…well, not much, anyway.

He heard the sound of horse's hooves beating out a rhythm on the dirt street. He turned, relieved to see the Archer family coming around the corner in a buckboard. He smiled and gave a big wave and waited for Simon to park the wagon. He was surprised to see Clara aboard. She was a right smart woman, that Clara.

"What's goin' on here, Simon?" he asked, as they made their way to the front porch.

"Big news about the horse rustler." Simon and John shared a look that told Joshua they were hoping the judge was going to throw the book at that no good son of a gun.

Simon knocked on the door while the others waited in a semicircle directly behind him, huddling close together on the cold, blustery morning. Joshua imagined there must be big news for sure, what with all the wagons parked out on the street. *Enough fer a small town meetin' that's fer dang sure.* He rubbed his hands together and then cupped them over his mouth and breathed warmth onto them.

A distinguished-looking young man answered the door. He greeted Simon with an enthusiastic handshake and stood to the side while the crew filed in. Simon introduced Marcus and Joshua. A right handsome woman he'd bet was Irish (if he was a betting man, that is) took everyone's hats and coats and lay them on the dining room table before showing the group to the parlor.

After a few minutes of visiting, Sheriff Johnson stood. The room fell silent as all eyes turned their attention his way. The tension was as thick as molasses in January. He dropped his head for a moment to gather his thoughts. When at last he spoke, he was as solemn as a judge. "Marcus and Faerie, thank ya kindly fer offerin' up yer home this mornin'. As ya kin see, prac'tly anybody whatever had any dealins with Reginald O'Keefe is right in this here room. Doc Fisher has some things t' share w' ya an' then we'll do our best t' answer any questions you'ns might have." He turned his attention to Joshua. "Joshua, we asked ya here t'day cuz it was you what shot O'Keefe. Word has it ye're a'feared charges'll be filed agin ya. Well, jest rest easy, m' friend. The District Attorney said t' tell ya t' stop yer worryin' 'cuz that ain't a'gonna happen. You wuz protectin' yersef, plain 'n simple.

"In case there's anybody here what don't' know how bad a crime horse rustlin' is, I'm here t' tell ya, it gits men th' noose in these parts. So Joshua, ya got nothin' t' worry 'bout. It's perty safe t' say ever'body here thinks ye'r a hero. Ya done what nobody else wuz able t'do. Ya took care o' Reginald O'Keefe once and fer all.

"Which brings me t' a whole 'nother point. As you'ns all know, O'Keefe is still in th' hospital with guards standin' outside 'is room, an' he's a'cuffed t' th' bed. Doc Fisher'll be kind enuf t' 'splain 'zackly what that means fer you'ns in a few minutes."

Sheriff Johnson coughed. Then he coughed again, this time rubbing his throat. Faerie excused herself and returned with a glass of water. "Thank ye kindly, Miz Wright." He downed the water before continuing.

"I won't lie t' ya. O'Keefe's trials an' tribulations have jes' begun. An' it won't only be 'bout him. Ever'body here'll hafta sit in th' courtroom an' tell their tale." He gazed at the ceiling and took a few deep breaths. "Doc, why don't ya take over fer me?"

Doc Fisher stepped up. The two men shook hands and Doc took his place. Sheriff Johnson sat and leaned forward and propped his elbows on his thighs and rested his head in his hands.

"Sheriff Johnson has worked diligently to find justice in this matter." He scanned the room and looked into the faces of the Archers and Clara, the Wrights and Somers, Joshua Benton, Nora and Dan, Myra and George, Lydia, Annie and Fred, and Augusta. "With few exceptions, it appears Reginald's fury has been isolated to this small group. There was another man in Silverton who bore the brunt of his anger. He's being protected by the sheriff's department up there. He had also been attacked by Reginald a couple of years ago here in Ouray. The District Attorney will question him, and depending on what he has to say, he may have to testify here if charges are filed; however, nothing is set in stone on that one. San Juan County has notified our Prosecutor they will be filing charges against Reginald, so that victim will definitely have to testify in Silverton.

"As far as how long it will take to get trial dates set, no one can say for sure because this is a real pickle. I wish it weren't so complicated, but let's face it. We have to do whatever it takes to right these wrongs, and at the same time make certain O'Keefe never hurts anyone again. I know there have been questions as to the charges against him. Well, let me tell you, there's quite a list." He took a sheet of paper from his vest pocket and unfolded it. "As of right now, the charges are as follows: two counts of conspiracy to commit murder, one count of solicitation to commit murder, one count second degree murder, two counts forcible kidnapping, two counts of assault with intent to do bodily harm, grand theft, trespassing, harassment, and three counts of breaking and entering." He took in a deep breath and released it with a heavy sigh. He then cleared his throat and continued. "That's quite a list. The District Attorney will be questioning each of you. Based upon that information, additional charges may be filed. Suffice it to say, Ouray County has never seen the likes of what this trial, or trials, will entail.

"I say trial or *trials* because nothing can be decided until the Prosecutor and I meet with Judge Lawson. And it's no secret Reginald has a history with Judge Lawson."

"I remember it well," Marcus interjected in a monotone.

"I'm sure you do, Marcus. One of the assault charges is for your broken nose and the other is for Myra's assault. Neither one of those assaults were dealt with in the original trial. And like I said, there may be one additional assault charge once the man in the Silverton case is interviewed here." then, "Back to meeting with the judge. We are going to try and convince Judge Lawson to allow an independent psychiatric evaluation of Reginald. I sold the D.A. on it; now we just have to sell it to the judge." He stared at the far wall and chuckled softly. "We all know he's old school. Still, I believe it's worth a shot. None of us wants to see Reginald back out on the street. Speaking as a medical professional, I also don't want to see him in the State Penitentiary for the rest of his life, or worse yet, sent to the gallows, if he's struggling with schizophrenia, as I believe he is. He'll never make it in prison."

Sandy raised her hand.

"Yes, Sandy?" Doc acknowledged.

"What is schizophrenia?"

Doc Fisher explained the different diagnoses under the schizophrenia umbrella, primarily touching on Multiple Personality Disorder. By the time he finished, everyone in the parlor was convinced he was talking about Reginald.

"I have a simple yet complex request." He tried to smile, but couldn't fake it due to the seriousness of the matter. "In order to make it through this ordeal, everyone in this must join together and become a unified force. Unfortunately, you've all been victimized by Reginald O'Keefe, some more than others. To endure the trial and come out on the other side whole, healthy individuals, you are going to need each other like never before. Let's face it. No one else will ever understand what has happened to you as individuals or as a group. He's attacked you in both ways. Stand firm; stand tall. Don't lean on your own understanding. Seek out one another in times of stress or heartache. If any person in this group should crumble under the enormous weight of it all, the others will need to stand in the gap and gird that person up until they are on their feet again.

"From what I've seen, you've been doing a pretty good job of this already. I'm asking you to be even more intentional about it than you are now. We were never meant to bear our burdens alone. Remember: 'greater love hath no man than this, that he should lay down his life for his friends'.

"I won't stand here and say this process will be easy, because it won't. It *absolutely* won't. In fact, it'll probably be the most uncomfortable, trying, tiring, sickening, hurtful experienceof your lives. If you thought being his victim was traumatic, just wait for court. I wish it weren't so, but it is."

Simon stood. "Doc, may I have a few words?" Doc nodded and turned over the floor.

"The year I was away was the most horrible time of my life, and the lives of my wife and boys. God knows I wanted to come home. The truth was that I couldn't come home. O'Keefe had paid people to find and kill me and if I had turned up at home before the appointed time, my family might have been hurt...or worse. In the end, O'Keefe went after my family anyway. He took John. And he took Sandy. The Somers know exactly how we feel. Am I right, Albert?"

Albert nodded soberly with his lips pursed and quivering.

Simon continued. "I agree wholeheartedly with Doc. We have no choice but to band together and become an emblem for good. From a personal standpoint, I can't imagine anyone I'd rather be aligned with than the folks in this room. We are all followers of the Word and the Word says, 'I can do all things through Christ who strengthens me'." He paused and scanned the room, trying to gauge what the others were thinking. Most everyone's expression was solemn, so he asked, "What do you say, folks? Are we going to do this thing? Are we going to walk this road together?"

Marcus and Faerie gave each other a look and a nod and then stood, holding hands. "We're with you."

The others followed one by one, and in so doing, pledged an unspoken vow of unity to the group.

With a tremble in his voice Marcus said, "I don't know how this will turn out, but I know whom I have believed, and I know that He is able to carry us through this time. We are not alone." Marcus paused. "When Reginald and I were kids, we were the best of friends. Now he believes me to be his enemy. He'll never understand what we're doing because he's unable to comprehend a holy alignment. He'll see our unity as an underhanded alliance intended to destroy him." Then: "Times will get tough and when push comes to shove we must rely on our faith to see us through. Trust is the key. Our Father will never let the righteous fall."

The group gathered close and stood in a circle holding hands. None could imagine the torment that was to come in the days and months ahead. None could fathom the kind of evil that brewed in the mind of a psychopath. None had begun to imagine what lay ahead as Reginald and his attorney began to lay out his defense. The truth would be told; however, Reginald didn't deal in truth…or reality. He would be out to discredit the band of friends and their reputations.

As they stood united in the circle, one by one they lifted their petitions to the Heavens, while outside the autumn winds whipped around the corners of the house, bending the giant spruce and aspen, bringing with it dark, ominous clouds that seemed to speak of trials yet to come. Trials that might very well challenge the mantra the band of friends adopted from a Prayer of David found in the Book of Psalms:

When I am alone, I will trust in Thee.

Epilogue

The holidays rushed in, taking the little town of Ouray by storm. Adding to the hustle and bustle of the season were the hours Annie and Faerie spent working on Annie's wedding gown. She wanted a simple gown of silk and lace "nothing too frilly"… with a floor length veil attached to an ivory comb. Faerie's sewing room was strictly off limits to anyone other than Faerie, the bride-to-be, and her mother, Beatrice. The three of them had a grand time cutting and sewing and sharing stories. The hours seemed to fly by and before they knew it, Christmas Day was upon them.

The band of friends gathered for Christmas dinner, each bringing an offering to the table. There was no mention of Reginald that day. It was a day set aside for family, friends and paying homage to the Babe born so long ago.

December gave way to the birth of a new year, 1893. The group collectively chose not to make New Years' resolutions, deciding instead to replace old worries and fears with an abiding faith in God's promises. For the band of friends, January brought with it a kind of strength none had experienced before. Doc Fisher was right. There was strength in numbers; there was solace in the open arms of comrades. Soon they would learn exactly how much faith they had both as individuals and as a unit. They locked arms and stood their ground, confident in the One who would see them through this time of waiting.

On the second day of January, 1893 the band of friends rallied around each other in support as Reginald O'Keefe was transferred from the hospital to the County Jail on a stretcher, surrounded by armed guards. The crisp, clean winter air filled his lungs, exhilarating him and filling him with renewed confidence. His mind was as clear as the blue sky above. During his extended stay in the hospital, he'd come to terms with the new pecking order. He and the Voices had become a unified force, each one knowing their place. He was as still as still could be as the guards carried him into the jail. He spoke not a word, secure in the knowledge that now was the time for Luke to put his plan into action.

And what a plan it was.

www.ingramcontent.com/pod-product-compliance
Lightning Source LLC
Chambersburg PA
CBHW070220260626
47160CB00002B/624